PROPHECY

BOOK ONE OF THE PROPHECY SERIES

BY LEA KIRK

Prophecy
Lea Kirk

Published by Heather Jarecki
Copyright © 2016, Heather Jarecki
Cover Art by Danielle Fine
Content Edits by Sue Brown-Moore
Copy Edits by Laurel C. Kriegler
Formatting by Nina Pierce

This is a work of fiction. Names, characters, places, and incidents are products of the author's imagination or are used fictitiously and are not to be construed as real. Any resemblance to actual events, locales, organizations, or persons, living or dead, is entirely coincidental.

All rights reserved. No part of this book may be used or reproduced electronically or in print without written permission, except in the case of brief quotations embodied in reviews. For information regarding subsidiary rights, please contact the author.

First Edition January 2016
California, USA

ACKNOWLEDGMENTS

As with any achievement in life, this one would not exist without the help and/or support of dozens of wonderful people.

- My family. My parents and sister, who have cheered me on even when I got so involved I forgot to call or visit. My husband and kids, who endured the messes and the questionable meals so I could make a memorable and positive first impression as a debut author.
- My critique partners, Dena and Dianne, who have been with me since before the start of this insanity. Carolyn and Peg, who read the first blundering attempts at a beginning and didn't beat around the bush to spare my feelings. Beth, JuNelle, and Melissa, who never complained about the rereads and kept me from wandering off this path.
- My beta-readers, Rachel, Laurie, Dawn, Janet...and, of course, Taron (for the "guy" perspective).
- My cover artist, Dani, who just *knew* exactly what I wanted, even though I didn't.
- My editors, Sue and Laurel, who both know how to use their red pens! Any, errors, in this book, are completely, on me.
- My proofreaders, Pippa and Stephanie who inspired and validated me, and held my feet to the fire...or *in* the fire.
- My formatter, Nina, who is a dream to work with.

- My sisters and brothers in the SFA-RWA and the SFR Brigade, whose support goes above and beyond. My first online class instructor, Karen, and Kickass Chicks Karen and Steph J., who helped me craft the blurb.
- My friends. All of you who have helped, supported, and listened to me over the last three years—and there are a ton of you—you are my cheerleaders.

I couldn't have done it without you. THANK YOU!

*In memory of
Ethel Kirk Kittleman
This one's for you, Grandma.*

CHAPTER ONE

Present Day Earth

Alexandra Bock opened her eyes. Faint grey light filtered through a woven black cloth over her face. Where the hell was she now? A chill from the hard surface seeped through the thin fabric of her hospital scrubs, and her muscles contracted, sending a violent shudder through her body. Had she really been chased by a giant, green-skinned alien through the streets of her hometown?

It happened. It really happened.

There'd been no escaping him either. He'd been fast, and unbelievably huge. Like ten-feet-tall huge—and pissed as hell. That might've been her fault. At the time, ramming the heel of her hand into his nose had seemed like a reasonable idea. It did distract him long enough for her to bolt.

But that freaking space invader had the decided advantage of being faster, and he'd had friends. They'd herded her through the rubble-strewn streets of Damon Beach like a pack of Australian Shepherds, laughing and shouting as if the thrill of the chase excited them. The last thing she remembered was burgundy blood dripping from Green Man's large nostrils, and the knuckles of his enormous fist just before they connected with her head.

Now she was...somewhere cold and metallic, lying on a hard floor with a sack over her head that stank like old cheese. That green bastard must've put it on her while she was unconscious. She swallowed against the first hint of acid at the back of her throat. Would she ever stand on the sandy, sun-warmed Northern California beach of her hometown again? Feel the cold Pacific waves rush around her feet? Was she even

PROPHECY

on Earth anymore?

She shifted her arms from behind her, but stopped when cords bit into her wrists.

Damn. Guess the disgusting hood is staying on for now.

She tested her feet and twisted her mouth in frustration. Tied at the ankles. Could this day get any worse?

That's a rhetorical question, God.

Although, there weren't a lot of things worse than an unexpected alien invasion. She may have survived it, but that didn't guarantee she'd remain among the living. Especially given her current incapacitation. But, knowledge was power. If she figured out where she was, she might find a way to free herself.

A steady mechanical whoosh, like air blowing, reached her left ear. And muffled voices, some of them moaning. They definitely sounded human. The invaders' voices had the rich tone of a deep gong. A child sobbed nearby, and she couldn't do a damn thing to help because she was trussed up like a pig. After what she'd seen and experienced today, someone here was bound to need a nurse.

You need a nurse, Alex. Or a doctor.

The fuzziness of her thoughts might indicate a concussion, and something was wrong with her right ear. It was possible the shot she took to the head could've damaged her eardrum. Getting herself untied was her first priority then she could deal with her injuries. If she wiggled around enough, she could loop her hands under her legs. Once they were in front of her, she'd be able to take the hood off. Magicians and escape artists did this trick all the time. How hard could it be?

You nitwit. You're a five-foot-eleven ER nurse who quit gymnastics when you were nine. She was so screwed. Unless someone nearby wasn't tied up and could help her. That might work. She pulled in a breath and raised her head to call out.

Pain exploded behind her eyes, and her stomach lurched like a drunken sailor. Bile burned a path up her esophagus, and her gag reflex kicked in. Crap. She was going to hurl inside the hood. This would be way beyond gross.

A gentle hand cupped the crown of her head. "*Paci*," a man's voice murmured, the language strange but beautiful and lilting.

The nausea receded, and her mind floated, as if buoyed by a gently rolling ocean wave. Tension drained from her shoulders. Peace. This she could deal with.

The hand vanished, and the tranquil waves faded, leaving Alex weak and gulping for whatever oxygen she could suck through the musty hood. What had just happened there? Cool fingertips rested against her neck. They must belong to a human. An alien wouldn't bother to check her pulse.

Unless they were checking to see if she was strong enough for experiments...

Her heart shot straight up into her throat, and she fought to contain the groan welling in her chest.

Breathe, Alex. You're overreacting again. This isn't a movie. First rule of disaster training: stay calm. If she ever got the chance, she'd make damn sure future training programs covered alien invasions.

"Is English your language?"

A man's voice, and definitely not alien. Low, calm, gentle—everything the alien invaders' voices were not—it wrapped around her like her favorite bathrobe, soft and warm.

"Yes." The word slipped passed her lips as she expelled a breath. "Help me."

"No fear. You are safe for the time."

A pleasant tingle fluttered through her core. He sounded so reassuring it must be true. Or maybe she just wanted it to be true. Capable hands assisted her with sitting upright, triggering a pulsing thrum that beat against her skull like Thor's Hammer. "My head...."

The floating sensation returned, but this time, instead of ocean waves, she drifted on a big, white, puffy cloud in a cobalt sky. Her head lolled, back and a strong hand cupped and cradled it.

"Concussion, severe tympanic damage, and dehydration, Captain," a second man's voice said.

So, her self-diagnosis had been correct: a concussion and ear damage. Hardly surprising after the abuse she'd endured at the hands of her captors. How was it no one on Earth had seen them coming? There should've been some warning. With all

PROPHECY

the satellites, telescopes and whatever else NASA used, they must've been blind to have missed the approach of those gargantuan space ships.

What a way to find out we're not alone in the universe.

"We will free you now."

Captain had a nice, melodic accent. Almost, but not quite Mediterranean. Or maybe Spanish. Hands worked at the cords binding her ankles.

"You're military?" Somehow imagining him as military was more reassuring than a cruise ship captain.

A second set of hands tugged at the bonds around her wrists.

"I am," Captain said.

"Then where were you guys during the attack?" She'd expected to see fighter jets streaking across the sky, coming to the rescue. But they'd never appeared.

"We were unable to help."

The military being grounded by the invasion was a scary thought. It made sense though. The aliens must've attacked more than just the California coast. Their space ship had spanned the horizon like a floating continent. It wasn't a stretch to assume they were capable of wiping out all civilization from the West Coast to the Rockies, and beyond.

She sucked in a ragged breath and fought back the tears of relief. If she cried anymore today she wouldn't be surprised if she shriveled up like a dry husk. Her feet fell apart, free from their bonds, and blood rushed to her toes with the sting of a hundred needles. "Ah."

"The ties of the hood are well knotted," Captain murmured. "To rest your head against me will keep it from moving as much while I work. Will you agree?"

Anything to minimize the pain. She made a small sound of agreement, and he drew her against him. His heart thumped steadily, strong—and, most importantly, like a normal human's—under her ear. Some of the tension in her shoulders seemed to melt away as he manipulated the hood's bindings.

"We are held aboard an Anferthian slave ship." Captain pitched his voice low.

"You mean those green bastards took us off Earth?" Like

hell she would spend the rest of her life as a slave.

"No. On your planet we remain as they collect survivors."

"I *hate* aliens." Especially ten-foot-tall, green-skinned, scumbag aliens.

Were Mom and Dad safe at his conference in New York, watching the attack from their hotel room? Or were they somewhere on this slave ship? And Nicky. Had her brother already left school to meet her for lunch? What if she was the only one in her family to survive?

Don't even go there.

Her family had to be alive. Life without them.... The pain of loss pierced her heart, and a small whimper caught in her throat.

"Your feelings are justified," Captain's words rumbled under her ear. "What is your name?"

He must be trying to distract her, a tactic she'd used more than once to calm upset or nervous patients. At this point, the change of topic was welcome. It was better than ugly crying in front of a complete stranger. Hopefully, once she was untied, she could find a corner to grieve in.

"Alexandra Bock." She pressed her lips together. Why had she told him that? Only her father called her Alexandra. Everyone else called her Alex.

"You are near free of your bonds, Alexandra Bock." Captain set her back upright, away from the comforting sound of his heartbeat.

The unknown person behind her slid the cords from her wrists. She brought her hands around, shaking them and wiggling her fingers.

Relief, relief, relief!

Now to get the hood off. She reached up, fumbling to find the edge of the hood with tingling hands that collided with Captain's. Together they shimmied the hood over her head.

Finally, freedom...oh. Sweat, blood, and body odor assailed her olfactory senses, and her stomach roiled in protest. Now the cheesy stink of the hood didn't seem so bad.

Squinting to ease the throb in her head, she took in the grey metal monotony of the walls and floor surrounding her. The long, narrow room appeared to be made of a single piece

PROPHECY

of molded metal, curved where the walls met the floor. A soft glow from the ceiling illuminated the space. Were they in a slave cell, or an alien version of a tin can?

Her gaze was drawn to a heavy-set man in a business suit laying on the floor nearby. Another man in some sort of graphite grey uniform knelt over the businessman's foot, as though examining it. Huddled against a wall, an African-American woman sat with her arms and head resting on her drawn-up knees. Nearby, a dark-headed boy, who couldn't have been more than six years old, was being tended by a woman with midnight black hair.

Alex's mouth dropped open. The woman appeared human in every way, except her skin was *blue*. She was an alien...a despicable alien. Not the same species as the invaders, but that hardly mattered. As of lunchtime today, all aliens had landed on her shit list.

"Alexandra, are you well?"

She turned back to Captain and met his deep sapphire gaze. Her breath hitched in her throat, and warmth spread through her chest. Familiar, and such a beautiful color. Unlike her own boring brown. And his skin...was blue. The same deep blue of the sky on a summer day.

A hunk of cold lead settled in her heart. This could *not* be happening.

"No. No, no, no." She pushed herself to her feet, and Captain rose with her. The room tilted, and she tottered sideways a couple of steps. Captain reached for her, but she jerked away from him, sucking air through her teeth with a hiss. "Don't! Just, don't touch me."

Captain lowered his hands to his side.

"You...you're an *alien*." A hint of red heat curled to life deep inside her, like the edge of a newspaper being lit for a campfire. How dare he trick her into thinking he was human!

He nodded slowly. "To you, yes."

"Oh, God." She flexed her fingers at side and fixed him with a hard glare. "Do you have any idea how many people I watched *die* today? I don't even know if my family is alive. My home, everything I ever knew, has been destroyed. *Aliens* did that." Aliens no one knew existed before today.

Captain's brows furrowed above wary eyes, and he tilted his head to one side. An errant curl of snow-white hair shifted onto his forehead. High cheekbones accented his patrician nose, like an ancient Greek statue come to life. A lapis statue with at least a week's worth of white beard.

"You are correct, Alexandra," he said. "The responsibility for the near annihilation of your people is mine."

She snapped her attention back to his eyes. *He* was the reason so many people had been massacred today? That her life had been upended like a derailed train car? That she had no idea if her family was even alive? The dry twigs burst into flame, ready to consume everything in its path. Her vision narrowed on Captain's face. This was his fault; he'd owned it. *That son of a...*

Alex balled her right hand, pulled back her arm, and swung. Her fist slammed into one gorgeous blue eye. Captain's neutral expression vanished, replaced by a look of astonishment as he staggered back a step.

Ow, ow, ow!

She cradled her fist to her chest and rubbed her stinging knuckles. A pair of large hands grabbed her from behind and spun her around. Two ruddy-red eyebrows drawn together above a pair of grey eyes froze her in place. Anger seethed from this new blue alien. *Uh, oh.* She was toast.

He jerked her close, and her head snapped back. A jab of pain shot through her head like an ice pick, and a cry escaped her. She squeezed her eyes shut as tightly as she could, waiting for the blow that was sure to come.

"Stand down, Commander." Behind her, Captain sounded calm, as though he hadn't just taken a right hook to the eye.

"Alex!"

Her eyes popped open at the familiar voice. "Nicky?" Her brother's anxious face blurred as tears flooded her eyes.

"Let her go," Nicky snarled at Commander Angry Alien.

Angry Alien didn't argue. He just let her crumple to the floor then stepped away.

"Ass-wipe," Nicky muttered as he crouched next to her.

What was her brother thinking going toe-to-toe with an alien built like a bouncer? At six-foot-one and eighteen years old, Nicky was pretty full of himself. They should have a chat about that before he got himself hurt.

What was she thinking? She was only four years older than him, and *she'd* just punched a guy as tall as her brother in the eye. A fact Nicky would probably point out if she went into lecture mode.

An ominous gurgling noise came from the vicinity of her stomach. She wrapped her arms around her middle and hunched forward. The gentle weight of Nicky's hand gliding over her back was the only thing keeping her focused. He was alive! And if both of them had survived, maybe there was hope for their parents.

A pair of black boots moved into her field of vision. "I may have deserved that," Captain said. "I truly am sorrier than you can imagine for the horrors visited upon your people and your planet, and do hold myself accountable for failing to avert this tragedy."

Tragedy? That had to be the understatement of the decade. Century. All time. She raised her throbbing head and gave him what she hoped was a nasty glare. He didn't look too happy either, but that might've had more to do with his already swelling eye than anything else.

"They've taken our planet away, haven't they?" The potential answer to that question scared the crap out of her, but she needed to know how widespread the invasion was.

Captain nodded.

No, not a tragedy. It was outright genocide. To top that off, she was imprisoned on an alien slave ship with a bunch of...other aliens. One of whom admitted he was somehow responsible for this slaughter. *Now* this day couldn't get any worse.

Her stomach contracted and her body tensed, as though conspiring to prove her wrong.

Oh, hell.

She threw up on his boots.

CHAPTER TWO

Senior Captain Gryf Helyg gazed at the ball of human misery huddled at his feet. It just did not seem possible, but after one Galactic Standard week, his situation showed no signs of improving. He had been betrayed by Vyn Kotas, his fleet destroyed, and his cousin killed. Then the Anferthians had incarcerated what remained of his crew aboard one of their slave ships. Had that not been enough? Now this Terrian woman, from a race he had sworn his life to protect, had accosted him.

And managed to vomit on his boots with unprecedented precision.

How had he been fooled into believing the worst was behind him? There had been something in the woman's eyes, an unspoken promise that all would right itself because she was here. Clearly, he had misread the situation. Taken in by a pair of bronze-flecked brown eyes, framed by lashes as dark as her hair. If only he had moved on to aid the next Terrian, his eye would not be swelling now.

He exhaled a deep sigh through his nose then bent to wipe the watery mess off his boots with Alexandra's discarded hood.

The one she called Nicky glared at him as he held Alexandra's dark hair back away from her face. The youth's body language bespoke familiarity with, and protectiveness of, her. Between that and his brown and bronze eyes—the exact match to Alexandra's—there was little doubt these two Terrians were siblings.

What a fortuitous coincidence for both of them to be incarcerated together in this deplorable slave hold.

Gryf paused mid-wipe. Or was it? The stench of Vyn Kotas playing them all contaminated the air.

PROPHECY

He straightened and shot a frown in Commander Graig Roble's direction. The scowl on his senior security officer's face was directed toward Alexandra. Her head now rested against Nicky's knee, her anger clearly spent.

"So who the hell are you?" Nicky asked.

Ah, so Terrian teenagers could be as belligerent as their Matiran counterparts. He must remember to apologize to his mother for any grief he may have caused her, provided he ever saw her again.

"Gryf Helyg, senior captain of the Matiran Guardian Fleet, captain of the Guardian Fleet Cruiser *Atlantis*. And an unwilling prisoner of the Anferthians, like you."

"You mean you're not with the freakishly tall green guys?"

Gryf winced at the question then squatted, bringing his eyes level with the boy's. "Most assuredly not. Unless you believe my crew and I incarcerated ourselves in this small, foul-smelling cell aboard our enemy's slave ship for an entire week just to trick you."

The Terrian youth studied him for a drawn-out moment, as if he believed that was exactly what they had done.

Gryf released another sigh. "And you are?"

"Nick Bock." The young man hesitated then extended his right hand.

Gryf stared at it. Terrian social protocol was not his area of expertise. Why would it be? Interacting with the Terrians was not supposed to happen during his life-time. Yet it had, and if there was to be any chance of establishing positive relations with these people, he must act. He gripped Nick's hand in his own.

"It pleases me to make your acquaintance, Nick Bock." Had he done it right? The Holy Mother had a wicked sense of humor, placing *him* on the front lines of this long-awaited, yet premature, reunion.

Nick tugged his hand, and Gryf released his grip. "Will you aid me in moving your sister to the wall, Nick? There she will be more comfortable while she awaits attendance from our healer."

"No." Alexandra's voice was a breathless murmur. "I'll do it."

This would not go well for her. "Your determination is admirable, Alexandra. At minimum, please accept my help as you take your feet." Her will might be as unbending as Tallinese iron, but she would need assistance to rise.

Gryf held out his hands to aid her, but Nick gripped her by one elbow. "I've got her."

Of course he did. Gryf compressed his lips and gave Nick a curt nod. Alexandra's body unfolded as she rose, long and lean, her feminine curves subtle under her loose clothing. If she stood to her full height, the top of her head would be even with his eyes. But with her head bent and shoulders hunched, she just reached his chin.

If only he could wrap his arms about her and allow his Gift to flow, comforting and strengthening her. But he had known her for mere moments, and to touch her so was a disrespect best avoided. He had no desire to have his other eye purpled.

Yet, had he not always known her? Not in reality, but in some deeper way? He drew his brows together; this conflict between convention and emotion was vexing.

Alexandra's legs buckled, and Nick's grip on her slipped as she pitched forward. Gryf moved quickly to catch her before she hit the floor. *Protect her.* Again, that voice in his mind—the same one he had heard earlier when she had rested against his chest. As a Guardian, he was already duty bound to protect her. So why did the voice ring with the authority of an official order from the Admiralty?

And why in all the hells was he hearing voices in his head at all?

He lifted her in his arms. "I will not let you fall, Alexandra." And he meant it—to the letter. A strange warmth eased into his chest, soothing, yet with an edge of anticipation, as though a wondrous event would soon occur. Similar to the feeling he had gotten as a child the night before Spring Festival.

Gryf sat her against the wall, cushioning the back of her head with his hand. The heat penetrating the thin fabric of her pink garment was a worrisome development. Could she be ill? If she were, his crew and the other Terrians were susceptible. He cast a glance around the cell and spied Dante attending the little Terrian boy.

"Chief, this one may be fevered."

Dante did not look up. "Worry not, Captain. Terrian body temperature is marginally higher than our own. Keep her comfortable. I will be there momentarily."

Nick laid his palm against his sister's brow then shook his head. "No fever." He leveled his gaze at Gryf. "What the hell happened this afternoon? Why are we here?"

Bold and direct. This must be a family trait. At least Nick used his words rather than his fists. How could Gryf respond without appearing evasive? "All your questions I will answer, Nick, once our healer has tended your people. This is my word to you."

The young man appeared skeptical.

Graig materialized at Gryf's side and handed him a water-soaked wad of grey cloth.

"What's that?" Nick jutted his chin at the dripping cloth.

"Water for your sister," Graig explained stiffly. "She is severely dehydrated. While Captain Helyg tends her, Nick, you may come with me. You have minor injuries which need tending."

The young man's eyes darted from Graig to Alexandra then back. "Why can't we do it here?"

"The only medical supplies the Anferthians allowed us are in Lieutenant Commander Zola's custody." Graig turned on his heel and strode in Zola's direction.

Gryf understood Nick's reluctance. Trusting the safety of his sister—possibly the only family left in his life—to a virtual stranger would be the last thing anyone would want to do in such a situation. If ever there was a moment to create trust between their peoples, it was now. Incarceration would be a living nightmare otherwise.

"On my honor, Nick, I will care for your sister until you return. I swear her safety."

Nick's mouth twisted with apparent derision. "You mean, you swear to keep her safe."

So much for establishing friendly relations. "That is what I meant, yes. My apologies for brutalizing your language. I strive to achieve improvement."

Nick's expression hardened even more, but in his eyes

lurked resignation that he did require aid. "Just don't get any ideas. I won't be long."

Gryf watched Nick make his way across the cell to where Graig waited. Alexandra was a treasure to the young man, and Gryf would not betray Nick's faith by treating her as anything less. No matter how obnoxious the boy proved to be.

Turning his attention back to the Terrian woman, he pressed the water-logged cloth to her lips. "Alexandra, here is some water. Drink."

As she sucked on the cloth, the tepid water dripped over his fingers. Her pale skin was so different from the standard Matiran blue. He glanced at the other Terrian woman nearby. She was as dark as Alexandra was fair. How must it be to live in a world with such a variety of exotic skin tones?

The darker woman's gaze met his, and she narrowed her eyes. There was no helping the anger and mistrust the Terrians carried. This day they had suffered so much with no understanding why. They would understand soon enough, though.

Alexandra turned her head to one side. "I'm okay."

Gryf focused his attention back onto her, but her eyes remained closed. A light spray of freckles dusted her cheeks, and the slight bump at the bridge of her nose. Even through the streaks of dirt, blood, and dried tears, she was an alluring young woman. Much younger than his thirty Galactic Standard cycles. No doubt she was too young to understand the burden of his failure to her people, and to his. It was clear she held him accountable for the destruction of her home world, and the massacre of her people. And rightly so.

Her head lolled, and Gryf raised his other hand to cup her cheek. If touching her was supposed to be crude and disrespectful, why did it feel so natural and right?

By the Holy Mother, cease this irrational behavior!

He lowered his hand. Brown and bronze eyes opened, and he swore his heart stopped. Her soul shone there, and he could not have looked away if his life depended upon it.

"I might have overreacted," she said in a rough whisper. "When I hit you, I mean."

He cleared his suddenly dry throat. "You did catch me

unawares."

"It's been a rotten day, you know."

Her lips scarce moved. She suffered, that much he could see. If only he could ease her pain. She wet her lips with her tongue. "I'm sorry I hurt you."

"I will recover." How would she react when Dante used his Gift to heal his eye? Or her wounds, if she allowed it?

"My mom says I'm passionate, but my dad says I'm a hothead." She made a huffing sound that may have been an attempt to chuckle. "I think he may be right, huh?"

"Perhaps they both are right."

The corners of Alexandra's mouth edged upward, and the pleasure of making her smile washed through him. Had he taken the first step to smoothing over their rough start? If he had learned anything from years of intergalactic relations and negotiations, it was that success or failure could hinge on the tiniest detail.

"This doesn't mean I trust you," she said.

Then again, perhaps not. "I will accept that, Alexandra."

"It's Alex." Her eyes drifted closed again. "And thank you for helping me, by the way."

"It pleases me to do so." He shifted in preparation to rise. "Our healer will attend you soon. I shall refresh the cloth to bring you more water."

Without awaiting her response, he rose and strode toward the small spigot, their only source of potable water. It mattered not if she did not trust him. She had respected him enough to apologize for her actions, and that was a start.

CHAPTER THREE

Alex kept her eyes closed and focused on the blessed coolness of the wall against her back. As long as she stayed still, right where the captain had left her, the pain in her head was less vomit-inducing. No moving, no talking, no throwing up on the nice captain's boots.

And he is nice, dammit.

His kindness made it difficult to stay angry. Although, she still didn't trust him.

And what about the healer? Would he be as nice? Hopefully this person had real medical training and didn't pull out alien leeches, or something equally archaic.

Don't be such a nitwit, Alex.

Any race with the technology for space travel must have far more advanced medical knowledge than Earth. A fizz of excitement bubbled up in her chest, and she slapped it back down. No sense in getting her hopes up. Until she knew the full story, these people were as much her enemy as the green aliens.

A soft rustle of cloth next to her reached her left ear. Sounded like someone had decided to join her.

A warm hand cupped her knee. "Hey."

Nicky. She forced her eyes open. Her brother squatted next to her, his forehead creased. "Hey, yourself."

"You okay?"

"I've had better days. But, yeah, I'm okay." Hurting but okay. That was more than a lot of people could say now.

Nicky jerked his head toward the man standing to his left. "This is the cell doctor, apparently."

A new blue alien, lanky and taller than the captain by a couple of inches, gave her a reassuring doctor's smile, his white teeth a vivid contrast to his dark-blue skin.

Captain Helyg stood at the doctor's side. "This is the *Atlantis*'s Senior Medical Chief, Dante Dacian. He is here to help you, Alexandra."

The newcomer crouched in front of her, knee-joints popping. "Greetings, Alex. It pleases me to meet you."

"Greetings?" She suppressed a chuckle. At least he hadn't asked her to take him to her leader.

And speaking of leaders...her gaze followed the lean, muscular line of the captain's legs up his body to his face. A runner's body. Had he run track in school like Nicky had?

Where had that stupid thought come from? He was from a different race, a different culture. They might not even have schools, or sports.

The ice-pick-wielding maniac in her head gave her brain another sharp jab. *Ow.* Was it too much to hope that Chief Master Medical—whatever—had an aspirin in his pocket?

Dante picked up her wrist to take her pulse, his hand cool against her skin. "You have probably guessed we are not from your planet."

Well, duh. Wait—was that supposed to be a joke? Did these aliens have a sense of humor? She raised her eyebrows at the man.

"Ah, I take it you have. Outstanding." There was a hint of amusement in his chocolate-brown eyes as he set her hand in her lap. "We are from a planet called Matir."

"Mah-teer." Was his planet as gentle as its name?

"Very well done. Despite our different origins, our internal anatomies are indistinguishable. Only our skin color is different. Rest assured, I am a competent master healer at the highest level." He paused and furrowed his brow as though a new thought had just occurred to him. "At least that is what the Collegium of Healers decreed, although they may have been trying to get rid of me."

Well, what do you know? Alex curved one corner of her mouth the tiniest bit upward. "Medical humor, huh, doc?"

Amusement lit Dante's eyes. Maybe this guy wasn't so bad. Besides, she needed medical attention and it seemed her options were limited to, well, Dante Dacian.

She shifted her gaze upward again. Angry Alien had joined his captain, a dour expression fixed on his chiseled face. Yup, Dante was definitely her preferred health care provider.

"Do you have any familiarity with concussions?" Dante asked.

"I'm a nurse." Given the look on Dante's face, nurses must not exist where he came from. "That's like a doctor's assistant."

Comprehension flashed in his eyes. "Then you know in most cases a concussion takes quite some time to heal."

Oh, boy, did she know. It could take weeks. Sometimes months.

"Alex, our medical knowledge is somewhat different than yours," Dante said.

Ah, ha. This must be the highly advanced medical technology she wanted to hear about. But why was Dante watching her as if he expected her to jump up and run screaming for the door? She scanned the cell, and frowned. Where *was* the door?

"While our anatomies are identical," Dante continued, "we have a Gift that your people do not. Our Gifts vary and are as unique as any individual. My Gift is to heal, which I am trained to do at a highly advanced level. I can heal your concussion within seconds with a single touch."

Her mouth dropped open. *No. Freaking. Way.* No one could heal with a touch. That was impossible. She cast a glance at Captain Helyg and read the truth on his face. Dante was serious.

"Wait. You mean like *magic?*" Nicky's question dripped with skepticism, but at least his brain and mouth were connected. *Her* mouth was hanging wide open, allowing all the emptiness in her head to seep into the cell. *Alexandra Bock, representing Earthlings everywhere.* She snapped her lips together.

"No, it is not magic or trickery," Dante replied, his eyes still on her. "It is truly a gift, and does have limitations. To us, it is as normal as the ability to draw is for some of your people. Some can draw very simple pictures, and others can create pictures with life-like clarity. Does this make sense?"

"Um." Unease skittered down her spine. "And you want to

use your healing Gift on me?"

"I would like to restore the full range of your hearing, heal your concussion and other injuries. If you prefer for me not to do so, I will honor your wishes."

Nothing but forthright honesty shone in his eyes. Still... "Your gift thing, can you use it to mind read?"

A smile lifted the corners of Dante's mouth, and he shook his head. "No, Alex. Mind reading is a myth."

It better be. The Matirans seemed genuine, and if Dante could fix her head, why not? Then again, did she really want someone messing around with her brain?

Dante's expression grew thoughtful. "Would it ease your fears if I healed someone else first?"

"Well, uh, I...." Exactly who did he plan to heal?

"I could heal Captain Helyg's eye first." Dante gave her a humorous quirk of his eyebrow. *Oh, right. That.*

Dante glanced up at his commanding officer. "Captain?"

"I would be grateful, Chief."

Captain Helyg moved with confidence and grace as he lowered himself to the floor at her right. She caught her lower lip between her teeth and clutched her hands together in her lap. If she didn't, they'd reach out and touch his well-defined, grey-clad thigh now resting inches from hers.

Good grief! She was reacting as though she'd never seen a man's leg before.

You don't even like him, remember?

She dragged her gaze away from the mass of masculine muscle only to get stuck staring into his sapphire eyes. Her thudding heart came to a screeching halt.

How much of her oglefest had he seen? Another hint of a smile touched his mouth. Nice. His bottom lip was just a little bit fuller than his top.

Oh, crap. She jerked her eyes down to her hands in her lap. She'd done it again. And the intense burning meant her cheeks and ears were scarlet. Maybe he wouldn't notice. *Yeah, right. What guy doesn't notice when a girl is staring?*

Dante moved closer, positioning his raised knee between her and Captain Helyg. The symbolic separation created some personal space for her, and she gave the healer a grateful look.

A knowing smile hung on his lips. *Marvelous.* She flicked her gaze upward and suppressed a groan. Angry Alien's narrowed eyes glared down at her as if he'd caught her with her hand in the cookie jar. He was so not amused.

"Proceed, Chief." Captain Helyg leaned his head against the wall and closed his good eye.

Alex moved closer so she could see over Dante's leg. Wow. The captain's eye was already swollen shut, surrounded by mottled black and purple bruising. Had she really hit him that hard? She flexed the fingers of her right hand. He hadn't even been angry that she'd hurt him. Instead, he'd taken care of her. She should've given him a chance to explain before she'd swung.

Dante's fingers hovered over the injured eye. "*Ocu.*"

Alex sucked in a soft, quick gasp. A faint aura glowed around the long-fingered hand. She glanced at the healer.

"You are not imagining it," Dante affirmed. "This is my Gift; to heal. Look." He lifted his hand a fraction. A pale-blue light swirled with tranquil grace between his palm and the captain's eye. Alex leaned farther over Dante's leg, tilting her head for a closer look. The swelling receded, and the bruising faded. It really looked like it was healing.

Her lips parted. The captain had ultra-fine laugh lines at the corners of his eyes.

The glow faded, and Dante pulled his hand away.

"Whoa," Nicky gasped.

Alex couldn't have said it better. The captain's eyes opened...so clear, so deep, and so blue. Her favorite color.

A deep desire to touch him—touch his soul—filled her, expanding until her heart trembled. What was happening to her?

Who cares? Just let yourself fall into the sapphire whirlpool.

"What are you doing to her?" Nicky's demanding question came from right behind her. Someone grabbed her by her shoulders and yanked her backward. Pain knifed through her brain, behind her eyeballs, and down her neck. A dry sob escaped her. Too much pain—and getting worse.

Nicky wrapped his arms around her in an awkward

embrace, and he scuttled backward, dragging her along the floor. Her head rocked against his shoulder, and she moaned.

"Nick." Dante reached toward her, concern marring his brow.

"Don't touch her!" Nicky snapped, adjusting his grip and pulling her tighter against his chest.

What the hell, Nicky?

Her mouth worked, but the words she wanted to say didn't come out.

"She suffers, Nick." Dante's voice remained calm and reasonable. "I can help her."

Sharp pain stabbed through her brain in time with her heartbeat. *Don't cry. It'll make it worse.* Dante continued to coax Nicky, but it sounded as though her brother wasn't having any of it. Blackness edged her vision. If they didn't stop arguing and help her, she would faint again.

She flailed her arm out, reaching for help that didn't seem to exist. Strong fingers entwined with hers. *Bam.* The sensation of ocean waves cradling her returned. A pleasant heat flowed through her ear canal then seeped into her head. It sped through her neural pathways, leaving nerve endings tingling, vibrant with renewal. Then, it funneled back out her ear and disappeared.

The heat and waves dissipated, and she blinked away the lingering haze of pain. Captain Helyg's concerned face hovered near hers, their hands still entwined between them.

What had just happened?

"Shall we try again?" he asked with a smile. "Hello, Alexandra, I am Gryf. It pleases me to meet you." His warm voice flowed as smooth as honey into her newly-healed ear, and didn't stop until it touched her heart.

◆ ◆ ◆ ◆ ◆

Gryf met Nick's glare. Surely the boy could see that his sister was now well.

"What did you do to her, you freaking Martian?" Nick growled, his arms tightening around Alexandra.

Did the young man seek to goad him? "I am *Matiran*, Nick, not Martian." He understood the reference and was not amused.

"I also should like to know what happened, Gryf." Dante's assessing look bordered on suspicion.

"I...." For the love of the Mother, what *had* he done to her?

He looked back at Alexandra. Had he truly just healed her? He had not the ability to heal anything more than minor cuts and bruises, yet she looked at him with eyes alert and pain free.

And she was the only one *not* glaring blades at him.

"Whatever you did, it worked," Alexandra said. "My head doesn't hurt, and I can hear."

"But you should not." How in all the hells had he managed this feat?

Alexandra appeared ready to protest, but Gryf cut her off. "I am not a healer, Alexandra, which means you should not be well."

"Well, you're wrong about that, because I'm fine. Nicky, let *go.*" She gripped Gryf's hand tighter and used it to lever herself upright, shaking free of her brother's hold. "And it's Alex."

"I am partial to Alexandra." It was a gamble, but he much preferred her full name. Would she find him worthy of the honor? He lowered his chin, quirked an eyebrow, and gave her a lopsided smile. Another negotiating tactic he had learned: the right facial expressions and body language often worked as well as his Gift to put another at ease.

A ghost of a smile crossed her lips, and she sighed. "All right, you may call me Alexandra."

His heart hitched in his chest. This Terrian woman wreaked havoc with his senses, and he *enjoyed* it.

From behind Dante, Graig Roble made a noise of exasperation. Gryf spared him a withering glance.

"May I check you, Alex?" Dante asked.

"Um...."

Then she did the most wondrous thing. She turned to him with a look as though seeking his assurance. It seemed too much to hope she trusted him to any degree already.

"He only checks to make sure I did it correctly. Nothing more, I assure you." If it were Graig asking to do such, she would surely balk. But Dante's nature instilled confidence.

PROPHECY

Alexandra nodded, and the healer laid his hand on her shoulder. Three heart-beats passed then he sat back frowning. "She is healed, Gryf. Completely."

"Wait a minute." Alexandra furrowed her brow at Dante. "You've done that before, haven't you? Used your Gift on me."

"I ran a diagnostic scan on you earlier." Dante's expression was wary.

Alexandra frowned. "But you...I feel different when you use your Gift on me, like I'm in the clouds. And, Gryf, you're like...an ocean wave."

It was true; each Matiran's Gift bore a natural signature of sorts. How had Alexandra picked up on both their signatures? She should not have been able to do that, any more than he should have been able to heal.

Dante stood up. "I apologize, Alex. Rare it is that I do not obtain a patient's permission first. Captain, a moment, please."

Gryf cringed, loath to surrender Alexandra's hand. But duty called. "Excuse me, Alexandra." He gave her hand a gentle squeeze and released her.

Dante led the way to the furthest corner, Graig following along. Apparently, both of them were in interrogation mode. It was their right.

"By your leave, sir." Gryf gave Dante an absent nod, and the familiar sensation of floating in the clouds filled his senses as the healer scanned him. "Completely normal." Dante spoke in Matiran, likely to keep the conversation semi-private.

"As a healer, I would think such a diagnosis would thrill you."

Annoyance flashed in Dante's eyes. "When my friend with no formal training heals a concussion and hearing loss for a woman from a different race—and shows no sign how he did so—I am far from thrilled. Sir."

Of course not. Who would be? In truth, these facts disturbed him as well.

"Sir." Graig moved closer. "As your head of security, I must remind you that at this time we are still prisoners of the Anferthians."

"I am rather familiar with our situation, Commander."

"Your personal involvement with any of the Terrians could

compromise the safety of us all."

Involvement? Had Graig lost all sense? "I need not remind you that the length of time the Terrians have been with us can be measured in hours. That is hardly enough time for any of us to become involved." Not that he would reject the idea as out of hand.

Graig's grey gaze did not waver. "Sir, I swore an oath to protect you, with my life, if necessary. You swore an oath to lead the Guardians. Right now we are in a volatile situation that requires you to be that leader. We cannot afford to have you distracted."

Gryf pinched the bridge of his nose and squeezed his eyes shut. No, none of them could afford that.

He dropped his hand and met Graig's stern gaze with one of his own. "It matters little, Graig. An hour from now, Alexandra will know my role in the events leading to the destruction of her people. Is it too much to allow me that time free of her glaring hate in my direction?"

Those were the most selfish words he had uttered in the two years since accepting his promotion to senior captain of the Guardian Fleet. Not that he held much hope of completing the three-year assignment, or resuming a personal life.

Graig opened his mouth then snapped it shut and gave him a curt nod.

Gryf shifted his attention back to Dante. "I am at a loss regarding the healing of Alexandra, Chief. Run regular checks on both of us, with her consent, of course. If anything unusual shows up, notify me immediately."

"Yes, sir."

"I do appreciate your concern, both of you. Dismissed."

Alone for the moment, Gryf massaged his temples. Friends did not come much closer than Graig and Dante. As children, Gryf and Graig had played together. They had gone to the same tutors for their schooling, and joined the Guardian Fleet together as young men.

Dante had fallen in with them when they were cadets. A couple of cycles older, and decades wiser, he had been their calming influence in their younger, wilder days. No one knew Gryf better than these two men.

PROPHECY

Except Ora. But she was gone now. The Anferthians had used the *Atlantis* to reduce her ship to dust. His cousin and life-long friend was no more. Mother above, had his aunt and uncle been informed of the loss of their daughter yet? His heart ached with an unbearable hollowness. He swallowed hard as regret rose up, threatening to consume him. He could not change what had happened, although he would give his own life to do so. But the universe did not stop spiraling, and he must let go what he could not control.

But, Alexandra. How could she touch him at his core when they had not known each other more than one Earth hour? If he was not mistaken, she was equally confused—fluctuating between accepting him and despising him.

In the end, though, it did not matter. She would pull away when the truth came out, and he would resume his isolated role as senior captain.

CHAPTER FOUR

Alex rubbed the heels of her hands against her teary eyes. If she didn't find something to focus on, she would completely lose control. She glanced across the cell at the four Matirans gathered in the opposite corner. It couldn't have been more than three hours since she and the other Earthlings had arrived in the cell, and it seemed that lines were being drawn. Besides her and Nicky, there was Simone, Dennis, and six-year-old Juan. A botanist, a banker, and a foster child. Talk about an eclectic group. But the bond of a shared trauma seemed to have drawn the five of them together.

The fourth member of the Matiran group was the woman Commander Roble had referred to as Lieutenant Commander Zola. She wore her black hair pulled back in a no-nonsense bun at the base of her neck, and her equally black eyes seemed to see right through a person. But, despite her severe appearance, she'd been kind to Nicky.

"It's every bit as awkward to use as you might think," Simone said, her lip curled with obvious contempt.

Alex refocused her attention on the petite African-American woman sitting next to her. "Sorry, what is?"

Simone's mahogany eyes regarded her with a hint of wry humor. "We're talking about the bathroom, Alex. Try to keep up. It's behind that partition over there, and it isn't easy to use knowing everyone out here can hear you. I know. I tried while that big blue bruiser, Roble, stood on the other side making sure no one walked in on me."

Alex studied the half-wall partition in the corner at the far end of the cylindrical cell. Grey, just like everything in here. Although, she'd revised her initial impression of their prison. The room seemed more like a smooth-walled Quonset hut than a tin can.

"I see your point, Simone." She gave her shoulders a small shrug. "I guess we'll have to make the best of the situation." Cripes, didn't she just sound like little Miss Mary Sunshine?

"At least no one has to help you to the bathroom every time you need to pee," Dennis muttered from where he lay a few feet away on the floor, one beefy arm slung across his eyes.

Of the five Earthlings, he was in the worst shape. Alex glanced at his injured foot. It was swollen and turning every shade of purple, blue, and black from being crushed under a large piece of concrete during the invasion. At least he'd allowed Dante to use that Gift thingy to block the pain. For the life of her, she couldn't imagine how the healer planned to fix it.

She glanced across the cell again. Gryf's blue gaze met hers. Something in the vicinity of her heart fluttered like the last leaf of autumn clinging tenaciously to its tree. What was it about him that caused such a ridiculous reaction? Sure he'd healed her, and that gave him mega-bonus points over the invaders, but she still didn't completely trust him.

And why not?

There wasn't a great reason other than she was just suspicious by nature. Until the Matirans gave a satisfactory explanation of their role in the invasion, she had to assume they might not be all they seemed.

"I'm hungry."

Alex started, and looked down at the little six-year-old boy sitting between her and Nicky. Juan wiped his nose with the back of his hand. "Do ya think they gonna feed us?"

As if in response to his words, her stomach growled. Her watch was gone when she'd woken up—probably being dissected in an Anferthian lab right now—but it had to be evening, more or less. Some food would be nice, she hadn't eaten since breakfast, and her morning coffee break had ended up on Gryf's boots. Heat rose to her cheeks. She really should apologize for that *faux pas*.

"Not sure how they're going to do that since there doesn't seem to be a door," Nicky said.

Huh? Oh, right, food.

She scanned the adjacent wall. Sure enough, not as much as a crack, or even a shadow of an outline. How the heck had they gotten in here?

"Maybe they can walk through walls." Juan scrunched his face at his own suggestion. "Nah. That's a stupid idea."

Whoosh!

A gasp escaped her even as her brother swore. Several spiraling lines appeared on the end wall opposite the bathroom, meeting at the center. Then the wall opened like a camera shutter.

"There's your door, Nick." Simone's tone was tongue-in-cheek.

"Cool," Juan breathed. The poor kid had been lost in the state foster system for most of his life, which could be why he seemed to be viewing their situation as an adventure.

A rush of cool air prickled Alex's skin as she stared at the large opening. Well, large to her, but just big enough to allow two of the green aliens to pass through. Which they did, and then stood on either side of the opening, weapons at the ready. As if they needed weapons. They had to be at least eleven feet tall. Even if everyone in the cell rushed them at once, there was no hope of getting past these giants.

A blue-skinned couple strode through the doorway, and Alex did a double take. "They're Matiran?"

"Wonder why they get to walk around free?" Dennis muttered.

She studied the strange Matirans. The man appeared to be in his early thirties, with medium brown hair and eyes, high cheekbones, and a straight, narrow, blade-like nose. Not drop-dead gorgeous, but he did pass as handsome.

The woman was...stunning. She wore a uniform similar to Gryf's crew's, but in better condition. Much better condition. The uniform pants accentuated her long legs, and the shirt fit snug over her full breasts. Her blue-green eyes had a hard, calculating look, and the features on her heart-shaped face were perfectly proportioned. She oozed *femme fatale*.

The man's gaze swept the cell before honing in on Gryf. "*Saltu, Capeto Helyg.*" There was a definite hint of mockery in his voice.

PROPHECY

"We speak English here, Kotas." Gryf stepped forward, placing himself closest to the newcomer.

Kotas shrugged. "As you wish. I hope you and your crew have found your new company here pleasing." His gaze met Alex's. "*Very* pleasing."

A chill slithered down Alex's spine. Being noticed by this guy couldn't have been a good thing, but it wasn't as though she could hide from him.

"And who do we have here?" Femme Fatale's gaze raked Nicky from head to toe, and his face flamed red under the Matiran woman's scrutiny.

"Leave him, Haesi," Graig growled.

Haesi's attention shifted to the Commander, and her perfect lips bowed into a seductive smile. "Jealous, Graig?"

Alex gaped. This drop-dead gorgeous bombshell was his ex. She had to be. Commander Roble's eyes narrowed a fraction, but he said nothing.

"No toys today, Lieutenant Velo," Kotas said, his gaze lingered on each of the Earthlings as though he searched for weakness. "You will be happy to know that your time in this pit is almost at an end, *Captain* Helyg." He spat Gryf's title as though it were a foul word.

"Indeed?" Gryf folded his arms over his chest and raised one eyebrow.

Kotas cast a glance back at him. "Indeed." His nose twitched into a sneer. "The merchant ships will arrive in fifteen Galactic Standard days. Then you and your crew will be moved to new accommodations with the Terrian slaves."

"*All* of my crew?"

"Of course, Capeto. It would be pointless to keep them here. The Anferthians want these cells available as they continue to collect their merchandise."

Did anyone else see the almost imperceptible tightening of Gryf's jaw?

Kotas's eyes narrowed. "As you can imagine, the Anferthians have a schedule to keep. Supreme Warden T'lik has given the invasion fleet one hundred days to collect all Terrian survivors. After that, you will be off to your new life."

An invisible band tightened around Alex's chest. Slaves.

The concept had seemed so abstract before, but somehow Kotas's words drove the truth home. This was real; they *were* slaves. She exchanged a look with Nicky. He appeared ready to vomit.

Kotas turned to Dante and said something in a lilting language. Lieutenant Commander Zola gasped, and Dante's face turned from blue to ash-grey.

"You cannot do such," Dante said.

"I assure you, Chief, I can. And I will," Kotas replied. Then he gave Gryf another oily smile before striding out of the cell. "Time to go, Velo. You will have a chance to play with them later."

The stunning Matiran woman eyed Commander Roble as she ran her finger down the center of Nicky's chest. Roble's eyes narrowed, as if a threat had been issued. With a smirk, Velo turned and followed Kotas from the cell. The Anferthians stepped into the corridor and the door telescoped in, the opening getting smaller until it was a solid wall again.

Alex gave herself a mental shake and pushed herself up to stand. It was time to set a few things straight. "What did he say to you, Dante?"

Dante hesitated, and Gryf said something in a foreign language.

Really? What the hell?

She jabbed a finger in the almighty captain's direction. "Don't you dare order him not to say anything. You *owe* us an explanation."

"Amen," Simone agreed, moving closer to Alex in a show of unity. Nicky rose too, and Juan with him, the little boy's wide brown eyes clouded with confusion. At six years old, he couldn't be expected to understand the tension between the adults in the room.

Gryf spread his hands in a placating gesture. "And that is why I asked Dante to wait."

"Who was that man, Gryf? And why is he walking around like he owns the place?"

His lips compressed into a thin line. "That was Vyn Kotas, a former...colleague."

"The Betrayer." Zola stood with her fists clenched at her

sides, a fierce expression on her face.
Note to self: Stay on this woman's good side.
"Karise," Gryf warned.
The Matiran woman closed her mouth, but the fire in her eyes didn't go out. "Sorry, sir."
Pain etched Gryf's face when he turned his attention back to Alex. "The Anferthians invaded your planet because I failed to recognize the depth of Kotas's animosity toward me after he was discharged from the Guardian Fleet."
Alex crossed her arms in front of her. "And exactly what is a Guardian Fleet?"
"Forgive my oversight, Alexandra. The Guardian Fleet is a sub-fleet of the Matiran Defense Fleet. We have guarded Terr—our name for your planet—for close to twelve thousand years."
Her mouth fell open. *Twelve thousand years?* Holy crap. "Um, guarded from what, exactly?"
"From races like the Anferthians. There are those in the galaxy who would have exploited your technologically-deficient ancestors. When the Matirans first discovered your home-world and made contact with its indigenous people, it was unintentional."
"But there was a good reason." Karise nodded. "Malfunctioning sensors showed no sentient life forms here."
"True," Gryf continued. "Yet from this mistake, a friendship between two worlds developed. For a time, our peoples worked well together. Eventually, some intermarried. Only a select few Terrians ever knew that we were not truly from a Utopian island in the sea.
"Then other races in the galaxy became curious about what the Matirans were doing on this tiny planet on the Edge, and our ancestors knew they must leave and allow your people to evolve naturally. But their presence here had drawn the attention of the galaxy, and the Matirans would not leave their beloved friends here unprotected. The Matiran government filed a Galaxy Claim for Mining Rights on Terr, and for twelve millennia Matir has been 'mining' your 'uninhabited' planet."
Alex snapped her mouth shut and gave her head a slight shake. It seemed far-fetched, but Gryf didn't strike her as

someone prone to making up stories.

Gryf swept one arm around the cell. "My crew and I have dedicated ourselves—our lives—to protecting your planet. Serving as a Guardian is a time-honored tradition."

They'd bald-faced lied to the rest of the universe in order to give Earthlings time to grow-up? Huh. Go figure. "If you...Matirans...*were* here, why don't we have any record of it?"

Gryf shook his head. "Great measures were taken to conceal our original contact with your people. Even so, there may be tales which have survived into your generation."

"You're right about that." Nicky looked from Alex to Gryf. "Didn't you say your ship is called the *Atlantis*?"

"It is." Gryf nodded.

"Then there is a record, sort of." Nicky twisted his mouth into a half-smile. "The Lost Continent of Atlantis."

If a ton of bricks had fallen on her, Alex couldn't have been more surprised. Why hadn't *she* thought of that?

"The *Atlantis* was large, but hardly a continent." Gryf shrugged. "Your lost continent was an early incarnation of our current flagship."

"Great earthquakes and an impassable mud shoal," Nicky paraphrased an account of the sinking of Atlantis. "I'm guessing your ship would've been big enough to create both those things when it took off."

"It was indeed."

Nicky looked at Alex again. "Dad would *love* this."

Yes, he would. Not only was their father the head of the history department at the university near their home in Damon Beach, he also had a passion for anything and everything related to the Atlantis myth. Not an all-consuming passion that tried to force the myth into recorded history, but he *had* filled their young heads with stories on the topic. She and Nicky had often made up their own stories, play-acting them out with the enthusiasm of children exploring their imaginations. And that had been Dad's point—for them to use their imaginations.

Dad wouldn't just love this; he'd be doing freaking back-flips.

"If being a Guardian is such a time-honored tradition, what the hell went wrong today?" Dennis asked from his spot on the floor.

Gryf shifted his attention to Dennis. "Former Commander Kotas was passed over thrice for captaincy. I was aware of the animosity he bore me after I was advanced to this rank ahead of him, though I was a full two years behind him. He challenged my advancement to senior captain of the Guardian Fleet, which subsequently led to his discharge. I failed to ascertain his whereabouts afterward. If I had, I could have prevented an Anferthian agent from corrupting him."

Graig Roble growled. "He was already corrupt. He blames you for something you had no control over."

Gryf narrowed his eyes at the man. "As the senior captain, it was my responsibility to assess *all* threats to the fleet and to Terr. I failed to do so," he replied in a clipped voice.

"If anyone failed, it was the fleet brass. *They* should have kept an eye on Kotas, not you. Blaming yourself—"

"*Enough*, Commander Roble!" Gryf cut him off.

Silence fell like a heavy blanket over the group. Something warm touched Alex's leg, and she startled. Juan's dark eyes gazed up at her, his hand pressed against her thigh.

"Why is Cap'n Gryf angry?" the boy whispered.

"He's not exactly angry, sweetie. He's had a difficult week."

Gryf closed his eyes briefly then opened them and gave Juan a gentle smile. "Yes, a very difficult week, Juan. I do not mean to upset you." He turned to Dennis. "Kotas did betray us, and the Anferthians managed to board the *Atlantis* one evening after I went off duty. It was the beginning of a night of blood-shed that did not end until my surrender."

Alex frowned. "Wait a minute. How did they get aboard if Kotas wasn't there?"

Gryf shot a quick glance at Commander Roble. "He had an agent aboard."

"That woman, Haesi?"

Another glance was exchanged between the two men, and Roble stiffened. "She was one of my people in security. She is...very good."

This time it was Karise who snorted. "Haesi Velo is *very*

good at one thing: deceit. She aligns herself with people who hold power."

Roble shot a glare at her, but Gryf interrupted any further exchange. "*Paci.* Peace, my friends. Speculation will get us nowhere."

The eyes of all the Matirans in the cell were on Gryf, their respect for their captain clear. That kind of respect was earned.

Gryf gave the healer a nod. "Dante."

Dante looked down at Dennis. "Kotas just gave me an ultimatum, Dennis. I must heal you in ten days, or he will kill you."

A knot of fear formed in Alex's gut. This was so not good.

"Alexandra."

She jerked her head up. Gryf had moved closer. His gaze bored into hers, sorrow and pain clouding the deep-blue depths of his eyes. "This will not be easy to hear, but almost the entire sentient population of your planet has been annihilated. You are among the few who survived. I know this because I was forced to watch the slaughter as it happened. Forced to watch the results of my complacence. And I will not ask for your forgiveness, because I do not deserve it."

She swallowed hard against the lump in her throat. "What are the chances that my parents are still alive?"

His gaze didn't waver, and her heart constricted. "The Anferthians are most interested in your planet—to what end, I do not know. Terrian slaves are merely a small bonus to be sold for profit to worlds that still practice slavery. The chances that your parents survived are less than point zero one percent."

The room seemed to shrink. Gryf's revelation was like a pile driver crushing her chest. She had so hoped the odds were better.

"Shit," Nicky hissed, balling his hands at his sides. "Shit, fuck, and goddammit."

"Nicholaus...." She clamped her lips together. What could she say? Nothing would make the situation better for either of them.

Her brother stalked away to thump his fists against the cold metal wall furthest from the group.

God help us all.

CHAPTER FIVE

The following morning, Alex lay on her back and stared up at the ceiling of the dimly-lit slave cell. She swiped away yet another tear with the back of her hand. They'd been leaking out all night, even after the air-gulping, soul-shattering crying session she'd shared with Nicky before they'd curled up next to each other to sleep. If anyone called drifting in and out of consciousness "sleep".

Things had gone from bad to worse with head-spinning velocity yesterday. And last night had been the longest she'd ever experienced. Which was fitting given that yesterday had seemed like the longest day of her life.

At least they'd finally received food. Some sort of hand-sized, orange protein loaf. Even though Dante assured them it would meet their daily nutritional requirements, she couldn't see how they'd maintain weight with once-a-day feedings. Especially Juan. The little boy had picky eating habits, which was age appropriate. But that made him the most likely candidate for malnutrition.

She pushed herself upright on the cold metal floor and rolled her shoulders to alleviate the stiffness in her muscles. Everything was lost. Her home was gone, her people slaughtered, and her planet occupied by hostile aliens. It was a freaking nightmare. She massaged her temples with her fingertips. If Gryf was right, she and Nicky would never see their parents again. The emptiness in her heart tore at her. Everything seemed so hopeless. Yesterday morning she was a first-year-nurse working in the county ER in Damon Beach. And now...now she was supposedly a slave. This kind of stuff didn't happen in real life. It couldn't.

Her gaze was drawn to Simone where she slept on the hard

floor, and a heavy ache settled into her gut. The other woman's dark skin was reminder enough that this kind of stuff *did* happen. Earth's history was full of such atrocities. Damn it. All she'd wanted was to care for people too sick to care for themselves. And maybe find someone to share her journey with one day. Now all that was gone.

Her bladder chose that moment to send her an urgent message. *Swell.* She turned her head to peer over her shoulder. The dark silhouette of the bathroom partition loomed, silently taunting anyone who dared to forsake modesty to come in and use the hole-in-the-floor toilet.

Alex wrinkled her nose. At least most everyone was asleep at the moment. Only Dante was awake, on watch. It was now or never…and never wasn't an option. As she climbed to her feet, she locked gazes with a pair of gorgeous sapphire eyes. It just figured that Gryf would be awake. He lay on his back with his head cradled in his arms, watching her.

Well, it wasn't as if she could ask him to plug his ears while she peed. She stepped over Nicky's sleeping form and headed to the bathroom.

When she emerged, she scrutinized the prone forms of her cellmates in the corner near the door. No part of her wanted to go back there. She turned toward the corner furthest from the others. According to Karise, in the week proceeding Alex's arrival Gryf had established that corner for private conversations, and as a place to retreat for personal meditation. Well, he wasn't the only one who needed private time. She lowered herself and snugged her bottom into the rounded corner. The floor dipped just enough to be comfortable. Now she understood why Gryf liked to sit here.

Nicky made a snork sound in his sleep and rolled over. Her mouth curved up a fraction. If Gryf was right, her brother was all the family she had left. Her heart contracted as though a metal band tightened around it, and she squeezed her eyes tight against the ever-present threat of tears. There was no going back.

She rested her arms on her drawn-up knees and buried her face against them. Gryf hadn't sugarcoated the situation—slavery still existed in the galaxy, and the Anferthians were one of the races who actively owned and marketed slaves. The Earthlings would be sold, and not necessarily to the same owner. Losing her brother to slavery just couldn't happen. There had to be a way out of here.

"May I sit with you?"

Alex startled then lifted her head and looked up at Gryf. As impossible as the situation was, his presence seemed to make it better.

She gave herself a mental shake. What was she thinking? Nothing could make it better, not even this man. She shrugged one shoulder. "Sure. Go ahead."

He sank to the floor to sit cross-legged in front of her. "You did not sleep."

It was a statement, not a question, but she shook her head anyway. "Not well."

"It is understandable."

"You haven't either, have you?"

"Dante makes sure I am rested, but no. I have not slept well on my own since the fall of the Guardians."

That wasn't healthy. "You mean that Dante uses his Gift to help you sleep?"

"Yes. It is called *dormio*, the healing sleep."

She shifted her gaze to the toes of her nursing shoes. They'd once been clean and white. What an odd thought. Did it matter how clean or white they'd been? Or that her rose-pink scrubs were now covered in dirt and grass stains—and torn in several places? She slid a finger into the ripped fabric at her knee.

Gryf raised his hand as though to reach for her, then he stopped and placed it back on his leg. A warm flush rushed to her cheeks and she frowned.

"I don't need your pity, you know." She wiggled her finger in the rip. "It's enough that I'm feeling sorry for myself, so just say whatever it is you want to say."

"I do not pity you, Alexandra," he replied softly. "I feel empathy for your losses, but I would never pity you. You are a strong soul, and deserve more respect than that from me, or anyone."

Her gaze met his again. No, there was no pity there. But

there was sincerity, and...admiration? She didn't deserve that. But clearly he'd meant what he said. She fought the smile that wanted out. If she wasn't careful, she could learn to like this alien.

Would that be so terrible?

Maybe not. Especially if he found a way out of here. But what did she really know about him?

"Truly, I am afraid of what you would do if I dared pity you." He touched his fingertips to the soft skin under his eye and grinned.

A soft snort of laughter escaped her. "Sorry. I had kind of a hard day yesterday."

"That you did, *yana*."

"And sometimes I react without thinking."

The corners of his mouth twitched, but he remained silent.

"What does *yana* mean?"

Gryf regarded her as though weighing his reply carefully. Were his cheeks getting darker? It was hard to tell in the dim light. He licked his lips. "It means my friend—gender specific to a woman. A male would be *ropo*."

She stared at him. His friend? Really?

"I will not use it again if it makes you uncomfortable," he offered.

Her heart thudded in her chest. On the one hand, the term was a little too personal. On the other, she kind of liked it. She caught her bottom lip between her teeth.

He nodded. "It does make you uncomfortable, this I see. I will refrain from using it in the future."

A pin-prick of disappointment poked at her heart, but she gave him a half-smile anyway. "How did you learn English?"

"Transmissions from your planet, both audio and visual." He rolled his shoulders as if to shake off stiffness. "It was a trickle at first, but as your technology grew, we had to scramble to block them from the ears of others. It was a nightmare when your people began sending unmanned probes into space. The information chosen to share with unknown races was a blue print to your own destruction."

Alex swallowed. He must mean the Voyager missions. There might've been others, but the space program had never held her interest. Nicky would know. "Pretty stupid of us, I guess."

"Not at all. You were curious, and learning quickly, which gave us hope that we soon would be able to contact your people again. We had estimated another two hundred years, and Terrian technology would be advanced enough to protect your planet should the need arise."

Two hundred years? Well after her lifetime. "If not for Kotas and what's-her-name, I guess."

"They did not act alone. There were others, and Kotas chose them wisely. His Gift is his ability to discern what is in the hearts of others."

"I wish...." She stopped herself. Wished what? That none of this had happened? That her parents were alive? That she'd go home tonight, open the door, and smell Mom's world-class lasagna baking? Of course she wished all that, but what good would it do?

Gryf shook his head. "To live dwelling in what could have been is not a life, Alexandra. This helps no one."

"I want to help." The words were out of her mouth before it hit her how true they were. She wanted—*needed* to do something to help.

Gryf's expression softened. "You are a healer for your people, and I know one who could use your expertise."

Moments later, Alex sat on one side of Dennis's sleeping form with Dante on the other. Gryf had taken a spot on the floor just behind her. "I know I don't have a Gift like you, Dante, and I feel a little primitive because of it...but, if there's anything I can do to assist you, I'd like to."

"I would very much welcome the opportunity to work with and learn from you, Alex." Warmth shone in Dante's brown eyes, and his expression was almost fatherly.

Her heart lifted. Dante had a power unlike anything she'd ever imagined, and he wanted to learn from her?

"In the ancient time before The Leaving, physicians from both our races sometimes worked together. Terrians could enhance the power of a Matiran's Gift, especially in difficult cases. You see, it was not only the guilt we bore for prematurely exposing you to the galaxy that drove us to protect you, it was also this connection we share. Our races complement each other."

"So you think that if I participate, you can put more power behind your healing, and we may have a better chance of fixing Dennis's foot?" Was it possible that what Dante wasn't able to do alone, they could accomplish together?

"My hope is such."

Her heart thrummed with excitement. "But how? What would happen?"

"I cannot say with any certainty, having never tried healing in this manner," Dante admitted. "It would be new territory for us both."

She wet her lips. Yesterday's experience with Gryf had been painless. She'd felt an awareness of him, and the sensation of ocean waves, but nothing nefarious. To the best of her knowledge, she wasn't under any sort of mind control, and her behavior seemed as normal as ever. Could she take a personal risk to help save a life? Alex checked over her shoulder. Nicky was still asleep. If he knew what she was contemplating, he'd blow a gasket.

It's not his choice to make though, is it?

Dennis sighed in his sleep.

"Time runs short, Alex," Dante murmured. "Dennis will awaken soon. *Dormio* will keep him from feeling pain as we put his foot back together."

Alex held Dante's gaze for a heartbeat. If there was a chance, no matter how unconventional, shouldn't she take it?

"Okay, I'm in."

Dante gave her a quick nod and patted the floor next to him, suddenly all business. "A point of physical contact is necessary," he explained as she moved to sit next to him. "Your hand on my arm should be enough. We will go slowly for all our sakes. Doing too much during a session could cause excess swelling, decreasing Dennis's blood flow, and leading to a whole new set of complications."

But what would it do to her and Dante? She rested one hand on his forearm, and Dante placed his hands over Dennis's foot. "When you are ready, Alex."

She licked her lips. Okay, this was a little intimidating, but medical advances weren't made by people who sat in their rooms picking their noses. "Okay, I'm ready."

The healer gave her a reassuring smile then murmured, "*Pes.*"

The faint healing light she'd seen yesterday glowed again in Dante's eyes and hands. It wrapped itself around her hand, and the white, puffy clouds she associated with Dante invaded her senses. There was a gentle pull at the core of her being, and she sucked in a sharp breath as the inner workings of Dennis's foot became visible to her like a full-color x-ray.

"I can see inside his foot. It's...all the bones are shattered. How could anyone fix this mess, Dante?"

"Just watch." Using his forefinger, Dante drew a line over Dennis's foot, and a bone fragment moved until it butted against and fused to another fragment. *Oh!* He was rebuilding the bone structure like a difficult jigsaw puzzle. Brilliant.

Ten minutes passed before Dante's light faded, and he released Dennis's foot. "That was excellent. Thank you, Alex. We are not yet finished, but I could not have done half as much on my own."

She couldn't help sharing his kid-like grin over their accomplishment. Successful healing session, and she felt perfectly normal. Didn't get much better than that.

Blackness swooped in like a vulture, tunneling her vision. Oh, crap, not again. A firm hand shoved her head down to her knees, and the gentle clouds were back.

"Come back, Alex," Dante's voice said.

Her vision cleared, and she blinked at the dull grey floor. The world stabilized, and the darkness whisked away in smoky ribbons. A hand stroked her back. Gryf. She'd all but forgotten he was there. Rats. He must've seen her faint.

"Alexandra?" Gryf's voice was gentle next to her ear.

"I'm sorry." *In. Out. Slow and steady.*

"Worry not. Even as a youngster first learning to use my Gift, I too fainted. It is not unexpected, and will get better with experience."

Gryf had fainted? That seemed hard to believe.

"Will you be ready to sit up?"

"I think so." As she straightened, Gryf kept his hand on her shoulder for balance.

"Why would Alex faint if she does not have a Gift?" Graig's grey gaze scrutinized her. How did he *do* that? Just appear from nowhere when she least expected him?

"Exposure," Dante replied. "As the Gift can overwhelm a Matiran child's first experiences, so can it overwhelm someone exposed indirectly. It is a potent force to anyone with no experience."

That made sense. The power which had drawn energy from her had certainly been potent.

Alex pursed her lips. "This won't *always* happen, right?" If it did, her ability to help would be limited, and that wasn't acceptable.

"I do not believe so." Dante gave her an understanding smile. "It may take several exposures, or just a few for you to adjust. We shall see. In the meantime, I do believe we have stumbled upon something that will be advantageous to both our peoples. Together, we made more progress today than I could have on my own in three days. It will still take several sessions to repair all the damage, but there is hope. Are you willing to try again later?"

"Of course." Dennis's life was on the line, and failure was not an option.

Dante nodded, satisfaction gleaming in his eyes. "Captain, I request permission to proceed with this project with Alex."

Gryf's fantastic blue eyes locked with hers, and he smiled. A genuine smile. Her heart thudded in her chest. *Wow.*

"Permission granted, Chief."

CHAPTER SIX

The Pacific Ocean sparkled brilliant and blue under the midday sun. It was a jackets-need-not-apply kind of spring day. A glorious time to be alive. Alex walked along the glittering sidewalk in her comfortable nursing shoes, closing the distance from work to lunch with her brother.

The sunlight dimmed. Her heartbeat pounded in her ears like a bass drum. Things were about to go wrong. Along the horizon, a white cloud billowed, separating the water from the sky. It stretched as far as she could see in either direction, accelerating toward the coast with more speed than any cloud she'd ever seen. The closer that cloud got, the darker the sky became, until the entire town of Damon Beach was engulfed in its sinister shadow.

The cloud evaporated, and in its place was a floating horror. A colossal foreign object blotting out the warm sunshine and bringing night to noontime. Lights strobed along the bottom of the floating nightmare, strafing the street, turning asphalt into rubble. Buildings imploded, turning to dust as they crumbled in on themselves. People screamed, ran, but there was no escape from the death raining down from above.

The metallic monstrosity's vibrations shook Alex to her core, as though determined to jolt her soul free and steal it away from her. She fell to her knees, begging for it to stop, but it didn't. A scream welled in her chest and rose to her throat, demanding release. Her lips parted—

A firm hand clamped over her mouth. "Alexandra."

Her eyes flew open. Eyes as deep and blue as the Pacific bore into hers. She knew this man.

"I am Gryf, Alexandra. It is over. The invasion is over, and you live. Your brother lives. Remember?" He kept speaking, repeating his words until a switch seemed to flip in her head and her brain tuned back into reality.

It'd been a dream; her memory replaying the events of the attack. Again. A tremor racked her. Four days in this cell, four days of horrific dreams every time she dozed off. It was getting to the point that she was afraid to fall asleep.

Gryf reached out and brushed her hair away from her face. Why was he so good at calming her after these bouts? Better even than Nicky. Could that have something to do with his Gift? She was still unclear what his Gift was, as Matirans didn't seem big on advertising themselves.

She leaned into his palm and let her eyes drift shut.

"It is okay now, Alexandra," he crooned.

"It's not." It never would be again.

"It is."

She opened her eyes and met his gaze squarely. "Gryf, have you ever *seen* an Anferthian? They're massive, cold-blooded killers, and they—"

"Shh. Not all of them are so."

Sure they aren't.

"I haven't met one I like yet." Not that she'd met many. Just the one who'd knocked her out.

"I imagine not."

And he *had*? Of course, he had a lot more intergalactic experience than she did, so maybe it was possible. But she wasn't buying into that one without absolute proof—which didn't exist. Those green bastards were evil. She drew a deep breath and exhaled the last vestiges of her nightmare.

"Are you well?" Gryf asked.

"Yeah, I'm okay." As okay as she could be, given present circumstances. He cupped her head just behind her ear. Just the touch of his hand eased the tension from her neck and shoulder muscles. Amazing. "Gryf, may I ask you something?"

"Of course."

"Is there any hope of escape?"

The grim line of his mouth wasn't a good sign. What would his lips feel like if she traced them with her fingers? Oh, cripes, what was she thinking? They were prisoners on a slave ship,

PROPHECY

waiting to be shipped off to God knew where, and she was fixating on this alien's lips?

"This cell is at the heart of the slave holds of the Premiere Warden's ship. Short of a miracle, escape is impossible. The Anferthians do not want to lose me. Yet, this does not mean I...*we*...are not watching for an opportunity."

She should be disappointed at the mixed news, but damn if she didn't want to keep him talking. And touching. "Why...." Her voice cracked, and she cleared her throat. "Why aren't there more people crammed in here with us?"

"This ship was originally a floating prison, not a slaver. It can hold thirty-five thousand prisoners." He moved his fingertips to her jawline and her heart rate sped up. "It may be there are not enough Terrians left to warrant more than ten people to a cell."

Gryf's words barely registered as she stared at his bearded face.

Wonder what he looks like under that facial hair.

Dad had worn a beard, felt it was part of his academic persona as a professor of ancient history. What were the rules regarding beards in the Matiran military? Gryf's beard wasn't full and kept like Dad's; in fact, it appeared to be a recent addition.

Gryf jerked his hand away, and she startled. "What?"

"*Dimmi*... Forgive me, Alexandra." Was that a note of panic in his voice? He rose and gave her a brisk nod. "I shall check on you later."

She blinked rapidly, watching his back as he strode away.

What just happened?

Had she fallen into a trance? If she had, it sure looked like he had too. And was he sorry for jerking his hand away as if she'd burned him, or because he'd touched her in the first place? She shook her head. That couldn't happen again. They were too different. Hell, they were different species. Right?

Her gaze trailed down the straight line of his back. He did have one fine-looking butt, though. Too bad it was attached to another planet.

A throat cleared next to her. She tore her gaze from Gryf's backside and peered up into the hard grey eyes of a less welcome cellmate.

Commander Roble regarded her with a cool look, his arms folded across his chest. Figured he'd show up now. Damn, his gaze was unnerving. Was he was trying to intimidate her? That jerk. Well, two could play that game.

She gave him a fierce scowl. "Did you want something, Commander, or are you just trying to dissect my soul?"

His eyebrows rose and surprise flickered in his grey eyes, but then the mask slammed back into place. "I must ask that you not distract Captain Helyg from his duty."

"Huh?" Had he really just said that? "What do you mean?"

"Am I not clear?"

Alex pushed off the floor to face him on more equal footing. She folded her arms across her chest and narrowed her eyes, imitating Mr. Wonderful to a T. "What I *hear* you saying is that your captain is easily distracted and incapable of doing his job, and that I'm some insipid woman who needs to be ordered about."

He looked utterly offended. Good.

"On the contrary, there is no captain more capable than Captain Helyg, and it is my great honor to serve as his security commander. Also, I hold women in the highest esteem. In my experience, insipid women simply do not exist."

Alex gaped at him. First he insulted her then—what? Was that supposed to be a compliment?

The commander inclined his head with stiff politeness, turned on his heel and walked away. *Argh.* How like an egotistical male. If *he* decided the conversation was over then it was over. Alex ground her teeth together and glared at his back. Well, this was fun. As if figuring out men from her planet weren't enough, now she had to figure them out from someone else's planet too. This had to be the greatest cosmic joke ever.

◆ ◆ ◆ ◆

Gryf frowned. Having a private conversation in the confines of this cell was difficult at best. Surely Graig's words to Alexandra had not been meant for his ears, yet he had heard them. And they had not set well in his heart, or mind. This must be resolved, now.

"Commander."

Graig met his gaze, and Gryf pointed two fingers at his friend then the far corner. An unspoken request for private speech that Graig would honor.

Once in the corner, Gryf pinned Graig with a hard glare. "Off the record, Graig, do you have feelings of the heart for Alexandra? Is that why you warned me away?"

"*Off or on* the record, sir, my answer remains the same," Graig replied. "I have no feelings of the heart for Alex. My heart remains my own, and I am disinclined to entrust it to the next female I meet."

Haesi's betrayal had come at a price for Graig. Of course he would not be interested in kindling a relationship with another so soon. Haesi had kept him apart from the others for several days after the fall of the Guardians. Whatever had happened between them during that time was still a mystery, and Gryf would not press his friend for details. The Oath of the Guardians ran deep and strong in Graig, and he would remain true to that oath, even at personal cost.

Yet, even as Graig spoke a thread of relief had stirred in the vicinity of his own heart. "I appreciate your honesty and concern. You are my right hand, Graig, but you must have faith in my ability to discern between my duty and my personal life. Now more than ever, we must work as a team if there is to be any hope of saving the few Terrians left."

"It will not happen again, sir."

"I trust it will not. Dismissed."

Graig gave him a nod and retreated.

Gryf allowed his gaze to drift to the knot of Terrians and Matirans in the opposite corner. Nick's arm lay across Alexandra's shoulders, the siblings no doubt deriving comfort from each other's familial closeness. Once, Gryf had shared such a bond with his cousin, Ora.

Sweet Mother, what he wouldn't give to be the one comforting Alexandra now.

Setting his back against the corner, he slid down the wall to sit cross-legged, and closed his eyes. Why had these five particular Terrians been incarcerated in this cell? There was little question of Kotas's hand in the arrangements. The traitor must have hand-picked each of the Terrians to use against Gryf. A desperately injured Terrian male, two beautiful women, a six-year-old child, and a youth with the potential to rebel against authority. It was even possible that Kotas was aware of Alexandra and Nick's relationship. A most unpleasant prospect. No doubt Kotas would bide his time and allow Gryf's natural instincts for guarding and protecting them to grow. And then....

Gryf forced his jaw to relax. If he continued to grind his teeth together, they would become nubs. There was only one thing he could do. He must not allow himself to become personally attached to any of the Terrians.

But it was too late, was it not? He frowned. Despite what he had told Graig, Alexandra's welfare concerned him the most. He could not stop this instinct any more than he had been able to stop the destruction of his fleet. But as long as he did not act on that instinct, she would be safe.

For now his duty was to protect the Terrian survivors until the Defense Fleet could arrive.

And find a way to escape.

"It must be pretty serious."

Gryf suppressed a sigh and opened his eyes. Alexandra squatted in front of him, her expression sympathetic. If only she knew the extent of the problem and how grim and far-reaching the consequences were, not just for him, but also his people.

"Far more dire than you could know." He tipped his head to one side. "How old are you?"

She blinked at him as though the question had caught her off guard. It had certainly caught him off guard. Yet, it had been asked and he did harbor a certain amount of curiosity. She was no doubt younger than him, but by how much? And did her age leave her with the inability to grasp the gravity of the situation?

"Um, I'm twenty-two," she replied slowly. Then she narrowed her eyes. "How old are *you*?"

A fair question. He more than deserved to have the star-chart flipped on him. There seemed to be no shortage of mettle within this woman. He liked that. "I am thirty Terr cycles."

PROPHECY

"A thirty-year-old senior captain of a decimated space fleet, and a twenty-two-year-old survivor of mass genocide. And, somehow, I'm *too young* to understand, huh?"

"I did not say so." He had thought it, but that was different.

"You didn't have to."

He struggled to keep the grin from reaching his mouth. How had he not guessed this spirit was in her when she had planted her fist in his eye? In retrospect, that had merely been the cone of the comet. The tail promised a wondrous, colorful spectrum, and he wanted to see that spectrum.

"Are you always this direct?" He should not engage her; it was too risky. But neither could he bring himself to cease.

Alexandra compressed her lips then shook her head. "No," she admitted. "Only when my planet is invaded, or my life feels out of control, or...." She stopped and looked down at her clasped hands.

"Or, what?" Perhaps the more he knew about her, the easier it would be to protect her. *You are an incredible fool, Helyg.*

Her gaze met his, and there it was. The answer to his question clouded her eyes, but she needed to say it out loud. She would find strength in her admission.

"Or when I'm scared." Her voice wavered.

He gave her a slow nod. "Would it surprise you to know that I am scared too?"

She regarded him with an intense look then shook her head again. "No. I don't think so. At least, not much. You have a lot of people to worry about. And I don't mean just those of us in this cell with you."

So she understood that the rest of the *Atlantis*'s crew was imprisoned in the cells around them. Shame stung his heart. He owed her more than a simple apology for underestimating her. "I give you my most profound apology for questioning you. I stand corrected. You are uncommonly astute for twenty-two years." He offered his hand, palm up in invitation. "Squatting is not comfortable long-term. Will you sit with me?"

"Only if I'm not intruding."

"Too late." He gave her a half-smile.

She made a small scoffing sound and placed her hand in

his, warm and soft. An effervescent tingle traveled along his arm to his shoulder, and his heart rate increased. Alexandra sat cross-legged facing him, surprise lurking in the depths of her unique eyes. Had she felt it too?

"I do worry about the rest of my crew, and pray constantly for their safety." There was no reason to admit this to her other than that he wanted her to know. "Talking with you would take my mind off these worries for a short while."

Her eyebrows rose. "Okay. What do you want to talk about?"

"Tell me about your life, before the attack. I would very much like to hear about Terr...Earth...as it was. And learn more about your customs and way of life."

Alex gave Gryf a crooked grin. "A lot of our customs are pretty different."

Gryf chuckled. "Learning has been entertaining, has it not?"

"I'd love for you to teach me more."

Their gazes locked, and Gryf's smile wavered, his eyes turning a darker shade of blue. Heat suffused her body, and her mouth went dry.

Ooh. Way to put your foot in your mouth again, Alex.

"About your customs, I mean. All of them. Okay, maybe not *all*, but...."

Oh god, there was no saving this conversation. Super Glue. That was what she needed to clamp her lips together so the wrong words wouldn't keep falling out.

Of course, gluing her lips together would make kissing him difficult.

Oh. My. God. Where did that come from? Shut up, shut up, shut up!

"My apologies," Gryf murmured. He appeared as discombobulated as her. "I did not...it was not...I...."

Gryf's gaze held hers. She couldn't have looked away from those sapphire depths if she'd tried. And she wasn't going to try.

He cleared his throat. "I put you in an uncomfortable

position with my response to your comment, and I apologize. There is...you...I have never...." Gryf plowed his hand through his hair with a frustrated growl.

This wasn't the self-assured fleet captain she knew, rather a man trying to sort out his own jumbled emotions.

He lowered his hands into his lap. "Matir means Mother, so-named for the Holy Mother of our race. Our women, we hold in the highest esteem. It is a sin for a man to force himself on a woman. *Any* woman."

"Wait. Do you think you just forced yourself on me?" The look on his face plainly said that was exactly what he thought. How had she missed that one? "But Gryf, you didn't."

"Perhaps I did not use force," he replied. "However, my actions made you uncomfortable."

"Maybe a little, but only because...." He'd made her examine her own feelings. *Yikes*. That was not something she should say. Not yet anyway. Maybe never. "No. I'm not the least bit offended by your actions." At least he saw her as a woman and not some stinky thing that had just crawled out of a swamp. Cripes, what she wouldn't give for a hot shower.

His gaze roamed over her face then he shook his head. "There are dangers in this, Alexandra. Mostly for you. It was not an accident that you and the others were placed in this cell with me. We are being watched, even now."

"You mean there are cameras in here?" That was a disturbing piece of info. She automatically scanned the featureless wall behind him.

"If a camera is a form of surveillance then yes. If what I suspect is true, Kotas has bought himself a cushion of time with the Anferthians, and they are allowing him the freedom to exercise his revenge for my slights against him, in exchange for I know not what. However, I believe his grudge goes beyond just me, and he plans to hand over the Defense Fleet to them. The result would be catastrophic for Matir."

Her belly made a queasy roll. "Are...are you sure?"

"That the Anferthians are using Kotas as much as he is using them? That Matir faces the same fate as Terr? Yes, I am sure."

Alex straightened her spine and frowned. How was it that

every time she thought things had gotten as bad as they possibly could, they got worse? "Um, would you excuse me? I need to go...." She pointed in the general direction of Dennis.

"Of course." Gryf's responding smile reassured her that he understood. "I will keep my crew apart so you may converse with your people."

◆ ◆ ◆ ◆

Alex cast a glance toward the Matirans congregated in the opposite corner. True to his word, Gryf had gathered his crew there, giving the Earthlings as much privacy as possible. Still, she had explained their situation to the others in a hushed whisper.

She turned her attention back to the tight circle of Earthlings and leaned forward. "My point is, Gryf is looking for a way to escape. If he does, I plan to go with him. I'm hoping all of you will too."

Nicky nodded, as expected, but Dennis made a skeptical face. "I'm too big a liability for them. I can't even walk much less run."

"But Dante is working on that—"

"I doubt they'll leave you, Dennis," Simone said, her dark gaze darting to the Matirans then back to Dennis. "Everything they've done since we got here has been for us. Taking care of our injuries. Making sure we eat our fill first before they do. Teaching us how to survive in this shit-hole. And did you see the way the captain put himself between us and those other two Matirans? If he finds a way to escape, he'll find a way to take you."

Dennis frowned. "I intend to walk out of here under my own power."

That was the kind of determination they needed from everyone. "Maybe Dante and I can increase the number of healing sessions we have with you. He was worried about over doing it, but you've responded so well I don't have a problem asking him."

A light touch brushed her arm. "Just make sure *you're* not over doing it, girl," Simone said. "That healing stuff is crazy weird to watch. I can't imagine what it's doing to you."

PROPHECY

It seemed trust went only as far as escaping. Everything else was still a crapshoot.

"I think it's pretty cool," Juan said. "It's like a super power. Cap'n Gryf used his when I was crying the first few days. And Healer Dacian helps me sleep at night."

"That sleeping thing works really well," Dennis agreed.

Alex caught her lower lip between her teeth. Obviously, she had some latent trust issues too. The idea of someone putting her to sleep scared her silly. What if she never woke up?

"I'm with my sister," Nicky said. "If she trusts them enough to try this then so do I. Anyone else?"

"Me." Juan bounced on his butt as though ready to bolt for freedom right that moment.

Simone nodded. "I'm in."

"Say we do get out of here," Dennis said. "Then what?"

It was a great question, one she'd asked herself several times in the last half hour. "Honestly, I'd like to find a way to get our planet back, but we can't do that alone. If we escape, hopefully Gryf can find a way to let his people know we're here. And hopefully they're willing to help."

The line of Dennis's mouth flattened then he nodded slowly. "I'd really like to blow those green assholes back to whatever hell they came from. Count me in."

Gryf could not stop the wide smile he gave Alexandra. "We welcome the partnership and trust of your people, Alexandra. I am correct to assume that you are their representative?"

"Umm...." Alexandra threw an uncertain look at Nick and Simone. Ah, so she did not know that her own people already looked to her to lead.

"She speaks for all of us," Simone said with a definite nod.

Alexandra clutched her hands together in front of her, but did not argue.

Life in this prison seemed less daunting, as if he had something to look forward to. Like more open and frequent conversations with Alexandra. It was a blade with two edges, and he would have to tread with care or Kotas might become more suspicious than he likely already was.

CHAPTER SEVEN

Alex leaned against the wall, worrying her lower lip between her teeth. Day ten had arrived. The tension in the cell was as thick as the walls that stood between them and freedom. She and Dante had done their best, and Dennis had taken a short walk this morning, unassisted. He was improving, but would it be enough?

"Relax, Alex," Dante murmured.

"Easier said than done."

Dennis's beefy hand covered hers. "Don't worry. I'll be ready to run when we find a way to escape."

She met his gaze and gave him a smile. His positive attitude, and active participation in his own recovery, made him the best patient she'd ever worked with.

Gryf climbed to his feet and extended his hand. "Come, Alexandra. Walk with me."

That must be code for "I'm distracting you before you drive everyone nuts." No point in arguing that, though. She took Gryf's hand, and he pulled her up. He set their pace at a slow stroll as they circumnavigated the cell. When they reached *their* corner, he turned to face her, halting their progress.

"Your service to Dennis has been invaluable, Alexandra. Thank you."

A flutter of butterflies took up residence in her stomach as heat rushed into her cheeks. "You're welcome. It's been an amazing experience, and I'm glad I've been able to help."

"How much—"

The cell door whooshed open, and ice crystalized in her veins, chilling her body, and soul.

Gryf jerked his head up. Two armed Anferthians took up positions on either side of the door. He flicked his hand in a circular motion and hissed, "*Custii.*"

Before she could blink, the other Matirans had moved to stand with their Terrian counterparts. Nicky, thankfully, stood with Graig. The commander may have been a pain, but he'd do everything possible to protect her brother.

Gryf moved to shield her from their view. "Alexandra, please do nothing to attract attention," he murmured.

No problem there. But she couldn't resist a peek over his shoulder. Kotas strode purposefully between his Anferthian escorts, followed by a third armed guard, who stopped in the doorway.

Gryf stood with his arms relaxed at his sides, a sharp contrast to the snapping tension in the air. Alex met Dennis's wide eyes from across the cell.

"Capeto." Kotas's calculating brown eyes fixed Gryf with a spiteful glare then he turned away. "Were you able to heal him, Dacian?"

"Dennis is able to walk." The icy contempt in Dante's voice could've frozen a lava flow.

"Ah." Kotas gazed down at Dennis. It was amazing that Dennis didn't flinch away from the Matiran traitor. She would've been freaking out in his position.

"Get up and walk, creature." Kotas's words dripped with contempt.

Dennis nodded then rolled onto his hip and levered himself off the floor. Alex squeezed her fists together under her chin.

Come on, Dennis.

He took one step with his good foot then his bad foot. On his fourth step, he collapsed to his knee. *Damn.* Karise moved to help him back to his feet.

"Leave him," Kotas snapped at her then looked at Dante. "I gave you ten days, Healer."

"He is able to walk a few steps now. In a few days, he will be walking without a limp, I assure you. All I need is time, Vyn," Dante replied. How did he keep his voice so calm?

Kotas took a slow step back, and Alex caught her lower lip between her teeth. Would he give them those crucial days? *Please, please, please.*

"Time is up." Kotas's weapon appeared in his hand in a

blur. It made a faint sound when he pulled the trigger. Dennis grunted, his face registering shocked surprise. Then his eyes glazed, and he slumped forward, blood seeping from the hole in his temple.

A hoarse cry of denial burst from her. Dennis's body toppled sideways, his eyes staring and vacant.

"You son-of-a-bitch." Alex stepped around Gryf. At the same moment, Dante roared, "*Dolonos!*"

Gryf grabbed her arms and hauled her against his chest, his eyes flashed with warning. "Think of the living," he growled.

But she had to *kill* Kotas. Rip his throat out for murdering Dennis. She pulled back, trying to free herself from Gryf's iron grip.

"Do you need my help to see reason?" he asked.

She froze. Did he mean using his Gift? She glanced toward Dante. The healer had closed the gap between himself and Kotas in three long strides. Angry words in a language she couldn't understand flowed from his mouth.

Kotas leveled his weapon at Dante's chest, responding in the same language. At six foot three, the healer was a good four inches taller than Kotas, and the traitor had every reason to be intimidated. But if they lost Dante....

"No, I don't." Her words gagged her. "But Dante might."

"Will you stay put?" Gryf's grip tightened a fraction.

She looked into his eyes. "Yes."

Gryf released her and moved toward the two men. "Stand down, Dacian!"

"That would be wise." Kotas's voice was cool.

"He could have been healed," Dante ground out through clenched teeth.

"Will you be able to heal yourself from a point-blank *telum* shot, Chief?" Gryf asked. "Stand. Down. Now."

The healer's expression changed from rage to reason in a blink. Alex frowned. Very weird. Dante took a stiff step back from the traitor. Even though he seemed in control, his fists were still clenched. Kotas did not lower his weapon as he eased back a few steps, putting himself out of Gryf's reach.

Alex narrowed her eyes. *He's afraid of Gryf.*

"It would seem I have solved a serious problem for you,

PROPHECY

Helyg. No thanks are necessary," Kotas gloated.

"None are given." Gryf's voice was as tight as the set of his shoulders.

"No?" Kotas smirked. "Pity."

The murdering scumbag turned and walked out of the cell as if nothing had happened. His Anferthian escort followed him, leaving morbid si

◆ ◆ ◆ ◆

Hunger gnawed at Alex. No dinner had come that evening. Whether it was because Kotas had ordered it or the Anferthians were retaliating against the prisoners for having to clean the bloody mess was anyone's guess. They hadn't done a thorough job of it either. She cast a glance at the thin smears of Dennis's blood on the floor where he'd fallen.

God, give him peace.

Damn, her heart hurt—no, burned. Kotas had so much to answer for, and she hoped she was there at his moment of reckoning. She let her gaze drift around the cell. Simone and Juan were asleep. It was the first time any of the Earthlings other than Dennis had gone to Dante for help sleeping. Dante too had retired to get a little rest before he relieved Graig from watch.

Karise sat where Dennis had lain for the last week and a half of his life, her thumb and first two fingers rested on the bridge of her nose. Gryf had once explained this was the way Matirans prayed.

Nicky covered her hand with his. He didn't say anything; he didn't need to. He was here for her, and she for him. God willing, that would never change.

She let out a soft sigh and leaned her head against her brother's shoulder. Gryf sat directly across the cell, head back against the wall and eyes closed. Was it her imagination, or was his skin several shades paler than normal? Must be the dimmed lighting. She furrowed her brow and frowned. No, it wasn't the lighting; he was flushed and haggard. The dark circles under his eyes appeared more pronounced.

"He doesn't look so hot, Alex," Nicky whispered next to her ear.

"I noticed." She pursed her lips. "And Dante's asleep."

"Then it's up to you to find out what's going on, isn't it, Nurse Bock?"

A tremor went through her hands. Was it? She wouldn't mind caring for him, but she wasn't his doctor, or a member of his crew. She was just a Terrian nurse with no special Gift. Unless.... She cast a glance to her left. Graig sat against the adjacent wall. His usual impenetrable mask had slipped, and his concerned eyes returned to Gryf with steady frequency.

So, he saw it too. And he was both Gifted *and* a crew member.

"Gag me," she whispered to Nicky and pushed herself upright.

Her brother gave her a mystified look. "What?"

"I have to swallow my damn pride and ask Commander Not a Chauvinist for help." She made a small choking noise.

Nicky scrunched his eyes closed, his shoulders shaking with silent mirth.

Alex pushed herself to her feet. "Yeah, well you just stay here, Chuckles, and I'll take care of everything."

"I have faith in you, Sis," Nicky choked out.

"Thanks." *Twerp.*

She started across the cell toward her intended patient. Half-way across, she shot a pointed look at Graig and jerked her chin in Gryf's direction. Graig's response time was impressive. He was on his feet in a blink, and they arrived on either side of Gryf together.

Gryf opened his eyes, their sapphire depths bright with fever. "I...had wondered...if you...." His lips barely moved as his words tapered off, and he closed his eyes again.

Pushing damp tendrils of white hair up, Alex laid her hand on his forehead. This was not good. He was hot by Earth standards, and more so by Matiran, but by how much?

She met Graig's concerned gaze. "Any idea what the temperature difference is between our races?"

"Terrians, 37, Matirans, 34."

So the Matirans used a system akin to Earth's metric system. She could work with that. "He's about a 39 or 40 now. Way too hot."

Graig's mouth pulled into a grim line, and Alex turned back

to her patient. "Gryf? Can you hear me?"

He nodded, breathing through his mouth.

"Can you tell me your symptoms?"

"Throat burns, my head aches, hurts to swallow," he croaked.

She ran her fingers along his throat just under his chin. "Lymph nodes are swollen too. Open your mouth please, Gryf... Got it. Okay, close it up."

"The spots in his mouth, what are they?" Graig asked.

Alex sat back on her heel. "Have you ever seen symptoms like these on Matir?"

"Never."

"I'm ninety-five percent sure it's strep throat. If treated early enough, it isn't serious. At least, not to Earthlings. Unfortunately, we don't have antibiotics, and it's highly contagious, which means all of us could get it. You Matirans are probably most susceptible."

"I shall wake Dante."

"Wait a minute." She tapped her finger against her thigh. "Dante said that all Matirans have the power of a Gift. Are you able to use yours for healing?"

"I am not a healer."

"Dammit." She cast a glance toward Dante's sleeping form. "This should be rudimentary, and I do know what to look for. I just lack the power."

Graig's gaze narrowed as if he were considering his options. Then his face relaxed. "I have the knowledge of a first-year healer. I will help you."

She opened her mouth then snapped it shut again. Asking him why he hadn't told her so in the first place was pointless. At least he hadn't blown her off, yet. There was still a chance he'd do so anyway and go wake up Dante. She gave him a quick nod and bent close to Gryf.

Blue eyes opened a slit as she explained what she suspected, and how she and Graig planned to heal him. Gryf gave her a vague nod. *I'm taking that as consent for treatment.* Not that she needed it. Who was left to sue her for malpractice?

At her direction, Graig placed his hands over Gryf's lymph

nodes, and she rested her hand on one of his wrists.

"Okay, let's do this." *Please let this work.*

The faint blue-white glow of Graig's Gift sprang to his hands and eyes. The familiar gentle tugging sensation of a Matiran's Gift drew from her reservoir of strength. She'd expected his signature to be different than Dante's, but *rocks?* Strong, steadfast, and sun-warmed rocks. Big ones. Boulders. How interesting. Were each individual's Gift signatures based on their personalities? She'd have to think about that later.

She focused on locating the bacteria inside Gryf. "There it is, Graig. Can you draw all the bacteria together and zap them?"

Graig gave her a peculiar look. "I could, but why do you not do it instead?"

A subtle shift of power fluctuated at her core. Was Graig really allowing her to control his Gift?

"Just focus and will it to do what you want."

Unbelievable. And that couldn't possibly be approval in his grey eyes, could it?

She gave him a nod and returned her focus to the illness infesting Gryf. It was so simple. She *could* do it. She moved through his body, drawing the bacteria together in one location. Then, with one blast of healing heat, she eradicated the illness. She ran a check for lingering pieces. The last thing she wanted was for Gryf to relapse.

"Looks good," she murmured for Graig's benefit.

Graig grunted acknowledgement. "Now withdraw like you have seen Dante do."

How was she supposed to do that with *his* Gift? An odd quivering sensation tickled inside her chest like a feather. Weird. Heat surged through her, flooding her body as though a dam had broken. The heat intensified and she was burning from the inside out. If it didn't stop she'd be incinerated. Dead.

She tightened her grip on Graig's wrist as a small strangled noise passed her lips. Gryf gasped raggedly, and his eyes popped open wide. God help her, she was free falling into them. What the hell was happening?

A wrenching sensation of vertigo jolted her. Graig had severed the healing connection as he physically dragged her

PROPHECY

away from Gryf. A guttural moan of tragic despair welled up and escaped her as black spots filled her vision. She looked up at Graig for help, but found fear in his grey eyes. Something must be very wrong. Nothing scared Graig.

"I am sorry," he murmured. He touched his finger to her forehead. A roar filled her ears, and the blackness swooped in.

◆ ◆ ◆ ◆

"What do you think?" Dante already knew the answer, as Graig surely must. He gazed down at Alex's unconscious form on the floor at his side. Under his fingers her pulse fluttered. Her face was paler than he had ever seen it, and her dark hair in disarray. Gryf lay in a similar position on the other side of Graig. Something had happened between them, and until he figured it out, it was prudent to monitor them.

"We have a problem," Graig replied in Matiran, his voice pitched as low as Dante's so as not to disturb the others pretending to sleep nearby.

After the initial excitement, the others had retired—Nick only after securing a promise to be woken up for regular updates on his sister's condition.

Dante released a soft sigh and shook his head. "With the two of you, when is there *not* a problem?" Did his friend have any idea how his presence comforted him?

Graig's mouth twitched. "Was it not your job to keep us out of trouble, oh, my elder?"

"How did I ever get sucked into the Helyg/Roble vortex?" This was a question that had plagued Dante for a decade. And still he had no answer, nor any desire to end his brotherhood with either of these men.

"Shall I summarize?" Graig offered.

"Please do not." Alex's pulse fluttered beneath Dante's fingertips.

"Gryf's pulse is fluctuating," Graig murmured at the same moment.

"Alex, too. *Anim tros*—soul mates." Heavenly Mother have mercy, could it be? It had been centuries since the last pair of *anim tros* had been brought together, presumably by the will of the Holy Mother. If only Ora were here. She had been a treasure trove of information and facts on the mysticism.

A V formed between Graig's brows. "But to what end?"

There was always a reason two souls joined in this manner, but the only one he could think of drove a blade through Dante's belly. "Do you remember the words of the *Profeti*?"

Graig's expression turned skeptical. "The Prophecy of the Guardians dates back almost twelve thousand years. Most consider it a legend, myself included."

Dante pinched the bridge of his nose. "As do I. There must be another reason."

"Or perhaps we are wrong, and they are not *anim tros*," Graig suggested.

"Perhaps. Their attraction may be driven by their hearts and not their souls." If only the evidence did not indicate otherwise. "Regardless, something is between them, and we must do what we can to protect them. Eventually, time will give us the answers we seek."

May the heavenly Mother protect them if Kotas as much as suspected. He would kill them both.

CHAPTER EIGHT

Gryf watched Alexandra from the corner of his eye. She had healed him. Granted, it was through Graig's Gift, but what they had done had worked. And this morning he had awoken to the most amazing sight: Alexandra leaning over him, her curtain of dark hair framing her face and her beautiful eyes clouded with concern. Then they had cleared, and she had smiled—radiant as any celestial body. He had yearned for her then, for her to press her lips to his in a kiss to last until the end of time. But she had not, much to his regret. That was her choice to make, and he must respect that.

But even now, hours later, he desired her company. Never had he been so drawn to any woman. What was it about Alexandra that gave him thoughts of eschewing all ingrained traditions and expressing himself to her? In her culture, men were free to approach women they were interested in, but the mere thought of doing so was distasteful. He would not disrespect her.

"You are staring," Graig murmured in Matiran.

Gryf drew his brows together then aimed a narrow-eyed gaze in his friend's direction. "Is there a problem?"

"Yes, a rather large problem." Graig kept his voice just above a whisper. "Your attentions will get her killed."

This he already knew without the reminder.

Graig moved a fraction nearer. "As your friend, Gryf, I see how this Terrian woman has affected you like none you have known before. She is intelligent, beautiful, and somewhat vexing. If you seek her invitation, I recommend you get her out of here."

"Escape, you mean?" If they were free, would Alexandra invite him into a relationship with her?

Graig gave him a single nod. "You know as well as I that Kotas will come for her. As he will come for each of the Terrians."

A muscle twitched in Gryf's cheek. The traitor had already come for Dennis. If he took Alexandra.... Fire flared in Gryf's heart. This must not happen. Damn Kotas to each and every hell.

Alex sat in the corner, her arms wrapped around her knees. Cripes, did Gryf ever look somber. What was Graig saying to him? Maybe they were working on a plan for escape, even though escape was unlikely. She shifted on the floor, snugging her bottom more comfortably into the corner. *Their* corner. She still liked the sound of that...and the time they'd spent talking, remembering, sharing.

Graig moved away, and Gryf pressed his thumb, index, and middle fingers to his brow. She'd seen this gesture often enough in the past two weeks, and had learned it was the way they prayed.

Gryf lowered his hand to his side, and his gaze met hers. One white eyebrow quirked upward, like a silent request for permission to join her here. Her heart fluttered. He must want to be with her, maybe to talk out whatever seemed to be bothering him. Even if he just wanted to sit quietly, she wouldn't mind. She liked having him around, as though weathering his illness together had somehow changed the dynamic of their relationship. She patted the floor next to her in invitation.

She gave him a smile as he lowered himself to the floor to her right. "Praying, Captain?"

"Always. And it is Gryf, remember?"

"You haven't been Gryf all day." Except when he first woke up and looked as though he might kiss her.

"I know." He leaned his head against the wall. "My apologies, Alexandra."

"Sorry. I didn't mean to come down on you." It wasn't his fault he led a life with dual roles, one as captain to his crew, and the other as Gryf. Could she live with sharing him with others? Would she ever have the chance to find out?

She lowered her gaze to her raised knees then looked back up to him. "Gryf, I need your promise. I know it's a lot to ask, but no matter what happens to me, please get Nicky out of here."

"Alexandra...." His eyes were bleak, but she had to know that someone would watch out for Nicky if she couldn't.

"Promise me," she whispered. "He's all I have left of my family. If something happens to me, swear you'll take him with you if you find a way out of this prison. Don't let him become a slave."

Counter-arguments rose in his eyes, and she gave him an unrelenting glare. He had to understand that she wasn't backing down. He sighed, and shifted around to face her. "Give me your left hand."

"You're not going to use your Gift to change my mind, are you?"

Gryf lowered his chin and raised an eyebrow at her. "Your insult is unintended, I am sure."

Ouch. Yeah, she knew better. There were limitations to the Matiran Gift, and mind control was one of those limits.

"I'm sorry." She extended her hand as requested, and he enfolded it between his. The strong, capable hands of a trusted leader—and a caring man. She stared into his eyes, her lips parting.

"*Veni.* Forgiven." Without breaking eye contact, he raised her hand...to his lips, not his forehead as Graig had. His warm breath feathered across the back of her hand, sending a thrill of goose bumps up her arm.

Oh, my. She swallowed. Karise had clarified Matiran traditions between the sexes. Women made the choices about who they did or didn't wish to have a relationship with. A man could express interest in a woman, but if she didn't reciprocate, he must accept her decision as final.

But, oh my god, was she ever interested. Was this his way of telling her he was also interested? Or was he just being polite?

Get a grip, Alex. As if relationships weren't complicated enough already. Now she was thinking about going intergalactic. Had she lost her ever-loving mind?

"This is how Matirans bind themselves with a vow." Gryf shifted so his hand cupped her elbow. "In the name of the Holy Mother, I do vow to you, Alexandra Bock, to do everything within my power to get your brother, Nicholaus, out of this prison and to safety. I further vow to do no less for you. So be it."

"Ah, so be it." *Please let that be the proper response.* A mild tingle wrapped around their joined arms, and she sucked in a sharp breath. "Wow. What was that?"

"That was the vow being sealed," he replied. His roughened fingertips slid down the smooth skin of her inner arm, and heat shot through her lower belly.

"So." She cleared her throat. "W-what happens if you can't keep your vow? You don't die or something, do you?" *Oh, god, she was such a dork. What a stupid question.*

Amusement lit his eyes, and he shook his head. "It is honor that will help me keep my vow, Alexandra, not the threat of death."

"Oh. That's good." *Focus, Alex. Focus.* "I, um, have a feeling that a vow is much more to you than the average promise. I will do everything I can to help you honor this one."

"Your help has been, and will continue to be, invaluable to me. Words cannot express my gratitude."

Well, damn. She'd read too much into that kiss on her hand. It was gratitude, not interest, he was expressing. She looked away across the cell in case her disappointment showed in her eyes. Nothing had changed, except now Dante and Graig stood in the middle of the cell, casting furtive glances at her and Gryf. What was up with that?

There was only one thing to do—shore up her defenses and carry on. She pursed her lips and looked back at him. "I think you should know something. The four of us...the Terrians, I mean...we don't blame you for what happened to Earth, Gryf. Dennis didn't either. He'd want you to know."

A crease appeared across his forehead, and she raised her hand to stop him from interrupting. He would hear her out. "I know. I get that you feel responsible for what's happened, and I completely respect your feelings. However, it wasn't you who put this plan into motion. It wasn't you who betrayed your fleet, or your people, or even my people. And it definitely wasn't you who broke your oath and sold out your honor so cheaply."

She paused for a breath. "I'm not telling you to let it go, Gryf; you have too much integrity to do that. What I *am* saying is that we believe in you, in your honor and in your integrity. And if we survive this, I assume that you will have some sort of accountability hearing on Matir. Expect us to be there. Expect us to stand up for you to clear your name."

The look in his eyes was unfathomable. Without breaking eye contact, he raised her hand to his heart. Was it her imagination, or had their breathing synchronized? He brushed the fingertips of his other hand over her cheek, and her heart pounded in response. He was so close.

"Again, I thank you," he murmured.

This was way more than appreciation. Her lips parted.

"Captain, someone is outside." Karise's stage whisper broke the spell.

Damn.

Regret flashed in Gryf's eyes then the efficient Senior Captain Helyg was back. "Stay behind me please, Alexandra."

He didn't need to tell her twice. The last thing she wanted was attention from whoever was coming into the cell. She let him haul her to her feet and tuck her behind him, his hand lingering in hers for a fraction longer than it should have. Fighting the urge to cradle her hand to her heart, she nibbled her bottom lip.

The whoosh of the door opening was followed by the click of booted feet—two sets of them, if she wasn't mistaken. Then the doors closed.

That's different.

She threw a quick glance at Karise, who stood nearby. The lieutenant commander wore an expression of surprise, curiosity, and mistrust. Not the sort of reaction Kotas or Haesi would generate, that was for sure.

Alex leaned to peek over Gryf's shoulder. The green-eyed Anferthian woman who'd brought them food and water many times, stood just inside the cell door. Her thick black hair was pulled back exposing her rounded ears. The Anferthian male accompanying her wore his hair similarly, except his ears were hidden beneath his wheat-colored locks.

Neither Anferthian appeared to be armed. The female addressed Gryf in a language Alex couldn't understand. Immediate sounds of protest came from Karise, Dante, and Graig. If only she understood what was being said.

Gryf quelled them into silence with a look. "Dante," he said, beckoning the healer with a flick of his wrist. He turned and placed his hand at the small of her back. "Wait with the others." He guided her toward Karise as Dante separated himself from the group. The two men joined the Anferthians.

Alex shifted from foot to foot, listening to the hushed voices conversing in a harsh alien language. Who was this woman and what did she want from Gryf? Clearly, none of the Matirans approved of the situation. Heck, she didn't like it much either.

"Her name is K'rona Zurkku," Karise whispered as the female Anferthian handed a small envelope to Gryf. "She is a factoress...the equivalent of a lieutenant commander. The man with her is Mendiko Gari, also a factor."

Alex acknowledged this new information with a nod. Gryf opened the envelope, his eyes flicking back and forth as he read the contents. His expression changed from rigid aloofness to flabbergasted amazement then he passed the letter to Dante. A moment later the healer murmured, "Holy Mother." Dante didn't sound upset, just surprised. Gryf took the letter back, and tucked it into the envelope.

What the heck was going on over there? Could it be that these Anferthians were trying to help them? Alex allowed her gaze to roam the walls in search of the elusive security cameras, or surveillance devices, as Gryf had called them.

Karise tipped her head close to Alex's ear. "K'rona said there has been a temporary malfunction in the surveillance system."

Alex jerked her gaze back to K'rona and her cohort. Malfunction, or sabotage? This could be the break Gryf had been hoping for.

A few more low words were exchanged with the

PROPHECY

Anferthians then K'rona and Mendiko left. Damn. It seemed like no one was going anywhere after all.

The tap of the envelope's edge against Gryf's palm was the only sound in the cell. What news was in that letter? Who was it from? And why did the Anferthians deliver it to him?

Gryf gave Dante a brusque nod, and they rejoined the group.

"It would seem," he told them, "that we are not as alone as we thought. There is a group of Anferthians who strongly disagree with the invasion of Terr. They call themselves dissenters. Factoress Zurkku leads them. She has offered their assistance to escape the slaver before it leaves the surface of Terr to rendezvous with the merchants in four days, as scheduled."

Graig snorted. "You *trust* those Anferthians?"

In response, Gryf handed the envelope to Graig. "The factoress has held this letter in her possession with orders not to give it to me until instructed. Read it out loud in English please, Commander. And hurry; we have about three minutes before the surveillance system comes back online."

Graig gave Gryf a skeptical look then removed the letter from the envelope. It was a piece of paper from a spiral notebook. A ragged edge ran down the left side of the page where it'd been torn out. Graig frowned at the handwritten words, a V creased between his brows.

"*Greetings, Cousin. If you are reading this letter, the situation has become desperate enough for K'rona to give it to you. I know you will have your doubts about the authenticity of this letter in light of the destruction of my command ship, Athens.*"

Karise slapped her hand over her mouth, her eyes alight with happiness. Graig raised his eyebrows at Gryf before continuing, "*I assure you this letter is real, and I am very much alive. I will share the galling events leading to my survival when we are next together. I have enclosed a golden gift for you as evidence of my continued existence, something which would not have been possible for any of our enemies to enclose had I truly perished with my ship. (Please resist the temptation to paint it purple, sobin.) I pray to the Holy*

Mother that this will be enough to convince you to hear K'rona with an open heart and mind. She is one of a handful of her people who are against the massacre of the Terrians, and is prepared to give her life to right this wrong. My coordinates will be passed to you when the time is right. Remain vigilant as the dissenters will act quickly. I await your arrival. Eni Terr, Ora Solaris."

Alex looked back at Gryf. "Oh!" She clapped her hand over her mouth. Gryf held up a lock of fine spun hair that shimmered like gold. *Beautiful.*

"Captain Solaris's hair," Karise murmured. "Her golden gift."

"That's *hair?*" Nicky blinked in apparent astonishment.

"Specifically, the hair of my cousin, Ora," Gryf replied. "Captain of the Guardian Fleet Cruiser *Athens*. Only a handful of Matirans have such hair. Of them, Ora alone currently serves in either the Guardian or Defense Fleets." One corner of his mouth rose in a crooked grin. "And I did once attempt to paint her hair purple."

A loud, undignified snort escaped Alex at the visual, and all heads turned toward her. Familiar heat crept up her cheeks. Again. She should be used to this by now. "Sorry."

Graig cleared his throat, drawing everyone's attention from her. "The letter is written in Ora's hand, and it was not written under duress." He returned the page to Gryf.

"*Eni Terr?*" Karise asked.

Gryf folded Ora's lock of hair back into the letter and nodded. "*For Earth.* Words from our childhood when we would pretend play that we were Guardians. I do believe that by the grace of the Mother, Ora is alive." He paused, as though struggling with his emotions before he continued. "Factor Gari will deliver our meal tomorrow. I am to signal him if we wish to proceed with the extraction tomorrow night. I must have agreement from all of you that you are willing to take the risks involved in this escape."

As one, his crew gave their assent. Even Graig seemed to have set aside his earlier objections.

"Alexandra?" Gryf gave her an expectant look.

She turned to Nicky, Simone, and Juan.

PROPHECY

"Are you kidding?" Simone responded adamantly. "I have a particular aversion to the whole slavery thing. Let's get out of this shit-hole before it's too late."

Alex gave Gryf a nod. "We're in."

CHAPTER NINE

Alex leaned her head back against the wall. The signal had been given to Mendiko Gari at dinner as planned. Now they waited for the Anferthians to devise a way to bail them out of this dump.

Why did I ever think volunteering for watch duty was a good way to pass that time?

"Volunteering" stretched the truth a bit. The reality was she'd nagged Gryf until he'd caved. Graig had given up his shift to her with an amused glint in his eyes. Now she understood why. Sitting in the semi-darkness of "night," trying to stay awake was comparable to watching paint dry.

Even though watch seemed like a pointless exercise in a slave cell, it did offer routine. Seemed that no matter where they were from, militaries liked to observe regular schedules. Not that she could argue the necessity of it. Even the county ER had established routines everyone adhered to without fail. And as boring as watch was, at least she was contributing something—like holding up the cell wall.

Karise had settled against the wall opposite Alex. They took turns walking the cell, and switched positions every hour. The others were asleep in the back left corner of the cell. The same corner she and Gryf had sat and talked so many times.

Alex clamped her teeth together and tightened her jaw to stifle the yawn trying to escape. How did the Matirans manage to stay awake? She never would've made it in the military. Although, being a spy might've been an exciting career choice.

Bock. Alex Bock. Double-O-You-Are-So-Fired-For-Sleeping-Through-The-Crown-Jewels-Heist.

She smirked. It was official; she was losing her mind. She glanced at where Gryf lay between the door and the other

PROPHECY

sleepers. His eyes were closed, but he probably wasn't asleep—not deeply, at least.

Simone sat up and disengaged herself from Juan without waking him up. Then she tiptoed away and disappeared behind the restroom partition.

Juan's head popped up, and Alex stifled a giggle. So much for Simone's covert maneuvering. The boy rubbed his eyes then got up and padded to the partition to wait his turn.

By the time Simone emerged from behind the partition, Juan was doing a pee-pee dance. He bolted in. Simone hesitated, and Alex gave her a shooing motion. There was no reason for her to wait for the boy.

The cell door whooshed open, and the lights blared on to full daytime mode.

What the hell?

Alex scrambled to her feet, blinking against the sudden glare. Several Anferthian guards pressed into the cell, one taking Karise to the floor with the butt of his weapon before stepping over her sprawled form. The others surrounded the prisoners rising from the floor.

Alex's heart sank to her toes. She, Simone, and Juan were cut off from the others by a wall of black uniforms. There was no hope of getting back into the fold.

Now what?

Vyn Kotas strode into the cell and paused just inside the door, his lips twisted into a condescending smirk.

Really, God?

On the eve of escaping this hell-hole, *he* showed up?

She edged toward Simone, meeting Gryf's gaze through a small gap between two Anferthians. A jaw muscle twitched and his eyes burned with tightly leashed fury. She gave a subtle shake of her head, sending him a silent message with her eyes. *Don't put the others at risk.*

"Kotas." Gryf growled the name like a warning.

"Greetings, Senior Captain." Kotas nodded in Gryf's direction. "I will not linger long. I have...questions about various topics, and wish to *borrow* one of your Terrians."

Gryf's eyes narrowed. "Leave the Terrians, Vyn. Your argument is with me."

"You believe *you* are the sole reason behind my decisions?" Kotas barked a laugh. "You are quite the egomaniac, *Senior Captain* Helyg."

Alex reached Simone's side in front of the partition. Strength in numbers wouldn't apply in this situation, but they had to try. Kotas's gaze raked them, and her skin prickled. Then the focus of his gaze shifted to something behind her.

A small frightened sound came from the bathroom entrance. *Juan.* The little boy clung to the edge of the partition with a white-knuckled intensity.

Kotas's lip curled and his nose wrinkled then a calculating gleam rose in his eyes. His hard gaze slid from Juan to Gryf. "Yes, I think so."

Gryf paced Kotas step-for-step from the other side of the wall of armed Anferthians. "Leave them, Vyn. It is me you want to hurt. Stop stabbing at random limbs, and strike at the heart, where you can do the most damage."

Was he crazy inviting Kotas to take him? The rest of them needed him...needed his leadership.

Kotas's smarmy smile didn't fade. "Oh, believe me, Capeto, I will strike at the heart soon enough."

Shit. He's going after Juan.

Who knew what unspeakable things he'd do to the boy? Kotas moved to circumvent her and Simone, but Alex stepped into the traitor's path. Surprise flashed in Kotas's brown eyes. He could probably sense her fear—hell, even see it written on her face—but she didn't care. He wasn't taking Juan.

A soft rustle came from behind her, hopefully Simone moving the boy back behind the partition. Alex was alone against Kotas now. Kotas's eyes narrowed to slits, and all the moisture in her mouth disappeared. She was in deep shit.

"Alexandra." Anger and fear burned in Gryf's eyes. But what would he have her do? Let Kotas take Juan? That wasn't an option. Besides, she wasn't doing anything Gryf wouldn't do himself had he been able.

Kotas studied her through narrowed eyes. "Very well."

Stars exploded inside her head, and she found herself on the floor. What the hell had he hit her with?

Someone grabbed her hair at the scalp and yanked her in

the direction of the door. "Come along, Terrian."

A small yelp squeak out of her, and she struggled to get her feet under her.

Nicky shouted her name, only to be drowned out by Gryf's roar. "*Kotas!*"

Progress to the door came to an abrupt halt, and Alex blinked against the tears of pain blurring her vision. Cripes, the room was spinning like a merry-go-round on speed. Gryf's enraged face hovered just beyond the guards. His arms were pinned behind his back by Graig, preventing him from charging the Anferthians, whose guns were leveled at him. She had to get his attention.

"Gryf!" That was enough to draw his tortured gaze to hers. Echoes of every tender moment passed between them with breathless clarity. "You promised safety. Remember? *You promised!*"

Gryf jerked as if she'd slapped him hard. His jaw clenched, and his eyes registered comprehension mixed with anguish. And maybe regret that he'd ever bound himself with that vow.

I didn't mean to hurt you.

Kotas's ominous chuckle filled the confines of the cell. "It would appear I found the favored pet. How...intoxicating." He stroked his fingers over her cheek. "I had wondered about you. I look forward to uncovering all your secrets."

Her stomach churned at his innuendo. Oh, god, what had she done? It was too late to change her mind now.

Nicky let loose a savage shriek and charged the guards, only to be taken to the floor by Dante.

Graig flexed his grip on Gryf's arms. "I advise you to watch your back, Kotas."

If Graig's warning had been directed at her, she would've listened. Kotas, on the other hand, just laughed again and dragged her from the cell. As the door closed, Gryf's enraged bellow filled the corridor.

Rage, pure and violent, boiled through Gryf. No one moved. The only sound in the cell was Nick struggling against Dante. Gryf growled deep in his chest and shook off Graig's death grip. Dante released Alexandra's brother to attend the unconscious Karise. Simone emerged from behind the partition, a terrified Juan in her arms.

Nick scrambled up and rounded on Gryf, fists clenched. "You let him take her," he screamed hoarsely. "Do you know what you've done? Do you know what he'll *do* to her? *She's my sister, god-dammit!*"

Red haze dropped like a curtain over Gryf's eyes, and a primal roar burst from him as he turned and slammed both fists against the wall. Pain shot up his arms like hot blades, but he did not care. He would rip Kotas into small bloody pieces with his bare hands.

Oh, sweet Mother. Alexandra.... He pressed his forehead against the cool wall.

"He knows, Nick," Graig murmured. "Better than you would ever imagine."

"You heard her, he promised her safety!" Nick's voice was thick with accusation. "He broke his promise and *betrayed* her." He faced Gryf. "You didn't even try to help her!"

Gryf turned and grabbed the front of Nick's shirt with both hands, yanking him so close they were nose to nose. "What I vowed to her was to get *you* out of here and to safety. A sealed vow that I am honor bound to keep regardless of the situation. It was *this* promise of which she spoke."

Nick gaped. "She did that?"

How could he ask such a question? He was her brother. Did he not know Alexandra at all? Gryf sucked air through his teeth as he glared hard into the Terrian's eyes, so like Alexandra's. *Ah, hells.* He shoved Nick aside with a snarl and stalked away to join Dante at Karise's side.

Gryf lowered himself to the floor next to the healer, rested an elbow on his raised knee, and pressed his forehead against his fist. Mother, his heart ached with a pain unlike any he had ever known, deep and searing. As if his soul had been mortally wounded. Not even Ora's presumed death had hurt this badly. He could not think. He could not function.

"Commander Roble must assume command," he murmured to his healer. "My ability to do so has been compromised by this incident."

"I can help you past this," Dante replied quietly. "Allow me to do this for you, Gryf."

"I do not want to forget, Dante. I will need this memory intact when I kill him."

"The pain can be set aside without compromising your memory. You won't forget, yet the rage will be suppressed. You will be able to function."

Would he? The weight of a solid, supportive hand clamped down on his shoulder. Graig knelt at his side. "Now is not the time for fractured leadership, Gryf. I will not assume command so long as there is something that can be done to restore you."

Gryf shook his head. Never had he been unable to comprehend his own reactions, make command decisions. "What is happening to me, Dante? The pain is physical, mental...spiritual. I am undone." His words made little sense to him. How could anyone else understand?

Dante rested his hands on Gryf's head. "Just say the word, Gryf, and I will help you."

There were no other solutions. If Dante could ease the agony, so be it. He gave the healer a nod, and uttered words wrenched from his soul. "Do it."

Hatred sustained him through the rest of that day. True to his word, Dante had blocked the all-encompassing, crippling anguish and rage. This gift from his friend allowed him to remain in command.

Ah, hells, but he could see Alexandra's face—the fear in her eyes, and the bravery. He had seen the moment when she had recognized the duty thrust upon her, and had accepted it with the valor of a warrior.

A growl rumbled deep within his chest. She should not have *had* to be a warrior. That was his lot. Kotas would answer for this, and Gryf would be no more merciful when that time came. But for now, his own duty must be met, and his vow kept, no matter the personal cost to him.

He took a visual census of everyone's location and stopped to gape at Graig and Simone. *Merciful Mother.* The brown-skinned Terrian had found refuge in the lap of his commander of security. Tucked under Graig's chin, she was almost hidden in the embrace of muscular arms. Graig cradled her like a child as he rocked her and stroked her short, wiry hair.

Graig may not have intended to give his heart to the next female he met, yet it appeared Simone may have taken it from him anyway.

Gryf turned away from the peaceful scene. Barring any unforeseen problems, K'rona would come this night, and even though he would see the others off the slave ship, he himself would not leave without Alexandra. His plan was clear in his mind. Graig would not like it, but that did not matter.

Only Alexandra mattered.

―――――◆•◆•◆―――――

It was the dead of night when K'rona slipped into the cell. Gryf listened as the Anferthian woman apprised them of the situation, Karise softy translating for the Terrians.

"With careful planning, we have been able to ensure any duty guards we encounter along our path tonight are dissenters," K'rona explained. "There is an air shaft that is open to the outside. It is there that Mendiko will meet us, and we will lower each of you through it to the ground. Once you are outside this ship, you will need to go southeast into the mountainous region. Use this directional device and follow Captain Solaris's coordinates. Any questions?"

"Factoress Zurkku." Dante addressed her in Anferthian, and Gryf frowned. There was only one reason he'd do so—he did not want the Terrians to hear what he had to say. "Captain Helyg and Commander Roble will remain behind until the release of the Terrian female taken from us has been secured. We will not leave her behind."

Gryf's eyebrows shot up. "Pardon?" He asked the question in Matiran. Now only his crew would understand. Rude, yet unavoidable. Something was going on here, and until he understood Dante and Graig's rationale, there was no reason to involve the others.

"We will not leave her behind, sir," Dante responded, also in their native tongue. "As Senior Medical Chief, I have given

Commander Roble orders to guard your health and welfare since you plan to retrieve your...Alex."

Karise had stopped translating, and stared wide-eyed as the conversation progressed.

"I will not allow it, Chief." There was no reason to risk any other lives besides his. If he failed, he failed alone. Ora was a competent leader and needed his crew. If the worst happened, *they* would succeed where he had failed.

Karise stepped closer. "Sir, Senior Medical Chief Dacian has the authority to supersede your orders in matters concerning the health and welfare of any member of the crew. Including the captain."

Mother have mercy, were they all in league together? They certainly had him well and good on this matter. "How did you know, Dante?"

The chief tilted his head. "It is not difficult if one knows the signs."

"Evasive. We will discuss this later."

"Yes, sir."

"Factoress, my chief is correct." Gryf switched back to Anferthian. "Commander Roble *and* I," he shot a glare at Dante, "will remain for Kotas's personal prisoner. We will not leave her behind."

K'rona's face was strained. "This will be difficult, yet not impossible. I have a thought, if you will give me time to work it through."

"We will not ask you to risk any more, Factoress."

K'rona raised her eyebrows. "Yet I choose to take the risk."

There would be no way to dissuade her. That much he could read in her dark green eyes. "We thank you. Lieutenant Commander Zola, please brief our Terrian friends of our change of plans."

Karise gave the three Terrians a brief explanation. Nick sent him a grudging look of approval, but there was no forgiveness in his eyes.

At K'rona's behest, they all removed their footwear. Shoes and boots in hand, they followed her out the door with silent footfalls. K'rona paused long enough to place a placard on it reading "Quarantine" in Anferthian. *Brilliant maneuver.* Gryf gave her ingenuity a nod of approval, and her mouth curved in a smug smile.

Their paths crossed with two duty guards, both of whom took no notice of the would-be escapees. It was as though they were invisible. As promised, Mendiko met them at the open-air shaft with a thick cord to lower them to the long wild grass below the slave ship.

Karise went down the rope first. Nick and Simone inhaled the cool night air of their home planet before following her.

Juan peered down the opening after them. "Aw. I wish we were in space."

"That would make this a long climb down, *agri*." Dante scooped up the boy then clasped arms with Gryf. "She is a gift, Gryf. Bring her to us safely, and yourself too. Ora will kill me, otherwise."

"Remember, do not stop or wait for us." Gryf took the compass and coordinates from his pocket and handed them to the healer. "Go straight to Ora's rendezvous point. Safe travels, Chief."

With a quick nod, Dante gripped the rope and disappeared down the shaft with Juan clinging to him.

"Come," whispered K'rona. "We must do this while my people are still on watch."

CHAPTER TEN

She didn't want to die here. Not sitting alone and naked in Vyn Kotas's private hell. Well, a hell for her, but Kotas didn't seem to be bothered by it. Neither had that freak-of-nature, Haesi Velo, with her needles and injections. Whatever drug that woman had injected into her was some kind of lie detector. Tell the truth, nothing happened. Tell a lie and, *god*, it was like molten lava filling her veins. At least there was no way Gryf could hear her screams.

A groan rose to her throat, and she rested her head against the wall behind her. There were moments when betrayal had been tempting. Just to end the pain.

"No. I won't do that." Her firmly spoken words sounded flat and hollow, absorbed by the sound-deadening walls of the small room. She was strong. Had to be, for Gryf. For Nicky.

If only being strong didn't hurt so much.

Who was she trying to kid? It was just a matter of time before she cracked. She looked up to where her hands were attached to the wall above her head by an invisible force-field. The same type of alien restraints anchored her to the floor by her ankles.

A wave of anger washed over her. This was barbaric. Shouldn't an advanced race capable of space travel be more humanitarian? She gave her arms a sharp downward tug.

They didn't move.

"Argh!" She thrashed, yanking her arms and legs, lifting her bottom off the floor, twisting her body from side-to-side trying to pull free. Pain burned along her ribs bringing her up short and gasping. She slumped against the wall, panting and fighting the blackness edging in to consume her. Damn, cracked ribs hurt like hell.

A lock of hair fell over one eye, but it didn't matter. There was nothing worth seeing in here anyway.

"My name is Alexandra Gaia Bock," she muttered then inhaled until stopped short by a harsh pinch of pain. "I am not...a fucking...*animal*!"

Silence. No one had heard her shouts. No one cared.

A tear slipped down her cheek. "Gryf cares."

Then why didn't he save you?

A small whimper of denial rose to her cracked and swollen lips. She couldn't think like that; it wasn't fair. He had the others to save, including her brother. That was what she'd wanted. Right? That's why she'd stood up to Kotas in the first place.

It was selfish of her even to pretend Gryf might crash through the door and carry her away. She was stuck here—the "pet" of a deranged monster. The slices on her chest where Kotas had cut his initials into her skin, marking her as his, was a tangible reminder that she'd never see Gryf again.

Had they escaped yet? There was no clock in this place, no way to tell how much time had passed. It seemed like an eternity, though. Maybe when Kotas came back she could piss him off enough that he'd kill her. Then she'd be free, just like Gryf and—

"It is not your time."

She startled at the unexpected voice then squinted at the bearded man standing near her feet. "Daddy?" He was frowning, like he did when he was unhappy with her. "Great. Now I'm hallucinating."

"You are a part of a much larger plan, monkey," her father said. "Soon you will be called upon to live up to your name."

"My name?" What the what?

She blinked, and he was gone. Panic seized her. "No." She pushed herself upright, her gaze darting around the space. Nothing was there, just the empty room. "No, wait! Come back, Daddy. Don't leave me with that monster. Please, help me." Even a hallucination was better company than the silence.

No answer. Her father was gone. He'd abandoned her, too. No one was coming to save her.

She sagged back against the wall and tears filled her eyes.

PROPHECY

Not that it mattered. Nothing mattered anymore.

───◆·◆·◆───

"Hurry up." Gryf narrowed his eyes at the security visual screens. According to K'rona, Kotas had a meeting scheduled with Premiere Warden D'etta three hours before first light, which provided a small window of opportunity for them to rescue Alexandra. "He should be leaving now, should he not?"

"Patience," K'rona murmured from her position behind Mendiko's chair. "He is consistently late to such meetings to annoy the premiere."

Behind Gryf, another dissenter, Ita B'aeja, paced the length of the security station. The room was small by Anferthian standards, but larger than the prison Gryf had resided in for far too long.

Gryf exchanged a glance with Graig on Mendiko's other side. His friend's gaze echoed K'rona's words.

"There," Mendiko said, and the others leaned closer. "Kotas's door opens and...he emerges."

The traitor walked down the empty corridor and turned the corner. Another surveillance device—what Alexandra called a camera—picked him up as he approached the conveyers.

"We go now," K'rona said. "Keep your heads down and say nothing."

Ita resumed her station in the chair Mendiko vacated and began the process of recoding the surveillance devices.

More time passed than Gryf liked before they arrived at Kotas's door. K'rona admitted them, and they left Mendiko in the corridor to run interference if necessary.

"She is in here." K'rona opened the closet door.

Heart pumping, Gryf hurried past the factoress. Alexandra sat slumped over, her bruised and battered body uncovered. Mother's love, Kotas had carved his initials into the skin of her breast! "Get something to cover her, *now*."

K'rona disappeared back into the main room, and Gryf knelt at Alexandra's side, smoothing his hand over her hair. His heart raged at the torments Kotas had subjected her to, and at his own inability to stop the traitor from taking her away in the first place.

She raised her head and blinked at him. A haunted wariness lurked in the brown and bronze depths of her eyes. "I'm dreaming again," she rasped. "You're not real."

"This is not a dream, Alexandra. I am here." His throat clogged, and he cleared it. "Even had I not so vowed, I still would not leave you." *Never.*

She stared at him, clearly trying to convince herself he was indeed real. "Nicky?"

"He is away with the others."

Relief softened her face. "Thank you." Her breathing was quick and shallow, as though taking in air pained her.

"For you, *compa*, I will not stop." If only he could hold her, cradle her to his heart. But that was not possible with her wrists pinned to the wall over her head.

Compa. Beloved. Would she guess that it was a term of endearment? Would she remember he had said it? It had come so naturally, and the feelings that had brought the word to his lips wrapped around his heart. By the grace of the Mother, this woman, this Terrian woman, had come to mean more to him than his own life.

K'rona reappeared, laid a blanket over Alexandra, then set to work freeing her from the energy field binding her wrists and ankles.

"Will your bio-signature not be recorded when you turn off the restraints?" Graig asked.

"Please do not fear for my safety, Commander Roble. At this time, my situation is not as precarious as it seems. There is an excellent chance I will be able to talk my way out of this situation."

May that be the Mother's will.

Putting K'rona in mortal danger had never been part of the plan. Gryf turned his attention to assessing Alexandra's injuries. By extending his Gift, he found the wounds on her body were extensive. Cuts, bruises, and burns. No broken bones, though, and she had not been sexually assaulted, thank the Mother. But, there was something else. Something elusive and unfamiliar.

"We must get you to the control corridor before too many others are about, Senior Captain," K'rona urged.

PROPHECY

Indeed, they must. K'rona assisted in securing the blanket around Alexandra's shivering body. For the sake of expediency, the factoress carried Alexandra into the control corridor.

Mendiko met them at the rendezvous point. Gryf cast a glance along the empty corridor as the Anferthian male opened the access portal and retrieved two packs. "Jandi was successful, K'rona-iad. A uniform, a *telum*, and several days' supply of protein bars."

K'rona received the packs and turned to Gryf. "Captain, the uniform belonged to one of your own who no longer has need of it, but Allazandra does. Your destination is remote and high in the mountains. It will protect her from the harsh elements there. The outer maintenance hatch is at the far end of the control corridor. That is your avenue of escape."

Gryf frowned. "Factoress, why not come with us?"

"Anferthians amongst the Terrians and Matirans would be treated with distrust and hatred." There was sadness in her voice. "In truth, I will be much more effective to our cause if I remain here for the time being. I do thank you for the gracious invitation, Senior Captain."

She turned to Mendiko, and he touched her cheek, murmuring something that made her smile. Then she swept back down the corridor to meet her fate. It was clear K'rona would not leave Mendiko unless she had no other choice.

CHAPTER ELEVEN

Dawn broke like red fire from the east. Scuttling clouds lit up like flames reaching for the zenith of the sky. It was by far one of the most awe-inspiring sights Gryf had ever seen.

The crisp, cold air filled his lungs—stale prison air gone, but not forgotten. If they were caught, they would be breathing the reprocessed air once again. That simply must not happen.

Supporting Alexandra against one side, he gripped the *telum* provided by K'rona in his free hand. The weapon was light and cool, and wholly satisfying to hold. When he had surrendered his own weapon to Haesi three weeks ago, he had had little hope of ever carrying one again.

But now, thanks to the dissenters, both he and Graig were armed. Alexandra would be too, had she the strength. Instead, her weapon remained in the pack. *Telums* were not difficult weapons to shoot, if one was able to raise their arm. Alexandra could not do much other than move her legs as she leaned against him for support.

As the sun approached its highest point, they were well into a forest, sheltered beneath the fragrant trees of Terr. Every step took them away from slavery and closer to Ora.

◆ • ◆ • ◆

Three days on the run. At least, that's how long Gryf said it'd been. To Alex, it was all a blur. She huddled in the blanket he'd wrapped around her before he'd left to scout ahead. The Anferthian protein bar she'd recently eaten sat like a lump of lead in her stomach.

If it had been three days, shouldn't she feel better? Hugging her knees, she ignored Graig's nearby presence and stared at the river rushing down the mountain. Between the blanket, the sun-warmed boulder she perched on, and the temperature-sensing Matiran uniform K'rona had provided, she should be overheating. Yet the bone-deep chill that had been with her since escaping remained untouched, sending shivers through her every few minutes.

Her malaise was slowing them down. Even *parvirtu*—the process by which a healthy Matiran shared their strength with an ill or injured companion by way of the Matiran Gift—hadn't helped. It was obvious even to her that Gryf and Graig were extending themselves beyond their limits trying to help. What she needed was real medical attention, which was still several days' journey away.

A violent shudder wracked her body, and Graig jerked his head around. For the first time since she'd met him, he watched her without masking the worry in his eyes. Odd that he'd be concerned, since he didn't like her.

"If you need to talk, *sora*, I will listen. Without judgment."

She doubted that. And reliving her torture was not an experience she wanted. Besides, how could he possibly understand?

There was only one safe thing she could say. "What does *sora* mean?"

The emotionless mask seemed to slam down again, but then Graig's expression relaxed. "It means sister."

Her mouth dropped open. "I didn't think you liked me." At all. In any way, shape, or form.

He shrugged. "I never disliked you."

Sure. "Then why...?"

"It is my duty to watch out for my captain," he replied. "And now you."

All this time his hard, crusty shell had been an act? It sort of made sense, though. So much had ridden on Gryf's ability to get them off that godforsaken slaver. She'd been a distraction he hadn't needed. But, the undercurrent of attraction had always been there between them.

Graig had made himself the counter-balance to that attraction. Good grief, he'd been *helping* them keep it under control.

She studied her blanket-covered knees. "It wasn't just

Kotas." Dammit, why had she said that? It wasn't like Graig could do anything about it, and he probably didn't care either.

Graig sat straighter, if that was at all possible, one hand fisting on his knee. "What do you mean?"

She looked back to watch the water rush and tumble over the rocks.

"Haesi," He growled the name through his teeth then muttered another word under his breath that she didn't recognize.

Swallowing hard, she met his gaze squarely. Both Graig's fists were clenched now. Then he seemed to force himself to relax, before standing up and crossing to her. Bracing his hands against the rock on either side of her, he leaned close.

"Then we both understand the evil of which she is capable."

She flinched at his cryptic words. The truth was there in his grey eyes. The shadow she lived with was in him too. "What did she do to you, Graig?" Tears choked her words.

Stay in control, Alex.

His jaw muscle twitched, and he stared into her eyes for so long she thought he wasn't going to respond. "For three days after the fall of the Guardians, she kept me prisoner. Her preferred means of torture was psychological. I will not tell you what passed between us, as you know better than most how she can destroy a person."

She did, and even understood Graig's desire not to relive the experience. A tear burned a line down her cheek. "I don't know how to get past it—to move on. For the first time in my life, I look at my future and I see nothing."

The hard look on his face eased, and he appeared to weigh his next words. "I think...." He paused. "I *believe* you have an extraordinary future ahead of you, Alex, one which you never conceived. You need time to heal, but once you have, I pray you will embrace that future wholly, and see it through with all your heart and soul."

He surprised her with a genuine smile. "You *will* get past it, *sora*, and you *will* move on." He pushed himself off the rock and stepped back.

"What...what about you, Graig?" She sniffed.

His face hardened again. "I will get past it, too. The

PROPHECY

moment I give Haesi our regards—just before I open her throat with my blade."

Five days, but it seemed like ten. Alex leaned against Gryf, snuggled close to his side for warmth. Peace and safety radiated from him, and the scent of pine clung to his uniform. The first time he'd climbed into the trees to check for Anferthian search ships had scared the bejeezus out of her. Him falling and breaking his neck was a real concern, until he'd proven what an adept climber he was. Or maybe she worried less because she felt like crap all the time. Weak and nauseated, with sharp pains in her abdomen. And every day was worse than the one before. What the hell was wrong with her?

Graig dozed on her other side, the blanket over all three of them to trap their collective body heat. A safe port in the storm. A swirl of snow blew past their small leeward-facing hollow; not quite a cave, yet more than an overhang. Outside, nature was working itself up to a full-fledged spring blizzard, a common occurrence in the high Sierra-Nevada mountain range. They must be near seven thousand feet by now.

"*Ithemba.*" Gryf's voice rumbled under her ear.

Graig stirred. "Outlawed five centuries ago. And the drug is very difficult to obtain even in the underworld market."

Alex frowned. What were they talking about?

"I doubt Kotas would bother," said Gryf. "But Haesi...it is conceivable that she would have connections."

It was too much trouble for Alex to raise her head, so she tapped her fingers against Gryf's chest. "What are we talking about here?"

Gryf brought his other arm around her and drew her closer. He idly stroked his hand up and down her arm. "A method once used throughout the known galaxy to interrogate prisoners." He paused to clear his throat. "This drug, *ithemba*, is injected. It intensifies the pain, making the victim more amenable to answering questions. As long as booster injections are given, the drug will not cause internal damage. But if left in the system unattended, the victim's internal organs will atrophy."

Nausea churned in her stomach. "You're right. Haesi does like her needles." She swallowed hard against the fear rising in her chest. "I'm dying, aren't I?"

Gryf tightened his arms around her. "Not if we can get you to a healer in time. We are only a day or two from Ora's coordinates. Dante should be there by now."

The tiny shelter seemed to shrink and the air became stifling, like Kotas's chamber. A slow rise of panic crept up her throat, and her heart thumped in her ears.

I'm suffocating. She shoved away from Gryf.

"Alexandra...?"

"Going to barf." Her words seemed muted to her ears, probably by the snow and the altitude, but their effect was instantaneous. Gryf released her, and she stumbled several steps away out of the hollow before falling to her hands and knees to retch the remains of her Anferthian protein bar into the fresh snow. Unbelievable. It tasted worse the second time around. And the third...fourth. *Ugh!*

The attack passed, leaving her panting. A cold sweat dotted her upper lip, and her arms trembled. She became aware of Gryf kneeling next to her, and the weight of his hand gliding up and down her back. He'd seen her at her worst more than once, and hadn't run away yet. At this point, there was probably nothing she could do that would scare him off. She flopped over onto her back and lay panting. The sting of the cold snow cooled her hot cheeks.

"*Compa.*" He leaned over her, lines of worry creasing his forehead as he smoothed his hand over her hair. "Come back to the hollow. I have an idea."

"But I can breathe out here." Her protests wouldn't work. He would take her back to the shelter.

Gryf wouldn't let up until she was on her feet and moving toward the hollow. If the ground didn't stop spinning—left, stop, repeat—he'd end up carrying her.

"Captain." Graig stood in front of the hollow, his *telum* in hand and trained on something behind them.

Oh, crap. Someone must be there—unless Graig had a history of pulling his weapon on imaginary snowmen, which wasn't likely. Gryf turned to look, keeping his body between her and whoever was there. She leaned forward just enough to see around his head.

Beyond him, two well-muffled, dark-clad shadows hovered in the failing light. Or were there four people there? Her eyes must be crossing. She reached up to rub them and blackness swooped in.

CHAPTER TWELVE

Ora Solaris shivered as she contemplated the swirling snow beyond the mouth of the main cave of the refugee camp. In the darkness, the sound of the wind roaring through the trees confirmed that the storm was intensifying. She had learned the names of many of those trees—aspen, cedar, Douglas fir, pine. Cedar was her favorite. The sharp scent of the bark was invigorating. Truly, Terr was a planet of incredible beauty. Not too different from Matir, although she did miss the lavender sky of home.

She compressed her lips and narrowed her eyes. Unfortunately, Gryf was out there in the storm. How was he faring in this blizzard? Her cousin had been in harsh climates before, and she could not bring herself to believe he was anything other than safe.

She had to believe Bodie was safe too. He still had not checked in. She nibbled her lower lip. Bodie was another invigorating life form on this planet. Not that she would share such thoughts with him.

"They'll be here, ma'am, don't worry."

She glanced at the army colonel standing with her, his feet apart and hands behind his back, relaxed but ready for action in an instant.

"I am that transparent, Gunner?"

"No, ma'am," Gunner replied, his breath fogging in the cold air. "Just a good guess."

Garrison "Gunner" Reed was a good man, and an excellent soldier. Thank the Mother that he and his platoon had been in the area on training maneuvers at the time of the invasion. They had gathered all the civilian survivors they could find. It was nothing short of a miracle that his ragtag group had crossed paths with Bodie and Duck two days later.

She gave him a nod. "I will feel much better once they get here, certainly."

Gunner grunted in apparent agreement, and a comfortable silence fell between them.

"Camp One, come in." Ora's handheld radio crackled to life. "Song Bird to Camp One."

Her heart rate leaped at the sound of Bodie's voice. Whether he was speaking, singing, or whistling, the effect he had on her was always the same. Sometimes just looking at him was all it took to mix up her head.

Maintain yourself, Captain Solaris.

Truly, she was a captain, and her response to this alien civilian entertainer was unseemly.

Ora yanked the radio off her belt and depressed the button. "Camp One. Go ahead Song Bird." The code words were not necessary, of course—it was unlikely the Anferthians would bother to scan for the weak Terrian band-waves the handhelds transmitted. But it had seemed prudent to err on the side of caution.

"We've located the treasure in Cave Twenty-eight—two, eight. One of the pieces is tarnished and may not make it back. She's a beauty, and worth sending in the expert."

Alex. Gryf's Terrian required medical assistance. It had been what the Terrians called a long shot, but Ora had so hoped they would all arrive unscathed. "What is the problem, Song Bird?"

"*Ithemba.*"

Ska! Her heart plummeted to her boots. Hells take Kotas. If what Dante had told her about Alex was true, there was more at stake than any of them imagined.

"Gunner, get Dante. Tell him it is a code one emergency and to dress warmly."

"Yes, ma'am." He turned and took a step in the direction of the tunnel leading to the infirmary, but stopped when she touched his arm.

"And Nick too. He will want to be with his sister."

"Yes, ma'am."

Gunner left to carry out her orders, and Ora lifted the radio to her mouth. "Song Bird, the expert is en route. Stand by."

"Standing by, Sunshine."

Ora suppressed a smile. Bodie had come up with her code name, and it pleased her ears to hear him use it now. She gave herself a mental shake then shivered. This would not be a pleasant hike, but the fates of two worlds depended upon Alex's survival.

◆ ◆ ◆ ◆

Alex fought her way through a thick, oppressive blanket of fog. Voices spoke around her, one of them Gryf's. And he held her right hand between his, chaffing her frozen fingers. She would've recognized his touch anywhere. But who had her other hand?

"Duck, move a *lutep* closer to her feet." Gryf's voice washed over her. As long as he was with her, she'd be safe.

"Would Dante have something to counteract it?" This voice she didn't recognize, the unknown man warming her left hand.

"It's been over two hours. We cannot afford to wait for Dante any longer." Gryf's response was harsh. He must be pretty stressed.

She forced her eyes open and blinked at the rocky ceiling above. A cave? And horses; she definitely smelled horses. How had they gotten here?

A familiar, wiry, dark-haired man in his mid-thirties sat on her left, massaging her hand. One brow winged up above his hazel eyes, and his mouth quirked in the midst of his rough goatee. "Never thought a face-plant could be graceful, but you did it—in the snow, no less."

Where did she know him from? Her brain didn't seem willing to cough up the answer, so she turned her gaze to the man sitting on her right. Gryf.

"I fainted." In case he hadn't figured that out already.

His I'm-in-charge-and-everything-will-be-all-right face faltered. "Indeed."

"How'd we get here?"

"Bodie and Duck." He indicated to the man next to her and another larger man setting a glowing cube by her feet. "They braved the storm to find us and take us to Ora's camp."

PROPHECY

"We're there already?" How long had she been unconscious?

A mixture of sympathy and regret rose in Gryf's eyes as he smoothed his hand over her hair. "Not yet. We are sheltering in this cave until the storm passes."

That made sense.

Warmth penetrated the blanket around her feet, and she glanced down at the glowing half-foot square cube. "Is that some sort of heater?"

"A *lutep*. It provides both light and warmth." Gryf returned to the job of defrosting her fingers.

Technology. Cool. God, her head hurt, and her stomach was empty. Would she ever eat real food again? Not that it mattered; she probably couldn't keep it down anyway.

"Beats starting a fire," the man named Bodie said with a grin.

She squinted at him. "Bodie...Jones?" Nicky's favorite R&B singer was here, in this cave, restoring circulation to her fingers? "How.... Never mind. My brother must've keeled over when he met you."

Bodie's grin widened. "He was a little tongue-tied at first. Good kid. I promised to get you back to him in one piece." His grin faded as he glanced at Gryf. "But your captain doesn't want to wait for the healer to get here."

"I have healed her before, Jones," Gryf growled.

He had, once. But the stakes were higher this time. Could he do it again?

"Dude, all I know is that this *ithemba* drug is some serious shit. It's out of control in her system, killing her." Bodie jabbed his thumb over his shoulder. "And Roble back there said only a trained healer can neutralize it. You are not a trained healer."

"Words I now regret," Graig muttered from somewhere behind Bodie.

The singer glared at Gryf. "I'm not letting you mess her up more."

"The choice is not yours." Gryf's jaw tightened.

Good grief. Alex allowed her eyes to close, shutting out the tunneling effect of her vision. "If you two don't shut up, I'm going to throw up again."

An unfamiliar snort came from somewhere near her feet. Must be the other man...Duck? "I'm thinkin' you should drop it, Bode. Ya ain't gonna win."

Bodie made a growling sound, but said nothing. Good.

"Gryf?" His name fell from her lips like a sigh.

"I am here, *compa*."

"Stay with me." *Fix me. Make me better*.

"Always."

Gentle pressure from his fingers squeezed her hand then darkness descended once more.

Alexandra's face relaxed as she once again faded into the realm where he could not reach her. It would have been better to have had her verbal approval before attempting a healing, but he had not the heart to push her past her endurance.

He lifted his gaze to meet Bodie's. "Step away. I will be using my Gift to heal her now. Commander Roble's orders are to stop you from interfering. By force, if necessary."

The smaller man's jaw clenched then relaxed. He threw his hands up with an exasperated sigh. "Man, it's on you. I hope this works."

As do I. Gryf gave him a nod, and the Terrian retreated to sit with his back against a stone wall.

Graig took the vacated spot at Alexandra's side. "I had hoped to have this conversation in private, but even so must share my concerns.... No, do not interrupt, Gryf. It is vital that you know what I suspect before you begin."

Gryf ground his teeth and bit back the acidic words vying to be spoken. Graig was his childhood friend, and a man of few words. Never had his counsel been detrimental or lacking. Why would this time be any different?

He gave Graig a sharp nod. "Continue."

"There is something unusual about your relationship with Alex. Would you not agree?"

Unusual was an understatement. Intense and soul moving were more apropos. He drew his brows together and frowned. "Soul moving." The murmured words teased at his memories. "At times, it is as though my soul reaches out for hers."

PROPHECY

Could it be? "If you are suggesting *anim tros*, I must point out that Alexandra is not Matiran. Therefore, soul mating between us is impossible."

Graig shrugged. "You say this only because it has never happened. But, unlike any other races in the known galaxy, Terrians are our genetic cousins. Only by our skin tones and Gifts do we differ. Why would soul mating be impossible between us?"

Leave it to Graig to find a sound counterargument. "But *anim tros* are rare, only occurring in times of desperate need. The last pair were joined two-hundred years ago, during the famine."

"During times of darkness, two are joined to right wrongs," Graig said cryptically.

Times of darkness. The Anferthian invasion of Terr could be considered a dark time. But he and Alexandra were stranded on her planet. What could they do to right this...? "Mother, help us." He stared wide-eyed at Graig. "Are you suggesting the *Profeti?*"

Graig's expression turned sympathetic. "It is the conclusion that has turned in my mind since your illness. Dante and I discussed and dismissed the possibility, but since then I find my opinion has changed."

Which meant Dante had likely had a similar change of heart. And Ora...holy Mother, she was an avid believer in the *Profeti*. There was little doubt where she would stand on this issue.

Like it or not, there was a certain logic to Graig's conclusion. And it would explain much about the depth of Gryf's relationship with Alexandra. *I cannot believe I am considering this.*

"What the hell is a *Profeti?*" Bodie asked.

Gryf released a sigh and shifted from sitting on his knees to his buttocks. "Ora must have told you about our history with your people." He paused long enough for Bodie to nod. "The *Profeti* is an ancient Matiran prophecy made a century after The Leaving. A dark time will befall Terr and Matir, and two will be chosen to reunite our peoples. One from each of our worlds." He cast a glance at Graig. "This is an insane idea.

What if you are wrong?"

Another shrug. "Can we afford to take that risk?"

"There is one large impediment you have overlooked. Alexandra and I are stranded here on Terr. There are no resources we can fall back on to win back her planet or save ours."

A rare mischievous grin brightened Graig's face. "As your cousin would say, who are we to question the will of the Mother?"

"Of that there is no doubt. I will consider your words." He allowed his gaze to rest on each of the three men. "None of you are to discuss this with Alexandra. As her potential *anim tros*, it is my responsibility to do so."

He pushed himself to his feet to stretch before attempting the healing. Chances were, the damage to her organs was significant and would take time to heal.

"One more thing, Gryf." Graig paused until Gryf made eye contact. "*Eno anim*—the soul mating—has not occurred for you yet. Each time you and she have a preternatural encounter, your souls have tried to bond. It is only by the blessings of the Mother that it has not occurred."

Here-in lay the problem. To heal her now, he would run a great risk of their souls joining without her consent. Alexandra should have a choice in the matter. To deny that her would rob them of the open and honest relationship he desired to have with her. It was vital that he not betray her trust in this manner.

He gave Graig a curt nod. "I shall do all I can to avoid this situation."

Gryf knelt over Alexandra, his knees cushioned by the rough horse blankets under her. He rested his hands on her mid-riff as he inhaled a deep, centering breath and allowed his Gift to flow over, then into, her.

His mind recoiled. It was one thing to talk about the damage caused by the *ithemba*, but quite another to be immersed in its oozing, sickening depths. There was not a chance in all the hells that she would survive until Dante arrived. Healing her now was the right course of action, even without her verbal permission. But, now that he was carrying out this plan, his path was not so clear. How would he remove the poison?

His Gift surged deeper, as though it knew where to go and what to do. Perhaps this would be easier than he had anticipated.

In his chest, something moved, pressing forward as though seeking egress from his body. Beneath his hands, Alexandra's body lurched and her eyes opened, glowing like warm amber.

"Fight it, Gryf." Graig spoke the demand next to his ear. "Close your eyes, and do not succumb to the desires of your soul."

Gritting his teeth, Gryf squeezed his eyes shut. The power of his Gift flowed through Alexandra's body, surrounding damaged organs and making them whole. Neutralizing the rampant drug. Healing her. As long as he kept his soul in check, all would be well.

The subtle shift of his Gift reversing its flow indicated that the trial was almost at an end. He allowed his eyes to open, and his gaze locked with Alexandra's. The flash of white light and stabbing pain through his head took him by surprise.

CHAPTER THIRTEEN

Alex gasped and sat up. *Crack*! Her forehead connected with something hard and she fell back again, stars flashing behind her closed eyelids. A moan escaped her as she held her throbbing head between her hands. "What the hell was that?"

"My head," Gryf groaned.

That's about right.

"*Ska*, Graig, did it happen?" Now Gryf sounded panicked.

"I would not know." Even Graig's voice had an edge to it. "Do you sense Alex's soul?"

Silence. Then, "I do not."

What were those two talking about? She opened her eyes again. How had she ended up flat on her back in a cave? Vague recollections teased the edges of her mind.

I was sick. But now I'm not.

Right. Gryf was going to heal her. That must have happened.

She turned her head. Gryf lay on the rocky ground nearby, holding his head too. She reached out tentatively to touch his raised knee. "Are you okay?"

He lifted his head and grimaced. There was a faint dark spot on his forehead where their heads had collided. "I shall be. Are you?"

"Yeah. You healed me again, didn't you?"

The smile he gave her was full of relief, and warmed her inside. He rolled to a sitting position and scooted over next to her. "Why do you always aim for my head?"

"Habit, I suppose." She returned his grin. "God, I feel so much better. Am I cured?" Even the stinging cuts and throbbing bruises from her captivity seemed to be gone.

"It is my hope, but I shall allow Dante the final word when

he arrives."

Graig rose to his feet in one abrupt motion, his *telum* in hand. "They may be here. Someone is approaching."

With those words, the light-hearted atmosphere vanished. Gryf matched Graig's motions of a moment before, stationing himself between her and the cave's rough triangular opening.

Bodie and Duck were on their feet too, cocking their weapons—a handgun and a rifle, respectively. If only she had a weapon. But, all she could do was sit here, useless, and pray it wasn't the Anferthians crunching through the snow toward the cave.

A heavily-bundled figure appeared in the opening. "*Bata Matir...*Gryf," a woman's voice breathed. She yanked off her snow-covered hood.

The Matiran woman appeared to be a few years older than Alex, and at least the same height. Short hair gleamed like a golden halo in the *lutep* light, unbound and wild. But the most beautiful thing about her was the unfettered look of love for Gryf in her tawny eyes. Then she closed the distance between them, and he embraced her.

"Blessed Mother, indeed," Gryf murmured then pulled back. "I did not think to see you in this life again, Ora."

Gryf's cousin gave him a cocky grin. "I am difficult to be rid of, as you know."

Gryf laughed, deep and clear. "I do, and am grateful for your tenacious determination to remain alive."

Alex's breath hitched in her chest. This was the first time she'd ever heard him outright laugh. The joyful sound was like a searchlight cutting through the darkness.

"Alex!" Nicky was suddenly there, pulling her into a fierce bear hug.

"Oh my god, Nicky." She clutched her brother's sodden coat, not caring if she got wet.

Dante squatted next to her. "May I run a quick check, Alex?"

She nodded. A moment later, the healer sat back on his heels and gave her a crooked grin. "I was told you were in dire need of a healer. But you are healthy enough to travel to camp. Gryf again?"

She released Nicky and gazed up at Gryf. "Yes."

Ora lowered herself to the floor next to Alex. "It pleases me to finally meet you, Alex. We have much to discuss once we get back to the camp." She opened her pack and the delicious aroma of real meat and spices wafted out. "But now, we brought evening meal to share with you. Have you ever had bear stew?"

Gryf cast a surreptitious glance across the cave. Alexandra appeared well rested this morning, but to put her on a horse alone after the events of yesterday?

He bent his head close to his cousin's ear. "How far is it to camp?"

"Three *kilots*."

He made the quick calculation in his mind. About six Terr miles over mountainous terrain. Too far. "I shall ride with her."

A sparkle lit Ora's eyes. "As you wish."

"May we have a few moments? There is something which needs attending."

"Of course. Bodie and Duck are still saddling the horses, so do not rush. We will wait outside." Ora nodded to Dante and Nick, and the three of them exited the cave into the bright sunlight beyond.

Gryf turned to Alexandra. What a difference from yesterday. Instead of the waxy pallor of death, her skin seemed to glow in the defused light coming through the cave opening.

Her fingers fluttered around her neck as though attempting to discern how to unfasten the uniform. The high neck and long sleeves were the style worn by engineering maintenance crewmembers. Which of his crew no longer had use for that uniform? Whose parents would grieve for her?

Gryf pushed the somber thought to the back of his mind. "Allow me to show you, *compa*."

She nodded, her tongue darting out to wet her lips. Then she lifted her chin, exposing the overlapping material at the juncture of her neck and shoulder. Applying gentle pressure, he ran his fingers along the smooth line of the uniform's seal, and it parted in response to the pressure until she could peel it back from her shoulder.

The soft swell of her left breast was exposed, smooth and unblemished. Gryf's heart stuttered, and he clamped his teeth together. With supreme effort, he lifted his gaze to study her forehead as if it were a rare treasure from which he could not look away. It was a good thing too because she raised her head almost immediately. Luckily for him, he still had his mouth curved in a smile. She could not be aware how difficult this was for him.

"It's gone," she whispered.

Now he did look down. She stroked her fingertips over the pale, delicate skin of her breast. The brutal slices of Kotas's initials were indeed gone, as they had both hoped. Awe filled Alexandra's eyes. However small, this was her victory, and for her sake, he would banish all thoughts of Kotas and Haesi to the darkest recesses of his mind.

He met her gaze again. She smiled and light filled his heart. "Not very long ago, I feared I would never see your smile again, Alexandra."

A faint tinge of pink highlighted her cheeks. "Thank you for saving my life."

She averted her gaze, and she resealed the uniform. When she looked up again, there was uncertainty in her eyes, and something else. Longing? In that moment, it seemed their breathing synchronized. Alexandra pressed her palms against his chest, and nothing in the universe mattered, or even existed, except the two of them. She raised her perfect, pink mouth to him, and he met her half-way. The softness of her lips against his sent his thoughts spinning. There was nowhere else he belonged but here, with Alexandra.

Her lips parted, and he deepened the kiss, exploring her mouth and caressing her tongue with his own. Wrapping his arms around her, he drew her close.

Sweet, so sweet.

A horse snorted outside. It was time to go. He pulled back and Alexandra smiled at him, her mouth a little pinker and fuller than before. "I think I'd like to keep doing that in the future."

He could not imagine hearing sweeter words from her. "Nothing would please me more."

A moment later, Gryf followed her out of the cave. Would she accept *anim tros* as eagerly as she had accepted his kiss? And how was he going to tell her? He could not imagine her reaction to their potential roles as fulfillers of the *Profeti*. Especially since he had yet to come terms with the idea. If only life would stop dropping asteroids on his head. A short time of peace would be appreciated.

◆ ◆ ◆ ◆

Ora's camp was nothing like Alex had expected. All the refugee camps she'd seen on T.V. had been tent cities. But here, there wasn't a tent to be seen. In fact, there wasn't much to be seen other than a snowy meadow surrounded by towering pine trees.

Gryf brought their horse to a halt, and Bodie appeared near Alex's foot. "We'll walk from the meadow. It isn't far."

"Excuse me, Jones." Graig stepped in front of the shorter Earthman, reached up and plucked her from her comfortable perch behind Gryf. She gripped his forearms to balance herself on legs that seemed made of rubber. "Steady, *sora*."

Over Graig's shoulder, Alex locked gazes with Bodie. He rolled his eyes and turned away.

A strong arm encircled her waist and gently extracted her from Graig's support. *Gryf*. Her entire body relaxed into him, accepting his assistance as they walked toward a path between the trees where Duck was waiting. Nicky followed behind.

"Yer cousin asked me t' take ya to the infirmary while she checks in with the crew on the transport," Duck told them as he led them up the path. "The camp's jus' up the way."

They emerged from under the branches, and Alex gazed up at the towering white granite outcroppings reaching toward the cerulean sky.

Nicky appeared on her other side. "Just like hiking with Mom and Dad. The air's pretty thin. We must be close to nine thousand feet."

"Feels like, huh?" Alex glanced at Duck. "I haven't seen any tents. What does everyone use for shelter?"

PROPHECY

"Sister Golden Hair an' her crew found a catacomb of caves under all this rock." Duck stomped his booted foot on the hard ground. "They're all under yer feet."

Gryf frowned. "Yet, I see people out. Like that group of Terrians and Matirans chopping wood over there. And...are those children?"

"Yup."

"Has she lost all sense?" Gryf growled. "The Anferthians could fly over at any time."

Duck's eyes narrowed. "There are watch posts fifteen miles in every direction, Cap'n. They're 'n constant contact. Ain't no 'Ferths gettin' anywhere near the camp without us knowin'."

"We got by," Gryf countered.

"How do ya think Bodie 'n I found ya so easily?"

The two men stared hard at each other then Gryf nodded slowly. "Indeed. Your point is valid."

A sudden grin creased Duck's weathered face, breaking the tension. "'Course it is. An' so is yer concern. C'mon. We'll go through the main cave."

They followed the grizzled mountain man up a steep, rocky slope and through the wide mouth of a huge, low-ceilinged cave. They crossed the space, which was longer than half a football field.

"Mind yer head, missy." Duck bent to pass through a low opening and into a tunnel. "Ya just follow them alien lights down a ways. The openin' ya need will be the first one on yer left."

"Thank you, Duck." She moved forward. Gryf slid his arm from her waist and enveloped her hand with his. The almost constant need for physical contact with him since he'd healed her should be disconcerting, but instead brought her comfort.

The tunnel was just wide enough for two of them to walk side-by-side, so Nicky fell in behind them. It was like following the yellow brick road...lined with solar-powered Matiran light and heating units. Wouldn't it have been nice if there were a great and powerful wizard at the end who'd get rid of the Anferthians?

"That must be medical." Gryf jerked his chin toward the light pooling on the ground outside an arched fissure twenty feet ahead.

Alex stepped through the arch and gasped. The back wall of the high-ceilinged cavity was lined with wire shelving units filled with medical supplies. Along another wall, microscopes sat on mismatched tables. Evenly spaced cots filled the center of the long room, which was easily forty feet long.

"Wow."

"A rousing endorsement, Alex. Thank you." Dante rose from one of the many stools dotting the room.

She gave Gryf's hand a light squeeze then slipped away from his touch to inspect one of the shelves. Picking up a small vial, she read the tiny print. "Insulin?"

Nicky chuckled from the doorway. "Well, now she's gone all glazy-eyed, Doc."

"I do not see the problem, Nick." Dante's voice was laced with dry humor. "Insulin was one of the medicines we could salvage, Alex. Many of the Terrian vaccination vials were worthless due to lack of cold storage. The ones that were salvageable are being kept in water-tight-containers in the underground cold spring."

"There's an underground spring?"

"Two, in fact," he said. "A cold one off the cave where perishables are stored, and a hot spring behind the horses' stable. You'll be happy to know they both test pure at their sources."

Yes, that was happy news. Refugee camps were notorious breeding grounds for disease.

"But, why keep them at all when you can heal most anything?"

"The ratio of healers to occupants of camp is one to one hundred nine, Alex." One corner of Dante's mouth quirked upward. "I could use some help."

"That's why I'm here." She returned his smile.

Turning the insulin vial in her hand, she checked the expiration date. The cool glass between her fingertips gave her a feeling of purpose. She was needed here. Useful. Able to do what she'd always wanted to do—help people. That was why she'd become a nurse in the first place.

She returned the vial to the wire shelf. "I can't believe how well stocked the camp is, all things considered. On the ride here, I heard there's also food, clothing, and arms and ammunition stored in some of the caves. It's just brilliant."

"Ora had everyone exceedingly busy prior to our arrival." Dante gazed at the rows of procured medical supplies with reverence. "The supply runners targeted medical, hardware, and sporting goods facilities, and it paid off. I am uncertain what a credit card is, but both Bodie and Duck claim to have maxed theirs out before the invasion."

Credit cards. Now there was something she didn't miss. "You're better off not knowing, trust me."

"Ah." Dante nodded. He reached into the pocket of his uniform and pulled out a slim knife. Without a word, he drew it across one palm, parting his blue skin in a thin line.

Alex stiffened and sucked in a sharp breath.

"Whoa! What the hell, Doc?" Nicky moved quickly to the healer's side.

Dante seemed unperturbed. "Come take a look at this, Alex."

She cast a glance at Gryf, but his narrow-eyed gaze was on Dante. All right then. She rounded a cot to stand in front of the healer. Red blood oozed along the slice. Only a superficial cut, which he could heal in an instant. "Okay, what's up?"

"A very simple test," he replied. "Place your hand over the cut. Yes, like that. Now, imagine the cut sealing itself closed."

"Excuse me?" Had she heard him correctly? "You mean like healing? The way you do?"

"That is what I mean."

"Explain, Dante." Gryf had moved to stand at her shoulder.

"A theory I've been contemplating since Alex healed you."

A snort escaped her. "I didn't heal Gryf. Graig did."

"I did not, Alex," Graig said from the entryway, Simone at his side.

Alex frowned. Somehow she wasn't surprised by Graig's sudden appearance. But if he hadn't healed Gryf, then.... "No. I can't believe you'd even suggest that I healed him, Dante. Humans can't do things like that."

"Terrians with Matiran ancestry might be able to, though," Dante replied. "And I believe that somewhere deep in your family history, you and Nick have at least one Matiran ancestor."

"You're shittin' me." The stubborn expression on Nicky's face would be comical if the situation wasn't so serious.

Dante raised his eyebrows at her brother. "I am not. Your reservations are understandable, Nick. I have had my own. But it is quite possible that the simple act of your sister allowing me to tap into her strength was enough to awaken her Gift." His brown-eyed gaze turned back to her. "Shall we at least try before we give up?"

Alex stared at him. It seemed unlikely that his theory was possible, but something weird had happened that night. What if Dante was right? If she could heal like him... Her heart thumped in her chest. She'd definitely love that.

She cleared her throat, squared her shoulders, and placed her hand over Dante's. "Okay. What do I do?"

Dante's expression turned neutral again. "Imagine the cut in your mind then imagine the edges reforming. You may say or think the word *dex*, but the most important part is to imagine part of you is flowing into the cut."

He made it sound so simple, but it couldn't be. She stared at the back of her hand and pictured the cut like a self-sealing plastic baggie. Put the two sides together and *zip*. A faint white glow surrounded her hand. Cripes, was it really working?

"Stay focused, Alex," Dante murmured.

In her peripheral vision, she saw Simone move closer. *Dex*. A gentle tug pulled at the center of Alex's body then a subtle prickling sensation ran down her arm and her hand glowed with a soft amber light. A breath later, the tug, prickle, and glow disappeared. Rats. She looked up at Dante. "I think I had it, but now it's gone."

He smiled. "Lift your hand and look."

She did. The lighter blue of Dante's palm greeted her, but the cut was gone.

"Holy shit, girl," Simone breathed. "You did it."

"Oh, my god. I did!" And it had been easy. Easy enough to try again. She whirled around and grasped Gryf's hands. The least she could do to repay him for taking care of her on their journey was to heal all the scratches he'd gotten climbing trees.

PROPHECY

She focused on the multitude of scrapes.
"Alex, no!"
Dex.

CHAPTER FOURTEEN

Gryf's breath wheezed out as his soul slammed against his chest. *Ska!* He had not anticipated Alexandra's intent as quickly as Graig. As she had taken his hands, he knew only joy for her and her newfound discovery. One unguarded moment, and now he was fighting to keep from joining his soul with hers, despite his deepest desire to bond with her.

"Release his hands, Alex." Dante's words were crisp and professional.

Alexandra's grip loosened then fell away, her eyes wide and face pale in the aftermath of an event she could not possibly understand. She sagged back against Dante, and he guided her to a stool.

Bending to place his hands on his knees, Gryf ran through calming exercises he had used since childhood to refocus himself. She deserved an explanation, but this was not the way he had envisioned telling her. It should be private, between the two of them.

But there was no going back now. Honesty was the best foundation to build from.

"Who's going to tell us what the hell that was all about?" Simone stood with Alexandra and Nick, her arms crossed.

Gryf raised his hands in a calming gesture. "Peace, Simone."

"Don't you 'Peace, Simone' me. Someone's gotta watch out for these kids, and it looks like that's me, since Alex is in shock."

Interesting how, when Simone was agitated, the inflections of her speech pattern changed. Even though brown-skinned Terrian was ten years Alexandra's senior, a friendship had blossomed between the two women. Much like his own friendship with Dante.

"I'm okay, Simone." Alexandra reached toward Simone's arm then pulled back before making contact. She stared at her hand, front and back, then set it on her lap. "I'm a little afraid to touch anyone in case that happens again, though."

"Do not fear, Alexandra." He must set her mind at ease before he could expect her to accept what he had to confess. "You may touch Simone, or Nicky, or anyone else without fear. I am your problem."

Dante held up a finger. "She may touch you too, as long as neither of you are using your Gifts."

"Can we get to the point, here?" Anger flared in Alexandra's eyes. "What just happened, and why?"

Gryf pressed the heel of his hand against his forehead then blew out a sigh and allowed his arm to drop back to his side. "It is called *eno anim*. In English, the mating of souls. The occurrence of soul mates is exceedingly rare among my people. Throughout Matiran history, soul matings—or *anim tros*, in our language—have come to pass during difficult or dark times. Two are chosen and bound together to work as one, to right wrongs and serve the greater good. We don't know how they are chosen, yet it happens."

Alexandra's mouth opened and closed twice then she gave him a side-long look. "Are you saying that we—you and me— are anim...whatever?"

"I am."

Her eyes narrowed. "I see."

This was the delicate part. No one truly wanted to give up their individuality. "When our souls bond, we become a new entity. We still have our individual bodies, but we will share each other's past experiences, and will be aware of the other's new experiences." He cleared his throat. "It is said to be rather intimate."

"You mean we share *everything?*"

"That is not all, I fear."

She scoffed. "Oh, please, do tell."

This was not going well. "Eleven thousand years ago a prophecy was made—"

"A prophecy?" Her voice dripped with sarcasm. "Great."

"Alexandra, please. This is part of my heritage, my people. Allow me to explain before you pass judgment." Even to him, his voice sounded harsher than he had intended. But, she needed to understand everything.

She blinked then seemed to settle. "Fine. Go on."

Gryf braced himself. Even if she heard his words, there was no guarantee she would accept her part in this.

Keep it as brief as possible, Helyg.

"The *Profeti* foretells a dark time befalling Terr and Matir. Two are to be chosen to restore order and reunite our peoples, or die trying."

It was as if a band tightened around his chest. Saying the words aloud instilled a clarity that he had lacked in the cave with Graig. As much as he wanted to discount it, the *Profeti* seemed to perfectly fit the series of events that had brought them to this point. This was their destiny. He and Alexandra were the *Profetae*—the ones chosen to fulfill an ancient oracle's vision.

"Is that it?"

Her abrupt tone was not encouraging. "Yes. That is all."

She seemed to study him then her gaze swept from him to Graig and Dante in turn, before returning to him. Without a word, she rose from the stool and strode out of the room.

Gryf thrust his hand through his hair. He had failed to convince her. And he'd thought getting her to see past his role in the invasion would be difficult.

Is he out of his ever-loving mind?

She was supposed to give up everything she was, her very identity, for what? To fulfill some ancient, alien *prophecy*?

"I *am* Alexandra Gaia Bock." Her words didn't even echo against the far bank of the river. They were flat, as if the earth, the trees, and the river had absorbed them.

She rolled a smooth rock in her palm. The size was all wrong, but the weight was near perfect. She gave it a little bounce. The roar of the river filled her ears as she scanned the opposite side for a target.

The tree on the left this time.

PROPHECY

She brought her arms in close, paused, then lifted her leg and pitched. *Smack*!

Nailed it. Good to know she hadn't lost her touch since high school. Baseball had been the one and only sport she'd played back then. She'd been the second best pitcher on the team, and the only girl. Definitely not a stranger to an occasional beanball when she was up to bat. But she'd been okay with that. Those opposing pitchers, who couldn't accept that a girl was a better player, usually got their comeuppance.

The corners of her mouth twitched, and she bent to retrieve another rounded river rock. Her male teammates rarely missed an opportunity to "defend her honor". Most of them were just testosterone-laden teenage boys looking for a brawl. Not that she'd been innocent. More than once, she'd jumped into the fray. And more than once, suspensions had been handed down.

But the joy of the game and the camaraderie had made the tough times bearable. It hadn't been easy, but she'd seen it through for four years. She wasn't a quitter, and they'd been a team, through thick and thin, come hell or high water.

For better or worse.

Dammit. If she could stop thinking about anything relationship related, she'd be one happy woman. She tightened her fingers around the rock. On the other hand, it would explain why she'd been attracted to Gryf from the start. Were they meant to be? Did she believe in fated love? Why did this have to be so complicated?

She posed, eyed the largest boulder across the roaring water, wound up and.... Something grey streaked past her head and hit the boulder with a crack. Who the hell had thrown that? Alex spun around.

"You like baseball, I think." Ora's mouth curved into a secretive smile. "Me too."

Huh? "You *know* baseball?" How could she?

Ora shrugged. "Officially, I have never heard of the sport. But, being a captain comes with certain advantages. And it helps to know someone in the Terrian Cultural Studies Department."

"Terrian Cultural Studies Department?"

"They process and study intercepted transmissions from your planet. Technically, I do not have clearance to view or listen to these transmissions." Her white teeth flashed as her grin widened, and Alex couldn't suppress a smile in response.

So, the good captain had a devious side. Nothing wrong with that. Alex turned back and fast-pitched her stone. *Crack!*

Ora appeared at her side, another stone in her grip. "That one *metra* patch of dirt, I think." She posed and pitched smoothly, as if she'd been born on the mound. The rock sunk into the soft mud and stuck there.

Game on, Captain. Alex scooped up another rock and pitched. *Crack!* Her rock struck Ora's, burying it deeper in the mud before bouncing away.

"Nice," Ora said. "How about the cedar, the second tree right of the boulder?" She let her stone fly.

Three more pitches went by then Ora said, "You have a Gift to heal, I hear."

Alex frowned. "Apparently."

"This is good. We need another healer in camp. Dante will be hard-pressed to care for all our residents." Ora struck the boulder again. "Please have him train you, Alex. We cannot risk having a rogue healer in camp, and he is an excellent *magister*."

"*Magister*." The alien word sounded almost like master, and Dante was definitely a master at healing. "Is that 'teacher' in Matiran?"

Ora grinned. "More than just a teacher. A *magister* invests themselves in their *disipula*, or student, much like a parent invests themselves in their child. They become your family."

That sounded intense, but now that the power flowed through her, it didn't take a rocket scientist to figure out what could happen if she couldn't control it. She let her arms drop to her sides. "All right. I'll talk to him."

The Matiran woman nodded. "We must speak about the other."

Great. Just great.

"Please, hear me out, Alex. You need not make any decisions at this time, but the choice you do make should be with full understanding."

PROPHECY

Fair point. "All right. Go ahead."

"Come. The meadow is quieter and still private."

Ora turned away and climbed up the bank and into the woods. Alex blew out a sigh.

Guess we're going to the meadow.

◆ ◆ ◆ ◆

Sunlight reflected off the snow-covered meadow, dazzling the eyes. Alex perched on a grey boulder, shoulder to shoulder with Gryf's cousin. Ora had not even broached the topic of the prophecy. Instead she'd talked about her rescue from her ship, *Athens*.

"The captain should go down with their ship. I believe it is much the same with your military." Ora met Alex's gaze, her golden eyes seeking confirmation. Alex gave her a nod, and the Matiran captain continued. "As I thought. Since I was unconscious, I was not given a choice. My second-in-command ordered Lieutenant Commander Laurentius to remove me from my ship. I woke up aboard the transport with Cassian, and twenty-four others from my crew."

Ora stared out across the field. "Sadly, Iantha, the Lieutenant Commander's wife, was not with us. She and Cassian had only just married. I was privileged to bind them. We lost most of the fleet that day."

"The *Atlantis* survived."

"Yes. And I believe two of the Guardian cruisers escaped. If *Delphi* and *Mu* were able to warn the Matir, the Defense Fleet will come. If not, they will still come. There will just be a delay."

Right, the fleet that defended Matir while the Guardians protected Earth.

"We wanted to warn all of you, Alexandra. But then we encountered Duck, and came upon Bodie the next day. Their initial reactions reaffirmed what we knew about Terrians. Keep in mind that we have monitored your audio and visual transmissions for several decades. In your stories, aliens seldom find acceptance. We opted to broadcast a warning to your governments, relying on them to share the message. After that, we started to bring Terrians to our camp as we encountered them. As we prepared for the probable Anferthian invasion and the resulting refugees, we prayed for intervention."

So what had happened with the broadcast? Had it been received and ignored?

"It would be best if the Defense Fleet did not come here," Ora murmured.

"What? We need them, don't we? If they don't come, we're screwed."

Ora turned to her. "They will be here, Alex, do not fear. This is why we have rotating crews aboard the transport scanning for them every hour of the day. But DF's arrival could leave Matir vulnerable."

Right. Gryf's concern as well. Not that any of them could do anything about it. Alex wiggled to alleviate the discomfort of sitting on the hard rock. "So, how did you land on Earth without us knowing?"

"Imagery." Ora smiled. "We projected the star field directly behind us in front of us. Anyone watching on Terr would not have noticed anything unusual. It is a common military tactic, and a technology that the Anferthians also used, only on a larger scale, of course."

Of course.

"You may wonder why I told you about my unsanctioned removal from my ship. The truth is it was a brilliant tactical maneuver by my second, Commander Damerys. By sending me away, he provided us an opportunity to rout the Anferthians." She dug into the snow with the toe of her boot. "I was furious at first. Furious with Damerys, furious with Laurentius, furious with all the others aboard the transport for allowing this to happen. But I was wrong. If not for them, this camp and its inhabitants would not exist. And you would still be in the custody of our enemy."

Ora reached into an inside pocket of her jacket and pulled out a folded piece of paper. "*Yana*, you are a natural leader. Truly, you are. I suspect you have been all your life. You are also a fighter. These are traits your people need. I understand that the Terrians aboard the slaver looked to you for guidance. It will be no different here, mark my words. Now that you have a sense of the larger picture, I have something you should read. Please consider these words, and how you can best serve your people. Unlike me, you have a choice."

The Matiran woman slid off the rock and met Alex's gaze. "It is in English, no fear." Then she walked away, the snow crunching under her boots.

Alex frowned and glanced down at the square of paper in her hand. It looked like it'd been torn out of the same spiral notebook as the letter Ora had entrusted to K'rona.

Curiosity spiked. "Ora?"

Gryf's cousin turned, a neutral expression on her face.

"How many Earth languages do you know?" It seemed like a random question, but Alex was curious.

Ora tipped her head, just like Gryf did. "Without a translator device, nine."

Wow. Heat rose in Alex's cheeks. Maybe she should've paid more attention in her high school Spanish classes. "Um, what about Gryf? How many can he speak?"

"He is fluent in twenty-two Terr languages of which I am aware. You will have to ask him about galactic languages."

Cripes. The man must be linguistically gifted.

Ora continued up the path through the trees. A snort escaped Alex then she unfolded the page and read.

Custii Profeti (Prophecy of the Guardians)
Beware! Betrayal, Destruction, and Despair.
The Knowing Ones gift us a single life from each Sun.
Two Souls sacrificed to unify.
Beware! Failure, Death, and Doom.

Alex stared at the neatly printed words. That was...depressing. And vague. What did Ora think she'd get out of this? That she'd be struck by an epiphany? If anything, she was more confused.

She refolded the paper and shoved it into her jacket pocket. Whatever hopes Ora had were not going to be met. Not by this Earthling, at any rate.

CHAPTER FIFTEEN

Gryf rolled over in his sleeping bag. That was the worst night's sleep he had ever experienced, and he had had some awful nights recently. And it had not been the result of the accommodations. No, the reason for his insomnia was wrapped up in a yellow sleeping bag across the cavernous sleeping dorm. Next to her brother.

He yanked the zipper down and pulled his feet free. Clearly Alexandra still harbored resentment over yesterday's *Profeti* debacle. In truth, she had spent the previous afternoon avoiding him. Then not graced him with so much as a glance when she had entered the dorm last evening.

Gryf thrust his feet into his boots with unusual force. The one positive occurrence in the past twelve hours was when Dante reported that Alexandra had agreed to begin her healer's training this day.

Graig appeared at his side. "Morning blessings."

"Indeed. Let us find our first meal." Gryf stalked out of the dorm, and Graig fell into step beside him. There was no call to be abrupt with Graig. Yet, he did not desire to apologize for his rudeness either.

"I will begin assessing and training Terrians in marksmanship and self-defense tomorrow. Shall I engage Alex?" Graig asked as they exited the tunnel and strode through the main cave. Surprising how many people had already risen for the day, even though it was not quite light outside.

"Yes. If nothing else, she must know how to defend herself. What time tomorrow?" He paused at the entrance to get his bearings. Cooking fire to the left in the circular outcropping. He headed in that direction.

"After midday."

"Do it in the morning, Commander." The words came out with the brittleness of a thin sheet of ice.

Graig's gaze narrowed. "Of course. Excuse me, sir." He veered away to take the path leading to the facilities.

This day was not beginning well. Not only was Alexandra ignoring him, now he had been rude to Graig.

"Senior Captain Helyg!"

Gryf glanced behind him and frowned at the young Matiran man approaching. One of Ora's crew. Lauris? No, Laurentius, Cassian Laurentius. "Yes, Lieutenant Commander?" How can I provoke you today?

"Captain Solaris's orders are to begin the process of transferring command of the camp to you. For that reason, I am reporting to you that a supply group is due back this morning from their latest assignment."

"Is Or...*Captain Solaris* incapable of remaining in command?"

Laurentius's eyes widened to the point Gryf feared he might have to catch his eyeballs when they popped out. "Sir?"

Why in all the hells was he so agitated? As the ranking officer, it was expected and appropriate that he assume command. His behavior this morning was inexcusable. "Never mind, Lieutenant Commander. I seem to be having an off day." And why would he admit that to a subordinate? "Dismissed."

Laurentius nodded and backed away, confusion in his pale blue eyes as he turned. There was something else in those eyes too. Something haunting, or...painful.

Ska. "Cassian."

The young man turned back. "Sir?"

"My heart grieves for the loss of your wife."

Cassian Laurentius's face relaxed. "I thank you, sir."

"Your attendance is requested at the staff meeting in the operations room this afternoon."

"Yes, sir." He turned away again.

Gryf compressed his lips. So much loss. So much pain. And there was very little he could do to alter the situation unless Alexandra had a change of heart.

Alex stood in the food storage cave glaring at a stack of fifty-pound bags of flour. Where had the supply crews even found fifty-pound bags of flour? Did anyone need that much flour? Okay, Maria Alvarez, the camp cook, did have an army to feed, but still.

"I got it, Alex." Her brother firmly grasped the humongous bag of flour on top, prepared to single-handedly move it from its shelf to the hand truck.

"Knock it off, Nicky. I can do it." There was no reason to snarl at him like that, but he'd annoyed the snot out of her all morning.

"Whoa." He backed off with his hands up. "Someone got out of the wrong side of her sleeping bag this morning."

"Really? That's the best you can come up with?"

"No." He dusted his hands against his jeans. "This is." He turned and stomped out of the food storage cave.

"Hey! Where are you going?" The twerp ignored her question as he clambered down the slope below the cave's entrance. She flung her arms wide. "Fine. Good riddance."

She turned back to the flour bags. They silently mocked her.

Argh. She'd been given one job this morning, and she needed to do it before meeting Dante to officially begin her training as a healer.

"Well, crap." Loading the flour and hauling it down the incline and up the rocky path to the cooking area was a superhero-sized job, and she was a mere mortal. A mortal deserted by her side-kick.

Bet Batman never had to deal with a situation like this.

Damn, but she wanted to hit something. Punching a flour bag lacked a certain amount of gratification. They didn't react, and she wanted a reaction.

A wave of dizziness slammed into her and she staggered forward until her hands connected with the cool granite of the walls. What the hell was wrong with her? She turned and leaned her back against the cool stone. Little sparkles of light danced in her vision. So not good. She needed help. She needed—

"Alexandra?"

Gryf! "In here." She stepped away from the wall toward his voice beyond the entrance, but her legs collapsed leaving her spread-eagle on the dirt. *Shit.*

Then Gryf was next to her, touching her as though checking for injuries. "Are you injured, *compa*?"

"I don't think so." What a time for her lips to turn into rubber. She'd slurred every word like a drunk.

Gryf pulled her upright. "I am sorry, so sorry."

Sorry? Sorry for what? "Off...dirt." That made as much sense as his apology.

Apparently, Gryf understood better than she'd thought, because he managed to get her seated against wall. Then he slumped next to her, panting. "I'm sorry," he said again.

"For what? Finding me?"

"No." He hesitated. "You will not like what I have to say."

"Can't be any worse than telling me I'm supposed to save the universe by fulfilling an alien prophecy."

"No. It involves the other topic."

Right. The soul mate thing.

"May I hold you, Alexandra?"

She gave him an open-mouth stare. "Why?"

"It should alleviate our mutual discomfort."

As much as she'd love to believe this was an attempt to get back in her good graces, there was nothing devious lurking in his eyes. In fact, all she could see was honesty, a trait he valued as highly as honor. And if she were also honest, there was no denying that she'd like to have him touch her.

"Um, how do you want to hold me?" A tremor ran through her.

In response, he opened his arms. Now the ball was in her court. She could either accept the hug or not.

She scooted next to him, and he enveloped her in his strong arms. Tension drained from her shoulders as though sucked down an invisible drain, and their breathing synchronized. This really did help. Snuggling into him and wrapping her arms around his waist was perfectly natural. Desirable, even.

"Are you better?" Gryf asked.

"Much. So, what's happening to me?"

"To both of us. I have suffered from a concerning lack of empathy and sound judgment this morning."

"You too, huh?"

"It has been shameful." One large hand stroked over her hair. "Can you deny feeling the discord within you ease now?"

"No."

"Our souls needed proximity to each other. It is called *anim loqui,* soul commune."

"Um, okay."

"Whether we are *anim tros* or not, our souls need time together each day to avoid a repeat of this morning's physical reactions." The warmth of his breath stirred against her hair. "Alexandra, I am sorry about yesterday. Truly. I will not lie to you. *Anim tros* is very real, but I will not demand your compliance. It must be given willingly."

His heartfelt apology washed through her. Since the air around them all but shimmered with honesty, then a little more from her couldn't hurt. "Ora gave me a copy of that prophecy yesterday."

He tensed but said nothing.

"I've given it a little thought, but Gryf, the whole idea scares me." She pushed back to meet his gaze. "I mean, I'd lose everything I am. Alex Bock would cease to exist."

He traced one finger along the side of her face. "It is not like that. Alexandra Bock and Gryf Helyg would continue to exist, but they would change. Grow. Become more than they are now. Their life goals would be shared, and they would live and die as one."

That almost sounded.... "Wait. You mean we'd die together too? Like, at the same time?"

"So it is with soul mates. They are a part of the same whole. Half a soul cannot exist."

"Like being married." For eternity. What if she wasn't ready to die when he did?

Gryf pressed his finger against her lips. "*Anim tros* does not equate to marriage, Alexandra. It is a mating of souls, not a secular union. There have been many before us who have not married, many pairs of the same gender. Even a few who were already married to their life partners when called to *eno anim*."

What would his finger taste like if she licked it? She shook off the deranged thought. He was trying to make it easier for her, she could read that much in his eyes. The least she could do was consider it.

She gave him a nod. "Okay, I'll think about it, but no promises."

He caught her hand in his and brought it to his heart. "Thank you, *compa*. There is nothing more I could wish for."

The truth of his statement was reflected in his eyes. How funny was it that her favorite color was blue? Heat rose to her cheeks. Cripes, she'd missed him.

Be honest, Alex. One kiss more than twenty-four hours ago isn't enough.

She ran her free palm over his smooth cheek. "You shaved." How had she missed that earlier?

"Shall I grow the beard back?"

"No. I like seeing your face." *Really, really like it.* His rough beard had hidden a strong, well-defined jawline. And he appeared younger—closer to twenty-seven than thirty.

"Alexandra, in Matiran culture, women—"

"Make the advances. I know. Karise was kind enough to explain all this to me in the cell." It was more of a "don't do this, and don't do that, and here's why" lesson than a matchmaking session. In hindsight, it was obvious that even they'd realized the dangers of her being involved with their captain.

But now there wasn't any danger—aside from their souls joining. And she was the woman here, so Gryf expect her to set the pace. "Be totally honest. If I kissed you, would that emo...ene—"

"*Eno anim.*"

"Yes, that. Would it happen?"

"It will not. It is possible if we use our Gifts on each other, but not from simple physical contact."

"Good." She shifted to slip her hand behind his head, burying her fingers in his hair. His eyes darkened to indigo as she drew his mouth down to meet hers. She peppered his lips with short, closed-mouth kisses. "Open for me," she whispered. He did, slipping his arms around her, drawing her closer. Sweet mint filled her senses, and a trill fluttered through her belly. God, he tasted...magnificent. She moved onto her knees, taking a dominant position, and splayed her other hand through his hair. Damn, it felt good to be in control. She slid her tongue against his as he delved deep into her mouth then sucked her in as he retreated. Cripes, the man could kiss.

A pleasant heat built in her lower belly as she flattened her breasts against him. Something stirred inside her as though awakening, and her eyes flew open. Pushing away, she pressed her hand over the center of her chest. "Whoa."

"Are you well?" Gryf's voice was laden with concern.

"I think so. I think I just felt my soul move inside me. It was weird. I've never been aware of it before, but now it's like another entity living inside my body." She scrunched her nose. "That sounds pretty freaky, huh?"

Gryf reached for her and pulled her to sit sideways on his lap. She moved her hands to his chest and he reverently covered them both with one of his. "I never imagined such was possible. Yet, that's not the only thing I've discovered was possible recently."

"Me neither." She drew her brows together and pursed her lips. "Did you just speak with contractions?"

He frowned. "What do you mean?"

"Putting together two words, like 'I' and 'have'...I've. And you used 'that's', too! I've only heard Graig try to do it, but he's been pretty awkward. You just used them and didn't even notice."

"I did." His face registered pleasant surprise. "Do I still have an accent?"

"Yes, and please don't lose that. I like it."

His warm chuckle went straight to her heart. "For you, I will keep it."

"Good." She tipped her head to one side. "May I ask you something personal?"

"Of course."

"What exactly is your Gift?"

His eyes widened slightly. "You don't know?"

She gave her head a shake, and he smiled. "It is unusual. I carry the Gift of Reason, which is very effective during political negotiations, or a hostage stand-off. For most Matirans—and yourself—touching a recipient is necessary to use their Gift. To use my Gift, I need only be in the proximity of the person or people I affect."

She frowned. "So you do...what? Release it?"

"In a manner. Have you ever seen a lake steam at sunrise?" She nodded, and he continued, "I let my Gift flow from me in such a manner. It calms those around me when they are agitated, and gives them the ability to make clear, rational choices. It has been a boon during tense situations aboard the *Atlantis*."

That made sense. "Can you direct their choices?"

"No. I cannot impose my will on others, nor would I, were I able."

Well, that was a relief. A power like that could corrupt anyone. "Did you use it in the cell?"

"Twice. Once to keep you from vomiting inside your hood, the other to aid Dante after Dennis's murder. Both touches were brief."

So brief she'd barely noticed. She gazed at their joined hands.

"It's not illogical that you would be curious," he said softly. "But to show you would risk our souls."

And she didn't want that.

Gryf gave her hands a gentle squeeze. "As much as I am loath to admit it, our presences will be missed soon. Are you ready to return to duty?"

She caught her bottom lip between her teeth and nodded. Gryf helped her transfer a bag of flour to the hand cart. At the entrance, he laid a hand on her shoulder.

"Thank you, Alexandra."

"For what?"

"Hearing what I have to say. I understand why you hesitate, and it is wise. To rush into anything without complete understanding rarely works out well."

CHAPTER SIXTEEN

Alex gazed across the warm, orange glow of the low-burning cooking fire, and laughed at her brother's dumbfounded expression.

"You mean you're not going to stop me?" Nicky's breaths hung like foggy puffs on the night air as he gaped at the tiny, paper hospital cup of peppermint schnapps she offered.

"I'm not your parent, Nicky. You're capable of making your own choices." She shifted her bottom on the small boulder. At least his choice was easy. Her brain still spun from her conversation with Gryf this afternoon. Clearly her feelings for him hadn't gone away, even in light of the *Profeti* thing. If anything, they seemed stronger. What was she going to do about *that*?

"Alex Bock, corruptor of youth." Simone leaned against Alex's leg, sipping from her own cup. It'd been Simone's idea to gather the Earthlings in the cooking alcove. A chance to bond, like a family reminiscing in a kitchen.

"Youth are rather good at corrupting themselves without *my* help." Alex ruffled her friend's tightly curled hair.

"I can agree to that." Gunner raised his cup in salute.

"I can *drink* to that," Bodie added, also raising his cup.

"You can write a song about that," Simone commented drily.

"I could," Bodie agreed. "*If* I could get drunk enough, which I can't with these puny paper cups. Damn Anferthians took out an entire block of pubs, but left the hospital standing. Seriously, where *are* their priorities?"

Sniggers rippled through the circle at his snark.

"Not anymore." Kelly, a buxom thirty-something with a thing for vengeance, frowned at the flickering coals. Everyone had lost someone in the invasion. Kelly had lost her eight-year-old son. "The hospital was gone when we went down there last week."

"*Sí*, it's all gone now." Ramon Alvarez cast a sad look at his wife, Maria. "The Anferthians turn everything we've built into piles of dust."

"Solaris tells me they're very adept at removing all evidence of the original occupants of a planet." Kelly's voice was bitter. "We're not their first conquest."

That she could believe. Alex passed her schnapps to her brother. "I hardly think twenty-one is the law anymore. One sip only, and if you like it, you can get your own cup."

Nicky took a sip, scrunched his face, then handed it back to her. "Maybe next time the supply patrol can find beer."

"Ah, no," Ramon disagreed, thumping his chest. "Tequila. That will put hair on your chest, *niño*."

"So *that's* where I've been going wrong." Nicky grinned, rubbing his chest good-naturedly. Another chuckle went through the circle.

"So we know what Ramon and Nick will miss the most," said Simone. "What one common everyday item do the rest of you miss most?"

"Chocolate," a young Chinese woman volunteered.

"Ooh, yeah, Li-Min," agreed Simone. "I've been missing flushing toilets."

Several heads nodded.

"My all-electric kitchen." Maria smiled at her husband.

"I will give you another one day, *mi amada*." Ramon took his wife's hand and kissed her knuckles. It was so sweet how in love the young couple seemed to be.

"The interweb," Duck said with a shake of his head. "I miss orderin' stuff online and havin' it magically appear at my door a few days later. Miss my door too."

LaShawn Butler gave Duck a surprised look. "No shit? *You* had a computer?"

"Yeah, ya know, us hillbillies need our ammo," Duck replied with a grin.

LaShawn shook his corn-rowed head and snorted. "Since no one's said toothbrushes, I will. Makes more sense than

Amazon Prime deliveries."

"Kid's got a point." Bodie crumpled his cup and zinged it into the fire. "I'd love to do some space travel."

Duck snorted. "After ya nearly fainted the first time ya laid eyes on them Matirans? Hell, I can't wait t' see you in space."

"Well, you can't blame me," Bodie protested. "I'd just found a nice quiet spot by a creek to write songs then suddenly I'm surrounded by escapees from Area 51."

Laughter erupted from the rest of the group, then Duck waggled his thick eyebrows. "Ya couldn' take yer eyes off Sister Golden Hair."

A chorus of "Whoas" and whoops rose into the thin night air, but Bodie just turned to open one of his guitar cases. "A little bird told me you can play, Nick. How about *Desperado*?"

Alex grinned into her tiny cup. This "little bird" might be seriously biased, but her brother could sing better than anyone she knew. And *Desperado* was one of Nicky's favorites. Bodie had all but handed him a pot of gold.

Nicky fiddled with the strings as if it was no big deal his idol had asked him to play with him.

That's it, play it cool, twerp. I know better.

Her brother gave Bodie a nod, the older man took the lead, and for three and a half minutes no one moved. It was like all the evenings she and Dad had sat in the den listening as Mom played the piano and Nick sang along with her. Evenings that would never happen again.

At the last chord, Simone wiped her eyes. "Well, I'm a fan. Alex, why didn't you tell us that boy could sing?"

An adorable deep-red rose on Nicky's cheeks, and he handed the guitar back, but Bodie shook his head and strummed the intro to one of his own songs called *From the Stars*. Bodie had written it five years earlier, and now it sounded almost prophetic.

Prophetic. Alex swallowed. Gryf was close by; she sensed his presence, but he'd refused to intrude on the Earthlings' time together. She slid off the rock to sit in the dirt next to Simone. Now was not the time to think about prophecies and all the baggage that came with them. She tossed her empty cup into the dying flames. Simone grabbed her hand, and they joined the others singing, their words of determination, survival, and hope hanging in the chilly night air.

An orange glow flickered through the narrow opening between the rocks. Gryf let the words from the Terrian songs wash over him. It was important they had this time. The bonding that brought them together tonight would keep them strong in the days and weeks to come. Thank the Mother that they were a resilient people.

Ora appeared out of the darkness and snuggled next to him on the flat rock just beyond the fire's light. He draped his arm around her shoulders, and it was as if they were children again.

The Terrians sang about a white bloom of snow and blessing their home world forever. The words touched him, leaving lingering warmth in his soul. And hope.

"That is beautiful," Ora murmured. "What are they doing?"

"Grieving." And his heart grieved with them.

The next morning, Alex headed up the path to the range with Nicky, Simone, and a handful of other Earthlings. Today would be exciting, and maybe even fun. She'd never shot a gun of any sort before, and to have someone as knowledgeable as Graig assess her minimal shooting skills was a not-to-be-missed opportunity. Hopefully she'd hit the target.

As they approached, Graig's grey gaze swept them. The stubble on his head had grown out enough for the morning sun to catch the coppery-red color.

She stopped in front of him and gave him a matter-of-fact look. "Just remember, despite the whole 'sora' thing, don't coddle me out there, okay?" The last thing she wanted was favoritism.

Graig's ruddy-colored eyebrows shot up to his hairline, quite a feat for someone who sported the Matiran equivalent of a buzz-cut. The apple in his hand slipped, and he made a sharp grab for it before it hit the dirt. Once the fruit was secure in his hand, the stony mask dropped back over his features. "I will remember."

"Great, thanks." Alex turned to continue up the path to the range with the others.

A tap at the back of her knee collapsed her leg under her. Her hands hit the hard-packed dirt, and a surprised "oof" escaped her. *He didn't just...? Of course he did. What a stupid question.*

She rolled over onto her bottom and glared up at the big, idiot Matiran. Graig bit into his apple. Even *his* steely eyes couldn't hide his amusement.

Well, hardy, har, har, Blue Man. "Shouldn't you teach us self-defense basics *before* jumping to practical application?"

Graig chewed thoughtfully. Then he swallowed and held up one finger. "Lesson number one. Never turn your back on your opponent."

He stepped around her and strode between the rocks and into the range. A wheeze of disbelief escaped her parted lips. *What a condescending little....*

Nicky guffawed, picked up a small stone and waved it under her nose. "Snatch the pebble from my hand, Grasshopper."

"Oh, shut up, Nicky." She slapped his hand away.

Simone chuckled. "Nice to see you two are warming up to each other."

"It's a love/hate relationship." Alex gained her feet, and dusted off her hands, then her jeans. "I love to hate the man."

That wasn't exactly the truth. She had a good deal of respect for Graig, and it irked when he treated her like a child.

◆ ◆ ◆ ◆

Alex curled her lip and glared at her target. Three hours earlier, Graig had claimed that *telums* were a stealth weapon. Virtually silent when discharged, and deadly accurate. Then he'd tossed his apple core into the air and shot at it without looking. His *telum* had made a whispering sound as a tiny projectile, called a *kagi*, shot out. The apple core had disintegrated, its juicy mist dispersing in the light breeze.

Now it was almost lunchtime, and she had yet to hit the bullseye. Her reusable practice rounds—christened "puff balls" by the Earthlings—were all clustered at the lower right section of her target.

It seriously pissed her off.

"'Clustering is not a bad thing, Alex.'" She mimicked Graig under her breath. *Deadly accurate, my ass.*

"Alex," Graig called from behind her. "Let's go."

She looked over her shoulder at him. His fingers were entwined with Simone's, a clear signal that he had lunch plans.

The hell with that. "How do I hit the center of the target?"

"Practice," he replied. What an infuriating answer. "Dante is expecting you this afternoon."

Alex blew a clump of overgrown bangs out of her eyes. "Even Dante knows that my medical knowledge isn't going to help once Kotas finds me."

A flicker of some unfathomable emotion flashed in his eyes. She'd found his Achilles heel. If she waited, he'd cave.

He murmured something to Simone and kissed the back of her hand. Simone nodded and moved to the entrance of the range.

Graig folded his arms over his chest and glowered at Alex. "Healing can be turned into a formidable weapon, if necessary."

"If I use my Gift for premeditated murder, I'll have nothing good left in me once this is over. I may or may not be the one to kill him, Graig, but I need to know that I *can*. I don't need to be a healer right now. I need to be a warrior."

He regarded her with an unreadable expression. Then he dropped his arms and closed the space between them, stopping inches from her.

Don't step back. Don't step back.

"The night Kotas took you from the cell, the warrior was born, *sora*. Everyone in the cell saw this. Gryf, me, even Kotas." He paused then added. "Are you unaware how much he fears you?"

"If he fears me, why—"

"Why will he search for you?" He finished her sentence. "Do you remember he referred to you as our 'favored pet'?"

She wrinkled her nose. How could she forget?

"Kotas is not a fool. He can read a situation and turn it to his advantage better than most. You confronted him to protect another, marking yourself as strong, courageous, and noble. Everything he is not. He also recognized that you are his key to getting to Gryf, and that knowledge will one day override his common sense."

Anger burned in her. Kotas must *never* get to Gryf. "Then teach me to defend myself so he can't use me against Gryf."

Graig's grey eyes hardened, but she raised her chin. Gryf's life might depend upon her ability to protect herself at some point, and she wasn't going to fail him.

Resignation registered on Graig's features. He shook his head and handed her his *telum*. "Five shots left. Go."

She suppressed a grin as she took up the proper stance and aimed the *telum* at the target.

"Slow breath in, now out," he instructed. "Relax. Good. Fire when ready."

She sighted down the barrel of the alien weapon and pulled the trigger. Two rounds slammed into the target, higher than before, but still too far right. She gave her shoulders a roll then repositioned, aimed, and centered her vision on the target. Everything else receded to nothingness except the black dot. She blew a slow release of breath out between her lips.

Thump, thump, thump. Her last three shots hit dead center. *Yes!*

"Well done, *sora*."

She bounced on her toes as she turned around. Gryf stood with Graig, and the smile on his face spoke volumes about how proud he was of her.

Graig held out his hand. "You may stay here with Gryf until you can hit the center of the target consistently. But remember, no coming here alone, or without my approval. I will have my *telum* now."

She presented Graig's *telum* over her left arm, butt first, per Matiran tradition. Then Graig turned away and strode toward Simone.

"Ridiculous rule," she muttered.

"He is the *magister* of this range." Gryf's voice was also low, but amusement lit his eyes. "I've already exchanged the *kagi* with practice rounds in my *telum*. Six shots then we're going to go eat."

PROPHECY

Ten minutes later, her last eight rounds hit the bull's eye. "That's more like it."

"Well done." Gryf hugged her shoulders, and she melted against him. "Now, for your next lesson, I'll teach you how to count to six."

A giggle bubbled up, and she met his gaze. Cripes, there they were again—those deep blue eyes that made her insides tingle. She licked her lips and studied his. "Before we leave, I think I need a refresher course."

Gryf's eyes turned a shade darker. "In what?"

Heat spread through her abdomen at the rough emotion in his voice. She lifted her face toward him. "This."

Their lips met with an unexpected surge of emotion. Before now, all their kisses had been tender and slow. But this time a sharp edge of hunger drove her, as if she were a famished woman who'd walked into a Smorgasbord restaurant. And Gryf responded in kind. His hand gently cupped the back of her head, holding her in place as his tongue explored her mouth. She gripped the back of his shirt, wadding in her fists.

Gryf slid his other hand along her spine to cup her bottom, drawing her against his erection. Heat blazed through her at the feel of him so intimately nestled against her. Dampness spread between her legs, and a moan of need rasped in her throat.

"*Compa*," Gryf murmured as he drew back. "We must stop now before this goes too far."

"Gryf...." His name hung between them, half plea, half moan. Was he really stopping when things were just getting started?

"No, Alexandra, I would never show you such disrespect."

But she wanted him to disrespect the hell out of her. Right here, right now. She opened her mouth to tell him so, and her stomach growled in a noisy protest of her neglect.

Their gazes met. *Awkward*. A giggle escaped her, and Gryf's deep laughter mingled with her own. He brushed back an errant strand of her hair.

"Midday meal is probably over, but perhaps Maria has saved us something."

"Maria always saves us something, even if it's beef jerky

from 7-Eleven."

Gryf tipped his head to one side. "Seven eleven?"

Alex gave him a wide grin. "Never mind. Let's go."

CHAPTER SEVENTEEN

Alex balanced on the rock next to the river, her knees aching. How had her ancestors tolerated doing laundry like this? Actually, what she was doing was more like a really good rinse, with a scrub brush to remove dirt and stains. Two weeks of warm, sunny days had melted most of the snow, but the chilliness of the water sunk through her fingers to the bone. She held up the dark grey Matiran uniform she was working on. Just a rinsing revived it to almost new.

"Whatever this material is, I want *all* my clothes made out of it."

"*Byssys*," Alta Imifa, a young, blonde crewwoman from *Athens* informed her. "It is a produced fiber on Matir, mimicking a natural fiber called *bys*."

"For this, I would join the fleet." Alex shoved the uniform back into the icy water for a final rinse.

Ora tossed a camp shirt over the rope line. "What an interesting idea—Terrians joining the Matiran fleet. We can never have too many healers, Alex. You should think on this."

Alex squeezed the uniform a section at a time. Damn, her fingers hurt. "I don't think so." She had other things to worry about, like what to do about the prophecy thing and watching her back for that whack-job Kotas. A chill trickled down her spine.

Ora waved her hand in the air as if to dismiss the entire conversation. "May I ask you something?"

"Sure, as long as you stop eyeballing me like I'm a puzzle that needs solving."

Alta laughed. "She has you figured out already, ma'am."

Ora flashed a grin. "Alex, have you...mm, pressed palms with Gryf?"

"Huh?" Sometimes talking to Ora was like trying to balance on a tightrope in a windstorm.

"Karise told me it did not happen in the cell," Alta volunteered.

"Truly?" Ora didn't even glance in Alex's direction. Almost like she wasn't sitting here listening. "Why not, do you suppose?"

Alta shrugged one slender shoulder. "There was danger of being discovered."

"But pressing palms is not detectable, like *eno anim*."

"Gee, I hate to interrupt this *riveting* conversation," Alex laced her voice with heavy sarcasm, "but what are you talking about? What's palm pressing?"

"The correct English translation would be Promise of Faith," Alta said.

"Yes, so it would be," Ora agreed. "Truly, you do not know of this?"

Alex raised her brows. "Things are a little different on Earth, Ora."

The hand wave again. Must be an Ora trademark gesture. "Maybe Terrians call it something else. Hear me, Alex—when a woman chooses a man for a relationship, she approaches him in a public forum. She raises her right hand, and waits for him to notice her. Most times he does so quickly, because she will have voiced her intention in advance, but not always."

"Okay," Alex let the word out slowly. "What happens when he sees her?"

"If he wants to pursue a courtship, which he usually does, he will raise his left hand and wait for the woman to approach," Ora continued, her eyes alight. "The woman then presses her right hand to his left. Once done, no other woman can claim the man unless the courtship is called off."

"So, courtship is like an engagement? An agreement to marry?"

The two Matiran women exchanged awkward looks then Alta shook her head. "It is more like a public declaration that you are together. A devotion to each other and your relationship."

Didn't the guy ever make the first move on *anything?* "And

you think I should do this with Gryf?"

"He is a highly eligible, unattached male." Ora gave her a pointed look. "If another woman is interested, and he turns her down in favor of you, you could have unintentionally made an enemy."

Wow, Matirans grew their women aggressive. "Why would any woman try this with an *anim tros*, though?"

Ora shrugged. "I'm not saying they would, necessarily. However, I do know that the gesture would mean an awful lot to Gryf."

Oh. Well, there was that.

An hour later, Alex perched on a stool in the infirmary. Remnants of the conversation with Ora and Alta spun through her mind, making it difficult to stay focused on the current conversation: did other Earthlings carry the Matiran Gift gene?

She gave Dante a speculative look. "I bet Nicky has a Gift too."

But her brother insisted he had no interest in finding out if he carried the potential. What was wrong with him? Who in their right mind would pass up an opportunity to help others?

"It is best to let him be on the matter, Alex." Dante's expression suggested she refocus her thoughts. "If he has a Gift, it will activate in due time, as yours did."

That wasn't what she wanted to hear. "I know, Dante. It's just, well, I don't want to be the only one. I feel like a freak."

Dante reached for her hands, holding them between his. "You are not a freak, Alex. And you will not be the only Gifted Terrian. Give it time."

"You sound like my mom. Has anyone else shown signs of having the Gift?"

"No." He squeezed then released her hands. "Not yet."

"Hey, Doc?" Duck's bulk filled the entryway.

"Hello, Duck," Dante greeted him. "What can we do for you?"

Duck took a step in, fingering his battered camo baseball cap in his hands. "I was wonderin', bein' ya have that power t' make things better, if'n...." He dropped off with a helpless look.

"Do you require Healing?" Dante asked him.

"Well, in a way."

Duck must want to talk to Dante privately. "I should go."

"No." Duck shook his head. "You c'n stay, missy. You have the power too, an' you need learnin' t' use it." Duck looked back at Dante with renewed purpose. "It's my eyes, Doc. They ain't good. That's why folks call me Duck. They say, 'If ya go ahuntin' with Duncan MacKay, make sure ya duck!' An' it's true. I miss more times 'n I hit the target. Traps is a whole lot easier 'n shootin'."

"I understand your concern." Dante nodded. "I am not sure if can help, but I would be happy to check your eyes for you. If I can fix them, I will."

The tension on Duck's face melted into relief, and he lowered himself onto a stool. Standing next to him, Dante placed his right hand over the grizzled Terrian's eyes. "Follow please, *disipula*."

Alex laid her own hand on Dante's shoulder, and allowed her Gift to flow through her. The best part of her education: observing as her mentor made his examinations. Whether human or Matiran, the internal workings of their bodies fascinated her like red lasers fascinated cats.

"Do you see it, Alex?" Dante asked.

"I do. It's like his eyes are wired incorrectly."

"Exactly." He straightened. "I can fix this, Duncan. The procedure will take about five minutes, however I will need to put you into the Sleep. Would you be all right with that?"

Duck's wide grin lit his face. "I'd be obliged, Doc. When?"

"Now would be fine."

A few minutes later, Duck was snoring on a cot.

"Are you excited, Alex?" Dante gave her a knowing look.

"You bet I am." Excited, giddy. She was about to assist in her first surgical procedure using her Gift to Heal. How could she *not* feel this way?

━━━◆ ◆ ◆ ◆━━━

Alex paced in front of the entrance to the main cave. The joy of helping Duck this afternoon had faded with the setting sun. Her gut churned, and she clenched and unclenched her

PROPHECY

hands. What if she couldn't go through with the palm pressing?

Maria and her assistants hurried passed, delicious aromas wafting from the cast iron pots they carried to the waiting camp refugees. The rich, meaty aroma lingered on the evening air, and a low rumble emitted from Alex's stomach.

Can't blame that on nerves.

It'd been two weeks since Ora had explained the Matiran Promise of Faith tradition, and Alex still hadn't done it. It should be so simple. Walk in, find Gryf, press palms. Done.

But, in front of *everyone*? She swallowed hard against the flare of panic. It'd be so much easier in private.

The low murmur of people gathering for evening meal drifted over her. Gryf was in there somewhere, waiting. He never ate without her.

But big, chicken-shit Alex doesn't have the guts to go in.

God, she hated having an audience. Public speaking had never been her forte, mostly because she wasn't comfortable being the center of attention. And the Promise of Faith would definitely put her smack dab in the center of the camp's attention.

A soft growl of frustration rumbled at the back of her throat.

Suck it up, walk in there, and do it.

She paused her pacing and gave her hands a narrow-eyed glare. Great, her palms were sweaty. How romantic was that?

"Alexandra?"

"Eep!" She swung around to face Gryf.

"What troubles you, *compa?*"

He stood so close, his eyes full of compassion and concern. Fuzz filled her brain. No chance of making a rational response now. Should she throw herself on him and have him for dinner? What would be really great was if *he* had *her* for dinner.

"Nothing." Heat rose to her cheeks. "I...I just have some things on my mind. You can go back in, I'll be there in a few."

"I will wait with you."

Oh, no, he couldn't do that. She'd never be able to work up her nerve with him standing right here. "Gryf, please, I just need to be alone for a few minutes."

He frowned at her. What if he didn't leave? Should she just palm press him here? No, that wouldn't work. Ora said it had to be public, and most everyone was inside the cave.

"I will wait for you inside," Gryf said then turned away.

He had the most beautiful set to his shoulders, strong and confident. The masculine line of his back tapered to a trim waist. Her lips parted. And his butt...mmm.

Gryf's step faltered, and flames erupted in her cheeks again. *Good grief.* Had he sensed her thoughts?

Don't turn around. Don't turn around.

He didn't, but she waited until he reentered the cave before she blew out her breath in a gust. Good thing mind reading was a myth. If Gryf knew some of the things she'd been thinking....

But sending him away was unfair to him. At the very least, she could've given him an explanation. He deserved so much better than her. Someone who would've palm pressed him the moment she'd found out about the tradition.

Get over yourself, Alex.

She straightened her spine and walked into the low, wide cavern.

The voices were louder inside, and the large number of bodies raised the temperature of the cave to a comfortable range.

Even in the crowd, her soul found Gryf like a magnet to steel. He had his head tipped to one side, his expression attentive but his eyes distant as Duck engaged a small audience with a story, probably his eye surgery.

Now or never. She stopped ten feet away from him, in full sight of everyone, and raised her right hand next to her. The volume in the cavern dropped as other Matirans noticed her. Gryf stiffened, his posture alert as his gaze roamed the space until he found her. Comprehension lit his eyes, and the corners of his mouth tipped upward. Then he did what she'd most hoped for. He raised his left hand, and—oh, my, that was a come hither look if she'd ever seen one.

A swarm of butterflies invaded her stomach as she stepped toward him. The Matirans present moved aside to allow her through, quick explanations being uttered to their Terrian counterparts.

By the time she came to a stop in front of him, the large cavern was silent. Gryf hadn't stopped smiling the entire time, and she loved that. *She* had put that smile on his lips. When she pressed her palm to his, the butterflies migrated to her heart. There was a sparkle in Gryf's eyes as he slipped his other hand around her waist. She leaned toward him and captured his mouth with hers.

The butterflies careened through her body, and her toes curled inside her hiking boots. *Oh, wow.* She moved her left hand up his arm and behind Gryf's neck to seal her mouth to his. A slow, pleasant heat blossomed between her legs.

Duck whooped, and the space around them erupted with enthusiastic approval. A bubble of laughter escaped Alex, and Gryf pulled back. "Now I understand why you needed to be alone. You were working yourself up to do this."

"This was a bit...different for me."

He brushed her hair back from her face. "*We* are a bit different."

That was putting it mildly.

"But, why did you not do it outside the cave?" He asked.

"Ou...outside?" She gaped at him. "Ora said it had to be done in a public forum." That meant a big group of people. Right?

"There were people outside. It would have been public enough."

Oh, she and Ora would be having a few words about this.

"I admire you for facing your fear of public notoriety for me, *compa*," he said. "Words are insufficient to express how you made me feel tonight. I am honored and blessed to love you."

Her heart lodged in her throat. "You...you *love* me?"

"Is that so hard to believe?" He touched his forehead to hers.

"No. I guess not." She gave him a smile. "Especially since I love you too."

CHAPTER EIGHTEEN

The afternoon sun warmed Gryf on the outside as the glow of Alexandra's Promise of Faith last night warmed him within. The chords from Nick's guitar were identical to the Matiran *chatarom* Gryf's aunt had played when he and Ora were young. The familiar sound washed over him, and the carefree days of childhood were within his grasp.

"Another one?" Nick asked.

Eleven children responded with a jubilant course of yeses. They loved Nick, of this there was no doubt. And Bodie too, when he wasn't out on supply runs. Nick's fingers fluttered over the guitar strings again. The children settled, giving Nick their full attention as he sang about a sailor, an air ship, and sailing away to the stars. Li-Min and the children joined in the chorus.

The weight of Alexandra's head rested against his shoulder, her arms around his waist.

Ah, compa. Are there words in English to describe how beautiful you feel to me? I can think of none in Matiran.

He moved his hand to the small of her back. In this peaceful setting, it was easy to forget they were at war.

"I love this song," Alexandra murmured and leaned close to him. Her lips offered an enticing invitation he would be a fool to ignore. Closing his eyes, he savored their soft warmth. If ever there was a moment in life he would remember with unparalleled clarity as an old man, this was it. He would kiss her all day if she would allow it.

A sharp whistle nearby cut through the peaceful afternoon, ending their romantic moment.

Or if the watch interrupted with a warning.

Gryf located Cassian at the top of a tower of white rock.

PROPHECY

Two fingers up, fist in palm...

"Double rider, incoming."

"Show's over, kids," Nick announced. "Follow Li-Min and me, and be very quiet."

It was impressive to see the children actually listen. The group quickly disappeared through the narrow gaps amongst the rocks as orderly as soldiers. Gryf drew his *telum*, and cast a glance at Alexandra. Her *telum* was in her hand, and she appeared ready to meet the intruder. A fierce sense of pride swelled within his heart. *Excellent.*

A familiar grey dappled horse appeared at the end of the narrow gully between the stones, heaving itself up the trail at a dangerous speed. Gryf glanced back up at Cassian for a signal. "Matiran. Cleared."

He squinted against the sun's glare. "Looks like Alta...carrying a Terrian child."

"But where's the rest of the supply patrol?" Alexandra murmured.

"Where, indeed?" Holstering his *telum*, Gryf stepped out as the horse came abreast their hiding place. Alta reined in, the beast's hoofs clattering against the grey-white granite.

Gryf grasped the halter. "Steady, friend."

Alta lowered a tiny, dark-haired Terrian girl into Alexandra's waiting arms before dismounting.

"Sir," she panted, bending over to catch her breath. "Anferthians...at the gas station. Double patrol."

His gut clenched. *Ska.* How had six Anferthians get this far into the mountains in just one day? Their intensive manual search pattern should have kept them at the lower elevations for weeks.

Alexandra's free hand glided over Alta in search of signs of injury. "Alta is clear, Gryf. The child is critical."

His heart sank to his toes. Dry flaky skin, distended belly, glassy green eyes...all signs that the girl suffered from malnutrition. The precious child did not appear to be more than three cycles of age. Too young to have suffered so much. Gryf cupped his hand to Alexandra's cheek. "I'll join you in the infirmary as soon as I am able."

She nodded, and took off running with the child cradled in

her arms. A movement between the rocks caught his attention. Nick gave a hands up shrug as if asking what was happening.

"A moment, Nick." Gryf turned to Alta. "Where are the others, Crewman?"

"Coming back from different directions to be harder to follow," she reported. "We took out two of the enemy patrol, sir, but they have Simone."

"The *Anferthians* have Simone?"

"Yes, sir. Commander Roble went after her."

All the hells. That was not what he wanted to hear. "Who did he take with him?"

"No one, sir." She straightened. She seemed to be recovering from her mad ride. "They appeared to be rogue, Captain. No communication devices, just weapons. As if they did not want to be found."

"They may be dissenters."

"No, sir. They fought back even after they saw our uniforms."

Just what they needed, rogue Anferthians roaming the mountains. Graig had been right to go after them, regardless of Simone being a hostage. They must be silenced.

"Alta, have whoever is at the stable bring in the horses. All hands are to return to the main cave immediately. After that, you are to report to medical."

"Yes, sir."

"Li-Min, see the children to the cave. Nick, find Ora. Tell her we're going to ground, and help her get the word out. Rogue Anferthians."

Alex rocked the silent girl from the gas station. Dante sat nearby, studying something projected on the tabletop by a palm-size gadget called a data device. A fascinating piece of Matiran technology that seemed to hold more information than the entire internet ever had. The current peacefulness in the infirmary could be interrupted at any moment by a medical crisis. It hadn't taken long for Alex to learn how to manage these times of low stress to her advantage.

Two days had gone by without as much as a whimper from

the small, dark-haired girl. And when she slept, she twitched a lot, emitting small mewls and an occasional sharp cry. Her REMs were almost constant, so it could've been nightmares. What had happened to her? How had she ended up at that gas station?

You know exactly what happened.

Alex brushed her hand over the soft curls. The Anferthians and Kotas had stolen the little girl's childhood. Deprived her of her family. Left her with no food except the crap she could find inside the gas station store. Candy bars, beef sticks, even coffee grounds, according to Alta.

I want to know your name. I want to listen to your voice, and hear you laugh like a child should.

A slow burning heat smoldered in Alex's chest. This little one's mother would never again hold her close and rock her to sleep. Her father would never swing her over his head as she laughed. In fact, none of the orphaned children in camp would share these moments with their parents ever again. And if the Anferthians succeeded, childhood as Alex had known it would cease to exist.

But what could be done to stop the invaders? It'd been two months since their horrific arrival, and so far no word from the Matiran Defense Fleet. What if the DF didn't even exist anymore? What if Matir was also under Anferthian control? That would mean more lives had been lost, more grieving survivors. More orphaned children.

"Miss Alex?"

Alex looked up, and her heart stuttered in her chest. Gryf stood in the entryway to the infirmary, his arm resting across the shoulder of one of the camp orphans. At seven years old, Flora MacDonald had the height of an average twelve-year-old. Despite the awkwardness of being taller than her peers, she was self-assured and confident; a natural leader in the eyes of the other camp children. Except, right now, she shifted from foot to foot as though nervous.

"Come in, Flora," Alex invited, welcoming the copper-haired girl. "What can I help you with, sweetie?"

Gryf patted the girl's shoulder, and Flora seemed to regain her resolve. She crossed the room, coming to a stop inches from Alex's knees. Her china blue eyes watched the tiny mystery girl.

"Has she talked yet?" Flora asked.

"Not yet, I'm afraid."

"Oh."

Something seemed to be on the girl's mind. A little coaxing couldn't hurt. "I hate to admit it, but Dr. Dante and I are almost out of ideas".

The freckled face lit up. "I have an idea!"

"We'd love to hear it," Dante said from his stool near the microscopes.

"I could sing to her." Flora paused, biting her bottom lip with sudden, uncharacteristic anxiety. "I think she would like that."

Alex gave the child a smile. "That's a great idea. Let's try."

Flora grinned and bounced on her toes. Then she leaned forward, bracing her palms on Alex's knees, her bright red hair hung like a curtain as if to block out the rest of the world. Then she softly sang *You are My Sunshine*. By the fourth note, the bright green eyes were riveted on Flora, as though drawn by the older girl's clear, sweet voice. Alex gave Dante a pointed look over Flora's head.

When the song ended, Flora looked up and grinned. "I think it worked, Miss Alex. Should I do another one?"

Shifting in the rocker, Alex pushed to her feet. "Most definitely. And, you should hold her while you sing."

"Can I?"

Are you kidding? Alex wanted to whoop. Their little gas station girl had reacted! "Yes, you may. Take my spot, sweetie."

Once the girls were settled in the chair, Alex stepped away to watch. The solid comfort of Gryf's body appeared at her side. Flora sang softly, as if no one else existed except the precious child in her arms. A moment later, the dark-haired girl reached up and rested her tiny hand on Flora's cheek.

Covering her mouth with her hand, Alex blinked back tears. A connection had been made! The older girl smiled, but didn't stop singing until she reached the end of the song.

Flora looked up, her gaze flitting from one adult to another. "Can I give her a name?"

PROPHECY

Alex gave Gryf and Dante a questioning look. Both of them were grinning. "I don't see why not."

"What name will you give her?" Gryf asked.

The girl lowered her gaze to the child in her arms. "She wants to be called Maggie."

"Maggie is beautiful, Flora."

"It is," Dante said. "Would you like to sing to her every day?"

Flora's eyes lit up. "I would love that, Dr. Dante!"

"The job is yours, *puella*. Please continue."

Flora turned her attention back to Maggie and began singing *Twinkle, Twinkle, Little Star*.

Gryf turned his head, his mouth next to her ear. "Would you be interested in joining me on watch duty tonight?"

His warm breath tickled her cheek, and her heart rate increased. "Isn't someone else already scheduled to watch with you?"

"Corporal Reyes from Gunner's platoon. He has...an affliction."

A vague sense of disquiet niggled at her, but she couldn't seem to focus on anything but Gryf's lips. "Is he...if he's ill, he should come to the infirmary."

"It's not something you or Dante can correct."

She blinked and frowned. "Not something..." Oh! Now she got it. "I'm sure his 'nurse' will take good care of him. And, yes, I can fill in for him."

"Excellent. Thank you. Our post will be Cave Twenty-eight, where Duck and Bodie found us. Since it is a fair distance to walk, I shall meet you at the main entrance one and a half hours before sunset." He turned away and strode toward the opening.

That was it? Was a simple peck on the cheek too much to hope for? And why, oh why, did his uniform always seem to accentuate his butt? Alex forced herself to look away. Every damn time that man had his back to her, she couldn't help staring.

She pushed away the unanswered aching need in her heart and returned her attention to the two girls bonding.

CHAPTER NINETEEN

After so many weeks in the constant company of her camp mates, the isolation of Cave Twenty-eight was a welcome reprieve. Perched at the crown of a huge rock above the cave, Alex gazed out over the shadowy points of the treetops. The starry July night wrapped around her like velvet, creating the illusion that she and Gryf were the only people in the world. She could almost imagine that the catastrophe of two months ago hadn't happened.

She pointed upward. "That line of three stars is called Orion's Belt. If you go down, you'll see his legs, there and there. And those stars make his body, shield, and sword."

The warmth of Gryf's arm pressed against hers from shoulder to wrist. This kind of skin-to-skin contact was both comforting and distracting, which didn't make it easy to concentrate on the amateur astronomy lesson.

"And he is hunting a bear, correct?"

"Ursa Major, the Big Bear. It's right there." Hopefully he could see where she pointed.

Gryf's low chuckle warmed her from the inside. "It is a shame Orion will never taste Maria's bear stew. It is exceptional."

A giggle escaped her. "Yes, it is."

There were so many things in her life Alex had never expected to eat. Bear stew was one of them.

She'd never expected to be sitting with such an amazing and giving man, talking about stars, either. She leaned her head on his shoulder. "Where's your home, Gryf? Can we see Matir's sun from here?"

He rubbed his cheek across her forehead. "Were we in Terr's southern hemisphere, then yes, we might be able to see it."

"You must miss your home and family."

"I do miss my parents, and Ora's as well." His breath tickled the fine hairs at her hairline.

"I bet they miss you too."

He was silent then, "I do not doubt they do, but they will be dealing with the shame I brought upon them with my negligence."

Not this again. "I meant what I said in the cell about this, you know. If we ever get out of this mess, Nicky, Simone, and I will testify on your behalf. And I bet most of the humans in Camp One will do the same."

The music of the crickets filled the night. "Thank you, *compa*."

Her gaze was drawn to a pinpoint of light rapidly rising on the western horizon. "By the way, what does—"

Gryf sat up, his body rigid. "Alexandra."

Her heart rate jumped at the warning edge to his voice. The light was now moving toward them. "What is that?"

"Nothing good," he replied. "Go. Get down to the cave and don't stop for anything."

The scrape of the walkie-talkie against its leather case at his hip reached her ears as she scrabbled across the grey-veined stone.

"Camp One, raptor incoming," he said. "Repeat, raptor incoming, northeast trajectory."

The handheld crackled. "Acknowledged. Northeast raptor. All stations go dark."

Where was the edge of the cliff? The ground sloped suddenly and her hands slid downward. "Whoa!" *Found it.*

"Alexandra?"

"I'm okay. Just found the edge." She sat on her bottom and scooted over the brink and down the steep slope. A brief sensation of being air borne preceded her final, bone-jarring landing. "Oof!"

Small loose rocks and dirt rained down around her. She looked back up the thirty-foot drop at Gryf's dark outline. "I'm okay."

"Then go. I am coming down now."

She scrambled to her feet and felt her way around the jutting stone perimeter. Her hand found the curve of the cave's entrance. A Matiran curse came from above then the scraping and sliding of Gryf's out-of-control descent. Cripes, he must be too far to one side of the cleared slope.

The distinctive thrum of the Anferthian transport vibrated against her eardrum. Gryf was still sliding, the swoosh of gravel marking his passage. There was no way he'd make it to the cave before the craft flew over. A thud and a shout of pain announced his uncontrolled impact with the ground.

The Anferthians were practically above them now. The last thing they needed was to be picked up by the enemy sensors, if they had them turned on. Maybe they didn't.

The transport flew over, continuing over the mountains in the direction of what was once Nevada. Alex waited until the thrumming noise faded to nothingness before emerging from the cave. She cast a glance in the direction the transport had come. Nothing but empty sky. No more transports, thank God.

"Gryf." Her whisper seemed like a shout in the absolute silence. Not even the crickets dared to chirp in the wake of the Anferthian's passage, and she couldn't blame them.

Light. I'll need my headlamp to see.

The last thing she wanted was to step on an unconscious Gryf in the dark.

It took longer than she liked to find one of their backpacks, and longer still to dig out a headlamp. Once she had it on, she hurried out of the cave.

He lay sprawled on his back, his right leg at an impossible angle. *Shit.* First thing first. His pulse seemed rapid, but at least he had one. Falling back on her nurses' training to examine his head, she found a large knot welling up on the left side. A peek under his eyelids confirmed a concussion. She was going to need help.

A brief search around the area turned up no sign of the walkie-talkie. *Double shit.* No way to call for help, and no way to get him back to camp. *Now what're you going to do, Alex?*

Gryf groaned, and she leaned over him. "Gryf? Can you hear me?"

His eyes opened as if in response to her voice. She switched the headlamp to red so he could see her.

"We're stuck here, honey. Help probably won't come for a while, and I'm not leaving you in pain like this until they can get here." They'd be lucky if anyone showed up before noon tomorrow.

He licked his lips. "Too risky. *Eno anim.*"

She gave him a wide-eyed stare. Screw *eno anim*. She wasn't going to let him suffer. "We both know this is inevitable, Gryf. Your leg is broken and you have a bad concussion. You need help now, and...and seriously, is being stuck with me for the rest of your life that bad?" She'd meant it as a joke, but her voice had cracked, ruining the delivery.

He cupped his dusty, scraped palm over her cheek. "My brave, *compa*." He visibly swallowed. "Never have I hurt so much. Not even the times Graig thrashed me as cadets."

"Once we're done here, I'll kick his ass for you, okay?" She grasped his hand and lowered his arm back to the ground. "I'm going to put you out while I work on your leg."

"No."

She gave him a sympathetic smile. "Tough luck, Captain. *Dormio.*" One tap of her finger to his brow, and he was out. "Sorry, honey, but screaming patients unnerve me." And even Gryf would scream when she forced the sections of bone back into alignment. This would be one unpleasant and tricky procedure.

It took at least an hour to line up the parts of the severed femur and reduce the swelling tissues enough to ensure a clean rebonding of the bone. The entire time, her soul moved restlessly within her, like a pacing tiger. A small piece of her urged her to fight against it when the time came, but what was the point? If she and Gryf were really the lives promised in the *Profeti*, it stood to reason that there was a way to beat the Anferthians. And she wanted that in the worst way.

Enough to give up your individuality?

Yes.

She paused and glanced down at Gryf's peaceful face. As much as the unknown scared her, she'd have him by her side to face it.

Good grief, Mom and Dad, I fell in love with an alien.

They would've loved him, too.

The healing light around her hands faded, indicating that the bone was mended. Her vision wavered then stabilized. *No passing out.* She repositioned herself near Gryf's shoulder. This was the part that scared her. Dante hadn't covered concussions, so she'd have to make it up and hope for the best. Besides, Gryf had done it for her without any healer training, so it couldn't be that hard.

She placed her hands on either side of his head. What word should she use? She didn't know the Matiran word for this type of injury... Would English work?

Only one way to find out.

"Concussion." She imagined her healing Gift flowing into his cranium, the bruising on his brain fading away, and swelling going down.

It's working!

She could see it. English words seemed to be as effective as Matiran for healing.

The flow of her Gift slowed then reversed, returning to the mysterious place it originated from deep inside her. Gryf's eyes opened, their pupils equal again, and his mouth curved into a small smile. The familiar signature of a gentle ocean wave washed over her as he released his Gift. A gasp escaped her as her soul shifted in her chest. This time, there was no reason to hold back. They'd waited long enough. She slowed her breathing, and allowed her shoulders to relax. A pin-point of pleasant warmth formed over her heart, and a palm-sized white sphere emerged like a star from the night sky. She'd never really thought about what her soul might look like. Finding it beautiful might be the height of conceit, but it really was.

Her soul-sphere drifted toward another, this one crystal-blue. Gryf's soul. It was just as beautiful.

The lights touched, merging with a brilliant flash. It was as though the entire universe tilted, and all sense of direction ceased to exist. Everything that was Gryf opened to her. Every experience he'd ever had become her own. His parents, his childhood, Ora, Graig, the loss of Graig's younger sister, joining the fleet, his first time with a woman, becoming Senior

PROPHECY

Captain, the fall of the Guardians, captivity, the first time he'd looked into her eyes. All the joys and sorrows that had molded him into the man he'd become were now memories she treasured.

There was nothing in her world but him. Them. Floating, joined as a single entity. She knew him as completely as she knew herself. All his strengths and his weaknesses, what motivated him, and what brought him to his knees, were laid out before her.

A universe of stars spiraled around them then their souls separated, returning to their homes. Hers held a dazzling nugget of sapphire at its center, and Gryf's blue sphere cradled a pure white core.

She exhaled a breath. That was *anything* but a dream. Gryf's presence was in her; there was no other way to explain it. She was aware of him in a way she'd never been aware of anyone.

Gryf sat up, taking her hands between his as though he held a treasure. "Alexandra Gaia, to you I give my soul. My life."

Two lives joined for eternity. Yes, this was right. The urge to sing, and cry, and laugh all at once rose in her. "Gryf Dimytro, to you I give my soul. My life."

The look in his eyes was unfathomable and his hands trembled. "I will never leave you behind, *animi*," he promised with his words, and his eyes. "And I will never let you fall."

"I'll never let you fall, either, Gryf." She swayed, and he drew her to his chest.

The familiar thump of his heart beat under her ear, just as it had that first day in the slave cell. They'd come full circle. She closed her eyes and exhaled long and slow. Life was good.

―――◆·◆·◆―――

Alex opened her eyes slowly. Dark. Cave. Warm. The soft flannel of the sleeping bag under her caressed her cheek. The weight of Gryf's masculine arm draped over her waist, and his blue-skinned hand covered her own. His body pressed against her back, solid and comforting under the second sleeping bag that half-covered them. Three Matiran *luteps* lit the immediate area.

She must've fallen asleep after *anim tros*. At least she hadn't fainted again. She'd never fainted before in her life until she met Gryf. A small sigh escaped her.

"How do you feel, *animi*?" Gryf's voice rumbled through her.

"I'm okay." And she was, as much as that surprised her. "Wide awake all of a sudden. How about you?"

"Grateful, and blessed."

Aw. She smiled. "What does *animi* mean?"

"My soul. And you are, Alexandra."

And he was hers.

"We did it." And it hadn't been so bad, after all. She wiggled and rolled over in the circle of Gryf's arms.

Her gaze met his, and heat erupted to life between her legs, its flame reflected in Gryf's gaze. "Oh."

"*Compa*," he murmured.

She reached for him and claimed his mouth in a kiss born of love and fueled by desire. He opened for her and she delved in, tasting, exploring, and caressing. Stroking his tongue with hers. Where this sudden need came from, she didn't care. She wanted him, all of him, here and now.

Gryf broke the kiss, nipping along her jawline then to the little hollow just below her ear. The warmth of his tongue and lips nuzzling her there sent tingles all the way down to her toes.

Cool air touched her skin as he skimmed his fingers under her sweater and up her ribcage to her breast. A moan escaped her, and she arched into his palm as he rolled first one nipple then the other, to hardness.

"Alexandra?" he whispered next to her ear, as if seeking permission.

"Yes, Gryf. I want this." There was no way she could stop, not now. The need to touch and be touched consumed her. If she never felt the friction of his skin against hers, she might go mad.

A moment later, both her sweater and bra landed with a soft thump somewhere in the darkness beyond the *lutep*. Gryf's uniform shirt joined them almost immediately. God, he was gorgeous. She reached out and ran the tips of her fingers across his well-muscled chest, trailing through the light dusting of white hair and around his dark blue areola. So similar, yet alien and exotic.

And probably delicious. She leaned forward and ran her tongue around each of his nipples in turn, tasting the faint saltiness of his skin. Gryf groaned, molding his hands to her head, he tipped her face up and covered her mouth with his. Then he pressed forward, easing her onto her back on the rough horse blankets.

The heat of his hard length pressed against her core, and she wrapped her arms behind his neck to deepen the kiss. If only this could go on forever. He pulled back, searing a path over her jaw and down her throat until he closed his mouth over her breast. He sucked hard, and a sizzling heat consumed her.

A gentle jerk at her waistband and the smooth grate of a zipper were the only warnings she had before her jeans slid off. Followed by her underwear.

"By the Mother, Alexandra." Gryf's eyes had turned a deep indigo, and his gaze touched every exposed part of her until he reached her eyes. "I am humbled."

He quickly removed the remainder of his uniform then knelt between her knees. She reached out to touch him, but he stopped her. "This time, allow me to honor you first."

All she could do was nod. He grazed his fingertips up and down the sensitive inner skin of her thighs. Each pass brought him closer to the part of her most craving his touch. If he didn't hurry, she would climax the second he inserted his finger, unless the anticipation killed her first.

He brushed over her clit, and she took in a sharp breath and closed her eyes. Another fleeting pass then he circled her entrance, but still didn't enter.

What was he doing? "Touch me, Gryf. Please."

"*Animi*, the first time you shatter, it will be around me." His voice was rough and above her, and the weight of his erection lay heavy on her belly.

Her eyes flew open. He lifted his hips then slid inside her, hard and hot. Her joy at their union escaped her in a cry that echoed off the rock walls. She wrapped her legs around his hips to take in all of him. This was home. This was where she belonged, and who she belonged with.

"Alexandra," he whispered. "My soul."

He moved with slow, even thrusts. Gradually, he increased his rhythm and she lifted her hips, meeting him stroke for stroke. A sweet tension coiled inside her, screaming for release.

"Please, Gryf." She was so close.

He shifted slightly, as if he knew exactly where to find her sweet spot. A growl started in his throat as he pumped his hips faster, his hard length driving into her, bringing her closer to bliss. She dug her fingers into the coarse material of the blankets and pushed up to meet him as she hurdled over the edge into ecstasy.

"Gryf!"

He stiffened and roared her name, filling her with his essence. The abyss exploded with stars, and they floated as one in the vast universe, joined both body and soul.

CHAPTER TWENTY

Gryf drifted back to his body, the glory of his union with Alexandra lingering. They were now truly joined on almost every plane of existence, even though they remained separate entities. It would not always be so. The day would come when their bodies ceased and their souls united. But not too soon. What they had just shared was worth staying alive for.

He opened his eyes to the cool glow from the *lutep*. While their souls had floated in another place, his body had collapsed atop Alexandra like the rag doll one of the camp orphans carried. He rolled off her then took her in his embrace.

Alexandra mumbled something against his neck. He grunted as he stroked his fingertips over the soft skin of her back. No idea what she had said, nor did it matter. Apparently neither of them had the capacity for coherent speech yet.

Five minutes later, she stirred. "Did we reverse the rotation of the galaxy?"

A chuckle rumbled through his chest. "It is possible."

She tipped her head back and met his gaze. "You glowed. Your eyes, your body...."

He gave her waist a light squeeze. "You did the same, through your climaxing. Seeing you like that was...." Was what? Like a vision as she shattered around him.

"Who knew it could be like this?"

"We do. Now." The light touch of her fingers against his chest was enough to stir his manhood. If he did not change the topic, someone could very well walk in on them. He gave the tip of her nose a kiss. "What does Gaia mean on Terr?" Likely there were as many definitions as there were languages.

Her chuckle was low and sexy. "Do you remember I told you my dad was a professor of ancient history? Well, he really wanted my first name to be Gaia, but my mom nixed that idea. So Gaia became my middle name."

"*Gaia* means earth in Matiran."

"Yeah, well." She shrugged one shoulder. "In Greek, too."

"It is appropriate then, as Dimytro means 'loves the earth'."

"Are you kidding me?" She made a small sound of amusement then cupped her warm hands over his cheeks. "I guess it is appropriate. I do love you, Gryf. I'm scared to death, but I love you."

"Is it *anim tros* that causes you distress?" There were things she should fear, but not their union.

"No, it's the prophecy thing. I mean, what are we going to do? I thought the *eno anim* would somehow show us what to do, but it didn't. It scares me not knowing, especially the part about sacrifice."

He drew one of her hands to his mouth and brushed a kiss over her knuckles. "Prophecies are unpredictable creatures at best. Attempts to interpret them before they are fulfilled are seldom successful. That being said, I believe the sacrifice was made when Kotas took you." Forty-eight hours of torture was sacrifice enough from his perspective.

Alexandra appeared thoughtful. "Or maybe it's all the people who died—in your fleet and here on Earth."

He stroked his thumb rhythmically across the back of her hand to soothe her. "Unpredictable."

Her tongue darted out, wetting her lips. "The thing that kept me sane in Kotas's chamber was thinking of you. At one point, in the middle of the night, I thought my dad had come to take me. Even then my thoughts went back to you, and I hoped you would forgive me for leaving you. But, then he told me I couldn't go, that I had something to do first. I think he meant the *Profeti*."

"A visit from a deceased loved one is not unusual among Matirans. Since you too carry the Gift, such a visit makes sense. Your father likely comprehends now why your name needed to be Alexandra."

Small, vertical lines appeared between her eyebrows. "What do you mean?"

"Alexandra means Defender of People. As *Profeta*, that is

essentially what you are doing."

"You *know* what my name means?"

"One of my grandmothers was named Alexandra." He gave her an impish grin.

"Really?" She gaped at him then laughed. "I'm glad you finally decided to share that piece of information."

A bark of laughter welled up be he bit it off when she tensed. "What is it, animi? Are you well?"

"Gryf, we didn't use protection. I could...we could be pregnant."

It was true, and a child now would be dangerous and detrimental to their roles as the *Profetae*. "Dante hasn't taught you *tinan* yet? The way we keep from conceiving children."

"Um, no, I guess not."

"Watch." He stroked his hand along the silky skin over her ribcage to rest over her womb. "*Tinan*." His hand glowed a faint blue then returned to normal. "It is done."

"Wow," she whispered. "It's that easy?"

Her innocent wonder at such a simple action filled his heart with delight. "Yes, that simple. It makes my sperm impotent inside you. And as I know you will ask, no, it does not work beforehand."

"Amazing."

Gryf cast a glance toward the cave opening. The pale grey light of dawn shone through the fissure. "As much as I wish to spend the rest of the day alone with you here, I fear someone from Camp One may walk in on us."

Disappointment flashed in her eyes, but she nodded. They dressed wordlessly. As he pulled on his boots, she broke the silence. "Gryf, what's my Gift signature?"

He reached for her and pulled her to sit in his lap. "We are well matched, Alexandra. Your signature is like a wave bubbling on the shore as it returns to the sea."

Gryf's gaze lingered on Alexandra's long legs as she passed through the opening to the camp's operations room ahead of him. The Terrian pants called "jeans" looked nice on her—as did the brown sweater, which complemented her eyes.

Maintain yourself, Helyg.

He gave himself a mental shake and stepped through the jagged fissure.

The operations room was twice the size of their prison cell, made both comfortable and functional with tables, camp chairs, stools, and rugs. Dante and Nick sat at a table just to the left of the entrance, a chess board—a game familiar to both their worlds—between them. At the table farther in, Bodie, Gunner, and Ramon filled long narrow metal casings with some sort of powder. They spoke together in amicable tones as they worked.

Gryf scanned the room for Graig and Simone. *Still have not returned.*

Ora rose from a loose circle of camp chairs and stools at the center of the room. She held a Terrian notebook in her hand and a Terrian stylus—pencil—tucked behind her ear.

"Senior Captain in the hole," she announced with a mischievous grin.

The Guardians present rose and stood at attention. Alexandra gave a soft snort of laughter as she sat.

"As you were," Gryf growled, claiming the seat next to her. "First order of business, we will dispense with *that* formality for these meetings. It has the potential of getting out of hand."

"Yes, sir." Ora's eyes twinkled. "Please so note, Lieutenant Commander Zola."

Karise used a Terrian stylus—a pencil—to write in her own notebook.

"Sorry we're late," LaShawn said as he entered, followed by Kelly.

Ora nodded as LaShawn pulled up a stool next to Bodie. Kelly took a seat apart from everyone, a brooding expression marring her otherwise lovely features. From the start she had kept her distance, as though the others were nothing more than an inconvenient necessity. She required watching.

Gryf turned his attention back to Ora. "Graig and Simone have not returned?"

"Not yet."

"Very well. Please carry on as we discussed, Captain." Upon returning to camp, he and Alexandra had gone directly to Ora to reveal *eno anim*. To say that his cousin had been ecstatic about the news was an understatement. After a brief discussion, the three of them had agreed that the news must be shared with the camp.

Ora launched into an explanation of *eno anim* for the benefit of the Terrians, all of whom appeared keenly interested. Even Kelly.

"As Matir has not had *eno anim* occur in over two centuries," Ora concluded, "word has traveled through camp faster than a rock burns in an atmosphere. I know the Terrians do not appreciate the significance of this event, so we will look to LaShawn, Kelly, Bodie, Gunner, and Ramon to explain it to the rest of their people after this meeting."

"We're on it," Bodie replied.

"Sure, why not," Kelly muttered.

"There is more news." Ora's gaze met Gryf's, and he gave her a nod.

"The dissenters report that there are four slavers on Terr's surface." Ora's golden eyes surveyed the room, touching on each person as though daring them to prove their worth. "And multiple pockets of resistance around the globe who might be willing to assist. The attacks will be timed to occur in unison."

Ora's plan to infiltrate the Premiere Warden's slaver—the ship closest to them—and free the prisoners aboard was flawless. The diversion would distract the Anferthian fleet still in orbit, and with any luck, they would be too busy to notice the arrival of the Matiran Defense Fleet. Once the DF arrived, of course. If they didn't, an alternate plan would be used.

"And we're expected to place our trust in these *dissenters*?" Kelly's voice was harsh.

Ora nodded. "I understand your concern, Kelly. Truly, you are not the only one in camp who has voiced their doubts to me. After the slaver nearest our camp landed, a reconnaissance mission went down to investigate. This was my first encounter with K'rona Zurkku—our contact—on perimeter patrol. I would have killed her, but she did something I had not expected. She handed me her Reliquary. As these are sacred relics, it is unheard of for an Anferthian to hand one to someone not of their race. Yet, K'rona did. She asked only that

I hear her out, and if I did not believe her, she would submit to death at my hands.

"Needless to say, she convinced me. If not for her, Gryf and his party would not have escaped."

Kelly gave a snort. "Convenient. Why hasn't she arranged to release the others?"

Gryf bit back a response. Ora was the youngest captain in the fleet for a reason. She could handle Kelly's objections without his assistance.

"If the dissenters did so, they would sacrifice not only themselves but also at least eighty percent of the prisoners. I am certain you are as appalled by that statistic as I."

Kelly flatted her mouth into a thin line then gave Ora a curt nod.

Gryf stroked his thumb over the back of Alexandra's hand. "Yet we lack two things to implement this plan: explosives and the Defense Fleet."

"That is correct." Ora nodded. "The Defense Fleet will be here, I have no doubt. There are some explosives aboard *Athens*'s transport, but not enough to disable the Premiere Warden's slaver."

Gunner exchanged a brief look with Ramon and Bodie. "I was going to make my report later, but it seems now would be better. After the gas station incident, Lieutenant Commander Zola and I took a circuitous route back to camp in case we were being followed. We passed a remote building belonging to the state avalanche control department. It appeared untouched by the Anferthians, and we didn't see any people."

Not seeing people did not mean there were none. "Do you think there may be Terrian explosives stored there?"

"Possibly. Since they're used to set off avalanches, it would be worth checking out. It's about a day's hike from here, if we take a more direct route than Karise and I did."

That sounded promising. "Ora, you had the transport scanners mapping as you came into the atmosphere, correct?"

"I did. It's how we found these caves. Laurentius, would you set up the data device, please?"

"Yes, ma'am," Cassian tapped the unobtrusive palm-sized black sphere sitting on one corner of a table. The table surface lit up as the data device displayed the images of several maps, and he swiped his finger through them until he found the correct one.

Alexandra vacated her chair, moving to peer over Cassian's shoulder. The four Terrian men trailed her. Gryf suppressed a smile. The Terrians always seemed hard-pressed to resist the lure of new technology.

"Capitán." Ramon pointed to a spot on the map. "My brother-in-law worked at this silver mine here—Silver Valley Mine, about twenty miles north of us. They used explosives. There still may be some, if it's not already destroyed."

Gryf joined the Terrians around the table. "Ora, assign two recon teams of four, with a Terrian-Matiran ratio of three to one. If there are people there, I don't want an alien presence to put them on the defensive. Team one goes to the avalanche facility, team two to the mine."

Gunner looked up from the maps. "I'll volunteer for team one, Captain."

Exactly what he had hoped Gunner would say. "Thank you, Colonel. Bring back anything you find there—explosives *and* people."

"Yes, sir."

"The mine team is to report back what they find. Any explosives stay there, but people they can bring back. We'll use the mine as our staging point for the attack on the slaver. Have both teams ready to go tonight."

"Yes, sir," Ora replied, scratching the page of her notebook with her pencil.

Alexandra met Gryf's gaze from across the table. "They can take some of the medical floats to transport the explosives. That'd be safer than carrying them, and they could bring back more."

"Excellent idea. How many can be spared?"

"Eight. We'll keep two here for medical emergencies."

"Thank you, Alexandra." Gryf blew out a sigh. "Now if the Defense Fleet would contact us."

"They will be here, Gryf," Ora said. "Even if Admiral Cael and Admiral Marenys have to steal ships and come themselves. They will not strand us."

Now that would be a sight: the two old friends

commandeering their own cruisers to come to the rescue. They would enjoy *that* experience.

Gryf grimaced. "Hopefully there will still be an 'us' when they arrive."

CHAPTER TWENTY-ONE

"So, what did I miss?"

Alex jerked her head around from watching Maggie sleep, and stared at the woman standing in the entry to the infirmary. "Simone!" She darted forward and grabbed her friend into a bear hug. "Oh my god, I was so worried. Are you okay? You've been gone for five days."

"I'm fine, just a little tired. Graig caught up with me quickly. Those 'Ferths didn't see him coming until it was too late." They drew apart. "So, how's the girl?"

Alex gave her friend a grin. "Improving, but still not talking. Flora comes in for hours every day to sing to her. She's also named her Maggie."

"Maggie?" Simone's expression softened. "Pretty." Then she jerked her thumb toward Graig and Gryf in the entryway behind her. "We brought a friend of yours."

"He says his name is James Trimble, from Damon Beach," Graig said. Both he and Gryf wore identical expressions of skepticism.

Alex's gaze fell on the familiar, hollow-cheeked Earth-man in Graig's custody. It was her former neighbor. But how? She took a step toward the man. "Mr. Trimble?"

The old man flinched then gave her a look of unbridled relief. "Alex. Thank God you're safe."

"I am, but you don't look so hot. Where did you find him, Simone?"

"Hiding in some bushes, in the foothills." Simone replied. She exchanged a glance with Graig, and her cheeks darkened. *So not going there.*

"Well, bring him in and Dante can run an exam when he gets back." Best not let Mr. Trimble know about her new-found ability until they knew more about his situation.

The old man sank down onto a cot with a strangled sob. "I think they have Megan in there, Alex. I saw them put her on a flying machine, and it took me weeks to figure out where they'd gone. She's fifteen. Just a little girl, a baby. My baby."

At fifteen, Megan wasn't a baby by a longshot, but she was Mr. Trimble's only child. Alexandra took his withered hand in hers and gave it a pat. "I understand, Mr. Trimble. Our doctor will give you a quick exam then we'll figure out what to do about Megan."

Dante returned at that moment, and after a brief explanation from Graig, greeted James Trimble as any friendly country doctor would've.

A light touch on her arm pulled her attention away from them, and Gryf motioned her to follow him. They stepped into the corridor with Graig as their shadow.

"What kind of man is he, *compa*?" Gryf asked.

She lifted one shoulder in a shrug. "He was always nice to Nicky and me, and a decent neighbor. He was in his forties when his first and only child, Megan, was born. His wife died when Megan was five, and he's been protective of his daughter ever since."

"Understandable." Gryf nodded slowly then his gaze flicked behind her. "Graig, put a guard on him for the standard eight days. Since the rogues have been dispatched, I will lift the 'go to ground' order this afternoon. However, I don't want Trimble wandering around, even under guard."

"Yes, sir," Graig replied.

"After that," Gryf wrinkled his nose, "go bathe."

A snort escaped Alexandra

"Yes, sir." Graig narrowed his eyes at her. "Meet me in the operations room in one hour for your verbal *telum* test." Then he was gone.

Gryf grinned. "The snort may not have been the wisest reaction."

"That would've been valuable advice thirty seconds ago." *Mr. Smarty Pants.*

"I shall attempt to be more punctual with my advice in the future. Do you think Maggie is up for a little rocking?"

PROPHECY

"Always. Come on."

Alex sat across a small table from Graig. She'd managed to evade his *telum* test for two days, but this morning he'd caught up with her at breakfast and dragged her to the operations room. That she'd ever thought he'd coddle her was laughable. He pushed her harder than he pushed any of the others, and for good reason. She was a valuable target for their enemy.

"And this?" Graig asked, pointing to another part of his *telum* with the tip of a pencil.

Easy. "That's the barrel. *Lindrim.*" Alex flashed him a smug look of triumph. Both English and Matiran, just as he'd asked. She was getting good at this.

Graig gave her a curt nod, and moved the pencil to another part.

"Ammunition chamber. *Rucubi.*" Alex shot a quick glance to where Ora stood across the room, an Earth book in her hands. Whatever she was reading, it must be good because she seemed to have forgotten that she was surrounded by empty camp chairs.

Graig cleared his throat.

"Oh, uh...muzzle." This translation always messed her up. What was the Matiran word?

The soft thump of booted feet entering the room came from behind her. Graig glanced up and stiffened. Huh. What could've possibly broken the almighty, perfectly focused Graig Roble's concentration? Alex turned in her seat.

Bodie stood intimately close to Ora, gazing into her eyes. He lifted the book from her hands, closed it, and set it on a table. Ora's lips parted as long, masculine fingers wove through her gold hair. Bodie slanted his mouth over hers.

Oh, good lord. Alex cupped her hand over her grin. A kiss didn't get much more romantic or passionate than that.

Graig pushed out of his chair, his hands balled into fists. Waves of anger rolled off him like heat off a furnace. So not good. He was going to kill Bodie.

Alex grasped his arm with both hands. "Don't."

"But he's forcing himself on her." Graig matched her low

voice, his eyes flashing. Whoa, was he ever pissed.

She gave a tiny snort. "Does Ora look like she's being *forced* to do anything she doesn't want to do?"

It was true. Ora's face had transformed from wide-eyed surprise to closed-eyed contentment. Every possible inch of her lean body molded against Bodie's, and she clutched the back of his shirt in her fists. There was no mistaking her low growl as anything other than a woman completely turned on.

Alex shot a smirk at Graig.

Now what, Mr. Prim-and-Proper?

Graig's jaw tightened. "Is this what Terrian females like? Their men *dominating* them?"

"Terrian females like it when males find them so desirable they'll take risks to be with them." There was no way to hide her wicked grin, so she didn't try. "You have to admit, coming in here knowing that you have a gun in your hand is pretty risky for Bodie."

Graig drew his brows together as though contemplating her words.

Alex leaned forward. "What's that sound, Graig? Could it be...Ora...*still* not protesting?"

His eyes flashed a warning that she was in danger of being throttled. All that was missing was smoke spewing from his ears. He yanked his arm from her grip. Holstering his *telum,* he scowled down at her. "We will continue your exam later." He strode out of the operations room without another glance at Ora and Bodie.

If Alex had to guess, Simone's afternoon was about to make an abrupt U-turn.

You're welcome, my sweet friend.

Ora moaned as Bodie brushed the backs of his fingers over her breast. Time to beat a hasty retreat. As Alex slipped past the table, she glanced at the now-forgotten book. Her breath wheezed out of her. Where the heck had Ora found a copy of *Men are from Mars, Women are from Venus?*

◆ ◆ ◆ ◆ ◆

Thirty minutes later, Alex walked among the trees, her fingers entwined with Gryf's. She stole a sideways glance at his profile. There was an aura of quiet authority surrounding the man. It flowed from him like his Gift, calming and inspiring those around him. He accepted life's experiences, working with them rather than trying to control them. No wonder his crew loved him.

Oh, he had his moments, that was for sure. Still, she'd never known, let alone loved, anyone quite like him. Or made love to anyone like him. Once. A week ago. They really needed to find a private place before she tackled him to the ground right here.

"How did your *telum* exam go?" Gryf asked.

Telum exam? Alex blinked, and the events in the boardroom flooded back. *Oh, that.* She grinned. "Didn't Graig tell you?"

Gryf frowned, a V forming between his brows. "Oddly, no. He seemed preoccupied."

"Hm, well, we were interrupted."

He raised an eyebrow, and she related the encounter between Bodie and Ora.

"Gryf, Bodie gave her the most passionate kiss I've ever seen." She smiled at the ground. Ora and Bodie had found happiness together. Who wouldn't be happy about that? Well, other than Graig.

Gryf's abrupt stop brought her up short. "Graig didn't stop him?" The words were pushed through clenched teeth.

Good grief, was he pissed about this too? She'd expected him to be a little...no, a *lot* more philosophical about the situation than Graig. "Well, he wanted to, but I wouldn't let him."

His lip curled. "Bodie should not have taken such liberties. That was Ora's choice to make."

"Are you kidding me? Ora's been on the fence about Bodie for weeks."

Judging by the look on his face, Gryf was clueless about his cousin's dilemma. In all fairness, Ora hid her feelings pretty well. Alex had found out when Ora confided in her at the hot spring the day Maggie arrived.

"That was Ora's decision as well," he said.

Did he have to be so blessed stubborn about this? Good

thing he didn't get like this often or she'd start carrying a frying pan. Maybe she should anyway. Never could tell when she'd need to knock sense back into the males in her life. Gryf released her hand to gaze back in the direction of the caves.

Alex crossed her arms in front of her. "What do you plan to do, Gryf—go back and give them pointers?" Ooh. That little bit of snark did not appear to be appreciated. "Bodie gave her the incentive to make her choice, and there's nothing wrong with that. He showed her that it's safe to move forward. Ora's a big girl, you know. She could've stopped him at any point. Trust me when I tell you, your cousin did *not* want to stop."

Narrowed sapphire eyes studied her. In their jeweled depths, his own desires warred with the customs with which he'd been raised. And just like that, this wasn't about Ora and Bodie anymore.

What incentive would Gryf need to make the first move? To commit to a true partnership as equals in all aspects of their relationship? She returned his narrow glare.

C'mon, Gryf. Break with tradition and make the first damn move for once.

She took a step away from him, and then half a dozen more. Gryf's stance went from indecisive to predator in a blink. A thrill raced through her. Was he about to answer her unspoken dare?

Gryf stalked toward her, and her heart fluttered like an autumn leaf on the breeze.

Oh, my god. He'd going to do it!

Anticipation numbed her hands, feet, and lips. Gryf reached for her, cradled her head in his hands, and claimed mouth with a searing kiss. A sense of need bordering on desperation rose in her as she pressed closer. All her thoughts pinged in different directions, crashing into each other, shouting until they coalesced into a single word: *Yes!*

He pushed his tongue deep into her mouth like an unspoken challenge. A dare for her to respond. She snaked her arms over his shoulders and returned his kissed with relentless intent, caressing his tongue with hers. Seeking, exploring, tasting.

Next thing she knew, she was on her back on a bed of pine

needles, Gryf's heated body covering hers. Every cell of her being clamored for his touch, ready to explode. She parted her legs to nestle him against her, drawing a ragged groan from him. He ground himself against her, and bolts of white hot desire erupted from the point of contact.

God, that feels good.

He stroked her nipple through her bra with his thumb. A moan escaped her and she arched against his palm. Her clothes needed to come off. Now. She needed to take him deep inside her again and again until she screamed. And she was going to scream. Just the thought of him filling her, hard and hot, stroking her so intimately.... She gasped against his mouth and rocked her hips up to meet him.

"Jesus, Alex!"

The sound of Nicky's voice crashed through the haze of sexual heat like ice water. She yelped into Gryf's mouth. Gryf jerked his head up, air hissing through his teeth. His eyes were glazed, but clearing.

"Dammit." Her chest rose and fell as she tried to focus. She reached up to cup his flushed cheek. "You're so lucky to be an only child."

"Not truly," Gryf growled. He turned his head to kiss her palm. "I have Ora. Sweet, merciful Mother, Alexandra. This will take me a more than a moment to master."

"Maybe aliens will abduct my brother, and we can finish what we started."

Gryf gave her a bemused look. "Very funny." He kissed her nose then lifted himself off her and helped her sit up.

Alex directed a glower at Nicky. "It's a huge forest, Nicky. Couldn't you have found another part of it for your walk?"

"You do know that this is the primary path to and from the main cave, right?" The little twerp spoke slowly, as if she were dense. Then he pointed above their heads. "And the watch is right above you. And believe me, they are watching."

Oh. She turned in unison with Gryf and looked up the side of the granite rock behind her. A Matiran ensign—was his name Ius?—looked down at them with a scandalized expression, but Duck gave them an enthusiastic double thumbs up. Weren't those two just the epitome of cultural differences?

Gryf turned back and rested his elbows on his raised knees. "Well, that was...different."

"Fun?" She thought so, but did Gryf feel the same?

He reached for her hand. "Empowering. Are you sure you are okay with this? If I did it again, you wouldn't mind?"

"Gryf, I am so turned on right now, you'd better do it again."

"Oh, barf." Nicky leaned back against a tree and folded his arms over his chest. For someone so grossed out, he didn't seem eager to leave.

Alex rolled her eyes. "There is no such thing as privacy in a refugee camp, is there?"

Gryf brushed his lips over her knuckles. "I am certain we could find privacy, *animi*."

Yes, they would. And sooner rather than later. "I'm talking about full-time, permanent privacy, Gryf."

When he tipped his head just so, she could almost see the little boy he'd once been.

"Pardon?" His face was incredulous, as if he hoped he was interpreting her words correctly.

He was. She placed their joined hands over his heart. "I'm ready, Gryf."

More emotions than she could track even with their soul link flashed across his face. She did catch one thing: conflict. Cripes, had she pushed him too fast? How could she gracefully retract her proposal?

"If you're not ready, it's okay." It would hurt, but she'd live with it.

"Are you kidding me?" he asked. His face cracked into an ear-to-ear grin.

She opened her mouth and stared at him. From time to time, he would throw out an unexpected, perfectly mimicked Earth phrase, catching her off guard. Like now.

He pulled her toward him and soundly kissed her. "Would this afternoon work for you?"

Relief flooded her heart. He *did* want this. She threw her arms around his neck. "Yes! Right here, right now. Let's do it."

"About freaking time." Right. Nicky was still here.

PROPHECY

"Nicholaus," Gryf said without breaking eye contact with her. "Make yourself useful and go find Ora. Tell her she has a binding ceremony to perform, per her duties as a captain."

There was no stopping the grin that rushed to Alex's lips. Somewhere above her head, Duck whooped. Gryf captured her lips again, and this time his kiss was slow and tender, stealing her breath just as he'd stolen her heart.

CHAPTER TWENTY-TWO

Gryf sat with his back against the trunk of a sugar pine and Alexandra reclined between his raised knees. Her warm back pressed against his chest and her arms rested on his thighs. The pleasant hum of *anim loqui*—soul communion—filled him as their souls celebrated their uninterrupted time together.

The pungent scent of pine needles wafted around him. They were no longer just unusual leaf-like parts of a particular Terr tree, or an exceptional fire starter. From this day forward, they would forever remind him of love, eternity, and Alexandra.

He moved his head a fraction closer to her hair and inhaled. *Ah.* In all the universe there was nowhere he would choose to be than here with her, waiting as Ora pulled together an impromptu wedding.

"...mean you can't find Simone? Have you checked both storage caves?" Ora's incredulous words drifted across the sun-dappled clearing. Alexandra stirred. A glimmer of amusement and ruefulness came across their link. He nudged his cheek against her temple and sent reassurance back to her. That Graig would allow anyone to catch him and Simone in a compromising position was inconceivable.

The hum of *anim loqui* tapered off, and his soul subsided. He moved his lips against her ear. "I have something for you."

"Mm? Do I have to move?"

Of course she would be reluctant. The peace of the forest had saturated his mind. Why would it be any different for her? If only they had time to snuggle and listen to the whispered song of the breeze in the trees all day.

But Ora had requested three hours to prepare, and there were rituals yet to observe. Nevertheless, this day shouldn't be steeped in just Matiran traditions. Alexandra's traditions must be honored too, and now was the time for the first of hers.

"Just a bit. Enough to face me."

Alexandra gave a good-natured grumble then complied, turning between his legs. His breath hitched in his chest. Terrians had a saying that the eyes were the window to the soul. At this moment, Alexandra was a living example of the truth in that saying.

He reached into his jacket pocket, closing his hand around the bit of cloth. "Shortly after we arrived in camp, I had the opportunity to speak with Cassian Laurentius."

Her brow furrowed. "Huh?"

He touched his finger to the tip of her nose. "Hear me out." She pressed her lips together and nodded. Gryf withdrew the folded piece of soft grey material and pressed it into her hand. "He gave us these. Go ahead and open it."

Alexandra unfolded the tiny bundle with tentative motions, exposing two grey-blue metal rings.

"Gryf, they're beautiful." She looked up at him with eyes full of reverence. "The wedding rings of Cassian and his wife?"

"Yes. They are given with his blessing."

"I never thought to ask, but Matirans exchange rings too, I guess."

"We exchange symbolic tokens, and often those tokens are rings." Gryf ran his knuckle along the smooth edge of her jawline. "Cassian learned of the Terrian ring-giving tradition from Maria and Ramon, and knew that Iantha would have wanted us to have their tokens."

"Which just happened to be rings?"

Gryf gave her a single nod.

"This is quite an honor, isn't it?"

"It is."

She leaned in and examined the entwined design. "It's a square knot. Although, the ancient Greeks called it a love knot. My mom had a lot of things from Dad with Greek love knots on them."

"A lovely tradition. Where do you suppose they got it from?

He loved the way her mouth dropped open when she was surprised.

"Are you kidding me? We got this from *you guys?*"

"Is that so hard to believe? These are made from *kri*, a Matiran precious metal similar to your gold." Gryf picked up the smaller of the two bands and turned it over between his fingers. In a short while, he would place it on her finger and wear the other himself. "Matirans call the design *aeter nom*, the eternal knot." It was an appropriate symbol. After today's ceremony, their bond would be even stronger.

"*Aeter nom.* That's so much more romantic than square knot."

Her smile lit his life. Would the Mother ever reveal what he had done right to deserve such a perfect mate?

A short time later, Gryf gripped the rock face and began the climb to the small cave where the perishables had once been kept. It was fortunate that there were hunters amongst the Terrians. Between them and Simone's knowledge as a botanist, hunger had not been an issue yet.

Boots scraped the stone behind him as Graig, Dante, and Nick began their ascent.

"Just because Gryf must be silent does not mean he cannot throw you into the cold spring if you are over-obnoxious." Graig's warning was directed at Nick.

"In that case, I'll be angelic," the young man replied.

Graig muttered something in Matiran that sounded uncannily like, "May I live to see the day."

Gryf suppressed a chuckle.

"To be asked to attend the bridegroom, Nick, is an honor of family and close friends," Dante explained. "It is our duty to be with him as he reflects on his worthiness to bind with Alex."

"Nobody's worthy of my sister, Dante," Nick replied. "But, Gryf's the closest."

There truly was no one worthy of her, but her brother's approval warmed Gryf's heart.

"Well said, Nick." Graig's words were measured and sincere.

"So, what do we do?" Nick asked.

"We accompany Gryf to the spring, divest him so he may

bathe, and pray with him afterward. Then we assist him with his wedding attire and present him to Alex just before the ceremony."

"He can't...." Nick stopped. "Never mind. Um, this isn't the way to the hot spring."

"No," replied Dante. "Alex occupies the hot spring for her own ritual."

"You mean Gryf has to bathe in the *cold* spring?"

A grin pulled at the corners of Gryf's mouth as he picked up a lantern just inside the cave's entrance. What would Nick say if he knew this wasn't the first time his future brother-in-law had used this spring? That sometimes it had been his only means of subduing the effects from time spent with Alexandra?

"Yes, he does," Dante told the young man.

"Whoa. You know, I don't think that's such a good idea, especially today."

"Why not?"

"Have your people ever heard of shrinkage?"

◆ ◆ ◆ ◆

Alex gazed into Gryf's eyes. Flora's angelic voice filled the space under the trees with sweet, heart-touching clarity as she sang a Gaelic blessing. The words flowed through Alex, and the deep peace they invoked settled over her. Reassurance flowed from Gryf through their soul link, as welcome as water in a desert.

As the final note of the song faded, Ora asked, "Have you tokens to exchange?"

Gryf drew a ring from his pocket and took her hand in his. "Alexandra Gaia Bock, daughter of Janet and Richard, sister of Nicholaus, I give myself to you wholly. You are the heart of my heart and the soul of my soul, eternally. So be it."

As the ring slid onto her finger, the accompanying effervescent tingle of a vow being sealed danced up her arm. The prickle of tears rose in her eyes, and her hands trembled as she accepted the second ring from him and took his hand.

"Gryf Dimytro Helyg, son of Charise and Zale, with this ring I thee wed, body, heart, and soul." Wet trails slipped over her cheeks, and her voice hitched. "I love you, eternally. So be it."

Again the tingle. Gryf wiped away her tears with the pads of his thumbs then leaned forward to kiss each of her eyelids. "Your tears are a gift I will treasure," he murmured.

Ora draped a chain of flowers made by the children over their joined arms. "Alexandra Gaia Bock and Gryf Dimytro Helyg, by the will of the Holy Ones of both your worlds, your paths are now fully joined in love. Your lives have already been ordained to the service of the Holy Ones. In your service to them, do not lose sight of one another, for you are each other's greatest gift. *Esto*! Let it be so!"

"Let it be so!" Their camp family cheered.

Ora plucked the flower chain off their arms and looped it over Gryf's shoulders with a grin. "Alexandra and Gryf, you may seal your vows."

Alex turned to Gryf. As the woman, she was supposed to initiate the kiss. But instead, Gryf pulled her against him. His lips met hers, feather soft then with deeper passion. How totally Terrian of him. And her toes were curling in her boots. Woots and cat-calls sounded around them, from the Earthlings, of course. By now all the Matirans must've had minor strokes over their senior captain's blatantly aggressive actions toward a woman.

"Are they supposed to do that?" Flora asked.

An odd question from a child. But who could concentrate when being so thoroughly kissed?

Don't let go, Gryf. Don't ever let go.

"Yes, Flora," Ora replied. "Soul mates glow like that."

"Cool," Flora breathed. "I want to have a soul mate when I grow up."

"That. Is. *Awe*-some!" Juan declared.

"Any day now. Some of us are hungry," Nicky muttered.

Alex laughed against Gryf's mouth, and they drew apart. He reached for her hand, and they started up the path leading to the main cave to the raucous cheers of their camp family.

CHAPTER TWENTY-THREE

The tunnel walls undulated. Alex squeezed her eyes shut then opened them again. She might've had a little too much of Bodie's wine with dinner. Crazy man had rescued the *entire* contents of his wine cellar before the attack. One thing was for sure: the Pinot Noir went perfectly with venison stew. Or was that the other way around? She gave a mental shrug and turned her focus to the masculine hand holding hers.

Gryf. A warm flush rushed through her. They'd done it. They were married, their union sanctified by both their peoples. And now they strolled together down a tunnel, off the main track to their honeymoon suite. Leave it to Ora, the Ever Efficient, to anticipate the future. She'd apparently found a tucked-away, cozy cavern for them the first day they'd arrived in camp. No more sleeping in the dorm, thank god.

The lantern in Gryf's hand lit the passage around them with dancing shadows. They passed another chalk arrow drawn on the wall, pointing the way to the suite. Alex swallowed, and pressed her free hand against her stomach. Soon she would join her body with Gryf's again. This time as husband and wife. A jolt of heat hit her right between her legs.

Think of something, anything else, before you jump his bones right here in the tunnel.

"The reaction of the kids when Nicky and Bodie played the airship song was priceless." She caught her lower lip between her teeth. Could she have sounded any lamer? Why was she so nervous? It wasn't as if they'd never done this before.

"It was a nice bit of bribery before sending them off to bed." Amusement crinkled the corners of Gryf's eyes.

A silly giggle escaped her. "And Simone got Graig to dance to *Desperado*. She loves that song."

"She's good for him," Gryf observed with a fond smile.

"That's what Graig said about me."

"That *you* are good for him?"

"No." Alex waved her hand to dismiss his teasing. "That *I* am good for *you*."

He gave her a side-long look. "How much of that wine did you drink?"

Another giggle bubbled out. "Maybe a little more than I should have. Do you know what Ora told me at the hot spring today?"

"Enlighten me."

She rounded on him, stepping into his path, and wrapping her arms behind his neck. "She said that our soul mate bond will deepen because we're married."

Gryf's eyes darkened, desire flickered in their depths. He traced the pad of his thumb along her cheek. "There are accounts of soul mates who could share their mate's pain, or help them through situations that would have otherwise killed them. Some have been able to hear each other's thoughts when in danger, heal each other without physical contact, or pinpoint where their mate is at any given moment. Even in the dark."

Oh, my. She swallowed hard. "You, um, knew that already?"

"Not verbatim," he murmured. "Dante gave me the same speech, sans the part about the dark."

She fingered the hair curling up at the nape of his neck and pressed closer. "Gryf, you're the best thing that's ever happened to me. And I'm only a little tipsy. I promise not to fall asleep."

"*Animi*." His voice was rough as he dipped his head closer. "If you fall asleep then I will need to reevaluate my technique."

Heat surged through her, and her legs filled with gelatin. *Holy freaking cow.*

He touched his lips to hers, and she opened to him. He tasted of wine, mellow and rich, and she deepened the kiss. A low growl vibrated through Gryf.

She pulled away, panting. "We need to find our room." Fast.

PROPHECY

Gryf glanced over her shoulder and shoved the lantern into her hand. "We are here already, *animi*."

She emitted a squeak as he lifted her in his arms. In two steps, he pushed them through a blanket-covered opening and into the warm room beyond.

Low light glowed from the *lutep* units placed at intervals along the walls. The furnishings were sparse; just two camp chairs, a small table between them, and an inflatable camping mattress covered with sleeping bags.

Alex raised her brows and nodded. "Homey. I like it."

Gryf lowered her until her feet touched one of the many soft rugs covering the rocky floor. "Only two things in here interest me at this moment, *animi*. You and the bed."

Oh. She couldn't seem to get enough oxygen.

Gryf cradled her head in his hands, leaning close until his mouth was centimeters from hers. "I can't believe we are here at last."

"Gryf." His name escaped her like a sigh.

He kissed her again, caressing and teasing as heat built again between her legs. The need to take him deep inside her returned with the force of a wildfire. She slid her arms around his waist, and drew closer until she felt his arousal pressed against her lower belly. Her channel clenched in anticipation of what was to come.

She broke off the kiss. "Gryf." She was panting like a dog in heat. But she couldn't help it, not while both her desire and his coursed through her. Her entire body was primed to explode with sexual bliss.

"I know. I feel you too," he whispered. He rested his forehead against hers, and grazed his knuckles down her back. "Don't move."

"Whatever you say." If he'd asked her to stand on her head and whistle Yankee Doodle, she would've.

He kissed the tip of her nose then moved away to walk the perimeter of the small cave, lowering the brightness of the lights. Damn. His dark-grey uniform accentuated his long, muscular frame—and his butt. Her gaze latched on to that particular body part and one corner of her mouth rose.

I'm married to that butt.

Gryf turned toward her, a faint blue glow shining in his eyes. He approached her with a slow, measured stride. Her love, her soul mate, her husband.

He stopped in front of her and traced one finger down her cheek and over her lips. "I will know you completely this night, Alexandra. And you will know me."

How was it that every time he spoke, her legs went numb? The low rumble of his voice seemed to touch the deepest, most secret places in her with a promise of more than a lifetime together.

"I think I forgot how to breathe." Her admission came out in a choked whisper.

"I am familiar with that feeling, *compa*." His gaze drifted downward, stopping at her sweater-covered breasts. His desire surged through their soul link, and she closed her eyes as she absorbed its intensity. Vibrations hummed along her nerves. God, what happened tonight would either kill them both, or be the most amazing sex she'd ever had.

His fingers grasped the hem of her sweater and lifted it over her head. Cool air prickled over her heated skin as his hand glided over the worn satin of her bra, cupping her breast. Then he stepped back, the expression on his face turning urgent.

"I need to feel you, your skin against mine. It overwhelms me." His hands shook as he worked the seal of his uniform shirt. "You can teach me how to operate your support garment later."

She made quick work of removing her bra. No sooner had she dropped it to the floor than Gryf enveloped her in his strong arms.

"Alexandra," he whispered.

"Eternally." The word fell softly from her lips.

"Eternally," he echoed.

He dipped his head to reclaim her mouth. This time, his kiss was thorough and slow, as though they had all the time in the world to "know" each other. He moved down to trail soft kisses along her jaw. A moan welled up, and she tipped her head back.

His lips and tongue fluttered against her pulse before

working their way down to take one nipple into his mouth. Every pull and nip sent electric jolts straight into her womb. How much more could she take? Wave after wave of hot pleasure moved through her as he turned his attention to her other breast. A coil of pressure built at her core, promising a release so sweet she might cry once it was over.

Cool air brushed her lower extremities, and she looked down. Gryf kissed her belly as he eased her jeans to her knees. When had he gotten the snap open?

Kneeling, he gripped her butt and lowered his head to delve his tongue between her nether lips.

"Oh, god. Right there. Yes." She dug her fingers into his hair as he sucked her nub. She leaned her head back and let out a guttural moan.

A few moments later, he moved back up her body until they were nose-to-nose. His grin was every shade of sexy with a dash of tease. "Can you handle just one more little ritual?"

Somehow she managed not to roll her eyes. "Do you Matirans have a ritual for everything?"

"Almost." He bent, lifting her in his arms as if she weighed nothing and settled her on the edge of the mattress. Kneeling at her feet, he removed her boots and socks before peeling her jeans and panties the rest of the way off. Then he sat back on his heels, gazing at her from her toes to her forehead, appreciation shining in his eyes.

He reached for a small, carved wooden box next to the bed and drew out an amethyst bottle. What new brand of sweet torture was this?

She leaned forward for a better look. "What's that?"

"Anointing oil," he replied, pouring a tiny dollop of thick, lavender-colored liquid into his hand. When he rubbed his palms together, a light spicy scent was released into the air. A deep throb began in her womb, and her womanhood clenched in response. *Wow.*

Gryf lifted her right foot, and smoothed the oil over it. "It is customary for Matiran newlyweds to bathe each other's feet with oil. It symbolizes their honor and respect for the other, and a commitment to the path they have chosen to walk together."

Romantic and symbolic. Sweet. The throb intensified, and the abyss loomed closer. "Can it...be used in...other places?"

Gryf grinned and ran his thumb firmly along her arch, eliciting a moan from deep inside her. "We shall find out."

He moved to her left foot, where his hands continued to work their magic. The unexpected foot massage felt so damn good. What else could she do but fall back on the mattress, her arms splayed straight out? "God, Gryf, that's amazing."

The mattress sank, and she opened her eyes. Gryf hovered on all fours over her. "And I'm just getting started."

She reached between them to run her fingers along the waist of his pants. "You're still partially dressed, Captain Helyg."

"Not for long." He skimmed a palm over her breasts. Her skin tingled with residual oil, and she arched her back.

They were so definitely using the oil in other places. But first things first. "Should I do your feet now?"

"As you are Terrian, I don't expect you to do so," he said.

"What's part of you is part of me, Gryf. My heart belongs to two worlds now. Teach me this custom."

Pleasure lit his eyes, and he pushed away from her, opened the seal of his pants, slid them off then sat on the bed.

Kneeling between his knees, she ran her hands over his shoulders and down his chest to the bulge in his underwear. Air hissed through his teeth as she feathered her fingers over it.

"*Animi*," he warned.

"Soon." She breathed out the word over him and he tensed even more.

"The oil. Hurry, because, Mother above, I need you around me."

He gave her brief instructions for applying the oil, then closed his eyes as she massaged his right foot. This custom must hold profound meaning for him. One she didn't understand fully right now, but she would eventually. She would learn everything about her husband and the culture in which he'd grown up, just as he'd been learning about hers.

She finished with his left foot, ran her hands up his arms and gently pushed him onto his back. She slid her fingers under the waistband of his underwear the pulled them down his lean, muscular legs. His shaft sprang free, and the low rumble from his throat brought her gaze back to his.

"Bronze," Gryf murmured. The appreciative gleam in his luminous eyes set loose the butterflies in her chest. "Your eyes glow bronze. Warm and beautiful. Come to me now, my soul."

She climbed over him, straddling his hips and gliding her soft parts against the ridge of his manhood. His heated gaze held hers as the friction stoked the burning desire within her. Then she wrapped her fingers around his hardness, covering him with the residual oil.

"Holy. Mother." Gryf's hoarse whisper hung between them, heavy with desire.

She sank down on him until he filled her completely.

A sexy, low growl came from his throat, and he grasped her hips and thrust up. A gasp escaped her.

In a blink, she was on her back. He pulled out and went deep, each time a little faster and a little harder, stroking her most sensitive spot with exquisite accuracy. The tension within her wound tighter and tighter. Her soul reached for his then the world exploded with wave after wave of glorious release.

Gryf thrust hard and strained, his cry of fulfillment echoed in her ears. Then all awareness faded until there were only two bodies and two souls, joined in perfect harmony.

Gryf stirred. How long had he lost consciousness for this time? Alexandra lay relaxed in his arms, her back pressed to his chest. He traced his fingers down the warm, satiny skin of his wife's abdomen, pausing over her womb.

Tinan.

His Gift surged and ebbed. He and Alexandra had taken turns running the pregnancy preventative each time they made love. It wasn't far-fetched to assume that she would eventually desire a child. She was a Terrian, and her people seemed to view children as an essential part of marriage.

Matirans, on the other hand, did not. His people loved children, but procreation was not a reason for a couple to bind their lives. Binding was a sacred devotion between each couple, the choosing of a life mate to share one's path. And he would have chosen Alexandra to share his path even without divine intervention.

His hand spanned her lower belly. Matiran couples traditionally had only one child, and a few had a second. How many would she want? No, it mattered not to him. If they survived what lay ahead, he would give her as many children as she wished.

Moving his hand up her body, he cupped the underside of her breast and gently rolled her nipple between his finger and thumb. It hardened, and she snuggled her bottom against him, stirring his loins.

Gryf pressed his lips to her shoulder. "Morning blessings."

"Is it morning so soon?" She rolled part-way over in his arms. Her sleepy smile nearly stole his breath.

"My stomach is telling me so."

Alexandra chuckled. "Mine too."

If he was not mistaken, first meal had been delivered to their door ten minutes ago. "Don't move."

He slid out of their warm bed and strode across the rugs toward the entrance. Alexandra's gaze warmed him, her admiration flowing through their link. He straightened his posture and stepped off the rug.

"Blazing Fires of Ata!" It was like walking barefoot onto a frozen lake. He danced back onto the rug. "We need more rugs."

Alexandra giggled. "Take your time. I'm enjoying the view."

Gryf cast a mock glare over his shoulder. "Hilarious." At least he had not shrieked loudly enough to bring the entire camp running to check on them.

"Well, go on," she urged. "The food isn't going to walk itself in here."

"You knew I was getting food?"

She frowned then shrugged. "I guess I did."

Interesting. Changes he had expected, but not so soon. He pulled back the blanket-door and reached through the opening to retrieve a tray from the floor. Fresh fruit and an Earth dish appropriately named scrambled eggs. Delicious.

"Ooh." Alexandra sat up as he approached. "Breakfast in

bed."

The blanket slipped to reveal the soft curve of her creamy breasts. Dusky areoles beckoned him, and his body's reaction went from mild arousal to full-blown desire. A low chuckle escaped Alexandra. Rather unhelpful to his current state. She walked on her knees across the mattress—sans blanket—and took the tray from his unresisting hands, placing it on the floor.

Sweet Mother, he wanted to feel her heat around him again. A shiver of desire coursed through him. "You should enjoy your morning meal first." That had to be the single most unconvincing argument of his life.

"I am," she murmured, her throaty reply testing his resistance.

She ran one fingernail lightly up the ridge of his manhood.

Oh, hells. What resistance?

Using his body weight, he carried her down to the mattress. He nipped and sucked at one breast while teasing the other with his fingers. Her soft whimpers flamed his desire even more.

Releasing her breast, he gave her a crooked grin. "Do you mind if I show you my idea of breakfast in bed?"

He didn't wait for her response before sliding himself lower and grazing his unshaven cheek against the smooth skin of her inner thighs. Ah, Mother, the scent of her arousal was more intoxicating than any alcoholic beverage.

"No." Her voice cracked with raw need. "I don't mind at...aahhh." She pushed her hips up as he explored her most intimate place with his tongue. Now *this* was truly breakfast in bed.

CHAPTER TWENTY-FOUR

Twenty minutes later, Gryf read aloud the note Alexandra had found tucked under the bowl of strawberries.

"It says: *No urgency. Senior Admiral Cael sends his congratulations on your nuptials. Viscomm this morning. Meet us at the meadow at third hour. Ora.*"

Alexandra slipped her arms around his waist from behind, and rested her chin on his shoulder. "She means the Defense Fleet, I hope."

She sweet breath tickled his ear. "She does." Finally. The Fleet was on alert and must be on their way. Ora would have told him if they weren't.

"Third hour is three hours after dawn, right?"

"It is, which leaves us less than ten minutes to get there." He leaned his cheek against her temple. "Admiral Cael is a close family friend, and the current senior admiral over both fleets. He recommended Ora and me for the Guardian Fleet."

"Really? I look forward to meeting him then."

"You may not like this, however. Protocol dictates that he address you by your title, which is 'Your Honor'."

She snorted. "From ER nurse to Your Honor in barely nine weeks."

Her discomfort radiated from the tense lines of her body. Given how much had happened since the invasion, she had every reason to feel more than a little overwhelmed. Knowing she was not alone in this was important.

He turned to take her into his arms. "From Senior Captain to soul mate and husband in the same amount of time. Yet, I cannot imagine sharing these changes with anyone else." He brushed his lips over hers. "An eternity with you, Alexandra, is not long enough."

PROPHECY

Alex walked hand-in-hand across the meadow with Gryf. The long, dew-laden grass soaked the hem of her jeans, and her heart was light. How could it not be? She was with the man that fate had destined her for. The one soul in the universe who complemented hers. Her gaze drifted to their joined hands. Alike in more ways than they were different.

Horses stamped and snorted at the center of the wide field, their ears cocking in different directions as they waited for the people amongst them to mount up for the ride to the *Athens* transport. Nicky waved to her before turning back to check his saddle's cinch. It appeared as though Karise and one of Gunner's men, Corporal Benji Reyes, would also be making the trip to the transport with them.

"Reed!" Gryf's voice was tinged with delight as Gunner strode toward them. "You have returned early."

"'Morning, sir. We got in last night. Captain Solaris told us you'd be leaving, so I thought I'd rendezvous with you for a quick report. Congratulations to both of you, by the way." Gunner grinned at Alex.

"Thanks, Gunner."

Gunner nodded at the man at his side. "This is Mitch Jamison, sir. We found him and thirty-seven others at the avalanche facility."

Gryf released her hand to clasp Mitch's. "It pleases me to meet you, Mr. Jamison."

"Likewise, Captain Helyg," a grinning Jamison said.

Alex studied Mitch. He had to be in his early fifties. His steel-grey hair was pulled back in a ponytail, and his tanned face reflected a lifetime of exposure to the outdoors.

Gryf placed his hand at the small of her back. "It pleases me to introduce my reason for living, Alexandra Bock."

She gave Mitch a smile and extended her hand.

"Pleasure to meet you, Alex," Mitch's pale-blue eyes twinkled as he shook her hand. "Your legacy precedes you."

Alex blinked. Now, what in the world did that mean?

"One minute," Ora called from atop her horse, giving Gunner a pointed look. "Get on with your report, Reed."

"Right." Gunner's blue-grey gaze returned to Gryf. "The Reader's Digest version is, we loaded all eight floats with the explosives from the avalanche facility without issue. Commander Roble, Mitch, and I have seen to their storage."

"Only a dozen of my people have experience handling explosives," Mitch interjected. "The rest are family members, all of whom are hard workers."

"It pleases us to have all of you here, Mr. Jamison."

"Call me Mitch, please."

Gryf inclined his head. "As you say, Mitch. I look forward to speaking with you upon our return this afternoon."

"Mount up," Ora called out.

An hour later, they rode out of the trees and into a rocky ravine. A tingle rippled over Alex, like a feather brushing her skin. She looked up and clutched her reins tighter. Cripes! She hadn't expected the transport to be so huge. The blue-silver craft was at least three times the size of a 747. And it hadn't been there a moment ago.

"Whoa," Nicky breathed.

"I know, right?" Benji Reyes rode up on the other side of her brother, grinning like a kid at Christmas. "Kinda a shock the first time you pass through the cloak, but trust me, the fun is just beginning. Wait 'til you see the inside."

A giddy thrill sprang into her stomach. *This is real.* She dismounted and looped her reins to a makeshift hitching rail under the transport.

Gryf appeared at her side and reached for her hand. "I don't even need to ask what you think. Your face says it all."

She gazed up at the side of the craft. "Like a child seeing snow for the first time. '*Guardian Fleet Ship Athens, Transport 103*'. You really *are* from another planet, honey."

Gryf stared at her, clearly astonished. Had she said something wrong? "I'm sorry. I was only teasing."

"No, it is not that," he replied slowly. "Where did you get the transport identification information?"

That was easy. She waved her hand toward the ship. "Well, it's right there on the side...of...the...." A knot formed in her stomach. *Cripes.* "Gryf, why am I able to read Matiran?"

"And understand Matiran, my soul?" he replied, using his

native tongue again.

The others stared at her, and her ears heated. Since she'd met Gryf, standing around with her mouth gaping open had become a normal activity for her. But to read *and* understand Matiran? How could this be possible?

"Interesting," Ora observed, also in Matiran. "Alex, try to introduce yourself in Matiran."

Speak Matiran? Well, it was worth a try. She dug deep to find the words, but they just weren't there. She gave her head a sharp shake. "Nothing."

Ora drummed her fingers against the wooden hitching rail, eyeballing Alex as if she'd become a riddle to solve. "Worry not. I wager it will come to you eventually. This soul mate stuff is fascinating."

Alex frowned. If she could read and understand Gryf's language, was speaking it such a far-fetched idea? Of course, three years of high-school Spanish had taught her that foreign languages weren't one of her strong points. Maria and Ramon were forever correcting her Spanish in camp. It was embarrassing.

The million-dollar question was how it had come to her seemingly overnight?

Heat surged into her face. *Next, on The Jerry Springer Show: I learned an alien's language overnight by having sex with him.*

If only everything were that easy. Or pleasurable. She cast a glance at Gryf.

Ora gave her a bright smile. "We can talk about this later. I have a ship to show you, and I am quite proud of it." She tapped the comm attached to her uniform. "Crewman Imifa, please lower the ladder."

Alex turned her body sideways. For all its size, the transport's passageways were as narrow as jet aisles. And they'd used a *ladder* to climb into the belly of the transport. Where were all the high-tech gadgets? Hollywood sure had set the bar high, but reality didn't seem to agree.

As they approached a blank wall, Ora touched her palm to

an iridescent-green rectangle. The wall scoped open, and Alex blinked. So *that* was how the doors worked. Walls turning into doors were disconcerting enough, but at least she couldn't accidentally lock herself in a room now. Ora breezed through the door ahead, and Alex followed, Gryf's hand at the small of her back.

"Captains on the bridge," Karise announced. The Matirans snapped to attention.

"As you were," Ora acknowledged then dismissed the outgoing shift. "Ensign Ius, our *Profeta* requires free access to the ship. Lieutenant Commander Zola, the same for Nick, please."

"Yes, Captain," the two Matiran officers answered in unison.

Ius rose from his seat. "*Profeta*, you may sit here, and I will scan you into our security network."

Alex slid into the seat. Rows of meaningless colored lights, solid and blinking, glowed from within the flat, black console. To her right was another glowing green rectangle. So this was where all the techno gadgetry lived.

"Whoa." Nicky sat with Karise, his face lighting up as his gaze roved over her station.

Alex allowed a grin to creep onto her face. Whoa was right. She glanced to her right. Even Benji Reyes appeared confident as he did...well, whatever it was he was doing at his console. Of course, he'd been with the camp since day one. Ora probably took all the help she could get those first few weeks.

This seemed so lax compared to the post-9/11 world she'd known for so long. "Ora, are you sure I don't need some sort of security clearance from the fleet, or something?"

"*Sobin*." The Matiran word for cousin fell from Ora's lips as though she'd called Alex that all her life. "You were cleared twelve millennium ago."

Alex parted her lips, and a shiver ran down her spine. *Someone* knew she would exist twelve thousand years before she was born. Mind blowing.

"Database scan." Ius leaned over her shoulder as he spoke the order to the computer in Matiran. Then he pointed to the glowing green rectangle and switched to English. "Place your

PROPHECY

hand in there, Your Honor, and the identification reader will scan you into the main database."

She suppressed a cringe at his formality. Was he still feeling awkward about the day he'd seen the *Profetae* making out in the woods?

A ripple of Gryf's amusement flowed over her. She gave her head a shake, stretched out her hand, and rested it on top of the rectangle. It sank into a shallow well of liquid. A laugh erupted from her and she yanked her hand back, flexing her fingers. Her hand was completely dry. "It's like oobleck, Nicky, except not grainy and without the residue."

"Kick ass, huh?" Nicky returned her grin, his hand also immersed in a green rectangle.

"It is a crystalline identification reader," Karise explained. "Please return your hand, *Profeta*, before Ensign Ius, er...has a cow, I believe is the Terrian term."

"Oh!" Alex spun in her seat and met Ius's blue eyes. He seemed to be at a loss as to what to do or say to her. It was too much to hope that everyone would remain calm and unflustered by her status. "It's okay, Ius. I'm not Oz the Great and Powerful." Cripes, that wasn't going to work. The poor guy had no reference. "Look, I'm new to all this *Profeta* stuff, and I really don't know what I'm doing. If you need something, just ask. Talk to me like I'm another ensign. It's okay, really."

"Yes, Your Honor," he murmured.

"No more 'Your Honor' either. Alex will work. Or ma'am." Not her number one choice, but it was unlikely he'd agree to call her Alex.

"Yes, ma'am." He still appeared rattled, but at least he hadn't passed out. "Will you put your hand back, ma'am?"

"Sure." She pressed her hand back into the cool crystals as far as it would go. The reader turned yellow, and there was a muted whoosh before it turned green again.

She looked up at Ius. "That was it?"

"You are finished." He coughed, and his cheeks darkened.

Ora tapped her fingers over another console. "Lieutenant Commander Zola, please hail Senior Admiral Cael on a secure range under my code, then direct him through to the viscomm room."

"Aye, Captain," Karise responded, her fingers flying over the panel in front of her.

"If the *Profetae* will follow me," Ora said. "We should be settled by the time the Commander puts through the Senior Admiral."

There wasn't much in the viscomm room. Just a narrow black table situated flush against the back wall. Eight black chairs lined one side of the table. Gryf pulled out a chair in the middle for her, and she sank into the seat. It conformed to her backside like memory foam.

"Ora and I will stand until we're given leave to sit," Gryf explained, his mouth next to her right ear.

A shiver ran through her, heating her most private parts. She raised her gaze to meet his. "Military protocol. I got it."

He brushed a kiss across her lips in response.

"Captain Solaris," Karise's voice came out of the walls. "Admiral Cael is standing by."

"Put him through, Lieutenant."

The wall opposite them glowed to life, and seven Matirans seated at a similar table appeared. The overall effect was as if they all sat around one table. But, wasn't there supposed to be only *one* admiral? Gryf had told her that seven admirals headed the fleets: three for the Defense Fleet, three for the Guardian Fleet, and one neutral. Were they *all* here? Alex looked up at him. A muscle twitched in his jaw.

"Did you...?" Gryf murmured to Ora.

"No!" Ora whispered back.

Cripes, it appeared that the Matiran brass had all come to meet the *Profetae*. A silent sense of apology flowed across their soul link. So, she wasn't the only one caught off guard.

CHAPTER TWENTY-FIVE

Alex's eyes were drawn to the grey-headed man in the center. "Please be seated, Captains," he said. He must be Senior Admiral Cael. The others, two men and four women of various ages, flanked him, three on each side.

"Thank you, Senior Admiral," Gryf murmured then slid smoothly into his chair next to hers. He reached for her hand under the table, lacing his fingers with hers. His face reflected professionalism—his game face. Beneath that façade, though, Alex sensed his uneasiness. She gave his hand a squeeze as reassurance. If nothing else, she'd learned to be flexible and adapt quickly since she'd met him.

"Senior Captain Helyg, on behalf of the Admiralty, I must express our relief to see you alive and well," Cael said.

"Thank you, Senior Admiral," Gryf replied humbly.

"Captain Solaris has shared much with me about the Terrian tragedy, and your role as this situation unfolds. She has quite convinced me, and subsequently all of the Admiralty, that you are one half of the long-awaited *Profetae*. How are you accepting your new role?"

"With more grace now than I did at first," Gryf admitted with an almost roguish smile.

Cael's lips twitched as though suppressing a smile. "Yes, we suspected as much. And there is further news you have to share with us?"

Gryf's gaze met hers, and his love surged through their soul link, warming her like a summer sun. "Admirals, it pleases me to be graced by *Profeta* Alexandra Bock, my beloved wife and *anim tros*."

The weight of seven pairs of eyes landed on her. Crickets chirped in her suddenly blank mind. How would she ever represent her people if her brain kept reverting to the intelligence level of a log?

As one, the admirals inclined their heads. "We are honored, *Profeta*," Admiral Cael said.

Rational thought flooded back, pushing aside the tension of the moment. "The honor is mine, Admiral. Thank you."

There. She'd done it—opened dialogue without sounding like an idiot. And after this was over, she would amp up her protocol lessons with Karise.

"It is true then, *eno anim* did in fact occur?" one of the female admirals asked. Her hair was blue like Haesi's, but there was kindness in her sky-blue eyes. She was also at least twenty years older than Haesi.

Alex nodded in unison with Gryf.

The fascination of the admiralty was evident on all their faces.

"Admiral Teris," Gryf murmured, and she shot him a grateful look. He picked up a stylus and began writing on the table surface in front of him.

Admiral Teris continued, "This is such a rare occurrence, Your Honor. You must be overwhelmed by these unfamiliar events."

"It *has* been unnerving from time to time, Admiral Teris. I am thankful that Gryf's been at my side from the beginning."

"The role of *Profeta* must have been difficult to accept at first." The man next to Admiral Teris gave her a speculative look. His blond hair was untouched by grey, and he appeared to be the youngest of all the admirals. In fact, he couldn't be more than five or six years older than Gryf.

Gryf released her hand then reached across and tapped the table in front of her. A screen set into the table lit up. It displayed each of the admirals' names in order of where they sat relative to her. Well, that was handy. She flashed him a smile before turning her attention back to the youngest admiral.

"It was difficult in the beginning, Admiral Milvus, but your prophecy gave me hope. And when hope is all you have, you embrace it fully."

The silver-headed admiral at the far-right end of the table

PROPHECY

leaned back in his chair. His vivid blue gaze seemed to be sizing her up. Then he raised one eyebrow in an all too familiar way. "And how do you feel about Gryf now, daughter?"

Her jaw dropped. *No way.* She glanced at the table-top diagram. *'Marenys (patre)'. Patre.* Father? Amusement danced in the admiral's eyes, and he smiled. The same slow smile as.... She whipped her head around and lasered her husband with a melt-you-into-the-floor glare.

It had zero effect.

"Alexandra." Gryf's eyes sparkled. "It pleases me to present Admiral Zale Marenys, my father."

"You have his smile." There was no denying it. She looked back at Admiral Marenys. "I have revised my initial opinion, sir. I am pretty attached to him now."

Her father-in-law's smile widened. "If time allows, I hope to have a private conversation with you and Gryf after this meeting."

"It would be a pleasure, sir." Right after she hyperventilated herself into unconsciousness.

The atmosphere of the meeting took on a serious tone as Admiral Cael brought them up to date. "Matir issued an official warning to Anferthia to stand down and withdraw from Terr. As expected, the time limit expired without a response. It took some time, but the Matiran Defense Fleet was recalled to Matir for rendezvous. Two thirds of the fleet is already en route to Terr."

Alex exhaled. Help was on its way. With any luck, Earth and her people would soon be free again.

"The fleet will arrive in the Terrian solar system in two weeks," Admiral Cael added.

"*What?*" The shocked exclamation rocketed from her mouth. She shot a look at Gryf. Why didn't he look outraged, or even mildly surprised? "Why so long?" There'd better be a stupendous reason.

Admiral Teris responded, "Mobilizing a fleet of battle cruisers is a longer process than readying a single transport, *Profeta*. We must remain close together through open space, or risk the same fate as the Guardians. If we fail to reach you intact, not only will Terr fall to the Anferthians, but so will

Matir. We leave behind only a third of our fleet to protect our home."

"But, all kinds of things could go wrong in two weeks."

What had happened to "Warp speed, Mr. Sulu"? Or "Punch it, Chewie"? The Hollywood versions of space travel were so much better than reality.

"*Cori*." Her father-in-law used the Matiran word for daughter this time. "Have faith."

Admiral Marenys's expression was sympathetic. In fact, all the admirals appeared understanding. But they were warriors, trained for times of peace and times of war. And trained to make sound tactical decisions. What else could she do but have a little faith that they knew what they were doing?

Alex allowed her shoulders to slump. "It's hard, *patre*."

Admiral Cael cleared his throat. "Senior Captain Helyg, Captain Solaris, we will reconvene in ten Terr days to finalize our strategy."

"Yes, sir," they replied in unison.

"Gryf...."

Alex covered her smile with her hand at the much-tested-parent tone of Gryf's father. Some things didn't change, no matter what planet you were from.

Now that Ora and the six other admirals had exited their respective viscomm rooms, the atmosphere seemed more relaxed.

Gryf shrugged. "*Patre*, you must agree that my entire life has been leading up to this point."

"It is rather clear to me now, *natu*," his father conceded in a dry tone. "You understand that there will be a Panel of Inquiry?"

"I do. How is Mother?"

"Strong, as always," Zale replied. "We stand with you."

Gryf bowed his head, murmuring his thanks. Then Zale turned to her. "*Cori*, welcome to the family."

The warmth of his words spread through her. "Thank you, *patre*. I will do my best to bring honor to your house."

"*Our* house," he gently corrected. "Your very presence is

PROPHECY

our blessing and honor. Never forget this, Alexandra. The loss of your parents weighs heavily on my heart. Charis and I can never hope to replace them, yet I pray we can help fill that void for you."

Swallowing against the lump forming in her throat, she gave him a nod.

Her father-in-law leaned forward. "It may seem premature, however, I do want you to consider the future. As the *Profeta*, what do you envision your role to be for the continued survival of your people?"

Clearly her father-in-law had not become an admiral by asking softball questions. She shifted in her seat. "I hate to admit it, but I've avoided thinking beyond winning our freedom from the Anferthians." There was no guarantee that they wouldn't fail. "I'd welcome your guidance here, *patre*."

His smile was the tender smile of a parent for his child. Her own father had given her that look many times. The memory squeezed her heart. "Daughter, you are the mouthpiece of your people, whether you wish it or not. It is possible you could even find yourself their chosen leader."

She gave her head a vehement shake. "I hope not. Leadership isn't something I aspire to."

"You did not aspire to be *Profeta* either, yet here you are," he pointed out. "Prophecies are unpredictable creatures."

She slid a glance at Gryf. "So I've heard."

"No matter what happens, you will have Gryf by your side, the Matiran Defense Fleet at your back and the unflagging support of the Matiran people. Should there be anything you require to aid you in your quest, you need only ask."

Wow. "I just hope I can live up to everyone's expectations."

"If you could not, you would not have been chosen," Zale replied then sat back in his seat. "Until next time, may the Mother guide your steps, my children."

The viscomm screen became a solid wall again. With a groan, Gryf leaned his head against the back of his chair. *"That was an unexpected adventure."*

"You didn't know your father would make the trip?"

"I did not. However, I am glad you both had the opportunity to speak. He's probably already viscomming my mother to tell her how wonderful you are."

"Oh, please." She gazed down at the row of names on the tabletop. How did this thing turn off? She pushed random spots on the table around the screen until it flickered off, blending into the black surface.

"I'm quite serious, Alexandra."

He did appear serious, and she couldn't help but smile. She curved her hand against his cheek. "I really like him too, Gryf. Is your mom as nice?"

"Nicer." His gaze held hers as he slid her hand down to his lips and tickled her palm with his tongue. Crazy shivers ran up her arm, into her heart, and straight down to the juncture between her legs. This could get interesting.

"Is there a broom closet aboard this old tub?" Her voice sounded oddly strangled.

Gryf's smile slowly widened, and he tucked her hand under his chin. "You make me feel like a teenage boy again, *animi*."

"Any small space will do." She willed him to understand that she wasn't kidding.

Desire flashed in his darkening eyes. He pulled her to her feet and towed her toward the wall-door at a brisk pace. Yup, he clearly understood now, and hopefully had a place in mind.

The ID reader turned green under his hand and the wall whooshed open. A harsh "wuff" escaped Alex as she plowed into his shoulder. What the heck was he stopping for?

She peered around him at the formidable figure in the corridor. Ora wore a fierce frown, her arms folded across her chest.

"Is there a problem?" Gryf asked his cousin.

"Truly?" she countered as if he should know. "I'm taking the two of you back to camp. I will not have you lighting up the *broom closets* or other small spaces on this *old tub*."

Alex slapped her hand over her mouth as heat flooded her cheeks. "How did you...?"

Ora's eyes flicked to her and narrowed even further. "You need to be more careful about which buttons you push on the table, *sobin*."

"Oh, crap. I'm really sorry, Ora. I didn't mean it like that, I just...well, you know." She gave the proud captain a helpless shrug. It was a good sign that Ora still referred to her as cousin, right?

Ora turned away from them, heading down the passageway in the direction of the ladder hatch. "Truly, it is as if you two are in love. Newlyweds, or some such thing. Nauseating."

Alex exchanged a glance with Gryf. Then he called after his cousin, "Speaking of nauseating, *sobin*, how is Bodie?"

"*Tacte*, Gryf!"

Instead of being silent, he laughed outright at his cousin's retreating form then glanced at Alex. "I did tell you that Ora is the Nick in my life, did I not?"

"Yes, you did." A chortle gurgled from her, and she wrapped her arms around his middle. "Do you think she'll forgive me for the old tub comment?"

"She did the moment you said it," he assured her, brushing a strand of hair from her face. "And I am certain the rest of the bridge got a chuckle out of it as well."

"So, no broom closet, I'm guessing." She gave him a teasing pout.

"There is more room in our little cave anyway, *compa*. If we leave now, we'll get back in time to watch the sunset. After that...." Gryf caught her bottom lip gently between his teeth, and nibbled.

Oh, yes. "After that" held a lot of potential.

CHAPTER TWENTY-SIX

Alex perched on a sun-warmed boulder next to her brother. Yesterday's viscomm with the admiralty still gnawed at her like a puppy chewing a shoe. *Two weeks? Really?* The kicker was that normal travel between Matir and Earth took about four days, or so she'd been told.

But that was for a single ship, not two-thirds of a fleet going to war. They had to be cautious at the velocity gates or the Anferthians could divide and decimate them, leaving Earth and Matir vulnerable. Gryf had explained that the gates were the entry and exit points for ships "flashing" through space. Apparently, flashing was the galactic equivalent of warp speed.

She puffed her cheeks and blew out a gusty sigh. It served no purpose to remain upset over something she couldn't change. Focusing on preparations was a better use of her time.

"Marriage seems to agree with you, sis." The spark of mischief in his eyes was at odds with his casual tone. "You're a lot calmer than you used to be."

Calm was an illusion. She gave her brother a speculative look. "Yeah, well, the sex *is* pretty awesome."

"Blugh!" Nicky gagged and slapped his hands over his ears. "TMI, Alex."

She reached over to pound him on the back. "Don't bait me then, twerp."

"No kidding." Nicky coughed once more then looked back up the trail. "Can you use the Force and find out what's taking Gryf so long?"

Smart ass. It wasn't as if they were in a hurry. "Relax, Nicky. Gryf'll be here when he's finished talking to Graig. No one's leaving until after dark anyway."

That was when the first wave of refugees headed out for the

Silver Valley Mine in preparation for the attack on the slaver. Over one hundred able-bodied adults in camp would make the trip during the next week and a half. With any luck, the small groups traveling at night wouldn't attract the Anferthians' attention.

The corner of her mouth pulled to one side. It was leaving the children behind that made her stomach ache as though she'd been sucker-punched. Duck had agreed to stay with them and Li-Min. Mrs. Beck, the camp's "grandmother", would also help, as would those from the avalanche facility who couldn't fight. Poor Mitch was still hashing it out with his sister Carrie. She'd been rather vocal about being left behind, even after Mitch threatened to tie her to a tree. Alex couldn't suppress a small smile. If Nicky ever did that to her, she'd bean him.

"Hey." Her brother nudged her and jutted his chin down the trail. "Isn't that Mr. Trimble?"

Alex shielded her eyes with one hand. Their former neighbor's gaunt silhouette lurched up the slope toward them. "Looks like. Something's wrong with him. C'mon."

"Need...help," James Trimble panted as they approached. Nicky handed over his water flask. While the older man drank deep, Alex slipped her hand over his shoulder to scan his vitals. Distressed, but not in danger. Good.

The older man wiped his mouth with the back of his hand. "The little boy, Juan...bit by a rattler...in the meadow." He pointed urgently back the way he'd come.

The blood in her veins turned cold, and her gut clenched. *No. Not Juan.* The child she'd protected from Kotas now had deadly venom coursing through him.

"You're a nurse, Alex," James said. "You can help him."

Even if she ran, she might be too late. But she had to try. She reached out to Gryf through their soul link, sending him a wordless message of urgency.

"Nicky, I'll need a float from infirmary. If you see Gryf, tell him what's happened and where I am."

"Should Dante come?"

"No time. I'll handle it."

"Got it. Meet you there." Nicky sprinted back up the mountain trail.

Not waiting to see if Mr. Trimble followed, she flew down the trail toward the meadow.

At the edge of the long, green grass just beyond the tree line, she stopped to take stock. The horses mingled at the far end of the meadow to her left, restless and snorting. The snake had probably freaked them out. She scanned the rest of the meadow, but didn't see Juan.

"Where is he?"

Mr. Trimble stumbled to a stop next to her, pointing to the far side. "See him...in the grass...near the trees?"

There he is. The early summer grass swayed gently, just higher than Juan's prone body. *Please let him be alive.* She bolted toward his still form, Mr. Trimble chugging like a train behind her. Good thing they weren't on a stealth mission.

"Juan." Alex dropped to her knees at the boy's side. "I'm here, Juan. It's okay. Where did the snake bite you?"

The boy's face was smudged with dirt and tears. "No, Miss Alex. Run, it's a trap."

"The back of his leg." Mr. Trimble pointed.

Alex gently rolled Juan toward her. *What the hell?* "His hamstring's been sliced."

Who would do such a thing? She turned to stare at James Trimble.

"I'm so sorry, Alex," he muttered, looking away.

"So this is where you have been hiding, my pet." Kotas's voice froze her blood in her veins.

She jerked her head around. He stood under the trees no more than a dozen yards away, smirking. Dammit, it *was* a trap. He'd finally found her.

"Run," Juan sobbed.

"He has Megan," Mr. Trimble whimpered. "He took my precious little girl, and she's all I have left."

So that was how it had worked. Kotas had used Megan Trimble, James's only child, to compel the old man to search for his escaped prisoner. Alex quashed a groan. Betrayed by a man who'd known her since she was born.

Gryf's seething anger crashed over her, and she suppressed a gasp. He must have sensed she was in trouble, and he was on his way. But would he get here in time?

"He said he'd release her." James's lips trembled.

"And you *believed* him?"

Kotas started through the grass toward them. How was she going to keep him away from Juan? *Think, Alex, think.*

"I...I...." James sagged and whispered, "I had no choice."

Megan being in Kotas's clutches was gut-wrenching enough. If Haesi was involved too, the girl would be lucky if she survived with her sanity intact. Assuming she was still alive. Alex curled her lip. "How proud will Megan be of your choice, James?"

Mr. Trimble's violent flinch was almost as gratifying as slapping him. She brushed Juan's dark hair from his forehead. "Don't worry, Juan. I'll do what I can, okay?"

The faith in his eyes bolstered her. She could do this. Rising, she stepped over Juan to face Kotas.

The former Matiran commander stopped in his tracks and gave her the once over. "You have been a very naughty pet, Alex. I'm afraid lessons must be taught. We shall begin with humility. Every pet needs a dose of humility, do they not?"

Kotas licked his lips and grinned.

Vile. Just vile. And closer than she'd hoped, but she still might be able to distract him. Her half-formed plan was risky, but mostly to herself.

She bolted to her right, away from Juan and the pathetic James Trimble and toward the far end of the meadow. She didn't need to look back to know Kotas gave chase. At the tree line, he caught her, slamming her against a tree trunk. The rough bark of the red fir scraped her cheek.

"Well, that was a merry chase, my pet." Kotas cooed in her ear. "But once again *I* am the master, and you are merely...my property." He thrust his erection against her bottom to emphasize his words.

"Please, no." As long as Kotas believed he had the upper hand, she should be able to distract him until help arrived. Where the heck was Gryf? She couldn't feel his presence anymore.

Kotas hauled her around to face him, bracing his palms against the tree trunk. There was no sure way to escape, but she might buy some time. As long as she didn't look him in the eye, and kept her hands behind her back. There was no telling how he'd react if he saw her wedding ring.

"Now you beg for mercy?" There was a hard edge to his voice. "Out of curiosity, if you could have only one mercy from me, what would it be?"

She swallowed hard. "Let the girl you are holding go."

"She amuses me." His shoulders rose and fell in a blasé shrug.

I just bet she does. "She's a fifteen-year-old child."

"If you had stayed put, I would not have had to find a replacement pet." He traced one finger down her left arm. "On the other hand, she is *so* much more compliant than you. Eager to please. Perhaps if you were a bit more...cooperative, I might find a nugget of mercy in my heart."

Cripes. No way to miss the innuendo in that suggestion. "If I come back with you, will you release the girl?"

"I said mercy, my pet. By now you know I do not part easily with what belongs to me." He grabbed her wrist and he raised her hand to chest level. "Interesting." He studied her knotted blue ring. "It would seem you have a new master. Matiran, if I am not mistaken." He met her gaze. "And I am not."

Remain calm. He couldn't know it was Gryf. And he definitely didn't know he was dealing with the *Profetae*.

He released her hand, brushing his fingers over her breast where he had once carved his initials into her skin. "Perhaps I still own your body?" A blade appeared in his other hand, resting at the neckline of her shirt. "Let us just check, shall we?"

Not in this lifetime.

She brought her arm up hard and swift, knocking his hand away. His blade cartwheeled through the air and landed in the grass with a soft thump.

"Let's not."

Kotas's face contorted with anger as he reached for her. She dropped under his arm and rolled away.

"You have learned some new tricks, I see." He grinned, his eyes alight at the challenge. "No matter. I shall still own you in the end."

"I doubt it." Alex gave him a grim smile and glanced

PROPHECY

purposefully beyond his shoulder.

It took half a heartbeat before Kotas snapped his head around to look behind him. "Roble," he growled.

Graig stood close enough to create discomfort for Kotas, yet far enough not to pressure him into doing something drastic.

"I warned you to watch your back, Kotas." Graig's tone was mild, and his stance relaxed. "You didn't listen."

Kotas snorted, his face lined with contempt. "So, you are Alex's new master."

Graig shrugged. "The *Profeta* is her own master."

"*Profeta?*" Kotas turned to gape at her, the look on his face borderline comical. But gloating was a waste of energy. She slammed her knuckles into the side of his neck, and he staggered back, gasping for air.

A well-aimed kick to the side of his head sent him sprawling. He was hers. In one fluid motion, she bent and snatched her blade from her boot. A grey-blue blur passed her. Gryf. She stepped toward the two men grappling in the grass but was brought up short by muscular arms pinning hers to her side.

"No! Dammit, Graig. Let me *go*." She owed Kotas pain. Not just her own, but the pain of the seven billion voices in her head screaming for justice.

"You will be a healer, *sora*," Graig reminded her, his voice calm next to her ear. "You *know* you can kill him, but let the soldier finish the job."

Her connection with Gryf slammed back into place as he rammed his blade home between her tormentor's ribs. Kotas grunted, his eyes wide and wild as Gryf gave the blade a vicious twist.

Alex clenched her teeth together. "Die, you bastard."

Gryf yanked the knife from Kotas's side, and levered himself off the doomed traitor. Crimson blood flowed freely into the wild grass, and Kotas shuddered. Graig released her from his iron grip.

She moved to her soul mate's side, and Gryf slipped his arm around her waist. "Vyn Kotas, you die this day for your crimes against the children of Terr. The *Profetae* deliver your soul for reparation."

Something akin to triumph flashed in Kotas's eyes, and he rasped a laugh.

That wasn't the reaction she'd expected. Hatred and defeat, yes, but laughter? "I think he's hiding something, Gryf."

Gryf nodded his agreement.

You know what you need to do, Alexandra.

She gave her head a shake. *Dad?* In her mind, a door opened like an epiphany. Beyond it, a secret room of treasures hidden for generations was revealed. Yes, she knew what to do, and it was terrible. But lives depended on her actions.

Hurry, monkey.

She dropped to her knees and grabbed Kotas's head between her hands. "Tell us." Her Gift surged through her, hers to command. And this time she wouldn't use it to heal.

"Nothing you can do." His voice was rough, as if he was certain of his final victory in death.

She moved within inches of his face and bared her teeth. "Then I will rip the information from your mind."

Panicked horror flickered in Kotas's eyes, and pink spittle formed at the corners of his mouth. "You...can't...."

"I am the *Profeta*. Watch me, you piece of shit."

Reaching out with her Gift, she invaded the traitor's mind, searching for the one thing they needed to know. A strangled scream gurgled in Kotas's throat, and the inhuman death knell crawled over her skin like a thousand ants. He pulled his thoughts away from her questing mind, but it didn't matter. It might take her a little longer to find the information, but she would win in the end.

Death's icy presence intruded, reaching for Kotas's soul even as she searched for his secret. Time was running out. She had to move fast.

"Alexandra." The firm, comforting weight of Gryf's hand rested on her shoulder. "I'm coming in with you."

Death's presence grew stronger. Every instinct for self-preservation screamed at her to withdraw, but if she did, there'd be no second chance to find out what Kotas hid from them.

"I'm going all in, Gryf. I may need your help getting out."

PROPHECY

"I will not let you fall, *animi*." Gryf's presence filled her, motivating her to move faster as she picked up and discarded Kotas's random thoughts and memories.

It had to be here somewhere. But if she didn't disengage before Death took Kotas, she'd be dead as well. And Gryf with her.

Her mind touched another memory, and it blossomed open. The Defense Fleet...ambush. They were flying into a trap.

I have it, Gryf.

Kotas screamed, his fingernails raking her arm. His dying mind slithered like the multiple arms of a cephalopod into her mind, dragging her toward the abyss with him. *Shit.* She snapped her eyes open, searching for a physical anchor to hold her to this life. Instead she gazed into the cowl of Death and saw....

"Mom?"

Her mother smiled, the promise of eternal peace in her soft brown eyes. Something hot and wet slid down Alex's cheek. God, she missed her parents.

Her mother reached for her...then she vanished, replaced by a faceless nightmare. The icy fingers of the hooded figure sank through Alex's chest and brushed her soul. A low moan escaped her, and her body jerked like a marionette. Air. She needed air but her body seemed to have forgotten the simple act of inhaling. She was going to die in this field with Kotas. And so was Gryf.

Fight it, Alexandra. Gryf's command echoed in her mind.

A low rumble shook her soul as pressure built in her head. Colors exploded around her, and her physical body flew backward.

She blinked up at the deep azure sky above her. *I'm on my back in the meadow.* Kotas's depraved mind and Death's eternal embrace were gone, but her body didn't seem to be able to obey the commands from her brain to move.

Gryf? Where are you?

No answer. Her pulse drummed in her ears and a violent tremor racked her body, pulling another moan from deep inside her. It wasn't over. Death still knelt at Kotas's head.

Horror filled her heart as it drew his soul out. *How am I able to see this?* The traitor's body exhaled its final breath then Death turned its empty cowl toward her. She clamped her teeth together and raised her chin. No way in hell was she going quietly. She had forcibly taken information that would save thousands, but not if she didn't tell someone. Where was Gryf?

CHAPTER TWENTY-SEVEN

Graig's face appeared above Alex, raw fear filling his steel-grey eyes. So not a good sign.

"*Sora*, can you hear me?"

Truthfully, no, not well over the sound of her teeth clacking together. Cripes, she'd never felt cold like this. Not even when she'd lain dying in that cave the day her soul touched Gryf's. "G-get Gryf-f-f."

Graig looked over his shoulder, swore in Matiran, and scrambled away. Nicky's face replaced Graig's.

"It's okay, Alex. I'm here, and I can help." Nicky's voice was confident. How could he be so calm? He should be freaking out. She would be if he were the one lying here. Dying. "Gryf will be here in a sec, and we're going to help you. Dad told me what to do, okay?"

Dad had told him? Another powerful tremor coursed through her, and she lost track of her thoughts. Then Nicky and Gryf were talking over her.

"...because she carries a piece of you, you *have to* let me control this," her brother said.

Gryf's expression was skeptical. "Nicholaus...."

"You're the protector, I'm the healer. I've never been more certain about anything in my entire life, Gryf."

Nicky a healer? She must've heard that wrong. Blackness played at the edge of her vision. The grey specter hovered by her feet. It was going to take her. She had to tell them what she'd learned. "Amb-b-bush. I know w-where."

The two men she loved most looked from her to each other. Gryf laid his hand on Nicky's shoulder. "Do it. I am right behind you."

Nicky cupped both his hands just below her collarbone,

and his eyes glowed golden. Alex gave him an incredulous look. *His Gift has awakened.*

"Let it go, Alex." Nicky's presence flowed into her like a gentle opening stanza. She hoped he knew what he was doing.

Then Gryf was there, his presence filling her, calm and strong. They were fighting for her life. If they failed, she was going to put up one hell of a fight before she let Death take her...or Gryf.

Alexandra, you are not breathing. Gryf's words caressed her mind, and the increased pressure in her lungs affirmed what he told her.

What do I do?

Relax and open your vital control to me.

How was she supposed to hand over control of an automated response? Wait. The medulla oblongata was automated response central in her brain. If she focused on that....

Her body took a deep, ragged breath, and oxygen expanded her lungs. *It worked!*

That's it, animi. *I will take it from here.* Gryf's presence and words reassured her.

Her heart fluttered. She just might survive this. Nick's healing Gift poured into her from his cupped hands like a song. The song reached its crescendo, and a flash of searing flame encased her soul. The icy feeling shriveled and vanished. Molten heat blazed outward, infusing every cell in her body before fading.

She forced her eyelids open, and her gaze darted to her feet. The grey figure was gone. Warmth filled her soul, and she inhaled deeply without Gryf's assistance. She was alive.

Her gaze found her brother's. "You *healed*, Nicky."

Nicky swayed where he knelt. His dark eyes stood out in stark contrast to his pale face. He may have healed, but without discipline, it had drained him.

"Yeah." His eyes rolled back in his head, and he pitched sideways into Graig's arms.

Gryf sat cross-legged in the long grass holding Alexandra

close to his heart. He'd almost lost her. His hand trembled as he stroked her hair.

"Captain Helyg." K'rona approached, Juan cradled in one arm like a precious piece of cargo, blood oozing from knife slashes to the back of the boy's thighs. Ora, Karise, and Ius walked with her. And there was the betrayer, James Trimble, being escorted by the dissenter, Ita, and another Anferthian woman. The old man's eyes were glazed with terror.

Let him feel fear. It was no less than he deserved for his actions.

Graig lowered Nick's unconscious body to the grass and rose to intercept K'rona. Incredible tenderness governed the Anferthian's movements as she surrendered Juan to Graig's keeping. Then she knelt in the wild grass in front of Gryf, her brow creased.

"Allazandra, you are well?" K'rona spoke through the translator attached to her ear.

Alexandra nodded, and the Anferthian woman's expression softened. Then, in a blur of motion, K'rona sprang to her feet. She whirled around and snatched James Trimble's shirt in one huge hand. A pitiful cry escaped the old man as she carried him to the ground.

"I am Anferthian," she hissed into Trimble's face. "I am *supposed* to be the enemy, yet I value her life more than you do, worm." She pulled her fist back, poised to deal Trimble a death blow.

"K'rona, no!" There was nothing Gryf could do to stop the unfolding drama, short of dropping Alexandra on the ground. And that wasn't going to happen.

Ora moved in, closing her hands around K'rona's raised fist.

"Do not do it, K'rona."

"He is a traitor. He meant to *kill* Allazandra," K'rona ground out.

"He did it to save *fyhen*." His own.

K'rona narrowed her eyes.

Alexandra stirred and raised her head. "Please don't give any of my people more reason to distrust you, K'rona. Let him go. We'll deal with him."

Her voice was steadier than he'd expected, given her recent ordeal. For several heartbeats, the Anferthian soldier did not move. Then she lowered her fist and relinquished her hold on Trimble. Curling her lip with obvious disgust for the elderly Terrian man, she stepped away. Ora helped Trimble to his feet and bound his wrists.

K'rona's dark-green gaze met Gryf's. So much pain and sorrow haunted the depths of her wide eyes. Whatever had happened to put it there certainly would be less than welcome news. She switched off her translator with the flick of her finger. "Captain, Mendiko has been exposed and executed. Premiere Warden D'etta is my mother's brother, and my status as his niece has protected me. But that cannot last. My position is precarious, and my usefulness to our cause can no longer be served aboard his ship."

"My heart grieves this news. Mendiko was a good man who stood true to his convictions. I honor him for this." Thank the Mother she had turned off the translator. Her kinship to the Premiere Warden was not something that should be common knowledge in camp.

K'rona reached behind her and unsheathed a long, wicked-looking bladed weapon from her back, and laid it on the ground in front of him. She repeated the process with a shorter blade at her hip. Her *fusil*—the Anferthian version of a *telum*—followed. Then she knelt in the long grass.

"I am faithful to my *ymero*, not the *Arruch*, Captain Helyg. I serve his interest to the best of my ability."

Ymero? Arruch? What's that? Alexandra's eyes were clouded with confusion.

So you understand Anferthian now, do you?

Her cheeks turned pink. *Apparently.*

Interesting. He stroked his thumb against the silky smoothness of her arm. *Since before The Leaving, the ymero have been the leaders of Anferthia, an inherited title. The last ymero was deposed several years ago during a coup by the Arruch Union.*

K'rona spread her open hands toward him, palms up. "The best way for me to continue serving my *ymero* is to take my place here with you and your own. My *luz-ba, labu-ba,* and *fusil* are yours to command. Will you allow me fight with you?"

Alexandra?

She gave him a startled look. *You have to ask?*

A smile tugged at the corners of his mouth then he met K'rona's green eyes. "K'rona Zurkku, the *Profetae* accept your long-blade, short-blade, and *fusil* to be raised in defense of our cause and our own. You honor us by fighting at our side."

A smile spread across K'rona's face, and she bowed her head almost to the ground. Then she rose to her feet and swept her hand in the direction of the other two Anferthian women. "Ita and Jandi will take Kotas's body to the Premiere Warden and tell him I turned on him and killed him. I then died at their hands and was left to rot, as is befitting of a traitor. My supposed death will resolve the problem of what he's going to do about me. He will have no reason to doubt Ita and Jandi's tale, especially after they present him with my *tirik*."

She scooped up her short-blade and handed it to Ita, who blanched. Then the other woman took the end of K'rona's heavy, waist-long braid, and sliced through it with one stroke of the sharp blade. K'rona turned and embraced Ita, murmuring words of consolation and encouragement.

Once Ita and Jandi disappeared into the trees with Kotas's body, K'rona turned back to face Gryf. The loss of her *tirik* signified dishonor, yet she smiled as though that dishonor did not touch her. And perhaps it didn't. Perhaps she found her honor in her actions, not in a ritual braid.

K'rona inhaled deeply. "Captain, I request a private audience with you. I have learned information vital to our cause."

Alex sat on an infirmary cot, her knees hugged to her chest. Gryf sat behind her, moving his hand up and down her spine. His Gift to calm was a godsend for her frayed nerves.

Nicky had healed. Somehow, something had triggered his Gift, and he'd snatched her from Death's grip. She glanced toward the cot where K'rona had placed her brother before she retreated to stand with Graig against a wall. He slept under the control of *dormio* until Dante could attend to him.

At another cot, the healer worked to correct the muscular tissue damage in Juan's leg. An occasional sniffle punctuated the quiet infirmary, but the little boy hadn't cried once since his rescue. It probably helped that Dante had diagnosed the wounds as one-hundred percent treatable.

Gryf shifted, drawing her back against his chest. For once his body felt warmer than hers. She closed her eyes and allowed herself to relax against him.

Are you comfortable? Rough stubble lightly scuffed her cheek.

This is...weird, Gryf. We're talking telepathically like it's nothing.

So it would seem. Gryf gave her a gentle squeeze as if to express his pleasure with their newest ability.

I should be freaking out. So should you. What's wrong with us?

His chuckle rolled through her mind.

"I am going to wake Nick now, Alex." Dante's passing created a gentle swirl of air.

Alex turned toward Nicky's cot, and Gryf moved with her.

Dante touched a finger to Nicky's temple. "*Evo.*"

Her brother's eyes popped open at Dante's command.

"How do you feel, Nick?" asked Dante.

"Um, okay, I think." Nicky rubbed his eyes then propped himself up onto his elbows and peered at her. His Adam's apple bobbed as he swallowed. "You okay?"

"Yeah, thanks to you." She gave her brother a grateful smile.

Dante sat on the edge of Nicky's cot. "I must compliment you on that extraordinarily advanced bit of work. Impressive for a trained healer; astounding for one who is untrained."

Nicky pushed himself to sit upright. "I'm going to make it then, Doc?"

"Indeed. So will your sister and Gryf, thanks to you." Dante furrowed his brow. "You understand that your Gift cannot be turned off, so to speak?"

"I'll live with it." Nicky's voice turned terse. Alex caught her bottom lip between her teeth. Live with it, yes. Live with it happily, not likely. He'd never wanted the ability in the first place.

"How did you even come up with the idea that you could accomplish such a feat?" Dante asked.

Nicky hesitated then blew out a resigned breath. "Ora and I got to the meadow just when Alex kicked Kotas in the head. I ran like hell to get to her, but then—it was weird—it kinda felt like something popped inside me." He looked over at Alex and tapped his temple with two fingers. "That's when I heard Dad's voice, in my head. He talked to me the entire way across the meadow, telling me what to do for you. And I *knew* I could do it."

So that was how it happened. "Sounds like Dad was a busy man out there. He was the one who showed me how to mind read Kotas." She shot a narrow-eyed glare at Dante. "Myth, my ass."

"What you did was not mind reading as much as mind ripping," Dante clarified. "There has always been much debate about the possibility of forcing information from another's mind against their will. However, no real evidence existed before today."

"You mean that in all the centuries since The Leaving, no Matiran has done this—even accidently?" That seemed hard to believe.

"Matirans are not able to do this, Alex. Healers can mind *browse* a newly-deceased person, though it is seldom done, as the results are often less conclusive than what you did today." Dante shrugged. "The potential ripping ability in descendants of a Matiran-Terrian union is only speculation."

"Well, there have to be some of *those* on Matir, Dante."

"Of course there are. However, all of them are heavy on the Matiran ancestry, whereas you are ninety-nine percent Terrian. My point is that there are no records of the mind ripping of anyone on Matir *or* Terr, until today."

Until her. Until she'd invaded the sanctity of another's mind, tore through it, becoming privy to memories that weren't hers. Memories she really didn't want, some deeply disturbing. Kotas had been ambitious. But then Gryf had come along and bested him at every turn. Unintentionally, Gryf had driven an already compromised mind over the edge.

And now she carried many of those memories. Although the information she'd obtained would save more lives than the one she'd violated, she was tainted.

"*Animi*, we all know that this act went against your nature. However, if you hadn't, many would have died," Gryf told her. "You may well have saved the entire Defense Fleet. And without them, there would be no hope for us."

"I killed a man to do so."

"*I* killed him."

Fair point. "How is what I did to him any better than what he did to me?"

"That's enough, Alex," Graig snapped, and she startled at the abrupt reminder of his presence. "If you think you will win your planet back without anyone dying, you are living a delusion."

Her mouth dropped open and she stared at Commander Reality Check. Crap, she'd been whining. Or starting to, at least.

"Well, I don't want a bloodbath, Graig."

"No good soldier does."

No, she supposed not. What she'd done wasn't right, but she'd been justified. "I don't think I'd change anything I did today, *magister*."

"I'm glad to hear it, *disipula*." Graig gave her a small nod.

A shudder passed through her, and she gave her head a shake. Thank God she'd let Gryf into the connection. Somehow, she'd known he'd be the only one able to get her out if things went bad.

She gave Dante a narrow-eyed frown. "But what about Gryf and I being able to communicate? That's mind reading, isn't it?"

Dante held his hands up in mock surrender. "I would call it telepathy, not mind reading. Either way, the ability does not seem as mythological as I had believed—for you and Gryf, at least."

CHAPTER TWENTY-EIGHT

Alex sat alone in the operations room, her elbows propped on a table and her head between her hands. What was wrong with her? Why was she so agitated? Ever since her encounter with Kotas in the meadow two days ago, she'd harbored a growing desire to rip someone's head off. She'd nearly done so in the main cave this morning when she overheard Kelly refer to K'rona as the "jolly green giant". And it hadn't been a compliment. It never was with Kelly. But did that justify tackling the woman to the cave floor?

This was worse than the day she'd shouted at Nicky about the flour bags. If only *anim loqui* made it better. But it hadn't.

And then there were the random memories of Kotas's that popped into her head with the unpredictability of an earthquake. And left her just as shaken, like now. She pushed away his memory of a young Earth woman with hair the color of honey. Her face contorted, and tears leaked from her eyes as Kotas....

Stop! Alex ground her teeth and clenched her fists in her lap until her fingernails dug into her palm. She didn't *want* to see these things, know these things. If that bastard weren't already dead, she'd gut him then sew him up and gut him again.

This hostility was spinning out of her control. Sometimes, she hardly recognized herself in her thoughts anymore.

"Allazandra?"

Alex startled as if someone had poked her with a stick. She lifted her head. "K'rona."

The Anferthian woman stepped through the entryway of the operations room. Graig hovered behind her, but remained in the passageway.

"May I sit with you?" K'rona asked through her translator. There were six such devices on the transport, unused. Even though Alex understood her just fine, K'rona did not know English.

"Of course. Your company is an honor."

K'rona smiled and lowered herself to sit on a rug. None of the chairs would support her almost-ten-foot frame. Alex moved to join her, but K'rona shook her head. "Stay in your chair. Our heads are more on a level."

That was certainly true.

"Thank you for helping me escape from the slaver, K'rona. You saved my life."

"It distresses me that my people serve as Kotas's tool for the destruction of your people. You still pay for the traitor's transgressions?" The gentle giantess tapped a finger to her own temple.

Kotas's memories. How had K'rona figured that out?

"It's my fault. I just *had* to know what he was hiding. I didn't realize there would be a price to pay."

"We seldom think about the price," K'rona murmured. "Yet can we put a price on life? Maybe you will find the lives you have saved are worth the personal cost."

Alex looked down at her hands. "Maybe."

"I will share with you, Allazandra," K'rona said. "I have a circle of people I call *fyhen*. My own. These are the ones in life I hold most dear, and would fight to the death to protect. They are as family. So it is for all Anferthians. So it is for you. Your people are *fyhen* to you."

Alex met K'rona's gaze. It was true. She'd *thought* she'd understood this when she'd accepted her part in the *Profetae*. But she'd only understood it in concept. Reality was far more intense. And she didn't want it anymore, dammit. If the Anferthians had just kept their *ymeros* and *fyhens* and whatever the hell else, this conversation wouldn't be happening now.

Whoa. Alex gave her head a shake to clear it of the negative thoughts. Had she somehow channeled Kotas during their confrontation? No, that wasn't possible. She'd seen Death take him.

"May we intrude?" Gryf stood in the entrance with Ora. They must've just returned from this morning's viscomm aboard the transport.

K'rona gestured to the empty chairs. "No intrusion, Captain Helyg. The fleet will be safe now?"

"They will," Gryf replied, lowering himself into the chair next to Alex. She pulled her hand away when he reached for it, and his eyes registered concern. She didn't want him to touch her. How messed up was this?

Gryf gave a barely perceptible nod. *I will fill you in later.*

He turned his attention back to K'rona. "Factoress, thank you for risking so much to join us. You know you are free to go anywhere in camp, but please have one or two of us with you at all times. There are some who are understandably resentful of Anferthians, and despite your good intentions, you may be a target for them."

"Most are tolerant, but some do give me hateful glares. Only one has engaged me verbally."

Alex startled. "Who?" She'd just bet it was Kelly.

"One of the children," K'rona replied. "Fearless, she is, with red hair. I admire her deeply."

That was unexpected. "Flora?"

"It must be," Gryf agreed. "Flora had the unfortunate experience of witnessing her parents' deaths at the hands of an Anferthian patrol."

"Her distrust of me is understandable." K'rona sighed then straightened. "Captain Helyg, do listen to what I have to say. It may be helpful to our cause."

―――◆ ◆ ◆ ◆―――

Gryf let his gaze touch each person sitting in the operations room. K'rona's news had been both welcome and disquieting, and had resulted in this hastily called senior staff meeting. It was unfortunate that only Graig, Dante, Ora, and Simone were in attendance. All of them stared back at him with varying degrees of surprise and skepticism.

"A resistance group in *San Francisco?*" Simone asked incredulously.

"According to K'rona, yes." A group who had lived in

constant danger since the invasion. They needed help. "K'rona reported that plans were being made to root them out and eliminate them. We need to get there first and offer them a way to safety." He tapped a stylus...*pencil*...on the table-top. "Mother knows these people must be fighters, and we could use fighters. We must also presume they have no way to communicate. I propose we send a recon team with Matiran technology to enable us to work together. Any objections?"

Gryf allow his gaze to take in each person sitting around the table. Counter-arguments were helpful to have when making critical decisions, and right now he heard none.

"All right. Captain Solaris, you're the lead on this one. Draw up your proposed team list and present it to me in two Terr hours. The team must be ready to go by dark."

"Recommendations, sir?" Ora asked.

"Take only one other Matiran, someone with technical expertise in case they require a viscomm with Camp One." He compressed his lips. "Senior Medical Chief Dacian and Commander Roble are already assigned to the *Profetae*. Also, Nick might be viewed as an anathema by his own people because of his Gift."

"Understood." She made a note in her ever-present notebook. "I will submit my list for your approval within an hour, sir."

"Thank you, Captain. The other item on our agenda is what to do with James Trimble."

Graig's gaze strayed to the entrance. "Should Alex not have some say in this decision, sir?"

"She's busy." It was unlikely this answer would appease Graig.

"Too busy for this?" Graig persisted.

Was it so inconceivable to him that Alexandra had found something more important? Something that would make his friend spit like a fire viper. *Tread lightly, Helyg.* "She has some things to work out." Gryf touched his fingers to his heart to reassure Graig that she was safe.

It took Graig all of two seconds before his lip curled. Had he figured out where she was already? The black look on his friend's face said he had. Graig stood up with such force his

PROPHECY

stool toppled over, hitting the stone floor with a hollow clunk.

Graig turned on his heel and stormed toward the door. Gryf could order him back, but to what end? The situation wasn't ideal, yet it was still possible to work it to his favor. Provided he could get to Graig before he engaged Alexandra.

Half-way to the exit, Graig spun around. "Permission to speak freely, and off the record, Senior Captain," he ground out through his clenched teeth, hands knotted into fists at his side.

Here we go. Gryf sat back in his chair and fixed Graig with a steady gaze. "Permission granted, Senior Commander."

"The rules were set for a reason: *no one* on the range without my approval. You let her go out there—*alone*—against my explicit wishes, you dumb-ass."

Simone covered her face with her hands and slid down in her chair. Not difficult to figure out who was teaching Graig new and colorful English words.

Gryf turned his attention back as Graig continued his rant.

"I know you two can communicate telepathically, but don't you *dare* warn her that I'm coming." Seething, Graig stormed from the room. In the tunnel just beyond the entrance he gave the air an angry punch with his fist. "*Argh!*"

Simone peeked between her fingers. "I'm sorry. I never imagined he'd use such language on you."

"Peace, Simone. It's only the first time he's done so in English." Gryf blew a gust of air out between his lips. "All of you stay here. I'll try to catch him before he gets to the range."

Ora gave him a dubious look. It was unlikely she'd enforce his request for long, but she would delay the others for a few moments. And a few moments were all he needed to catch up with Graig and explain what was really going on.

Alex blew her overgrown bangs out of her eyes. Only six lousy puff balls remained in the chamber of her *telum* before she'd have to collect them all and try again. What she really wanted was to load her *telum* with *kagi* and shoot at....

Oh, God! What was she thinking? Coming out here alone was supposed to ease the anger, not inflame it. The concept of having taken in Kotas's hatred without realizing it didn't seem so farfetched anymore. Between that and her new-found Gift, she was a powder keg for a supernatural event of nuclear proportions.

Raising her *telum,* she breathed in and out as Graig had taught her. She applied pressure to the trigger. One shot...two.... Megan Trimble's face rose in front of the target. An involuntary twitch of her left arm sent the third shot wide.

"Argh!" Why didn't Graig have a punching bag somewhere on the range?

She froze. How long *had* she been here? Graig was going to be royally pissed if he caught her out here without his permission. He was such a stickler for his precious rules. She should call it quits and get back to camp before she was missed.

"Again, *disipula.*"

Her heart launched itself into her throat, and she spun around. Graig stood close behind her, his arms crossed over his chest. Busted. Why was he so damn good at the whole stone-face thing? How was she supposed to know how deeply she stood in the Roble shit pile?

She ground her teeth together hard enough to make their roots ache. "I can't do this, Graig. I'm too angry all the time."

He shrugged. "Anger happens."

Alex flung her hands in the air. "Don't you get it? I'm a ticking time bomb. At some point I'm going to explode, and when I do, I might kill one of *us!*"

No reaction, just more unnerving grey gaze. Then he reached out and lifted the *telum* from her hands. Setting the safety, he slid it across the ground to the base of the rock wall surrounding the range. She almost groaned out loud. What had she been thinking, waving the *telum* around like that? As far as stupid actions went, that one took the—

Graig moved fast, his hand closing hard over her wrist. Reflexively, she yanked her arm toward her to unbalance him, aiming a hard kick at his midriff. Graig evaded her foot, and she twisted free of his vise grip.

He came after her again in a heartbeat. She dodged another direct advance before he landed a well-placed kick to her side. An *oof* escaped her and she staggered. Graig swept her legs out from under her and she landed on her butt in the dirt. *Damn.*

"Have I taught you nothing, Bock?"

Her vision sharpened, and she curled her hands into fists. How dare he taunt her? She scrambled to her feet and circled him. *Time for a little offense.* She launched herself at him. It made no sense, and she had no plan other than to hurt him. Badly. She aimed, and the heel of her hand connected with the cartilage of Graig's nose with a satisfying crunch.

Graig staggered back, blood dripping from his nostrils. "Well, that was pretty chicken shit, now wasn't it?" He bent and drew a blade from his boot. A strange gleam lit his eyes. "Let's see you try that again."

"Do you have a death wish, Roble?" Had those words just come out of her mouth?

Graig smirked. "You couldn't kill me if your life depended on it."

Take him down. Kill him! She rushed forward, but before she touched him, Graig grabbed her, spun her one hundred eighty degrees and slammed her back against his chest. The cold flat of his blade pressed against her throat, and one of his legs was planted firmly between hers. If she moved, he would trip her up. Now what?

"Yield," he demanded.

Yeah, right. Not likely. She would get out of this and finish the job.

"Yield," he demanded again, impatience lacing his words.

Not on your life. Alex swung her free arm backward and grabbed his balls. Graig grunted, and loosened his hold just enough for her to twist free.

His knife was in her hand. How had that happened? *Don't give him time to recover.* She plowed into him, and they fell together. Graig stared up at her. A shout of laughter escaped her, and she raised the blade.

Something large broadsided her like a truck, knocking her off Graig. She landed on her back, and air whooshed from her lungs.

Gryf sat on her stomach, his hands pinning her wrists on

the dirt. "Fight it, Alexandra, long enough to let me in."

Anger roared through her with the force of a freight train. Panic rose, clogging her throat. Her gaze locked with Gryf's. "Can't escape it."

Gryf's soul burst from him, blinding her with its brilliance before it plunged into her chest. His soul enveloped hers, the anger pummeling him. Searing heat stole her breath, and her body arched with unexpected violence. A scream echoed in her mind, sounding frighteningly like Kotas's.

Then it was gone, the heat, the anger. Only Gryf's soul lingered before he too pulled away to return to his own body. Exhaustion crashed over her like a breaker on the shore. She gasped in rapid, ragged pants.

"Please tell me it's over." She couldn't manage more than a whisper.

His face relaxed, and a smile curved his mouth. He released her wrists. "I do hope so."

A small sob escaped her, and she reached for him. He leaned forward over her, and they clung to each other.

"Why am I so weak?"

Gryf stroked her hair. "Likely it's the effect of holding two souls in your body. We should probably avoid doing that again, okay?"

"Okay." Soul-to-soul encounters were much more pleasant done externally. Gryf propped himself up with his hands to look at her.

Alex swallowed. "Wa- was I possessed by...?" *Kotas.* She couldn't say his name. It might bring him back.

"Not exactly." Gryf cupped her cheek. "After you expressed concern that you'd taken in Kotas's memories and psyche, I spoke to Ora. She told me it was entirely possible. She was kind enough to remind me that there was nothing anyone could do, though your *anim tros* should have the knowledge."

"And you did."

"*Compa*, I had nothing until the moment I knocked you to the ground and sat on you."

The blood rushed from her head. "I almost *killed* Graig."

"Not even close."

"You saw what happened, right?" She frowned. *Come to*

think of it, Graig had gone down rather easily, even after her ball-grabbing move. "Did you guys set me up?"

Gryf quirked an eyebrow and shrugged.

"You did!" He had let Graig incite the anger until it reached near irrational rage before he came in to obliterate it. Alex pushed her hands against his chest. "You can let me up now, Gryf."

He obliged, offering her his hand. She took it only because he owed her for his deception. Graig sat on a nearby rock, holding his bloody nose. A sheen of sweat dotted his forehead. Yeah, she'd gotten him good. Best to get this over with quickly.

"Hey." She bit her lower lip.

"Where did you learnd that mube?" Graig asked. "It's not oned I taught you."

"My mom."

His eyes widened. "I hab imbense respect for your mudder."

Alex couldn't hide her smile. "Sorry about breaking your nose."

Graig gave her a cocky grin. "Dat wad the best brawl I'b had in a long timeb, *sora*."

She couldn't stop the chuckle that bubbled up. "May I heal it for you?"

He lowered his hand and nodded. In less than thirty seconds, she'd set everything back in place. He scrunched his nose a few times then leaned forward with a grimace. No matter how badly *that* body part hurt, she wasn't going to offer to heal it for him. He'd have to endure, or fix it himself.

Graig stood, a resolute look in his eyes. "Your enemy will show no mercy, Alex, and neither did I. I'd be a piss-poor teacher if I had. You may have been influenced by Kotas's anger, but the skill you displayed was entirely your own. I would be honored to fight at your side any day."

Her mouth fell open. He would? Wow.

"Alexandra Bock," Graig said. "You have earned the privilege to come to the range *unaccompanied*." He raised his left hand, fingers curled to his palm, touched the back of his thumb to his forehead and then to his heart, inclining his head in her direction.

Ectu belltur, the respect of warriors. A Matiran salute used between soldiers and warriors, and Graig had just honored *her* with it. She returned the honor with the requisite slow, deep inclination of her head.

Graig received his blade from Gryf, and it disappeared into his boot. "As much as I would like to say *my* ass-kicking went unnoticed, I am afraid that's not the case." He jerked his head in the direction of the entrance to the range. Simone, Nicky, Ora, and Dante were all there, watching. "I strive not to make mistakes, Alex," Graig continued. "Yet I made one today by not giving you full credit for your capabilities. You understand that won't happen again."

Oh, she knew all right. Today their relationship had changed. He'd given her his friendship out of duty, but now she'd earned his respect. And that felt good.

"I think Dante will want to check us both now." There was a smile in Graig's voice.

She swept her arm in the direction of the target. "What about the puff balls?"

A smug look crossed his face, and he gave a sharp whistle. Three camp children, Juan, Wilson, and Kunao, scampered onto the range. The boys immediately set to collecting the practice ammunition.

Well, that was just about right. "You think of everything, don't you?"

"I don't believe in doing things half-way, *sora*."

Alex smiled at him. "Thank you, *magister*, for not allowing me to wallow in self-pity."

"Thank you, *disipula*, for keeping me humble."

CHAPTER TWENTY-NINE

Gryf ran his palm over the silky smooth curve of Alexandra's bare shoulder. Her hair fanned over the pillow and her pale skin glowed in the soft light of the *lutep*. And, sweet Mother, her skin seemed to glow from their earlier love-making. His loins stirred.

"So, what did Admiral Cael have to say today?" she asked.

Not exactly the topic he wanted to pursue at the moment, but she was entitled to an answer. "Even though we were on a secure channel, we did not discuss details. Cael will handle the fleet. Our assignment is to disable and infiltrate the slaver."

"And free the prisoners?"

"Yes, and free the prisoners. If we fail, the fleet will do everything within their power to rescue the children and anyone else remaining at Camp One."

"Good. But we won't fail, Gryf. We can't."

He wanted to believe that, with all his heart. But he had been a soldier long enough to know the unpredictability of even the most carefully laid plans. "We can only do our best, *animi*."

Alexandra cupped his cheek, and the flame of desire flickered to life in her eyes. "For now—"

The chime of his personal comm cut her off.

"*Ska*. Only one person in the universe could have such timing." He leaned over the edge of the bed to grope through his discarded clothing. *Where in the hells is that comm?* His hand closed around the tiny device. *Ah.* "What is it, Ora?"

He hadn't meant to snap, but private time with his wife had been harder to come by since their first viscomm with the admiralty. Behind him, Alexandra snickered. He reached for the sleeping bag covering her and gave it a yank. She yelped and grabbed it back, her eyes narrowed in warning. Sweet Mother, he loved this woman.

"Gryf, we found them." Ora's voice came from his personal comm. "Or, more accurately, *they* found *us*."

"You're in San Francisco already?" He rolled himself into a sitting position on the edge of the bed. They had only left four days ago. Even on horseback, it should have taken a minimum of six days.

"No, we're in the great agricultural valley between Camp One and San Francisco. That is where they found us."

He exchanged a concerned look with Alexandra. "Any problems?" Perhaps it was more than he should hope for, but he had to ask.

"Nothing we could not handle," Ora replied.

This meant *something* had happened. Gryf frowned at Alexandra, and she made a calming motion with her hands.

"Their leader is Moises Alexander," Ora continued. "A former military man who knows how to keep people alive."

"How many are with him?"

"Seventy-eight." He heard the smile in Ora's voice. "All of them trained to handle weapons at a level even Graig would deem acceptable. Plus eleven untrained due to age or physical impairments. We are on our way to the rendezvous now."

His mouth fell open. Eighty-nine more people? This he hadn't expected. "Ora, I don't like this. It almost sounds as though they were expecting you."

"On my honor, *sobin*, these people are no threat."

"On her honor" and "cousin" in Matiran—the code words she was to use if all was well. So it must be. "All right. We will meet you at the rendezvous in six days. And, Ora...be safe, *sobin*."

◆ ◆ ◆ ◆ ◆

The silence of the empty tunnel surrounded Alex, and she rolled her shoulders as she approached the operations room. The camp was so much quieter now that eighty percent of the refugees had migrated to the mine. Tonight's group was ready to depart after dinner. It was hard to believe she'd be leaving in four more days with the final group. Damn, she would miss the kids.

She ducked through the operations room entrance, ready to absorb more silence. After a week of upheaval, she needed a break. A few minutes to reenergize before she jumped back into the chaos.

"*Hola*, Alex."

Her gaze darted in the direction of the unexpected voice. *Crap*. Were a few moments of alone time too much to ask for? "Hi, Kelly. You ready to leave tonight?"

"Pretty much," the other woman replied, her feet propped on a table, ankles crossed.

Now would be a good time to clear the air. Despite their differences of opinions, they were on the same side in this war. "Look, Kelly, I'm sorry about attacking you the other day."

Kelly waved her hand in a dismissive gesture. "Ancient history. I understand you weren't quite yourself."

"No, but that's not an excuse."

"It's not your normal MO either, so don't worry."

This was too easy. Kelly must have an agenda; she always did.

"You can sit if you want." Kelly gestured to a vacant camp chair.

Want, yes. Want with Kelly around, not so much. Alex's wariness warred with her need to take a load off for a few minutes. She allowed an internal sigh. It wasn't as though she couldn't defend herself if Kelly attacked her. And Kelly wasn't that stupid. Alex sank down into a chair away from the table, and swallowed a groan. Cripes, it felt wonderful to be off her feet.

"I *am* wondering," Kelly said. *Here we go.* "What do you plan to do about *her*?"

"Her?" Kelly would, of course, be referring to K'rona. Kelly hated the Anferthians in the way Sarah O'Conner hated the Terminator. And it appeared she was also a vendetta-wielding stalker.

"The 'Ferth woman you've become so chummy with." This time Kelly's voice dripped acid.

Bingo. "I'm not sure what you're getting at, Kelly. K'rona is on our side, and has proved herself a valuable asset to us."

Kelly dropped her feet to the floor. "She's an Anferthian—an *alien*. She can't be trusted. She'll turn on you, you know. And when she does, we're all screwed."

Talk about having your words come back and bite you in the butt. Had she really felt the same way about aliens once upon a time? What an idiot she'd been. But that was before Gryf...and soul mating...and the *Profeti*. Before she'd fallen in love with an alien and bound herself to him in ways deeper and more profound than she'd ever imagined.

Kelly didn't have that experience. All she had was her bitterness and guilt over the death of her son. It was a devastating story, but who in camp didn't have a similar one? They'd all lost everything they'd ever known. And Alex wasn't Dr. Phil; she couldn't fix *everybody*'s problems. Kelly would have to find her own peace.

Alex blew out a sigh. "You know, I came in here to get away for a few minutes."

"I just knew you had sold out." Kelly's words were laced with bitterness. "You've bought into the whole prophecy thing. You think you're 'the great voice of your people'." She threw air quotes around that with her fingers. "You've been blinded by what you've been told by *aliens* and have ignored what's best for *your people*."

"Are you kidding me?" She gaped at the insanity of Kelly's words. She could almost hear her mother say, *"Close your mouth, Alex, sweetie."*

Kelly slammed her fist on the table. "Do I *look* like I'm kidding? You're their sheep, Alex, and they're leading you—*us*—to slaughter!"

Alex compressed her lips. *Don't let her get to you. Remain calm.* No, nix that. She needed to get away from Kelly and her brand of poison, fast. "Let me give you the cold, hard facts, Kelly. Without the Matirans—and even the Anferthian dissenters—we have *zero* chance of taking back our planet. We simply do not have the resources or people to do so.

"As for K'rona, I don't plan to *do* anything about her. She sees our goal, and shares it. She is willing to fight to the death for it. The real question is, what will you do? Do *you* stand with your people?"

PROPHECY

Kelly's eyes glittered with malice. "I am with *my* people until we have our planet back. After that, the rest can all go to hell. And you, Alex, are *not* my voice."

"I can live with that." And she could. Her goal was to free her planet and spare Gryf's from the same fate. There were plenty of people in the universe who were not happy about that idea already—namely the players on the opposing team. "For the record, I haven't bought into anything, Kelly. I never asked for any of this. Once this is over, I intend to live a quiet life with my husband."

Kelly barked a short laugh. "You won't live that long. They'll make sure of it."

There was no getting through to someone who didn't want to listen. Alex pushed out of her chair. "I gotta go, Kelly. See ya."

She stomped up the tunnel to the main cavern, and paused. Gryf would want to know about that little conversation, and K'rona would need an extra person or two for protection. She wasn't going to like that, but tough. Since joining Camp One, the Anferthian factoress had become something more to Alex than just a dissenter. She'd become a friend.

◆ ◆ ◆ ◆ ◆

Alex sat on the ground outside the main cave. She sighted down the inside of her *telum,* making sure it was clean and clear, then reloaded her *kagi.* Tonight was it. She'd leave at full dark with Gryf, Nicky, Graig, Alta, LaShawn, and K'rona. The final group.

I'm going to miss this place.

Around her, the others prepared for departure. The late afternoon sun was warm, the atmosphere subdued. Nicky sat a short distance from her sharpening his knife. He'd grown up. Become a man through circumstance. And she was so proud of that man, although her heart grieved for the abrupt loss of his youth.

"Miss Alex?" Thin, pale freckled arms snaked around Alex's neck from behind, and a bright red head pressed against hers. *Ah, Flora.* And where Flora was.... Maggie slipped into Alex's lap and snuggled. This was one of life's happy moments. If only she could've clung to it for all eternity. Holding these girls in her arms brought her peace and contentment, and she could almost forget what lay ahead. Almost.

"Hey, girls." She kissed each of their heads.

"I wish you didn't have to leave," Flora declared, her voice small and sad.

"I know." Alex swallowed against the lump in her throat. "Me too. I'll miss you both."

"Maggie wants to know if you'll come back. I told her you would."

Since Maggie had yet to utter a word, it wasn't a stretch to figure out which of them really wanted to know.

"I hope so, Maggie." She wasn't going to make promises, not about this. The girls would know it rang false anyway, and they deserved better than that.

Flora snuggled against her side, and Alex drew her into the protective circle of her arm. "You girls listen to Miss Li-Min, Grandma Beck, and the other adults who are staying behind, okay?"

"Except for Mr. Trimble," Flora said. "We know he's a bad man."

Maggie nodded vigorously.

Alex stroked Maggie's dark curls. "He's not *bad*, really. He's just scared. Sometimes people make wrong choices when they're scared. Captain Gryf and the rest of us will do everything we can to get his daughter back to him."

"Will that make him not scared again?"

"He will be better." But never not scared. James Trimble would live in fear for his daughter's life until the day he died.

"At least he has his family still." Flora's blue eyes tracked K'rona as the Anferthian woman walked the perimeter of the gathered Terrians and Matirans.

It was time to plant another seed. "We're lucky to have K'rona and her dissenters, Flora. With all the information they've given us, and the risks they've taken...our attack on the slaver wouldn't be possible without their help."

Flora remained silent, as expected. Would her words germinate and take root in the young girl's mind?

"Look, Miss Alex." Flora pointed up at a dark spot making

lazy circles above the camp. "Is that a bald eagle?"

Alex blinked, and a slow sense of wonder filled her. "It sure is, Flora."

If there was such a thing as a good omen, this was it. Five minutes later, the bird of prey disappeared beyond a stand of pines, and the girls excused themselves to finish saying their goodbyes to the other adults.

Alex studied the deep alpine-blue sky. Somewhere not too far away, the Matiran Defense Fleet lay in wait for their signal. It was wishful thinking that everything would go perfectly. Glitches were inevitable, and once the attack began, there would be no going back.

And no time to grieve the fallen until it was over.

But she was a warrior for her people now. A scared warrior. How did Gryf, Ora, and Graig deal with the gnawing fear? Or Gunner and his platoon? They were all trained soldiers, so they must have their ways. Little rituals, maybe? Good luck charms? A lot of prayer?

"Miss Alex?"

Alex turned her head toward the small voice. Juan stood a few steps from her. This brave little boy had never known a family. He'd been a foster child until the Anferthians unwittingly freed him from the system. What would happen to him if they were successful in routing the invaders?

Juan's bottom lip trembled. *Oh!* She opened her arms, and he collapsed into her embrace.

"We've been through a lot together, haven't we?" She stroked his dark hair as she rocked him.

Juan nodded against her shoulder. "I'm sorry, Miss Alex."

She tilted her head to one side and frowned. "For what?"

"For what happened in the meadow."

There were tears in his voice, and she pushed him back far enough to make eye contact. "That was *not* your fault, Juan. You were tricked, and I'm not angry with you. In fact, I'm very relieved that you're safe."

He nodded and sniffled, but doubt lingered in his eyes. What could she say or do to convince him?

Nothing.

"Promise me one thing." She waited for him to nod again.

"Don't blame yourself. You are a good person, and you're going to grow up into a fine young man. I want you to focus on growing up to be that man, okay?"

"I will, Miss Alex," he promised. "Will you be careful too?"

"You have my word, Juan."

He leaned in again, and she hugged him close.

CHAPTER THIRTY

Alex gazed at the gold and orange wisps of clouds glowing in sunset. Their first day at Silver Valley Mine had been grueling. Plans reviewed, revised and reviewed again ad nauseam. Assignments dispersed, weapons cleaned and loaded, target practice. The quiet and solitude of the Sierra foothills, and the toasty warmth from the rock under her bottom, were her reward for the tedium.

But even though her day was done, Gryf's wasn't—not by a long shot. When she'd left him an hour ago, he'd had a strange gleam in his eyes as Mitch explained how gel pack explosives worked. One corner of her mouth twitched. Guys and blowing stuff up—a universal phenomenon.

There wasn't much else to do but make herself comfortable while she waited.

She raised her gaze. The first stars already twinkled in the indigo sky above. What was it like out there in space? Would she get a chance to see it for herself?

The hair at the back of her neck prickled. Someone was close by, and it wasn't Gryf. She turned her head to look over her shoulder. Moises Alexander, San Francisco resistance leader extraordinaire, stood several yards from her, his face raised to view the stars. She'd met him after she'd arrived this morning, and had been impressed with his humble demeanor. For a man who'd pulled nearly a hundred people out from under the Anferthians' noses, he seemed so calm. The man was a freaking hero, yet his attitude and appearance weren't at all super-heroesque. He was probably in his early fifties. Definitely Latino in heritage. Trim, but not tall—a good couple of inches shorter than herself, in fact. Handsome, with a deep tan and salt-and-pepper hair brushed back from his face.

And no cape. A grin tugged at the corners of her mouth.

"They look different from space," he said.

"What? The stars?" Now how would he know that?

He looked at her, his dark eyes twinkling. "Yes. Or so I'm told. I do wonder about it, don't you?"

"Yeah." Did she ever.

"Don't worry, you'll find out."

"Are you a resistance leader *and* a psychic, Moises?"

He chuckled. "No. My parents instilled in me unusual amounts of common sense."

"And courage."

Moises tipped his head to one side, almost exactly like Gryf. His expression was far-away and reminiscent. "Yes, they had uncommon courage." He blinked, and gave her a smile. "I hope a little of it rubbed off on me."

"I think it did." She patted the rock next to her. "Want to sit?"

"Only if you're up for company."

A soft snicker escaped her. "I already have company. K'rona's around here somewhere, standing guard over me while Gryf and Graig play with explosives."

Moises grinned. "Then I'd love to sit." He moved around the rock and sat next to her. They gazed at the stars for a few minutes before he pointed up. "You will go there because you are the *Profeta*."

"Oh, really?"

"Well, that's less intimidating than saying you'll go there because you have to meet your in-laws."

Ooh, yeah. There was that. She did admire her father-in-law, but Gryf's mom was an unknown entity. Gryf and Ora had both insisted Charise was a warm, wonderful woman, and Alex hoped she'd get to meet her. "How about you, Moises? Do you see yourself going out there?"

"I hope so." The far-away look was back.

"Traveling in space would be pretty interesting. Boldly going where no man...okay, *Earthling*, has gone before." A small spark caught in her heart at the thought. "Do you *really* think I'll go out there, Moises?"

"Alex, my star child, I have no doubt."

PROPHECY

───◆ ◆ ◆ ◆───

Gryf crouched on the floor of the narrow control corridor aboard the Anferthian slaver. Never had he wanted to come back to this place, yet here he was. And this time not only were Alexandra and Graig with him, but also Dante, Nick, and K'rona. Their assignment: to escort the unsuspecting Premiere Warden D'etta off the slaver and into the custody of the Matiran Defense Fleet. Hopefully, without being discovered, and having the Anferthians attempt to lift off from the planet's surface. It would be preferable not to have to use the explosives to cripple the slaver.

"Just like old times," Graig muttered, his gaze moving around the control corridor as though watching for any sign of foul play.

Betrayal from the dissenters did not concern Gryf as much as Alexandra's current frame of mind. He couldn't sense any misgivings from her through their soul link, so perhaps she didn't remember the last time she'd been in this room as they made their escape.

He studied her profile. She had become adept at concealing her thoughts from her face. Graig's training was above reproach, but had he managed to turn this Terrian healer into a true soldier? All indications pointed to success. This would be her final test.

He reached up and smoothed his hand over her hair. *Are you well?*

Her look turned quizzical. *Of course. Why?*

This is the place we hid during our escape.

Oh. She looked around the cramped space then she shook her head. *I don't remember.*

That was good. Gryf gave K'rona the signal to proceed, and the Factoress crept past him to the closed maintenance hatch. She scratched her fingernails across the floor in front of it, sounding uncannily like a scampering rodent. Twice more she did this then a noise came from the other side of the hatchway.

This was it. The moment of truth. He raised his *telum*, and the others followed his lead. The latching mechanism on the hatch whirred, and the door fanned opened. Ita peered through. Relief flashed across her face, and she hugged K'rona. Gryf reached for Alexandra's hand, weaving his fingers through hers. Then they followed the Anferthian dissenters into the main part of the ship.

◆ ◆ ◆ ◆

Alex's eyes moved constantly, taking in every inch of the corridor. It was only a matter of time before something went wrong. She fixed her gaze on the back of Gryf's head. Of course, there was an equal chance they'd make it through the entire ship to the Premiere Warden's war room without incident. If they were lucky.

Prickles of warning ran over her scalp. Something hit her shoulder hard, slamming her to the ground. On her back, she looked up into the aquamarine gaze of her first "oh, shit" moment of the day.

Haesi's eyes would be exquisite, if not for the murderous intent in them. The Matiran woman raised a jagged-edged blade of lethal beauty, its hilt the same shade as its wielder's eyes.

The blade flashed downward toward Alex's throat. She shot her hand up to intercept Haesi's wrist, but before she made contact, the Matiran woman was gone. *What?*

Gryf landed on top of her, forcing a whoosh of air out between her lips.

"Stay down," he ordered.

"No problem." Alex turned her head.

Graig tussled on the floor with the bitch from hell. He'd said he would kill her if the opportunity arose, but would he really?

Alex pushed against Gryf's chest with her hands, and he growled. *You will stay down, animi. Haesi's a knife thrower.*

"But...."

No!

"Haesi!" Graig tore down the corridor like a maniac. Haesi had broken free, her lithe form disappearing around a corner.

Gryf covered Alex's ears. "*Roble!*"

His battlefield command voice rumbled through her like a military jet buzzing a building. Cripes, he could bellow.

Graig stopped dead in his tracks, his fists balled at his sides. He turned back to face his captain, air hissing through his teeth.

"Let her go, Graig. There will be another time." This time Gryf spoke gently, as a friend.

Graig's jaw worked, and he clenched and unclenched his fists half a dozen times before nodding. His gaze flicked to Alex.

"I'm okay." She pushed on Gryf's shoulders. "Get off me, you big lug."

A strange vibration began under her back, and Gryf froze. "The engines are powering up."

Alex met Gryf's gaze. They were about to find out if the dynamite they'd used would cripple the slaver, or blow it to hell with them inside.

K'rona breathed what sounded like a curse word in Anferthian.

"Everyone down," Gryf roared.

The others hit the deck just as the first explosions went off.

CHAPTER THIRTY-ONE

The wall scoped open, and Alex gripped the edge of the doorway. The slaver now listed to port, its legs apparently useless. She entered a cavernous, circular chamber with the others.

It looks more like a royal audience chamber than a war room.

At the heart of the room stood an immense Anferthian man, watching them with pale-amber eyes. He raised one hand, setting off a multitude of soft clinks as the medals decorating his black uniform bumped against each other.

"Hold your fire," he growled at the soldiers lining the wall behind him.

Alex raised her eyebrows. She risked a glance at Gryf. *Premiere Warden D'etta, I presume?*

Gryf gave her a slight nod. His tightly controlled emotions roiled beneath his calm exterior. She couldn't blame him. The last time Gryf had stood in this room, D'etta had forced him to watch the destruction of the world he was charged to protect.

The premier's hair may have once been light brown, but now it was streaked with liberal amounts of grey. He wore it in the traditional *tirik*, his ears hidden under the thick mane. Why all the Anferthian males covered their ears and the females didn't was a mystery. She'd have to ask K'rona about that sometime.

D'etta's eyes narrowed. "I have been expecting you, Senior Captain Helyg."

I just bet he has. How could he not after the explosives had crippled his ship, making takeoff impossible?

"Ah, K'rona, my dear. Welcome back to *fyhen*, sweet niece." Nice words made completely worthless by the scowl he gave K'rona.

Swell guy.

K'rona's eyes narrowed. "I am not part of your own, Premiere Warden. Your abusive treatment of me turned me against you years ago. You are not worthy of many titles, including Uncle."

Rage suffused the Premiere Warden's face. "You are a disgrace to your family—a traitor! I gave you *everything*. I even stopped visiting when you took that simpering Mendiko as your lover." He stopped suddenly, as though remembering he wasn't alone. Several of his guards stared at him with narrow-eyed disgust. A few had paled to near-white.

Alex's heart jumped to her throat. *Gryf.*

Steady, compa.

Alex clenched her teeth. *But, he molested her. Maybe even raped her.*

Another reason we are here.

"Mendiko and I have stood against you for years," K'rona bit back.

The slick smile crept back onto D'etta's face. "Then his execution was necessary. How sad there are no other traitors here to help you now."

A full two-thirds of the Anferthian guards turned their weapons on D'etta and his compatriots. Alex also directed her *telum* at the Premiere Warden, relief coursing through her. The dissenters had managed to infiltrate the Premiere's personal guard.

D'etta's face darkened, and he raised his own *fusil* in K'rona's direction. One of the dissenters broadsided him, knocking him to the floor. His *fusil* discharged, but the shot went wide.

Pain exploded through Alex, and something warm and wet hit the side of her face.

Ska. Gryf's voice echoed in her mind.

She sank to her knees. *I've been shot?* God, she hurt.

The premier rolled to his feet, *fusil* in hand. He again raised his weapon in K'rona's direction, but she wasn't looking at him. Instead, she gazed over her shoulder, an expression of abject horror on her face.

Alex touched the trigger of her weapon. The whispered hiss of the projectile seemed at odds with the resulting violent explosion of blood and grey matter. D'etta's body stiffened then slumped to the floor.

Gryf had warned her that her first kill would be hard, but it hadn't been. Shouldn't she feel some sort of remorse, or be puking her guts out? There was none of that, only the searing pain in her chest. She raised her fingers to the source of her pain, but her hand came away clean and dry. What the hell?

K'rona grabbed her by the shoulders. "It is not you."

If not her, why did she hurt so badly? Unless.... Her mouth went bone dry, and she whipped her head around.

Behind her, Dante and Nicky dragged Gryf away from the fray. Blood from the hole in his chest soaked his shirt.

A scream tore from her soul like a wounded animal, and she scrambled forward. Her feet slipped, and she slammed spread-eagled to the floor, air whooshing from her lungs with the force of the impact. She blinked at the trail of blood under her. Gryf's blood. *God, no. Please.*

Graig hauled her up by the back of her shirt and slid her across the smooth surface into Nicky's arms. Her brother pushed her into a sitting position near Gryf's head. Dante's cupped hands glowed bright over the wound, desperation etched into his face. This couldn't be happening.

Alex took Gryf's face between her hands. "No. Not yet, Gryf. It's not time yet, my heart. My soul."

"There's a medical bay just down the corridor," K'rona said.

"No time," Dante replied. He gave Alex a look of devastation. "He's almost gone." Once Gryf was gone, there would be nothing Dante could do to stop her own demise. Not that she cared. Without Gryf, her life would have no purpose.

Something cold and familiar slithered down her spine, and her eyes were drawn across the room. The shrouded grey figure next to the body of the Premiere Warden watched her. Then it took a step forward.

A sharp chill settled over her like a mantle, and her chest tightened. *No. Not again.* If she didn't come up with something fast, all hope would be lost with the deaths of the

Profetae. She refused to do that to their peoples.

"N-Nicky." Her teeth chattered as she grabbed her brother's arm. So cold. "H-h-hook in with D-Dante, and k-keep Gryf breathing."

"What are you planning?" Nicky asked.

She held her shaking hands above Dante's. "T-t-to c-catch something."

"*Sora*, the tremors...."

"B-b-blank-kets, Graig. K-keep me warm." She would be using every ounce of herself to hold Gryf in this world. Consigning her body to Graig's keeping was the only way she could focus on saving her husband.

"There are blankets in medical," K'rona said. "What else do you need, Healer?"

Graig gripped her shoulders as though his strength alone could keep her anchored in this life. Dante's voice faded from her hearing. All that mattered was the pale blue light with a crystal white center, rising now from Gryf's chest. She cupped her hands around his soul, and drew it toward her heart. Once he was in place, she met Dante's wide eyes. "Two souls in one body doesn't work well, but I will hold him as long as I can."

Understanding flashed across his face, and he nodded. She curved her body inward to protect Gryf's life force. All her energy focused on the place he occupied next to her own soul. *God, please let this work.*

"What is she doing?" K'rona asked.

"Buying us time." Dante's voice was incredulous.

Gryf.

Alexandra.

He was cognizant, thank God. *You're safe for the moment. I'm not letting you get away that easily.*

What happened?

The Premiere Warden tried to shoot K'rona, and hit you instead.

Forever has he been a notoriously poor shot. Is K'rona safe?

Yes. Dante's going to surgically remove the...oh, cripes, whatever an Anferthian kagi *is called. Nicky's working with him.*

Then we're in the best hands.

A wave of hopelessness crashed over her. What if all this was a farce? What if the damage was too extensive and they couldn't be saved? And if Gryf died, would she slip away with him, or would she have a moment to warn the others? The two of them were about to die together in the most literal way, and she so wasn't ready for this.

It can't be over yet, Gryf. There's too much left to do. Free the prisoners, rescue the slaves, negotiate with the Anferthians to keep their freaking hands off Earth and Matir. Hot tears slipped out from under her closed eyelids, burning their paths over her cheeks.

Peace, Alexandra. Maybe all we were supposed to do was start the process for others to carry on.

"Sora." Graig's worried voice was at her ear. "Is Gryf still with you?"

She opened her eyes. She was curled on her side now, a blanket under her and another over. Definitely warmer, but tremors still rocked her. Dante was well into the surgery, and Nicky sat astride her husband's abdomen, his dark head bowed, eyes closed and glowing hands on Gryf's rib cage. Beyond them, the dissenters appeared to have subdued D'etta's men and were watching.

"He's here." She touched her fingertips to her heart. "Safe for the moment."

"Why are you crying?"

She turned so she could see his face. "If we don't make it, Graig, please don't give up. Don't let anyone give up."

"I won't, *sora*, but this isn't where it will end." He sounded so certain, but how could he be sure? "If you could see your face right now, you'd know too. Your eyes are glowing with your Gift, and you have that inflexible set to your jaw when you're determined to get your way."

He didn't understand. She glanced at the dark figure closing on them. "Death is here. I know you can't see it, but I can. It's standing where Gryf was shot."

Graig glanced across the room then back. "It doesn't matter. You fight to win, Alex."

He's right. Gryf agreed.

PROPHECY

She looked at Gryf's body. His face was chalky, and so pale. She reached out and placed her hand on his bicep. If she had any energy to spare, she'd flood him with healing.

Death moved another step closer. A cold sweat broke out above her lip, and her stomach clenched. It was better to close her eyes and sink into the comfort of Gryf's presence than to watch it approach.

Her concentration faltered. She was sinking under a blanket of exhaustion. *I'm starting to feel the drain, Gryf.* Supporting both their souls was becoming too difficult for her body. How much longer did they have?

Alexandra, will you do something for me? Gryf asked.

Anything.

Sing a song for me.

Have you lost your ever-loving mind?

Gryf's amusement warmed her. *Not completely, yet.*

What song?

Any song. I just want your voice to be the last thing I hear if things don't go well.

A moment later, Graig said, "She's singing." She'd never heard him speak with such awe.

"What song?" Dante's question was followed by a plink of metal against metal. Probably the *kagi* dropping to the floor.

"The airship song the children love." Graig's tone was now amused.

"I'm closing. Nick, he needs a massive regeneration of red and white blood cells stat."

"On it," Nicky replied.

"Alex, Gryf," Graig murmured in her ear, and she slitted her eyes open. "We're almost ready. Just hang on a little longer."

Her hand slid slowly off Gryf's bicep, as though it were now lead instead of flesh and blood. She stared at it, limp on the floor, for a couple of heartbeats. It seemed too much effort to put it back. Instead, she continued to sing under her breath.

Between one breath and the next, Gryf was gone. A strangled cry escaped her, and she sat bolt upright, her head catching Graig under his chin. Nicky's eyes popped open, and he shot her an alarmed look.

The light of Gryf's soul floated above his own heart. Death stood just beyond Nicky's shoulder, its cupped hands reaching between her brother and Dante to pluck Gryf away.

"Whoa, shit!" Nicky jerked back. He must be able to see Death's hands too. "Grab him, Alex! Now!"

Even as she launched herself from where she sat, there was no way she could stop Death. It was too late.

Gryf opened his eyes. Nick sat on his stomach, grinning down at him.

"Welcome back, brother-in-law."

Gryf frowned and raised his head. "What happened?"

"Don't move, Gryf," Dante ordered. "If you don't let me finish, you will bleed out internally and undo everything Alex did to save you."

He gave Dante a nod then turned his head to his right. *What in all the hells?*

Graig straddled an unconscious Alexandra, his glowing hands resting on her shoulders. Ora knelt at her head, bent close, with her fingertips pressed to Alexandra's temples.

"It isna wha' it looks like, Captain," Nick said in an odd, thick accent, a mischievous glint in his eyes.

"Nick, stay on those blood cells," Dante warned.

"I haven't stopped," Nick replied, not sounding the least chastised. "Close your eyes and relax, bro. She's okay. She just needed a double dose of *parvirtu* after holding onto you so long. You'll both be all patched up in a few more minutes. After that, we'll fill you in."

All Gryf could do was nod again. Sweet Mother he ached. If he did not know the truth of the matter, he would've sworn he'd been hit by a maintenance shuttle. He allowed his eyes to drift shut. Dante had said to be still, not quiet. "Report?"

"You just don't quit, do you?" Nick muttered.

Gryf permitted his smile to surface.

"The admiralty reports their campaign to be mostly successful," Karise began in her no-nonsense style. She and Ora were safe, thank the Mother. "Five of the eight Anferthian warships have surrendered, and two were crippled beyond usefulness during battle."

"Effing A," Nick muttered. Whatever that meant.

Karise continued, "Two slavers from the surface have escaped and are fleeing in the general direction of Anferthia, along with the remaining warship. Admiral Cael's cruiser, *Olympias,* is already in pursuit with half the Defense Fleet. Admiral Marenys awaits the arrival of the *Profetae* before he too sets course for Anferthia. A transport will be here shortly. And, sir," Karise inhaled deeply. "Defense Fleet Cruiser *Polarus* will be the escort ship for the *Atlantis.*"

Gryf snapped his eyes open. *Atlantis?* His ship was intact? Spaceworthy? And his father's cruiser would travel with her—as her escort, no less. A great honor.

"Yeah, you heard that right." Nick's grin was wider than before. "And by the way, you now have a full count of red and white blood cells. Glad you chose to hang around with us a little longer."

"Thank you for making sure I could."

"I wasn't the one who snatched your soul from the hands of Death. Literally." Nick jutted his chin in Alexandra's direction. "Everything Dante and I did would've been for nothing if not for Alex. By the time we got the dog pile of people off your chest, you were breathing on your own again."

Gryf drew his brows together. What in all the hells was a dog pile? He shook aside the question and met Dante's gaze. The healer shrugged. "She will be all right, Gryf, fear not."

Closing his eyes, Gryf swallowed around the hard lump in his throat. *Dearest Mother, thank you for gifting me this amazing woman as my soul mate.*

Nick's weight disappeared from Gryf's abdomen, and he took in a deep breath then exhaled, before opening his eyes.

"That should do it." Ora straightened and gave him a severe look. "We must stop trying to die on each other, *sobin.*"

"I couldn't agree more."

Dante laid a hand on Gryf's shoulder. "Now go thank your wife for saving your soul."

Gryf turned his head. Alexandra watched him from where she lay at his side, a smile curving her lips.

"Ah, Mother." He rolled toward her and pulled her hard into his embrace.

CHAPTER THIRTY-TWO

This is chaos. Gryf suppressed his irritation as he strode through the mass of humanity outside the slaver. A transport had landed, disgorging the remaining refugees from Camp One, per Admiral Cael's orders. Despite the brief yet frustrating delay, it was logical to gather together as many Terrians as possible in one place. If the negotiations went sour, a hasty evacuation would be necessary.

Maggie clung to him, her skinny arms tight around his neck. Thank the Mother he'd had time to wash up in the slaver's medical bay. The child did not need to know how close he'd come to dying barely an hour ago.

Gryf ground his teeth together. Nick had once explained a fictional device in Terrian folklore called a transporter beam. If only such technology were possible, they would be underway by now.

Every moment that passed put more distance between them and the Anferthian ships on the run. While Admiral Cael and the pursuing Matiran fleet should be able to overtake and stop them, the fact remained that the Anferthians would only be willing to negotiate with a Terrian for the Terrian hostages. And the greatest chance of successful negotiations lay with Alexandra. The *Profeta*. Those were her people, and she wanted them back. Alive.

His gaze lit on two people standing together just beyond the main group. James Trimble and his daughter Megan. Their father-daughter reunion could not be easy. Megan said something to her father then placed her hand over her womb. They stood facing each other before James folded his daughter into his embrace.

The poor girl. Fifteen Terrian cycles and pregnant with the

offspring of an alien traitor. It would be difficult for them. However, there was hope. Perhaps this child would be the first visible sign of their worlds becoming one.

Heavenly Mother, please don't let it take after its sire.

A small hand touched Gryf's face, and suddenly nothing seemed as important as the petite, green-eyed child in his arms.

"No go," Maggie whispered.

Gryf curved his mouth up. "So you do have words, *puella.*" The Mother be praised. This knowledge would bring tears to Alexandra's eyes, and joy to her heart.

Maggie's bottom lip trembled.

"Shh, sweet Maggie. Nothing could keep me away from you for long." Gryf wiped a tear from her cheek with the pad of his thumb. "Will you promise me something now?" She nodded. "Promise that when I return, you will keep talking? I want to hear everything you have to say."

Maggie threw her arms around his neck and squeezed. Why was he in such a hurry to leave?

"There you are, Senior Captain Helyg." Moises's greeting cut through the tender moment. "The Earthling translators are onboard the transport. You'll be leaving in about five minutes."

"Excellent news, and congratulations on your new appointment, Lead Councilor Alexander." Gryf gave him a quick grin.

Moises cringed at the reference to his newly acquired title as the head of the hastily seated Terr council. "*Temporary* Lead Councilor Alexander, until they find another sucker to take the job permanently. Come on, Maggie. Let's find Li-Min. The sooner Captain Gryf leaves, the sooner he can come home."

Gryf kissed Maggie's cheek and transferred her to Moises. As they walked away, moving with the others to a safe distance from the transport, Gryf rubbed his chest over his heart. Home. He liked the sound of that.

Are you okay? Alexandra's question filtered gently into his mind.

He turned and found her a fair distance away, standing near the rear of the transport. She must have felt his emotion.

I'm fine, animi. Have you seen Ora?

She's over by the oak tree on the other side of the transport.

Odd place for her. Gryf gave his soul mate a nod. *I'll meet you on board.*

I'll be waiting. Alexandra blew him a kiss, and he touched his cheek as if it had landed there. Then he ducked under the belly of the transport and immediately located Ora, exactly where Alexandra said she would be. Alone under a tree, gazing out across the valley.

"Ora?"

Her head moved slightly in his direction, but she didn't respond. Something was amiss.

"*Sobin.*" He stopped in front of her, but she still kept staring out over the valley. Her eyelashes were damp, and her nose red. What could possibly make a woman as strong as his cousin cry? "What has happened, Ora?"

She shook her head then whispered, "Bodie didn't make it."

◆ ◆ ◆ ◆

Alex shook her head at her reflection then smoothed her hands down the front of her dress. The sage-green gown had an almost medieval cut. The square neckline fell just below her collarbone, and long, fitted sleeves ended in a point over the backs of her hands. A cream-colored sash hung slightly loose around her waist, accentuating her curves. Very plain and unassuming, which was the point. After all, she represented a people who had lost everything. Karise had even nixed accessories, except for Alex's wedding ring.

She turned away from the mirror, her gaze drawn to Gryf's bed...their bed...which they hadn't even had a chance to test out since arriving aboard the *Atlantis* four days ago. Granted, she'd suffered gravity sickness during the transport ride and hadn't been in the mood the first day. But since then, debriefings, strategic planning, diplomatic and foreign policy training, a crash course in the art of negotiating, and garment fittings had occupied her days. It was no wonder she was practically asleep when she fell into bed every night.

"Maybe tonight." But that wasn't even certain. Now that

PROPHECY

they'd caught up to where the rest of the fleet surrounded the Anferthian ships, it was time to negotiate for the lives of her people. If she was successful in convincing the Anferthians to return the captive Earthlings, she'd probably be up all night caring for the refugees.

On the other hand, there was always the possibility that the Anferthians would decide to blow up the slavers and plunge the three worlds into war. A shiver ran down her arms. She must tread very carefully today, because neither Earth nor Matir could afford that.

She let her gaze sweep the bedroom. Gryf had excellent taste. Although sparsely furnished with only a bed, dresser, and desk, the entire cabin was done in relaxing greys, blues, and creams.

The door chimed, and a soft feminine voice announced the caller. "*Admiral* Roble."

Alex gave her head a shake and rolled her eyes. So her escort to the negotiations had given himself a promotion. "Well, let the *Admiral* in."

She moved into the living area as the door opened and Graig stepped inside. Crossing her arms over her chest, she gave him the stink eye. "You didn't happen to do a little work on our announcer, did you?"

"I can't imagine what you're talking about," Graig replied, a mischievous twinkle in his eye.

"Hm, I bet you can't." She twisted her mouth into a teasing smirk. "By the way, you clean up *almost* as nicely as Gryf."

Gryf had looked like an Earth girl's hot-hunk-from-outer-space fantasy before leaving for the bridge thirty minutes ago. His ankle-length navy-blue cape draped over the standard grey uniform, held in place at one shoulder by his broach of rank. Somewhat reminiscent of a Trojan warrior's cape. Shiny black calf-hugging boots completed the look. No doubt about it, the Matiran full dress uniform was a thing of art.

"I *almost* take that as a compliment." The man never missed a beat. "And you look every bit the *Profeta*."

"I look like an extra from The Lord of the Rings."

Graig raised his brows. "This time I really don't have a clue what you're talking about, Alex."

"Oh, so you admit to fiddling with our announcer?"

"I admit nothing," he replied coolly, offering his arm. "Shall we?"

Alex swallowed, her throat suddenly dry. In fifteen minutes, she'd be face-to-face with the Anferthian Supreme Warden. Cripes, how was she going to pull this off? She rested her hand on Graig's arm. She couldn't fail; the survivors of Earth—her people—were depending on her.

Graig covered her hand with his. "Don't worry, *sora*, you will do fine."

"I hope so."

Tapping his personal comm, he said, "Senior Captain Helyg, the *Profeta* is departing her quarters for the negotiation."

"Thank you, Commander," Gryf responded. "We will meet you at the conveyor."

"Yes, sir." He met her eyes and grinned. "It's showtime."

A laugh bubbled up at the Terrianism, and let her shoulders relax. Graig swept her through the door and in the direction of the conveyor. It was silly to be this nervous. Gryf would be at her side the entire time. He had faith in her, and whatever divine power had chosen them to be the *Profetae*. Her father-in-law, Nicky, and Graig would also stand with them. Even the Administer—the elected leader of Matir—would hologram in for the meeting. What could possibly go wrong?

"I hear the Supreme is an asshole." Graig's tone was conspiratorial as they rounded the first corner. "But don't allow that to bother you, Alex."

"Are you trying to make me laugh, or just scare the crap out of me?"

A group of six uniformed Matirans appeared at the far end of the passageway. What were *they* doing here? The entire level was supposed to be cleared until she reached the viscomm room.

"*Ska*," Graig muttered. He body-slammed her into a control panel alcove along the wall just as the mysterious Matirans opened fire.

PROPHECY

◆ ◆ ◆ ◆ ◆

The conveyor doors slid open, and Gryf narrowed his eyes at Nick waiting to board the lift.

"Morning blessings, Nicholaus," Gryf's father greeted the young man.

"'Morning, Admiral," Nick stepped into the conveyor and jerked his chin in Gryf's direction. "Hey, Q-tip."

Gryf raised an eyebrow. "I know what a Q-tip is, Nick." He reached into his breast pocket and pulled out the little blue flexible stick with white fluff on the ends. Thankfully, Alexandra had warned him that Nick might eventually tease him in this manner. It was good to stay ahead of his brother-in-law.

Nick grinned. "I guess you do."

"And I know who...or what...Papa Smurf was." He gave the youth a smirk.

The doors closed behind Nick, and the conveyor began its descent to Epsilon level. "Damn. Those were my two best ones."

Nick didn't appear overly disappointed. No doubt he had others tucked away in that devious brain.

"You may call me either." Gryf tapped the swab against the shell of his ear. "But if you do, make sure you watch your back—Nich-o-laus."

"Gotcha, old man."

Zale cleared his throat.

"No offense, sir." Nick certainly knew how to use his easygoing charm.

The conveyor slowed as it approached their destination. Fear, raw and primitive, permeated every part of his being. His heart rate spiked, and he gripped the wall to keep from folding to the floor.

Alexandra. Danger.

"Gryf?" His father's voice seemed to come from sectors away.

Gryf's comm beeped.

"Code Red! Code Red!" Graig's voice filled the conveyor. "Level Epsilon, Section Twenty-seven. Repeat, Epsilon Two-

Seven."

Graig's comm picked up a woman's sharp cry. Alexandra's cry.

Gryf slapped his comm. "On our way."

By the Mother, he didn't want to withdraw from their soul connection, but he had a job to do. He swore in Matiran, sent her his reassurance that he was coming, then withdrew. Cold isolation descended. If his soul could cry, it would.

He punched his code into the small control panel to enable the ship-wide transmitter. "Code Red. All available and armed personnel to Epsilon Two-Seven. Code Red." An instant later, the message repeated a constant broadcast of the order.

"What's happening?" Nick's face was pale.

Gryf slammed his hand into the crystalline ID reader on the wall. A panel snapped open to reveal a small arsenal of *telums*. "Someone is attempting to assassinate Alexandra." He pushed one of the weapons into his brother-in-law's hands. "Take this, and remember your training."

The conveyor came to stop at Level Epsilon, and Gryf shoved through the doors before they were fully open. Given all the noise, it wasn't difficult to figure out the assassins were around the first corner. *Please don't let me be too late.*

He rounded the corner, and opened fire. One assassin fell before Gryf's shoulder slammed into the far corner bulkhead. He grunted at the impact before dropping to his stomach on the floor. Nick rolled into the middle of the opening and flattened himself next to Gryf just as the remaining three assassins opened fire on them.

"They're Matiran," Nick shouted.

"Not any of mine."

One traitor yelled something indecipherable, and the rest turned their attention back down the corridor where Alexandra and Graig must be taking cover. This made it ridiculously easy to pick them off. But they were assassins, and their goal would be to eliminate their target at any cost.

The last one fell. Gryf held his position on the floor, weapon ready, watching for movement. Everything remained still. He signaled his father and Nick, and they rose together in silence. Nick walked over to the closest dead assassin. He gazed down at her dispassionately, then crouched and splayed his fingers across her forehead.

"Go, Gryf. I will watch your back," his father said.

Gryf strode through the debris-ridden corridor. If any of the assassins as much as twitched, his father would cut them down.

The outline of a body lay in the control alcove. A male. The cape of a dress uniform draped over the still form as if protecting something. Or someone.

Graig. Mother have mercy.

Gryf moved forward quickly, his stomach knotted. In a blur of motion, Graig flipped over on his back, his *telum* appearing from under the folds of his cloak, aimed at Gryf's heart.

"Peace, Graig." Gryf raised his hands. The tension in Graig's face drained away, and he laid his head on the floor with a gusty sigh. Gryf dropped to his knees next to him. "Are you hit?"

"No." Graig nudged Alexandra. "Alex, it's over. Gryf's here, *sora.*"

Alexandra was curled in a fetal position against Graig's side, her head covered by her arms. Graig moved aside, and she peeked between her elbows. "Oh. My. God," she whispered with ragged disbelief. "Someone tried to *kill* me, Gryf."

"They tried." Tried, and failed.

She stretched one arm toward him. Relief and post-adrenalin rush slammed into him, and he grabbed her hand, hauling her into his lap. He peppered kisses over her face, her mouth, touching her everywhere. She was alive. Safe. "*Animi.*" He cradled her against his chest. *Thank you, Mother.*

Behind him, his father gave the stand-down order to the armed personnel arriving, and put them in charge of taking the bodies to the morgue. Alexandra shivered. Shock must be settling upon her. Her warm palm rested against Gryf's chest, over his heart. "Gryf, who was the dumbass who insisted I go unarmed to these negotiations? You should throw her in the brig."

He half-smiled against her hair. "Perhaps after the negotiations, when you are feeling more yourself."

Nick squatted next to him, balanced on the balls of his feet. Placing a glowing hand on his sister's head, he murmured,

"Peace." Instantly Alexandra's body stopped shivering, relaxing as it was released from the effects of shock.

Nick's gaze hardened. "I got some information I think we can use. I couldn't understand the words, but the actions were pretty clear."

CHAPTER THIRTY-THREE

Barely ten minutes later, Alex strode through the corridors of the *Atlantis* toward the viscomm room they'd use to negotiate with the Anferthian Supreme Warden. Her husband and her brother flanked her. The former looked like a Category 5 hurricane waiting to be unleashed, while the latter seemed grim and determined. Ahead of Alex was her father-in-law, and at her back, Graig. All five were now armed with *telums*.

In the viscomm room, she stood between Gryf and his father. Zale touched a spot on a console inside the door, and a realistic 3-D hologram of Administer Navigand, the elected leader of the Matiran people, appeared on the other side of the admiral.

Now that's damn impressive.

"Admiral Marenys." Navigand's hologram nodded then bowed to her and Gryf. "*Profeta, Profetu,* it is my honor."

Alex inclined her head in unison with Gryf. "On behalf of the Terrian people, Administer Navigand, I thank you for arranging and supporting these negotiations."

"I am thankful that you are safe, honorable one. Arrangements are in place for the members of your Earth Council to listen in to these negotiations. They have been briefed, and know you came to no harm during the attempt on your life."

"I know they appreciate that assurance. Thank you, sir." As the head of the newly-seated Earth Council, Moises had probably demanded it. He had begged her to be careful during this trip, but she hadn't seen where there'd be any threat. She'd be aboard the *Atlantis*, after all, and couldn't have been safer. Boy, had she been wrong.

Zale extended his hand to her, and she placed hers in his.

His face softened. "As deeply as I regret the events which have brought you to our family, Alexandra, I cannot regret gaining you as a daughter. Please remember this always."

Some of the tension drained from her shoulders, and a smile tugged at the corners of her mouth. Best father-in-law ever. "Thank you, *patre*."

He released her hand. "Are you ready, *cori*?"

"Just let me know when they can see me."

Zale gave her a wink. "You will know by their shocked expressions."

No doubt she would. The wall screen flickered to life. Supreme Warden Antaro T'lik and his coalition council appeared.

"Administer Navigand," he greeted the Matiran leader. The vibration in his voice had a nasal quality. "I trust there is a good reason for this delay in communication."

"Our *Profeta* came under attack by a group of assassins," the administer told him without apology.

"I see." T'lik tapped his long fingers on the table in front of him, his face a mask. "Then the negotiations are over before they begin."

"Not even remotely, Supreme Warden," Navigand assured the other man.

"With your *Profeta* gone, there is no one to speak for the Terrians."

"Why would you think that, Your Excellence?" Zale asked.

T'lik visibly stiffened. "Surely you do not suggest that your *Profetu* negotiate for both peoples? We will not negotiate with a *Matiran* for the Terrian prisoners."

"Forgive me, Supreme Warden, for my poorly-chosen words." Zale smiled thinly. "I meant to ask, why would you think the *Profeta* is gone?"

Amazing. This is going exactly as planned. Alex sent the thought to Gryf. *I hope I do half as well. It'd be shame to mess up all your father's groundwork.*

Gryf rubbed his thumb against the back of her hand. *I won't let you fall.*

She gave him a grateful smile. *I know.*

"Terr's *Profeta* is alive and well, I assure you, Supreme

Warden," Navigand said.

Hm, that's an awful lot of surprised faces. Only a few of the Anferthians did not seem affected by this news.

Gryf's chuckle rolled gently through her mind. *Are you ready, animi?*

As I'll ever be.

"Then where is she? Show her to us." T'lik smirked. His arrogance was mind-boggling.

Gryf squeezed her hand before releasing it. Her father-in-law ran his finger across the flat control panel in front of him. All sets of Anferthian eyes settled on Alex. She smothered a grin. It was clear they saw her now.

The administer extended his holographic hand in her direction. "Supreme Warden Antaro T'lik and esteemed Coalition of Anferthia, it pleases me to present the honorable *Profeta* of Terr and the *Profetu* of Matir."

She and Gryf inclined their heads when introduced. About half of the Anferthian Coalition returned the acknowledgement. One of them, an elder coalition member, asked, "Admiral, is this not your son?"

"It is, Member K'nil. And as fate would have it, he stands at the side of my daughter-in-law."

Member Fynn K'nil and my father share a mutual respect for each other, Gryf explained. *Of all the coalition members, his heart is the most true to his people.*

"So you are the *Profeta* of Matiran legend." Supreme Warden T'lik leaned back in his seat. "I had expected more."

"I had not expected it at all." *Take that, you condescending weasel.*

Member K'nil's black eyes focused on her, as though measuring her up.

T'lik frowned, his coarse, pale brows drawn together over his glare. "Let us dispense with formalities and get right to the point."

This is a grave insult, Gryf warned. *Force official acknowledgment of your status.*

Well, that was easier said than done. She pushed her shoulders back and raised her chin. "Supreme Warden and esteemed Coalition, I greet you as the *Profeta* and the voice of the people of Earth."

For several heartbeats, T'lik clenched and unclenched his jaw. "Greetings, *Profeta*, on behalf of this coalition and the Anferthian people," he ground out.

"Thank you, Your Excellence, and Coalition."

Member K'nil addressed her, "*Profeta*, I would be remiss if I didn't say that I am glad you survived your ordeal this day."

"Thank you, sir." She felt herself warming to his tactful diplomacy. But only a little.

T'lik narrowed his eyes. "Clearly Senior Captain Helyg has scant control over his crew if they are attempting to assassinate his wife."

Whoa. Had he just said that? "We never said that my attackers were Matiran, Supreme Warden."

Dead silence. T'lik's face went from a condescending sneer to horrified panic. And there was no way he could retract his ill-chosen words. He stood up and pounded his large fist on the table in front of him. "These negotiations have ended. We will not negotiate with you. End the transmission."

The Anferthians disappeared, and Alex gaped at the blank viscomm wall. *Well, shit. Now what?* She turned to Zale. "Can you get them back?"

He shook his head. "If we did, they would take it as a sign of desperation. We would lose credibility in their eyes, and weaken our position."

Double shit. "But trying is better than doing nothing, isn't it?"

"We must try something different, *cori*," her father-in-law murmured, staring hard at the blank tabletop in front of him. "What we did did not work."

She pressed her hands to her cheeks. "I screwed it up. I can't believe it."

"You did no such thing."

Yeah, sure. "So, now what?"

His gaze flicked up, and he gave her an apologetic look. "We wait." Then he went back to contemplating the blank table.

Dammit. We almost had them. How had she been so horribly wrong?

Gryf touched her elbow. "Come with me, *animi*."

He led her to a corner of the room, the others seemingly oblivious to the *Profetae*'s retreat. Stepping into his embrace, she touched her forehead to his as comfortable warmth spread through her chest. Strength, well-being, and peace flowed through her. His love wrapped around her heart, setting her universe in balance once more.

"You did nothing wrong, *animi*. Such is the nature of negotiations." The rhythmic stroke of Gryf's hand over her hair drained away the tension and her shoulders relaxed. "In the worst case, T'lik will realize that negotiation is the only way he will get out of this with his life. Unfortunately, the Arruch Union will use this to convince the Anferthian people that duress was involved in the negotiations, and that the agreement is not in Anferthia's best interest."

"What's the best case?"

"We pray that Member K'nil can turn coalition opinion in our favor."

Alex drew back and locked gazes with her husband. "You mean Member K'nil is on our side?"

Gryf shrugged one shoulder. "I believe your people would refer to him as the ace in our pocket."

Well, that was unexpected. "But, Gryf, what if he can't? We have to have a back-up plan." She pulled away from the comfort of his arms and paced the floor. What could they do?

Nicky moved to take a seat farther down the table. Alex came to a stop behind Zale and squinted at her brother. There *was* something they had that the Anferthians did not. Nicky met her gaze, furrowed his brow, and mouthed, "What?"

"I think I've got something." She tapped her father-in-law's shoulder. "I need to talk to Moises."

Her father-in-law gave her a curious look then nodded.

"Alex, my star child." Moises grinned at her from another screen a moment later. "We've been listening in like Big Brother. Anything you need, just tell me."

No doubt about it. Moises had just rocketed to the number one position on her Most Favorite People list. If this worked, it would be because of him. And it had to work, because they were out of options.

The moment T'lik had cut the transmission, the coalition chamber had burst into a cacophony of noise, everyone vying for vocal dominance. Amid the impassioned words of retribution against Terr and Matir, Fynn K'nil remained seated. He glanced down the table at Antaro T'lik. The slimy ball of muck would be the downfall of the Anferthian people. Too many had lived in fear of the political party known as the Arruch Union since the untimely death of the last *ymero*, Zular B'aq. More deaths would come if the Arruchs were not stopped, and that did not sit well with Fynn. He and his daughter had sacrificed much to ensure a future for his grandson, and he would fight to the death for the boy.

Fynn exchanged a look with the only other member not participating in the uproar, Holt Hunnu. Having an ally was a dangerous luxury, but on more than one occasion, the much younger man had proven his allegiance to breaking the iron grip of the Arruch Union.

"They avoid the one question that would end this," Holt murmured, his words cloaked by the shouts around them.

Fynn nodded. "Patience, Holt."

T'lik banged his fist against the smooth, jade-colored tabletop. "We will turn our firepower on them. They must be reduced to space dust!"

Some of the others roared their approval, but not all. It seemed the division of ranks had begun. Fynn shifted and leaned forward in his chair, catching T'lik's defiant gaze. "Do you truly believe Divine Warden T'orr will approve this action, Antaro?"

"I have his ear, K'nil," T'lik sneered. "Why would he not?"

Fynn gave his shoulders a casual shrug. "There is the matter that our few ships are surrounded by a full two-thirds of the Matiran fleet."

Member Pren worried her bottom lip between her teeth. "They do outgun us, Antaro."

"Silence! Or I will have your tongue cut out, Pren," T'lik snapped back.

Pren flinched. If she, T'lik's staunchest supporter and

frequent bedmate, was questioning him, far be it for Fynn not to sow that seed of distrust. "Do you still have the authority to do such, Antaro? I am of the opinion that your presence here no longer serves the best interest of Anferthia. I fear what other damning words might escape your mouth."

T'lik did in fact open his mouth, but the words everyone heard were from a far more beautiful voice.

"Citizens of Anferthia, I greet you as Alexandra Gaia Bock, a citizen of the planet Terr, and the *Profeta* chosen to fulfil the ancient Matiran Prophecy of the Guardians."

The young Terrian woman's image appeared on their viscomm. Fynn fought to keep his face impassive, though his heart rhythm near quadrupled in his chest.

A wordless shout of rage came from T'lik. "Stop her! Cut her transmission!"

"It's not being directed at us, Supreme," Member Pren reported. "It's being sent to all of Anferthia."

"Jam it then." T'lik's eyes bulged. If the situation were not so serious, Fynn would have let go the laugh building within him.

"Not possible. The source is shielded," Pren replied.

"...came in good faith to negotiate for the release of the Terrian and Matiran prisoners being held aboard those slavers. Unfortunately, on my way to these negotiations, there was an assassination attempt on my life. We have indisputable evidence of who masterminded this treachery." The words of the *Profeta* filled the room.

T'lik roared and slammed both his fists on the table. "She spews lies like the Lokat'a Tar Pit spews its black ooze!"

Holt leaned back in his chair. "I find the lady has an enchanting voice. Like stream water flowing over rocks. Much nicer than the gravel you expel, Antaro."

Fynn tensed, bracing for the tirade that was sure to come.

"I'll have you brought up on charges of treason for helping her, Hunnu!" Spittle flew from T'lik's lips.

Holt moved with the speed of youth. Fynn had hardly blinked before T'lik's throat was in danger of becoming intimately acquainted with the lethal *labu-ba* pressed to it.

"Stand down, Member Hunnu." Fynn used the same

soothing voice as he did when reading to his grandson. As much as he'd like to be rid of T'lik, he wouldn't condone bloodshed in this chamber. "Supreme Warden T'lik, it does not appear we have as superior a stance as you hoped. We must listen to the *Profeta*'s message in order to run an effective negotiation."

Holt gave him a slow grin, and the short-blade disappeared. "You are fortunate Fynn likes you, Antaro."

"...not to mistake Terrians as easy prey for conquests. Even though we find peace preferable, we will fight with our souls to defend our home world. And I will defend *fyhen*, my own."

That caught the attention of everyone in the room. She knew of *fyhen*? If only Zale's daughter—and she was a daughter to his old friend, Fynn had seen it in the Matiran's eyes—knew how much chaos her words were causing in this room. And, likely, all over Anferthia.

"It is important that you know, since the annihilation of seven *billion* of my people, we Terrians have been experiencing preternatural changes in ourselves." The *Profeta* raised her hands, her palms toward them. Fynn squinted then leaned closer. A faint golden glow surrounded them. And in her eyes as well. Did she carry the Matiran Gift? How was this possible?

"It's a trick," T'lik spat. "A Matiran is lighting up her hands and eyes."

Fynn shook his head. "If that were the case, wouldn't her hands glow blue like a Matiran's?"

"My Gift was discovered before I came into my destiny as *Profeta*. But there will be doubters. So...." A young Terrian male stepped next to the *Profeta*, his eyes and hands glowing as hers did. Golden, like clouds at sunset. "This is my brother, who also carries a Gift. And finally...."

The screen split at the center. To the right of the split were a group of Terrians, at least a dozen. And every last one of them demonstrated the Gift they carried.

"So, Terrians carry the Matiran Gift," Holt breathed. "In Matiran, *terrania* means kindred. No wonder the Matirans have guarded them so well. They are kin."

"The people you see on the opposite screen are being viscommed in from Terr." The *Profeta* lowered her hands.

PROPHECY

"They are only a small sampling of our remaining population, and as Gifted as my brother and I. We expect to find many more Gifted Terrians in the future."

T'lik made a scoffing noise.

"Cease, T'lik, and let her finish," Holt snarled.

"I will not!" T'lik slammed his hand down on the viscomm control, and all the Terrians disappeared. "We must attack now, while they're distracted."

"Enough of this," Holt snarled. "Someone gag the Supreme Warden. For the sake of Anferthia, I want to hear what this *Profeta* has to say."

There was a brief struggle before T'lik was subdued by the Coalition Guards and forced to sit in his chair. Fynn tapped the control, bringing Alexandra back to the viscomm wall. The effect of her presence, even filtered through a transmission, was mesmerizing. But was she aware of the one damning piece of evidence that would end T'lik's career—and possibly his life, once he faced Divine Warden T'orr?

Divine Warden. Fynn suppressed a derisive snort at the title Isel T'orr had bestowed upon himself. Elevating himself even above the *ymero*, and one mere step below the Creator. Would it be too much to hope that this was the beginning of the fall for the self-anointed demi-god?

"Citizens of Anferthia," the *Profeta* said. "I'm sure some of you have heard of the term mind-browsing—the ability of a healer to scan the brain of a person recently deceased. My brother has an extraordinary gift for healing. An hour ago, he browsed a dead assassin and retrieved a memory, which he corroborated by mind-browsing three others. He does not speak or understand a word of Anferthian, but you will not need your translators to understand."

This could be it. Fynn clenched his fist in his lap and held his breath. The Terrian male closed his eyes and, in flawless Anferthian, repeated word for word an assassination order for the *Profeta*, down to the signature...one Antaro T'lik. A cold silence fell in the room, and all heads turned to Supreme Warden. Even his most loyal supporters, who were likely just as guilty, were sure to desert him now.

Fynn gave the putrid mass a narrow-eyed look.

"Assassination is a coward's game, T'lik, one played by the skulking Nightshades, not Anferthians. Is what the Terrian tells us true?"

Antaro T'lik's face turned a sickly greyish-green. His mouth worked, but nothing came out. That was all Fynn needed. He signaled the Coalition Guard. "Remove the Supreme Warden. Place him in a holding cell. The Divine Warden will decide his fate later."

T'lik didn't utter a word—a small blessing, to be sure. The doors closed after he and his escort passed through, and Fynn returned his attention to the brilliant young woman on the viscomm who now called on the Anferthian people for justice.

CHAPTER THIRTY-FOUR

"Two birds with one stone." Alex turned her back to her husband, and lifted her hair from her neck. It was so nice to be back in the privacy of their quarters, even if it was for just enough time to change into their uniforms.

Gryf smoothed his hand lightly down her spine, opening the seal of her dress. "And that means...?"

"That I accomplished two things at once today."

"More than that, I would say."

"Well, yes, but two things I *wanted* to accomplish. Winning the release of the Earthling prisoners, and securing a safe sanctuary for K'rona and the dissenters on Matir." As much as she wished K'rona could live close by, there was already a faction of humans on Earth bent on ridding the universe of Anferthians. Her friend wasn't safe on Earth.

"Both of monumental importance. There, you're free," Gryf said, pushing her dress down her arms. Goose bumps marked the trail of his hands.

"Mm. Thank you." She stepped out of the dress, turned to him and reached for the clasp holding his cape. "Chin up. I'm really sorry one of my assassins turned out to be the son of your father's friend. Does anyone know how that happened?"

Gryf frowned. "Matiran policy has always been to keep military families together. Hence, we do have children aboard our ships. My understanding is that Sergious Roma was an infant aboard the Defense Fleet Cruiser *Luna* when it disappeared twenty-two years ago. Apparently, he was taken and trained from childhood to be an assassin, as we discovered today."

"Along with the other children from *Luna*." She released the cape, and it slithered down his back to puddle on the floor.

"It's heartbreaking, Gryf. I can't even imagine what his childhood was like."

Certainly not a loving one. The Anferthian Supreme Warden deserved a horrific punishment for his part in enslaving those children. She ran one hand along the overlapping sections of Gryf's dress uniform, exposing the shirt underneath. "Can I do anything to remove the mark of shame on all their families?"

Gryf shrugged out of his over-coat. "They must come to you for forgiveness."

"Can I go to them?"

"It's rarely done, but yes." Gryf reached for her hands and brought them to his lips, kissing one palm then the other. Then he traced his tongue down to her wrist, making little whorls against her sensitive skin. Oh, boy. They had to be in the transport bay in a half hour to meet the ships transferring the prisoners. And the gleam in Gryf's eyes was anything but platonic.

She cleared her throat. "Well, ah, then I'll do it when we get to Matir." How could she concentrate with him nipping his way up her arm? "Oh, what the hell. We have time for a quickie."

Gryf raised one eyebrow. "I hope that means what I think it means."

"You bet it does." She moved her body against his, burying her hands in the soft, white curls behind his head. "And up against the wall means what you think it means too."

His eyes darkened, and a sultry smile played on his lips as he backed her against the wall. "The *Profeta* has spoken. How can I deny her?"

"Don't even try," she murmured against his mouth then the satin smoothness of his tongue slid against hers.

We'll be late. Gryf slid her panties down far enough for her to free one leg. Then he freed his shaft.

So?

With a firm grip, Gryf lifted her thigh and hitched her leg over his hip. The hardness of his erection pressed against her entrance, and the building heat at her core blossomed into a flame. Her soul shifted in the now-familiar way it did when preparing to reach out to Gryf's soul.

He entered her with one swift thrust.

Oh God, Gryf.

"*Animi,*" he whispered next to her ear as he pulled out and surged back in, each plunge rocking her against the wall.

Heat built at her core as they moved, as if each stroke was designed to give her the most pleasure. She dug her nails into his back and bit down on his shoulder as her orgasm burst over her in intense waves of pleasure.

Gryf thrusted hard, his body tensing from his own release. In that moment, their souls merged and she catapulted into oblivion with him.

Gryf rose from his seat at Admiral Teris's signal, and Alexandra stood up with him. It had taken the better part of a week to convene the Panel of Inquiry, and another two days for the Panel to hear testimony both for and against Gryf. Now they were ready to render their ruling.

The warm touch of Alexandra's hand in his was a blessing. No matter what decision was handed down, no matter what they stripped him of, they couldn't take the most important and precious part of his life away. She would likely rip them a new one if they tried. He liked that Terrian phrase. Nick had taught it to him last night, along with how to cough and say 'dick-wad' at the same time. Gryf was still unclear on exactly what a dick-wad was, but something about saying it was satisfying.

Alexandra gave his hand a squeeze, and his heart soared. The girl who'd despised him at first sight had become the woman who loved him. And, true to her word, she and the others from their cell had spoken on his behalf today. Winning her trust had been a defining moment in their lives.

And now they stood on the precipice of another life-defining moment. The decision the Panel of Inquiry handed down would set them on a new path.

"Senior Captain Gryf Dimytro Helyg," Admiral Teris intoned. "This Panel of Inquiry has heard the evidence and deliberated over today's proceedings. We have reached a decision."

From behind Gryf came a soft rustle. Alexandra glanced over her shoulder. *Everyone is standing up.*
All of them?
Even your father and Admiral Cael.

Gryf closed his eyes and swallowed. She didn't know it, but by standing, those who served in either Fleet subjected themselves to whatever sentence he received. He blinked his eyes open. So be it.

"Senior Captain Gryf Helyg, you are charged with failure to prevent the hostile invasion of the planet Terr, also known as Earth, by the Anferthians; the near annihilation of the sentient inhabitants of Terr; and the near complete destruction of the Matiran Guardian Fleet. This Panel would impress upon you of the severity of these allegations."

Gryf gave the Admiral a nod. "I do understand, ma'am, and will abide by the Panel's ruling."

"Terr's newly-seated council was invited to sit in judgment of these charges against you, but they have been steadfast in their insistence that you are not guilty of any of these crimes, and that the Panel should 'spend less time investigating false accusations and more time at the beach with their families.'"

Alexandra made a small choking sound, but Admiral Teris continued her discourse.

"Due to this, and subsequent evidence from various sources, and the events and risks to which Senior Captain Helyg has subjected himself, including near loss of life, this Panel votes to dismiss all charges."

He blinked. *All* of them? Alexandra wiped her eyes with her free hand. He longed to crush her against him and hold her there forever. But Admiral Teris wasn't finished speaking. Regardless of the dismissal, there would still be a sentence.

"We further vote to decommission the remaining Guardian Fleet. We charge Senior Captain Gryf Helyg to oversee this process, and give him one Galactic Standard cycle from today to complete the process. At the end of said year, all remaining Guardian ships and personnel will be augmented to the Defense Fleet. The Matiran Defense Fleet will be retasked as the *Unified* Defense Fleet, which will be open to all Matirans

PROPHECY

and Terrians."

His stomach lurched, and numbness tingled in his hands and feet. Disband the Guardian Fleet? He met Admiral Teris's blue gaze.

She gave him a pointed look. "Do you understand your duties, Senior Captain?"

"Yes, ma'am."

Teris nodded. "You have your orders, Senior Captain. This Panel of Inquiry is dismissed. So be it."

The Panel rose and exited in silence. No one else moved. It was as though they had all been frozen in place. After twelve millennia, the Guardian Fleet would be no more. A lump lodged in Gryf's throat, and he swallowed around it.

"Did that just happen?" Ora's murmured query broke the spell.

Gryf took in and expelled a deep breath. He was still the senior captain of the Guardians, and the others would look to him to set the tone of this final year. He turned to face them, laying his arm around Alexandra's shoulders. "Guardians, we have one last duty to perform for our beloved Fleet. You are the final Guardians of a great legacy."

―――◆・・◆――――

Simone held her new puppy close and frowned at Graig standing a short distance away. Something was not right. He'd seemed distant since returning to Earth. He hadn't been like this before he'd left with Alex and Gryf to chase down the Anferthians. Something must have happened out there. It wasn't like him to just stand in the field outside her cube leaning against that single section of wooden rail fence. He'd been there for a solid half-hour.

"Is something wrong, Graig?"

His intense grey eyes seemed to study her. The hot autumn breeze ruffled his russet hair. The stubble it had been when she'd first met him had grown out over the last few months, and she loved running her fingers through it.

"I'm going back, Simone." His words were soft, yet they cut like a jagged knife through her heart. This was what she'd always feared. That he would leave her, fly away in the *Atlantis* when the ship left. And it was leaving at the end of the week, taking Alex, Gryf, and now Graig away.

"You have to go where your heart calls you." *I wish it called you here.* "My heart calls me to stay and help my people rebuild."

Graig came around the fence and stopped in front of her. Why did he have to look so damn fine in his uniform? She wasn't going to look at him; it hurt too much. Instead, she cuddled the puppy in her arms—a gift from Graig just two days ago.

"The next transport to the *Atlantis* will be leaving from the port in New Damon Beach soon."

"Then you'd better get to town so you don't miss it." Her words came out sharper than she'd intended, but really, did he expect her to beg him to stay? Even though the *Atlantis* wasn't departing for another four days, it was better to make a clean cut now.

He reached out as if to touch her, and she stiffened. He dropped it back to his side. "Take care of yourself, *dele*." Darling.

He turned and strode away through the long grass. The horse snorted as he mounted then he snicked and the animal moved out of the tiny yard in front of her equally tiny new home. What she would've given to feel his arms around her once more, to have one last chance to inhale his masculine scent.

"You too, space cowboy." He couldn't possibly hear her whispered words, and it was just as well. The last thing she wanted was his pity.

Ranger whimpered in her arms as both horse and rider disappeared over the next hill. He would go back to space, where he was happiest. Why had she ever been stupid enough to believe she could compete with that?

She set Ranger on the ground then placed her hands on the top rail where Graig had been leaning. Somehow the fence had survived the pounding the Anferthians had dealt her planet. Their relationship had not been as fortunate.

Simone rested her forehead on the bare rail between her hands and allowed her heart to shatter.

PROPHECY

From the top of the bluff just outside of New Damon Beach, Alex could see her husband wading in a tide pool, as any respectable Fleet captain would: barefoot, uniform pants pushed above his knees, peering into the clear water with the three remaining Camp One orphans, Flora, Juan, and Maggie.

Too bad her cell phone was long gone. This would've made a great picture.

A Matiran transport whooshed softly overhead, disappearing over the coastal hills in the direction of the new Matiran station being built. Terr Base One. Gryf had already secured assignment to be the first commanding officer of the station, a post he would take up in a year after completing his current assignment.

Little Maggie picked up some creature from the water and held it out for Gryf's inspection. Then she shrieked, dropped it back into the water, and clawed her way up his leg and into his arms. The once-peaceful tide pool erupted into a boiling cauldron as Flora and Juan tried to recapture the creature.

Gryf said something to Maggie.

"No, no, no!" Maggie pointed to a rock well back from the edge of the pool.

Alex's heart did something like a flip-flop in her chest. If only she and Gryf weren't going into space.

By the time she reached the sand, Maggie was safely settled on the rock. Gryf met Alex, and pulled her against him.

"Dante asked me to remind you...mmm." Delivering messages wasn't easy to do with her husband's mouth exploring hers. Not that she would complain. Cripes, the man was becoming more Terrian by the day. They parted, and she gave him a smile. "You need to go see him before we leave."

Gryf snorted and shook his head. "He is aware that the *Atlantis* does not leave for another four days, is he not?"

"I think he wants to show off his new infirmary."

"All right. I will be there tomorrow morning to submit myself to his poking and prodding."

A giggle bubbled up, and she entwined her fingers with his. "Good."

"I need your opinion." His serious tone drew her attention back to his face. "Let's sit."

So this was a "sit down" talk. Hmm. She lowered herself next to him on a sea-worn log.

"Okay. On what?"

Gryf's hand made an all-inclusive motion in the direction of the kids. "You know we've come up with zero DNA matches for then?"

"I saw the data when it came in, yes." How heartbreaking that none of their biological family members had survived.

"Fortunately, Li-Min and another young woman named April Boruski have set up a home for youngsters like them."

"Yeah, Nick goes to the orphanage a couple times a week to teach music and help out." She met his gaze. "Gryf, wouldn't taking children on a spaceship be, well, risky? Remember what happen with *Luna*?"

He appeared only mildly surprised that she'd figured out where he was heading with his thought process. "Living is risky, *animi*," he replied quietly. "Firsthand experience has taught you this."

"I see your point." Her gaze drifted back to where Flora and Juan were trying to coax Maggie back into the tide pool with them. Maggie wasn't having anything to do with that idea. "You realize that's *three* children, right?"

"Would you rather we create our own?"

"Having a baby ourselves should sound terribly romantic and fulfilling, yet it doesn't feel right to me, somehow."

"I think our children have arrived by more unconventional means, *compa*."

She glanced in the direction of the children. "To deny them would be to deny everything we've stood for the past several months."

He brushed his lips across the back of her hand. *Then we are in agreement?*

Warmth flared in her heart, and she gave him a smile. *One-hundred percent.*

EPILOGUE

Gryf lay in bed; the soft, slow breathing of his soul mate sleeping at his side filled him with peace. Down the hallway of their recently expanded quarters, Juan murmured in his sleep. Underlying the night noises of Gryf's family, the barely perceptible, steady hum of the *Atlantis*'s engines proclaimed smooth sailing.

All was well.

Even their trip to Matir had been without incident, with the exception of his mother and her grandchildren. Who knew how much work it was to reprogram three children after such excessive spoiling? He certainly did not.

A warm internal glow crept into his chest. His children. Flora, Juan, and Maggie. The most important assignments of his life. For a short time, he had feared he was in over his head with parenting, until he began taking his cues from Alexandra. She handled them with ease, just as she handled her new duties as Terr's first ambassador to Matir.

When Moises had extended the request for her to fill this role for the next year, Gryf had not expected her to accept. But she had. Then, surprise of all surprises, Senior Admiral Cael and Administer Navigand had placed the *Atlantis* at her disposal. It was now the official residence and flag-ship of Ambassador Bock. In hindsight, this was an ideal situation as the dismantling of the Guardian Fleet did not require the constant presence of its Senior Captain. If the unlikely event of conflict occurred, his new second-in-command, Ora, would step in to cover for him.

Gryf glanced at the framed image on the bed table, a gift from his parents to Alexandra during their month on Matir. In it, Vyn Kotas's mother, Adra, knelt at Alexandra's feet after pleading for the *Profeta*'s mercy. Alexandra had pardoned Adra for the crimes of her son—publicly, no less. The two women in the image gazed into each other's eyes at the moment of absolution.

The image of this historic moment had been broadcast galaxy-wide, but his father had imprinted Alexandra's copy with the words *"Two worlds become one"*, in both English and Matiran. A special message from Gryf's parents to their beloved daughter-in-law.

Alexandra sighed and snuggled her bottom against him. Her desire teased at their soul link with sleepy suggestion. A suggestion he was not inclined to ignore. He reached for her, gathering her warm body against his own. Brushing her hair aside, he tasted and nipped from her shoulder, to her neck, and then her ear.

No words were needed as their souls had already engaged in *anim loqui*, humming together in their mysterious language. Gryf positioned himself and slid into her from behind. *Mother above.* Would there ever be a time when he wouldn't have to struggle to maintain himself when he entered her? He closed his eyes to better savor her heat around him. Then he moved with long, slow strokes, caressing her tightening bud.

Her breathing became pants, and she arched her back, meeting his quickening thrusts. Her cry and release flooded over him. He surged into her and stiffened, his own groan escaping his lips as he filled her. Their souls touched, and he lost all sense of time and place.

Reality slowly reestablished itself with each beat of his heart. He was still buried deep inside his wife's warmth, and there was no reason to withdraw. Instead, he touched his thumb and forefinger to the bridge of his nose and sent yet another prayer of thanksgiving to the Mother for bringing the two of them together. It was a daily benediction for his lifetime; how could it not be? Alexandra was his heart and soul, and the treasure of his eternity.

The End

GLOSSARY OF WORDS

A
Ades – (Matiran) Brother.
Aeter nom – (Matiran) Eternal knot. Most often used as a wedding ring.
Agri – (Matiran) young boy, lad.
Animi – (Matiran) My soul.
Anim tros – (Matiran) Soul mate.
Anferthians – The alien race which invades Earth. Lanky and tall 8-12 ft. on average. Skin color: various shades of green from sage to olive to forest green. Military wears black uniforms.
Arruch Party – The political party in power on Anferthia.

B

C
Capeto – (Matiran) Captain.
Compa – (Matiran) Beloved.
Conveyor – Elevator or lift within a Matiran ship.
Cori – (Matiran) Daughter.
Custii – (Matiran) Guardians.

D
Dele – (Matiran) Darling.
Dex – (Matiran) Healing command for hand injuries.
Dimmi – (Matiran) Forgive me.
Disipula – (Matiran) Student.
Dolonos – (Matiran) Murderer.
Dormio – (Matiran) Slumber. Healing command to put a patient to sleep.

E

Ectu belltur – (Matiran) A salute used between soldiers and warriors to show respect.
Eni Terr – (Matiran) For Terr, or For Earth.
Eno anim – (Matiran) Union of Souls, or the birth of soul mates.
Esto – (Matiran) Let it be so.
Evo – (Matiran) The command to wake someone from an induced slumber (dormio).

F

Fusil – (Anferthian) An Anferthian gun similar to a Matiran telum.
Fyhen – (Anferthian) My Own. A person, or persons, so important and treasured by an Anferthian that they'd lay down their life for them.

G

H

Healing – The vocation or calling of a particular Matiran's Gift.

I

-iad – (Anferthian) An endearment added to the name of an Anferthian's love, lover, sweetheart.
Ithemba – Outlawed drug historically used to torture or interrogate another. Originally from a planet called Zuatia.

J

K

Kagi – (Matiran) The ammunition used for *telums*.
Kilots – Matiran unit of measure equal to a kilometer.
Kri – A grey/blue Matiran precious metal.

L

PROPHECY

Labu-ba – (Anferthian) An Anferthian short-bladed knife.
Lindrim – (Matiran) The barrel of a telum.
Lutep – (Matiran) Portable solar-powered units which provide light and heat.
Luz-ba – (Anferthian) And Anferthian long-bladed knife.

M
Magister – (Matiran) Teacher.
Matir – The mother world of the Matiran people; very much like Earth, except the sky is lavender instead of blue.
Matiran – The indigenous peoples of Matir; hair & eye colors vary but all have skin in some shade of blue.

N
Natu – (Matiran) Son.

O
Ocul – (Matiran) The Healing command for eye injuries.

P
Parvirtu – (Matiran) A means for healthy Matirans to share strength with those who are injured.
Pas – (Matiran) Peace.
Pes – (Matiran) The Healing command for foot injuries.
Profeta – (Matiran) Alex's title as the female half of the Profetae.
Profetae – (Matiran) Alex & Gryf together as the fulfillers of the Profeti.
Profeti – (Matiran) Prophecy.
Profetu – (Matiran) Gryf's title as the male half of the Profetae.
Puella – (Matiran) Young girl, lass.

Q

R
Reliquary – A pendant worn by Anferthians. Very little is known about the purpose of a reliquary, but it seems to have

an almost holy meaning to the Anferthians.
Ropo – (Matiran) Male friend.
Rucubi – (Matiran) The cylinder of a *telum*.

S
Saltu – (Matiran) Greetings. A salutation.
Ska – (Matiran) An all-purpose swear word.
Sora – (Matiran) Sister.
Sobin – (Matiran) Cousin. One of the few gender neutral words in Matiran.

T
Tacte – (Matiran) Silence. Be quiet. Hush.
Tallinese – The ore smiths of the planet Tallin, known for providing the highest quality metals to the galaxy.
Terr – Matiran for Earth. Short for Terrinia.
Terrania – (Matiran) Kindred.
Terrian – What the Materians and the Anferthians call Earthlings.
Telum – (Matiran) Gun. It is a stealth weapon and is virtually silent when shot.
Tinan – Matiran word used with their Gift to prevent pregnancy.
Tirik – (Anferthian) The ritual plait or braid traditional plait worn by Anferthian adults.

U

V
Veni – (Matiran) Forgiven.
Viscomm – Intergalactic word for long distance Visual Communication.

W

X

Y
Yana – (Matiran) Female friend.

PROPHECY

Ymero – (Anferthian) A dynasty of leaders who have ruled Anferthia for millennia. Overthrown in a coup by the Arruch Party. (Fem.: Ymere).

Z

NOTE FROM THE AUTHOR

To my dear readers:

Thank you for the privilege of entertaining you for a while. I hope you enjoyed reading Alex and Gryf's story. I started writing Prophecy when I was in high school. At the time, I was testing my wings and not very confident. But, I knew two things: I'd wanted to be a writer since I was in third grade, and I loved science fiction romance.

But, after many stops and starts, the story seemed to fizzle. I finally chalked it up to being one of my "practice pieces" and put it away.

Flash forward thirty-something years: Alex and a certain blue-skinned, white-haired alien dropped into a fevered dream for a visit. Next thing I knew, I was sitting at the computer madly typing even though I had a 102 temperature. That was three years ago. Now Prophecy is a completed manuscript, and has been released on the unsuspecting universe (a terrifying prospect for me, but hopefully a wonderful experience for you).

It's appropriate that Alex and Gryf's story is the first book I've published. These two characters were my first "babies"—even before my own real-time children came along—and I have loved them since their inception.

If you want to spend more time in their world, I have great news for you. Nick's story is out! *Salvation* picks up seven years after the Anferthian invasion. Lives are on the line, and Nick must come to terms with the Gift he's managed to studiously deny for far too long. I don't want to give away too

PROPHECY

much, but Dante will be back, and K'rona returns with her dissenters.

Keep an eye on my website and other social media sites for excerpts and progress reports for Salvation. Also, I've included a special chapter from Prophecy at the end of all this back matter. My gift to you.

Until next time, happy reading!

~Lea Kirk

ABOUT THE AUTHOR

Lea Kirk loves to transport her readers to other worlds with her romances of science fiction and time travel. Her fascination with science fiction began at six-years-old when her dad introduced her to the original Star Trek TV series. She fell in love with the show, and was even known to run through her parents' house wearing the tunic top of her red knit pantsuit and her white go-go boots pretending to be Lieutenant Uhura. By nine years, old she knew she wanted to be a writer, and in her teens, she read her first romance and was hooked.

Ms. Kirk lives in Northern California with her wonderful hubby, their five kids (aka, the nerd herd), and a Doberman who thinks he's a people. She's also proud of her seven times great grandson. Apparently, her stories will serve as the inspiration for James T. to join Star Fleet Academy. She learned this in the 1980s when James sought out her counsel on where to find a pair of humpback whales.

ALSO BY LEA KIRK

The Prophecy series

Salvation: Book Two of the Prophecy series

Collision: Book Three (Coming in 2017)

All of Me, a Prophecy short story

Pets in Space Anthology: Space Ranger, a Prophecy short story

DESPERADO

As a parting thank you to my readers, here's an extra chapter that didn't make the final cut. I thought you all might like to know what happened to two characters I love, Graig and Simone. ~LK

Simone closed the door of the study cube—her makeshift lab, courtesy of the Matiran government. The modular buildings served as homes, offices, and stores—even barns, like the one behind her tiny living cube. The beauty of the instant buildings was their ability to interconnect. If she ever wanted more lab space, she could have more cubes attached to the existing building.

She glanced across the open yard to her home cube. That would always be small. No reason to expand when living alone.

Crap. She despised self-pity, and refused to wallow in it ever again. Her life was about recovering local agricultural seeds and plants. A thankless job sometimes, but necessary. At least she wasn't the only one working toward the goal of making Earth's people self-sufficient again. It would take decades, at best. Eventually, she'd take on students and teach the next generation to continue her work. Talk about job security.

The late spring evening was cool and clear, and the sun hung low on the western horizon. Ranger danced around Simone, barking as her awkward teenage puppy legs tripped her up. But she still wagged her tail in frantic anticipation of their evening outing. No shortage of enthusiasm here. Buck galloped across the field to greet Simone, nuzzling her hand for a small horsey treat.

Simone gave his neck a pat. "I think I'll walk tonight,

Buck."

The horse nodded and snorted as though he understood. At least there was one guy she could always count on being there for her. Not that she needed any guy. The past eight months had proven that she would be fine on her own. And she really wasn't on her own. She had a dog and a horse to talk to.

You just keep telling yourself that, Simone Campbell.

She struck out across the field toward the hill behind her cube. Her four-legged companions fell in step, trotting along loyally. At least they never questioned her evening ritual. Even *she* didn't want to know what possessed her to return to that little piece of fence on clear evenings and watch the stars appear in the indigo sky. Or why some nights she stayed until it was full dark, unafraid because she had Ranger and the deadly accurate *telum* Alex had sent her from Matir. Simone had used it a time or two to drive off coyotes.

Maybe she was just bat-shit crazy.

Ranger barked and ran up the hill. Simone's gaze followed the dog's path straight to the fence...and the stranger sitting on the top rail.

Well, now, who the hell is that?

The man was dressed in boots, jeans, and a long-sleeved plaid shirt. A cowboy hat rode low over his brow, shielding his face from the setting sun. Gloved fingers methodically shredded a long piece of wild grass. Ranger danced in circles around the section of fence barking then tore back down the hill, presumably having caught the scent of something more interesting. Hopefully not another skunk.

Simone pressed her lips together and frowned. Some crazy-ass stranger had invaded her sanctuary, and he had to go. She'd try nice first, but if he came at her, she had her *telum*. What was the worst that could happen?

Stand tall, shoulders back, walk with confidence. At least Graig had been good for something. She closed the distance, prepared to start with sweet talk.

"You should have your *telum* out by now," the stranger said.

Simone's heart lurched in her chest, and she came to a dead stop. "Say what?" Holy crap, she *was* bat-shit crazy. He sounded like....

The man pushed the brim of his hat up with one finger to reveal a dead serious, and all too familiar, face. "A woman alone approaching a strange man in the wilderness of this planet should have her gun trained on him."

A heartbeat later, she did exactly that, *and* released the safety. Graig's stare remained impassive.

"I didn't get that weapon for you to wear as a decoration, Simone."

"Son of a bitch." The words came out in a whisper. *He'd* picked out the weapon? Shifting slightly to her right, she shot a hole dead in the center of her homemade rain gauge nailed to the far post, for no other reason than because she could. The can obligingly shattered with the force of the *kagi*.

Graig didn't even flinch a muscle, but a slow grin appeared. "That's my girl."

"That could've been your head, dumbass, and I am not *your* girl." She set the safety and holstered her weapon. "What the hell are *you* doing here?"

He spread his hands in a placating manner. "I was in the solar system and thought I'd stop in to see an old friend."

"And maybe get a little whoopee while you're here, I bet?"

He raised his eyebrows as if the thought had never crossed his mind then shrugged.

"Go to hell." Not the same three little words she'd once felt for him, but she meant every letter of them.

She turned on her heel and marched back down the hill. That man had a hell of a lot of nerve coming back here. What was wrong with him? And, what was wrong with her? The second he peeked out from under that damn hat, her heart took off like a horse running the Kentucky Derby.

Shit, shit, and shit.

Buck watched her as though confused that their walk was over early tonight then trotted in the direction of his stall behind her cube. Ranger perked her ears up and cast a worried look at Graig before running ahead of Simone. The mutt zigzagged through the grass as though sniffing out imaginary threats. Smart dog.

It was amazing how fast a beautiful evening could be

torpedoed. She didn't hear Graig following, but that meant nothing. She'd seen him in action, and he could be quieter than death when necessary. If fact, he had been death for more than one unlucky soul. He'd knifed four Anferthians, one by one, when they'd attempted to take her back to the slave ship. They'd never heard him coming.

Heat jolted through her belly, and her step faltered. Jesus. It was what had happened after he'd disposed of the 'Ferths that still got her hot and bothered. She'd thrown herself at him...on him.... *Whatever*. He'd filled her desperate need right there in the golden summer grass of the Sierra foothills. Not her first orgasm ever, but definitely her first honest-to-Jesus, thank-you-God-for-making-me-a-woman orgasm.

Was he following her? She had to know. She whirled around. Graig stopped five paces away. She pulled her lip up in a snarl.

"I thought Matiran men weren't allowed to pursue women."

"Since when did we ever observe Matiran protocol, Simone?" He asked drily.

True. Things changed the day Bodie kissed Ora, knocking all the Matiran men in camp onto their proverbial asses. Graig had adapted. Quickly. He'd stalked her like crazed paparazzi, finally coming out of hiding, throwing her over his shoulder and carrying into the black passageway behind the storage cave. And in the dark, it was all about feeling....

Shit. It was his fault she was reliving those painful memories now. She shot him her best fuck-off look, and resumed her angry stomp toward home. Turning the door handle, she was brought up short. She wiggled the handle again. It was locked.

What the hell? She never locked her door.

"Your ID reader works again," Graig said behind her.

The damn thing hadn't worked since last Christmas. "How did you know it was broken?" The words were barely out of her mouth when the answer hit her. "You've been *stalking* me?"

"Surveilling is a much nicer word."

Oh, this was just getting better and better. Not. "How long?"

He gave her a vague shrug. "Long enough to learn your routine."

She made a growling noise in her throat. "I don't have enough food for both of us."

"I'd be happy if you would just lock your door while you're out."

"Yeah, against whom, exactly?" She swept her arms in the general direction of all the great empty nothingness surrounding her tiny home.

His slow, suggestive smile reached his eyes. *Shit.* She slammed her palm against the ID reader. Oh, yeah. That was how it had broken the first time. It must be okay this time because it still glowed green. No glow at all meant bad news.

She gave the door a yank, stomped inside, and came to yet another abrupt halt. Two place settings and a glass jar full of her favorite flowers—hibiscus—adorned the bistro-size table in her kitchen. The most mouthwatering scents came from her microscopic oven. All this for a little nookie while he played hooky? It seemed over the top, and she had no intention of saying yes. Never mind that her body registered strong opposition to her brain's decision.

"Where'd you get *those*?" Her voice dripped with sarcasm as she pointed to the flowers. "Hawai'i?"

"Yes." His response was so matter-of-fact, she could only gape at him. He shoved his gloves into his hat and hung them on the coat hook just inside the door. Simone swallowed against the sudden attack of nerves bubbling in her stomach. So, he planned to stay for dinner. And what could she say about that, especially since he'd cooked it?

His large presence filled her tiny cube, and she curled her lip and huffed. "You're impossible."

He raised one brow. "So are you. Sit down."

"I need to feed Buck and Ranger."

"The animals have been cared for. Sit. Your dinner's ready." He spoke English like a native Terrian, no trace of an accent. Was there anything he wasn't good at doing?

A flush rushed up her neck, suffusing her face and numbing her lips. She knew from personal experience just how good he was at so many things.

PROPHECY

There was no getting out of this. She huffed again, and plopped into a chair as Graig retrieved the cooking pot of savory-smelling meat from her oven. He sat across from her and began serving. "This is a Matiran dish, and yes, I did bring it all the way from Matir. The meat is from a native animal you've never heard of, and bears no resemblance or relationship to koalas. It's not even remotely cute."

He remembered she adored koalas? That was sweet. She took a bite, and her eyes watered as the tender meat melted in her mouth. Why couldn't she cook like this?

"This is good, Graig. Really good." No sense in going overboard with the compliments. He might think she was caving. Which she wasn't.

He smiled, and they ate in silence. They were almost finished before she finally dared to ask her most burning question. "Why did you come here, Graig? Honestly."

He appeared to consider her question for several seconds before placing his utensil on his plate. Leaning his arms on the table in front of him, he met her eyes squarely. Even now, his ice-grey eyes that intimidated so many others, sent her heart racing. Right over the same cliff it'd been over more times than she could count. Her hands trembled, and she dropped them onto her lap, out of sight.

"All my life, every time I've done anything, it's been well thought out. Something I am good at, and something that makes me happy, or at least satisfied. After leaving you out there at the fence, it took me two months, and a sound thrashing from Alex, to figure out that I was no longer happy. It took five months more to secure my early discharge from the Guardians."

"That's seven months, space cowboy. You've been gone for eight."

His gaze never wavered. "I spent most of the last month on Matir with my family. Saying good-bye."

He was? "Why?"

"I don't plan to go back. I made a poorly-thought-out choice eight months ago because it *seemed* like the right thing to do. I enjoyed being a Guardian and in charge of security, and was damn good at it. There was no reason I shouldn't continue on that path." His lips pressed into a thin line. "It's the most miserable I've ever been.

"Simone, never in my life have I been happier than when we were together. Everything I have ever had or done pales compared to the time I spent with you. I don't expect you'll take me back, certainly not easily, but I had to at least let you know how it's been for me. And how sorry I am for tearing us apart. I love you, and that will never change. However, if you want me to go, I'll go."

That was more honesty than she'd ever received from one person in her life. Including her mother. She studied him for several heartbeats then collected their dishes and deposited them in the sink. She should scrap them into the compost, but his words kept replaying in her mind.

What could she say? There were so many things to think about. "You know, I've never heard you say that much at once, ever."

"Do you need time to think?"

Yes. No. Why didn't she just *know* what she should say? Or do?

She gave him a nod. "Meet me at the fence in one hour."

The chair slid against the floor, and she listened to the rustle as he rose from the table. He paused for his hat and gloves then the door opened and closed with a soft thump.

Simone approached the fence. Again. Graig was a shadowy figure in the moonlight, sitting where he'd been when she'd discovered him earlier. His hat hung over one fence post. This time, she stopped about ten feet away, and he stood to face her.

No sense beating around the bush. "It gets pretty dull around here. If you stayed, what would you do?"

"You still need greenhouses for your work. As I recall, you wanted to make your home self-sustaining by planting and raising your own food. I can make that happen." He paused then added, "I've also been told I'm a fairly decent self-defense *magister*. It would be a good way to give back to the people who have given me so much."

PROPHECY

She raised her eyebrows. He *had* given this some thought, yet she still wanted him to sweat a bit, so she stood silent for several heartbeats.

"You love me?" She held her breath.

Graig's eyes glittered silver in the moonlight. "With every fiber of my being, Simone."

"What if you discover you've made another mistake?"

"Mistakes can get a man killed. This one's been killing me for eight months. I am not making another mistake."

They stood facing each other in silence. Now for the moment of truth. "For life?"

Graig nodded. "For life."

Her heart fluttered. "We're doing it right this time, you know."

"Anything less would be unacceptable."

Slowly, she took her right hand out of her jacket pocket and raised it, palm toward him. His response was instant. He raised his left hand. She stepped toward him, closing the distance step by step until her palm pressed against his. His hand glowed with his Gift, and by its faint light, she could see the softening of his entire face.

"I love you too, Graig." Her admission came out in a choked whisper.

She stood on her tip-toes, and he bent down to oblige. The warmth of his breath fanned her face then he captured her lips with his. She tasted the exotic, alien spices from the dinner he'd cooked for her, and opened her mouth to him for more. The tender kiss went on and on. Their fingers entwined, and he slipped his other arm around her waist. She relaxed against him. This was home. The only place she ever truly wanted to be. Tears welled against her closed eyelids, seeping out and down her cheeks. After eight long months of living with an empty heart, she still loved him. Maybe even more than before.

When they pulled apart, she discovered that he'd picked her up and her legs were wrapped around his waist. His most intimate desire pressed against hers, and her flame ignited.

Graig touched his forehead to hers. "I brought you a gift."

She tightened her legs around him. "What's that, space cowboy?"

His low chuckle vibrated through her. "Not that. Not yet." He balanced her with one strong hand cupping her bottom, and reached his other hand into his shirt pocket. Simone frowned at the small device he pulled out. He was gifting her with the Matiran version of an MP3 player? Wasn't *that* just so romantic?

Graig tapped the device and returned it to his pocket. "Let's see if you can guess who this is."

The first strands of acoustic guitar filled the night air, and then a male voice began to sing, "Desperado...."

"Nick?" The kid's voice still blew her away.

Graig nodded. "He recorded this in Dante's infirmary."

She gave a derisive snort. "Bet Dante had a cow."

"Very nearly." He chuckled. "Dance?"

"I would love to."

He slid her down the length of his hard, muscular body until her toes touched the ground. Then her space cowboy danced them home.

Made in the USA
Columbia, SC
21 November 2021